THE BLOOD AND THE WIND
BOOK ONE

BLOOD
OF
THE
CROWN

A . G . W I C K E R

BLOOD OF THE CROWN

First published in Great Britain in 2022 by Fulmar Press.

Copyright © 2022 A.G. Wicker.

All rights reserved. No portion of this book may be reproduced, copied, distributed or adapted in any way without prior written permission from the author, with the exception of non-commercial uses permitted by copyright law.

The moral right of the author has been asserted.
A catalogue record for this book is available from the British Library.

ISBN 978-1-3999-3423-7

For all those who have ever felt the struggle to belong.

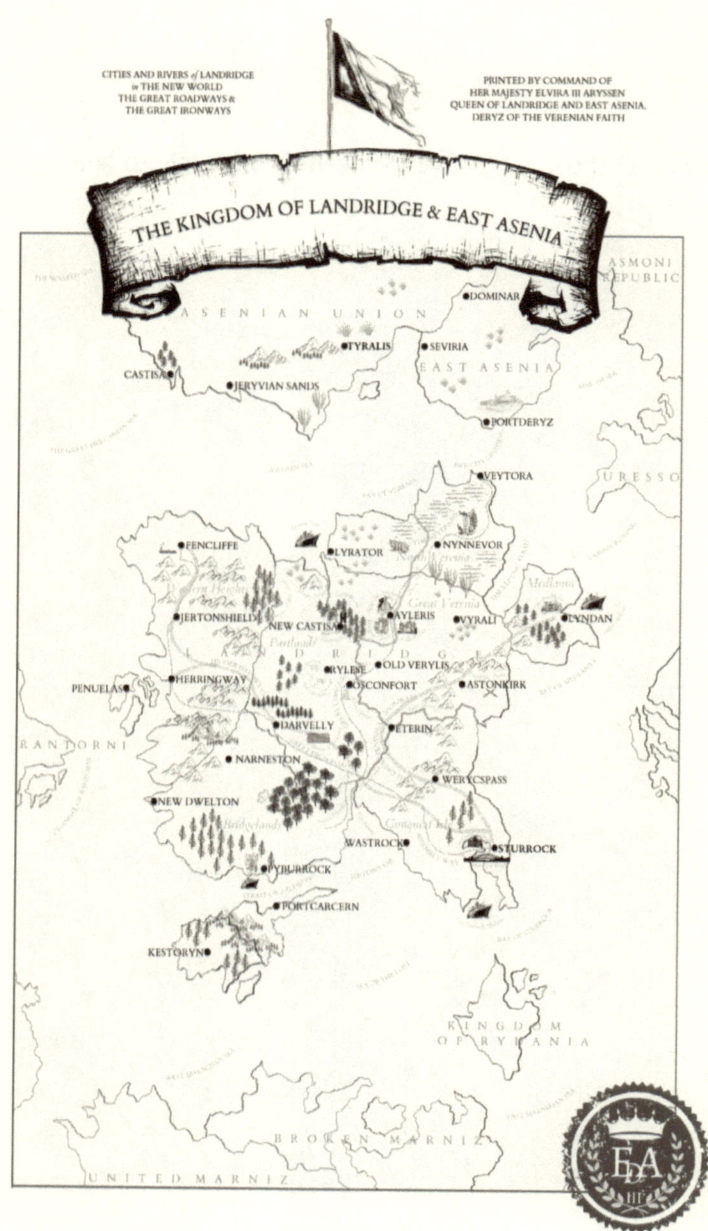

CITIES AND RIVERS of LANDRIDGE in THE NEW WORLD THE GREAT ROADWAYS & THE GREAT IRONWAYS
PRINTED BY COMMAND OF HER MAJESTY ELVIRA III ARYSSEN QUEEN OF LANDRIDGE AND EAST ASENIA, DERYZ OF THE VERENIAN FAITH
THE KINGDOM OF LANDRIDGE & EAST ASENIA
ASMONI REPUBLIC
ASENIAN UNION
DOMINAR
TYRALIS
SEVIRIA
EAST ASENIA
CASTISA
JERYVIAN SANDS
PORTDERYZ
VEYTORA
URESSO
FENCLIFFE
LYRATOR
NYNNEVOR
JERTONSHIELD
NEW CASTISA
AYLERIS
VYRALI
LYNDAN
LANDRIDGE
HERRINGWAY
RYLESE
OLD VERYLIS
PENUELAS
OSCONFORT
ASTONKIRK
DARVELLY
ETERIN
RANDORNI
NARNESTON
WERYCSPASS
NEW DWELTON
WASTROCK
STURROCK
YBURROCK
PORTCARCERN
KESTORYN
KINGDOM OF RYHANIA
BROKEN MARNIZ
UNITED MARNIZ

A Different Path
Rhedas

The heat was the worst part of it. Rhedas Sandaerzi put his hands on the beige stone wall ahead of him and bent over, panting, his rucksack weighing him down. He turned around and looked at the view beneath, seven hundred and fifty six steps spiralling down into a valley. It was a deep, vast valley, the Nevebaris, and as the sunlight glimmered through the mist of its waterfalls, all seven of them, it painted the sky violet and green and orange too.

"Good God, will you get a move on!" came a voice. "Half of Nynnevor is waiting for you, idiot."

Rhedas looked down at them. Nynnevor must have been a tiny village then.

"Move!" came another voice, shoving him.

"Stop!" said Rhedas, losing his balance. "I'll fall." It was a holy place, blood need not be shed here. Not for his clumsiness.

"Well, then, get out of the way." came a gruff voice. He had a thick accent, even for Rhedas.

"Now, now," came an old woman's voice. "We're all going to the same place, there is no need to rush."

She reminded him of his mother, just as calm. Not quite as mad, t hough.

"Aye, but if we take too long none of us will get to see her."

"If it is written in your stars, you shall meet her today," said Rhedas. "I know that it is in mine."

"And what else is in your *stars*?" said the man, pushing him again. Rhedas stumbled backwards, clinging on to the rocky edge of the wall tightly, before landing on his two feet once more.

"Leave him!" cried the old Verenic woman as the filthy looking oaf laughed to himself. "I need to catch my breath for a few moments anyway."

"Yes, leave me!" shouted Rhedas. "I have a role to play in the wars to come."

"Wars?" The man looked back at him with his eyes narrowed. "Has the old hag declared war? On Ashcrest?"

Rhedas had said far too much.

"Don't call her that," the old woman exclaimed. "After all, she is our queen."

"She's absolutely useless, that's what she is. As useless as her son, *His Highness Aren the Absent*. She could learn a thing or two from Her Eminence."

"The child is ill," said the woman. "None of us can blame her, any mother would do what she can to protect her son."

"He is no *child*," said the oaf. "He was a child maybe fifteen odd years ago, no more. The man spends his time in Asenia, living in luxury on *our* money."

"He lives in no luxury," said the woman. "He fights, for Verenia, for Landridge."

The oaf spat. "Fuck Landridge."

"Is it cold in Asenia?" said Rhedas. *He fights*. Rhedas had seen him fight, but in a dark, dark room.

The man crossed his arms. "It is a desert. Even hotter than it is here."

But Rhedas had seen no desert in his dreams. It was a cold, grey land where he'd seen Prince Aren Aryssen. A cold, grey land with beautiful trees and shiny motorcars, like they have in the chilly south. But it wasn't the south, it didn't look like Landridge at all.

"Are you seriously thick?" the man said once more.

"You shouldn't trouble those of us that have come here to devote ourselves to the North Parydon," said Rhedas. "Especially not in times like these, where we should stay as one." *Stay as one*.

"Ah, you've come here for all that have you?"

The woman smiled. "He looks like it! Do you want some water? It must have been such a long walk."

"Twenty seven days," said Rhedas, looking down at his bruised and battered feet. Even with his shoes, the rocks and thorns and heat had been rough. *The heat had been the worst*. "No water."

"Have it your way," said the man. "Mother, we don't have time for chitchat. We don't want to miss her, you saw how many people there were last time."

"Alright, alright!" she shouted. "Under whom are you studying, my boy?"

"Hmm?"

"Which minister?" she croaked.

"Master Tamuz Sandaerzi," Rhedas replied.

"Hmm, I can't say I've ever met the man."

"You'd better get going," said Rhedas. "The clouds are darkening."

"Mother, let this madman be," muttered the foul-tongued son, looking up at the speckless blue sky. "Let his clouds consume him in his own madness." And very quickly they disappeared beyond the stone wall and into the Courtyard of the First Falls. Rhedas needed a moment though, to catch his breath…the journey ahead was not an easy one. *Key of Blood. Stone of Sacrifice. Shield of Mankind. He mustn't let them know.*

"Move, you idiot!" shouted another. It had barely been a moment since the last.

"I'm sorry," said Rhedas. "Move past me, for I must rest."

"You'll miss her," said this one, a fair-haired man, his cheeks red and burnt from the sun – probably Weslin. "Her Eminence." *How'd he find his way this far north?*

"If it is written in my stars, I will see her."

"Yeah, well, good luck," said the Weslin man, shuffling past. "Do you need help?" he said once more, turning back.

"I have a different path ahead of me."

And then the Weslin man disappeared too, into the Courtyard.

"It's the first time she's come all this way," came a familiar voice. It was the old Verenic woman again. "Develyn Asellar, from Veytora. She's never come here before, so it's only natural we're all aching to see her."

"Where is your son?" Rhedas replied, not looking at her.

"Busy," she said, and he finally looked over at her. Her hands were on her hips and she looked tired and weary. Her eyes had bags beneath them, and her skin was cracked. "You should drink some water."

"Is that why you came back?"

"Yes," she replied. "It is the Sandaerian way, after all."

He took the flask from her and downed it one go. "Sorry, I shouldn't have done that."

She sighed. "It is fine, I have faith I will be okay."

Rhedas had more than faith though, for the rains would come down all at once. Any moment now.

"Don't bring yourself down over my son," the woman said. "He means well, he is just worrisome and, well, he really needs to see her."

"He will see her," said Rhedas. "We will all see Develyn Asellar." He took a moment, shuddering at his dream. *The blade, the blood.* He couldn't rid his mind of it. "But why is he so impatient?"

She sighed again. "For me. We've heard about her…her powers. Her Eminence has, well, healed hundreds up in Veytora hasn't she?"

"And what's wrong with you?" Rhedas choked on his words as he let them out. Sometimes he had no control over them.

"Glint's Dusk. They told me I have months left," she said, pointing to her chest. "That I should relish every breath I take."

"I thought Glint's Dusk…"

"Kills you quicker than that, yes, it does," said the old woman. "But I caught mine early, by the grace of the One. And I took some medicine, something my neighbour gave me. But it just slows the process, it doesn't stop it."

"So, you think Her Eminence can help you?"

"She's my last hope," said the woman. "Same as a lot of us here."

"Hmm?"

"Why do you think there's so many of us here, desperate to see her? The rot, the rot that plagued Jertonshield and Fencliffe, it came to Nynnevor. So did the droughts. We're suffering up here, where have you been?"

He mustn't let her know. "I shall pray for you," said Rhedas, handing her back the empty flask.

"Thank you," said the woman. "I'd better get going again, he's waiting for me."

"That, you should," Rhedas muttered under his breath. "As should I." He drew a deep breath and yanked his aching arms up, stretching them far above his head and behind his back until they cracked, and then he carried on, following the spiral path to the very western edge until he was far away from the Sandaerians climbing up. He tightened the strap of his rucksack around his waist and turned around, making sure there weren't any others.

Then he grabbed onto the top of the wall and hoisted himself up with the little strength left within him, his arms trembling all the while. He clambered sideways over the top of the wall and lowered himself carefully till his trembling arms finally gave way and he fell on his arse on the other side.

"Ow," he muttered, rubbing his stinging thigh. But the drop had barely been that of his own height, of course. *Nobody can know.* He got up and dusted himself off, before glancing around at the hidden path. It was clear from the cobblestones and the overgrown bushes dotted along it that the path had seen very few over the centuries. Nothing like the worn-down cobblestones and dusty path he'd just seen above.

He followed the path around, desperately searching for the crack in the stone wall. *It had to be here.* He'd seen it in his dreams. He wished it didn't have to be like this, he wished he could have it as easy as the rest of the men who'd be sworn to the Parydon, but he *had* to help. If he didn't help the Panderer, then who would? *Each had a role to play.*

There was a ferocious roar, and the ground beneath his feet shook as the hairs on his arms suddenly rose up. He felt the chill on his neck too, as the skies above him darkened. And then there was a flash, brightest light he'd ever seen, and he felt his lips curl into a thin smile. Seconds later, another white flash, and this time he saw the lightning strike ahead of him, maybe atop the First Falls. A moment later, another louder roar, thunderous. And then the skies opened up and the cold rain pattered against Rhedas' skin as he looked up, his mouth open and his tongue out like a dog. It tasted almost sweet. He squinted through it, wiping the water away from his eyes as the grey clouds above parted, ever so slightly. If he'd blinked, he might have missed it, the white thing darted past in a flurry, soaring back up into the dark clouds. There was another crack and lightning struck down fast, almost right in front of him, setting ablaze the trees and bushes beside the path in the distance. The rain poured down again, harder this time and the flames hissed and fizzled out, smoke rising from the burnt leaves and twigs left below. The creature swooped down lower still, gently this time. He gazed at the magnificent beast, its beady eyes sparkling, its white and golden feathered wings spread wide as it glided over the path and climbed straight back up, disappearing into the clouds. It was just as his mother had described, all those years ago. Just as he'd seen in his dreams. Just as beautiful, just as breathtaking. The clouds parted quickly as the Verenic sun peered through once more, burning him where it kissed his skin. Just as swiftly, the grey in the sky dwindled till it was no more, and an azure mist was all that was left above, save a few wispy white clouds here and there.

He missed her, his mother, he really did. She'd been wise, so wise. But that wisdom had driven her mad, by the end. *They can never know*. She'd turned them all against her by the end, every single one. It was a different path that Rhedas would take, a more careful one. There was far too much that hung in the balance. *They can never know*.

He unbuckled his rucksack and swung it off of him. He opened the clasps carefully and retrieved it, the dusty old thing. He held the scroll tightly in his hand for a moment, before unravelling it to reveal the madwoman's frantic scrawls, possibly some of her last. *One who shall rise from the dead. One who shall wield the blade. And one who shall dwell amongst the darkest of clouds*. But not yet, no, he mustn't be hasty. He folded the scroll up again, and shoved it in his sack, and hurried on. It was here somewhere; he could feel it.

Home
Aren

The low sun glistened through the evening mist, seeping through cracks in the dense grey clouds. Aren looked around him, the road ahead seemed clear. He walked cautiously down the hill, wading through the auburn leaves that the autumn chill had left behind. He stuck to the edge of the path, hugging the hedges that lined the front gardens along the road, careful not to dwell.

Avoiding the busier streets had seemed like the better idea, but he was now increasingly conscious of how long this meander was taking. He'd never hear the last of it…Cyneric would be sure of that.

He stopped in his tracks, his ears pricked up at the noise. He was quick to react, sliding calmly over to the left, behind a parked car. He turned to look around him. A cat? No, too large to be a cat, far too large. A tall woman appeared from behind the curve in the road, beside a child who looked to be about six, maybe seven. Not too much older than Daria would have been. He cleared his head.

The roar of a jet engine soared high above him, in the dark, misty skies. He looked up, smiling. The skies had always called to him, ever since he'd come here. Perhaps one day Cyneric would let him fly. Perhaps. But today was not that day…today Aren had only his training to worry about. He sighed, crossing the road and stopping just short of the tall brass fence opposite. Perhaps he *should* take the shorter route through the park. It wasn't too far now. It wasn't likely he'd be spotted. Not this late after the school day. Even if he did stumble into someone, he'd worked up quite a list of excuses over the years. A list he could rely on. So many times, they'd ask him what he was doing in the park so late, why he was lingering by the school…why he hadn't gone home yet. Of course, it wasn't a home at all that he was walking to, not then and not now. He knew he'd never had a home here and he'd never let himself believe otherwise.

It would have to be the park; he was already so late. It had been at least the good part of an hour since he'd left, so at least he had the cover of night to thank, which was good because Cyneric had said not to be followed.

He shuddered at the thought of it…being seen here. It was a small town and he'd always stuck out like a sore thumb. He decided he didn't care. They already thought he was peculiar, they always had. Nobody had ever tried to hide it. Of course, he'd always tried his best to fit in. But even with Cyneric's lessons, he knew in his heart that he'd never belonged – nor did anyone every try to make him feel like he did. Nobody, that is, except Shannon. She was the only one who had tried. Sometimes her company, as little as it may have been, was enough. More often than not though, it was overshadowed by the bitter truth in the whispers echoed by the others. In the beginning the words hadn't hurt him nearly as much as they did now, after spending years in this foreign land he still couldn't call home. It had taken him quite some time to understand how things worked here, amongst the Panderers. He'd always told himself it was temporary. It was a temporary hindrance and as soon as he was of age, he would rid himself of this place he'd never quite understood. Of course, he hadn't an idea when that might be.

It seemed that his mother's plans were always changing. *"Just a couple of years more,"* she'd say each time. He'd given up now. There was no changing anyone's mind. Clearly, they all had a plan of their own for him. A couple of days here and there were all that his mother would allow. Visits, really. Visits, knowing he'd be ripped away from it all just as quick. The few moments he had with his friends from home, his real home, were moments he cherished with all of his heart. He looked forward to those days. It was an escape from this life, a chance to go back to where his real friends were. Olivia, Jaspyn, Lara, all of them. How he longed to play cards with them or watch as Vidalia and Lara painted pretty pictures of the sunrise, or just sit and talk and let the hours go by. It hurt him that he'd already missed so much. It hurt him that each time he was going home, he didn't know if all his friends would still be there. They were all growing up now, living their own lives. Sometimes their paths took them away from him. Without a chance to say goodbye. He missed Eyan sometimes. It had been so hard, he hadn't seen him for months, given what had happened…and now, he was afraid it was all happening again. He was seeing Olivia less than ever and it terrified him.

In the distance he caught a glimpse of the top of the bare flagpole behind the thick of the trees outside the old library. A gentle glimmer of scattered light shone dimly through the frosted windows on the ground floor. A sigh of relief…at least he hadn't missed Cyneric altogether. He crossed the narrow road, careful to stay clear of the dull streetlights.

"Did you misunderstand the urgency in my message?"

Cyneric's deep voice pierced through the night's cold silence. He turned to face his mentor. A pale, thin man, not too tall nor too short, dressed almost entirely in black. A dark black vest, a charcoal jacket over it. He looked like he was tired. A lightly overgrown stubble shaded his face and his sleek black curls, though parted to one side, were not nearly as neat as they usually would have been.

"I stayed back after school, as we discussed," said Aren. "I didn't want to be followed though so I took a slightly longer way."

The response seemed to be enough for Cyneric, who nodded, stepping forward towards the old library doors. "Come on then," he said. "I got worried, so I thought I'd go looking for you."

"What's on the agenda tonight? I didn't think to bring my sparring gloves if we're training."

Cyneric laughed, holding the grimy wooden doors open. "We aren't training tonight."

Aren gave him a puzzled look. There were dusty books sprawled all across the floor and the old stone bust of a lion's head that had once hung proudly from the tall wooden doors was tipped over on its side, chipped and scratched, on the rotting wooden desk below.

"Don't worry about the gloves, I have some grave news for you from the capital."

"What's going on over there?" he replied, his voice shaking. "Has Sturrock…fallen?"

"Heavens, no." Cyneric pulled out an old key out of his inside jacket pocket. "Couldn't have left it unlocked, could I?" he muttered quietly. He opened the door to the derelict library basement, and prodded him in. He was extra cautious sealing the door behind Aren, as if expecting them not to have been alone. It wasn't unusual of course, not for Cyneric.

They made their way through the dirty corridor to the abandoned cellar that they usually trained in. A dark, rather melancholy room if not for a single bulb that provided a quiet glow under which they could just about see each other's faces, as well as the little furniture in the room. There were no windows, just the door they'd entered through, an old chalkboard on one wall and a small, round table that had been pushed up against the other. The wall behind them had shelves, once home to a collection of phonebooks from a different time – all which Cyneric had been quick to rid the room of when they'd first started using it. There were no books on it now, there were far more important possessions. Artefacts they'd use for training – but nothing too suspicious of course, just in case somebody were to happen upon the dingy room. The majority of *those* sorts of items stayed in a bag, which Cyneric brought with him from his quarters every time they were to train. Aren, on the other hand, kept his things in an old, forsaken cupboard he'd made use of at school. His sparring gloves, any little keepsakes from his mother, anything to remind him of home. Of course, Cyneric did not have his bag with him here today and hadn't asked him to bring any of his things, so Aren was a little bit bemused about what was planned for him.

"I think it best to be as direct and transparent as possible," said Cyneric, his arms now crossed. "So, I'll be quick about it. We aren't staying here for much longer," he said, giving one of his rare smiles.

Aren gave him a perplexed glance. "Has the library basement been compromised? I thought it could never–"

"No, no. Not the library. This realm. This life. For good this time. It is time. You're ready." Cyneric gave him no time to gather his thoughts. "There's suspicion stirring amidst the nobles at court. Not just the nobles either, even the commoners are starting to ask questions. Why their Crown Prince makes such…such few appearances in public, why the appearances are so bleak, so short."

"And they've been asking those questions for years. What's changed?"

"What's changed, is that the sentiment has now more grievously plagued the palace itself, the Crown Council. Her Majesty fears it could brew into a deeper conspiracy, especially with everything…*else* that is happening there right now. She feels the capital needs a certain stability and that you might just be ready to take that on."

Cyneric must have noticed his eyes widen as he placed a hand on his shoulder. "Everything is fine, Aren. Everything is fine."

"But it isn't, is it? The Federation is gaining support, the papers are calling for a war, an uprising. First it was just Eyan's father, now Olivia's too… anyone could be next."

Cyneric raised one eyebrow. "What is life without challenges… it isn't anything you haven't been prepared for," he said. "Now, have you got your father's watch? Your mother and Mr. Runeval said that it would be good to wear that at the Recedon. And the pendant your mother gave to you?" Cyneric asked. He was frantically moving around the room, creating space in front of the wall. "Come on now, we don't have too much time. Lights out within the hour."

"Well, no. I haven't got anything, I wasn't sure whether or not we'd be training today, everything was so rushed…"

"Don't worry about it. Your things can be retrieved later, especially those damn sparring gloves of yours!" he chuckled.

"What do you mean by retrieved later? Are we leaving tonight? I can get them now, if we rush back to school, they're in the cupboard, I can –"

"It's alright, Aren. Your mother wants you back tonight. As soon as possible, in fact. We can come back for your other things, the bloodgate isn't going to close on us. Besides, I'm sure such trivial matters won't place too highly on her agenda for the Recedon."

"Wait – so it is happening soon, then? If I had known, I would have kept the watch on. I only put it in the cupboard so that it'd be safe."

"Sooner than you imagine. But as I said, we can come back for your things, not to worry. Now, your mother will be expecting us very soon. Shall we make our way home?"

After years of feeling imprisoned, Aren was finally headed to where he felt most comfortable. Surprisingly, a part of him felt some sort of sorrow, as if deep down he had somewhat accepted this life, however wretched it had been. Perhaps some part of him even felt like he should say goodbye properly. It was a silly thought. But then, it dawned on him that he would never see

Shannon again. He felt a lump in his throat. The one person here that had made an effort to reach out to him…did she not deserve as much as a goodbye? An explanation?

There was no time. Even if there were, how would he even explain it to her? Of course, he'd always known deep down that it would be this sudden. That had always been the cost of his homecoming.

"I thought you would be more excited than this," said Cyneric.

"I am," said Aren, his palms sweaty. But he knew he'd never prove his worth if he didn't act with seriousness, with purpose. "Yes, let's go home."

"Perfect. I have the dagger ready," said Cyneric, reaching inside his jacket pocket. "This part never seems to get any easier," he sighed.

He pulled the old thing out. In all the years Aren had seen it, it had always looked exactly the same, the shine had never faded, not even slightly. The same bronze hilt encrusted with burgundy garnets. The blade was covered in an ornate charcoal scabbard, an intricate golden engraving weaved around it. Cyneric unsheathed the weapon, revealing the blade – a sleek, silver thing. He handed it over.

They stood side by side next to the old chalkboard, facing the bare red bricks that remained uncovered, except a thin film of dust that had gathered. Aren cleared his throat and Cyneric nodded at him. Holding the dagger in his right hand, in one smooth, practised movement, Aren lifted it to his forehead, moving its flat edge across from left to right slowly, as though marking a straight line across the top of his face. The blade kissed his skin, gently gliding over his face but drawing no blood. He muttered the words, the words he'd practised so often. Words that were clearly still nonsense to Cyneric, who stared blankly at the wall.

"After all these years, it's still foreign to you?" said Aren. "Old Verenic."

"It's a complicated tongue."

"It didn't take me that long to learn yours," said Aren. "The tongue of the Panderer, it's no easy feat either."

"You never had to learn it," scoffed Cyneric. "You were brought here as a child, surrounded by thousands who spoke it."

"So?"

"If thousands in Sturrock and Astonkirk spoke Old Verenic, heck even just Verenic, perhaps I'd have picked it up just as easily," said Cyneric, scowling. "But they don't, do they? It's more like four of you."

"Now," said Aren. "But it wasn't always that way."

"And how many thousands of years do you think I've lived in that world?" said Cyneric. "Just be pleased I'm fluent in Landridgian, vile tongue."

"I'm going to have to start again," said Aren.

"Well, get on with it, and this time don't interrogate me on my tongue!" Cyneric shouted. "Your mother is waiting."

Aren nodded, passing the blade over his forehead once more before gently raising it to Cyneric's forehead. He repeated the same soft action, still muttering the ancient incantations under his breath. He drew back the dagger and held it firmly in his hand, blade facing forward. He looked over at his mentor, who nodded. The two of them closed their eyes, and Aren took in a deep breath and counted to three. He plunged the dagger straight forward into the bricks. They opened their eyes to see dark crimson blood dripping from the edge of the blade, where the point met the brick. The blood flowed down the dagger, staining the mortar and dripping to the cold ground beneath. The bloodgate before them was opening.

Aren held up the dagger between them, gripping the hilt tightly whilst Cyneric held the stained blade. Aren took in another breath, deeper this time and turned around to face the room, Cyneric followed. He inched backward, ever so slowly, closer and closer to the wall behind them. As they leaned further back against the wall, it fell further away from them. Each time he did this, it was just as astounding as the first. It felt as if they were sinking and stumbling into a hole in the ground, except they were stood perfectly still. A high-pitched droning sound pierced the silence of the cellar, getting shriller as they fell. The world seemed to crumple and fold in on itself around them, spinning and hurtling at infinite speeds until what seemed to remain was a blur of black and red... an immeasurable emptiness with vermillion shooting stars painting the shadows, fading in, fading out.

The noises stopped. The shooting stars slowed down and eventually faded away entirely, leaving a mist of burgundy, golden and a very deep blue. The mist slowly cleared as the world began to take shape around them. The all-too-familiar smell of his mother's lemon scent from the Waters of Léoree filled the air. Aren rubbed his eyes and squinted at the familiar burgundy carpets of the cellar under the Western Quarters of the Valecrest Palace. On one end of the room stood a tall doorway with a dark mahogany frame, an almost identical doorway opposite it at the other end of the room. Lights hung down from the ceiling, bouncing off the pale, beige wallpapers which surrounded them. Each wall itself was decorated with ornate, golden frames, housing paintings of the Rivers of the Nevebaris and mountains of the south that he recognised so well. Aren was home.

"You took your time, didn't you?" came his mother's familiar voice. She was wearing a violet dress, intricate golden lacing along the collar. A tall woman, her height wasn't something that Aren had inherited, much to his regret, though her dark curls definitely bore some resemblance to his own wavy hair. Her golden skin glistened under the hanging yellow lights. He walked over to her, and she embraced him at once, running her fingers through his hair.

"Sorry we're late, Your Majesty," said Cyneric.

She held back her laughter, then she kissed Aren on the forehead, gently cupping her hands on his cheeks. He wasn't used to it, it was rare for her to give more than a thin smile, she was the sovereign Queen of Landridge, after all. She'd raised Aren to be the same way, emotions were weakness…something personal and not something to show others.

"I have missed you so very much, Aren. You've no idea how much I've missed you. I yearned for your trips home, and every time you had to leave again, I'd… I'd quietly shed a tear in the palace Parydon, praying for your safety in that godforsaken place…praying for your quick return. Now, Cyneric will have told you about the Recedon, I trust?"

Aren quietly nodded back. He'd been dreading it for weeks. He cast his eyes curiously around the largely empty room, reminiscing his childhood. It was, of course, a cellar only in name. A few crates of wine sat in the corner, the rest of the cellar was largely empty, though the walls and carpet were decorated lavishly as if it were a foyer. In a way, he supposed it *was* a foyer. It was the first thing he'd see each time he came home. All that time he'd spent a world away, waiting to be back here for good – and he was finally here. No more counting down the days until he had to go back, to live with the Panderers. He drew a deep breath as he took it all in, relishing each moment.

It was short lived. A silhouette appeared in the doorframe at one end of the room. It was too dim for Aren to see his face, but there were only a few in the palace that might be seen this far beneath the Western Quarters. The figure appeared too tall to be Pennyn Runeval, the Crown Chancellor, and he didn't know why any others in the Council might be down here. He squinted but it was useless, all he could make out was the man's brown hair. It was longer than Aren's and lighter too, with fair streaks that glistened in the feeble light.

The figure disappeared behind the wall of the doorway just as quickly as he'd appeared, perhaps noticing Aren's stare. His mother was quick too to note his wandering glances.

"I trust you will be tired tonight; I'd suggest getting an early rest to be ready for training tomorrow. You have three days to perfect your technique and practice with Cyneric. Mr. Runeval and I were discussing perhaps opening the doors of the Crown Foyer to the common folk," she said, smiling proudly. "You'll have plenty of people to impress that night, so make sure you rest! I'll leave you to it, then. You remember where your room is. The quarters haven't changed, but Mr. Porter, I ask that you accompany him just in case he has forgotten." she said, turning to face Cyneric who nodded back promptly.

"Thank you."

She raised her brow. "And before you go, I know how difficult it has been for you…not quite here, nor quite there. Constantly stuck between here and the Panderer's realm."

"It was nothing," he lied.

"Just know this. My dear boy, you will always belong somewhere," she said. "A home at court, a home with your friends – Olivia, Jaspyn, Lara, all of them…" her voice trailed off. "No matter where they might be. A home with Cyneric, obviously. And with your family – your aunts, your uncles, cousins. And of course, you will always have a home with me." And with that, she wrapped her arms around him, in the warmest of embraces, gently kissing his forehead again.

She left the room out of the doorway where the figure had stood just moments before, whilst Cyneric pointed Aren to the opposite end of the large cellar, one that led to a spiral marble staircase, if

Aren remembered correctly. It hadn't been too long since Aren had visited home, but this time felt different. He eyed the ancient paintings of skyverns and sunrises that hung on the walls all around the marble steps, Cyneric trailing behind silently, as Cyneric often did. He didn't mind it, though. It gave him time to himself, to ponder over his thoughts – to take it all in. There was a carpet neatly laid down on each landing, bordered with a fine golden stitch-work on a field of deep burgundy. Aren knew to take the second-floor landing; there were several routes that led to the royal quarters, many that only those very close to the sovereign herself were privy to, but Aren knew that this one was the quickest.

A lot had changed in the palace, even in some of the corridors – parts of the walls were freshly plastered and painted, the ceiling in the West Parydon Pass looked as if it had just been repaired and the marble and granite all looked speckless. A lot, however, was exactly how Aren remembered it. The corridors and halls of the Valecrest all had carpets of distinct, specific colours, for example, which all meant different things.

The corridor passing on his right had a charcoal carpet with golden embroidery. He shuddered at the thought of where it led. The corridors leading to the Hall of Krelis all had black carpets. He'd not been in there very often, there was something about it that he didn't really like. This particular corridor led to the balcony overlooking the hall. Large tapestries hung on the brick wall below it; one depicted a battle, with large fires burning in several clusters, then there was one which bore a silhouette of a ship with a rising sun behind it. The third depicted two lynxes springing towards each other under a field of stars, a bolt of lightning striking down between them. The beauty of the palace was unmatched by anything Aren had seen in the Panderer's realm. Legend had it that the tapestries foretold of great prophecies, but Aren had of course been taught better than to believe in that sort of thing. A lot of Landridgian culture revolved around fables and prophecies, it was foolish to pay attention to them all. The hall was alluring nonetheless, even if a bit eerie. The ceiling also donned at least hundreds of bronze stars, carved by the greatest smiths of Kestoryn, hanging on thin, barely visible fibres. Looking up at them often felt like looking up at the night sky itself. The room had always struck Aren as a bit peculiar. Fortunately, though, he had no need of going down that corridor today. Instead, he turned back towards the royal quarters.

Another set of marble steps across from the Central Courtyard were dressed in a maroon runner. Hanging from the roof by two metallic chains was a bronze crest, one that he knew all too well – one that filled his heart with pride.

"What's got you thinking?" said Cyneric, making him jump.

"Oh, erm, nothing," said Aren. But Cyneric must have already noticed the sparkle in his eyes.

"Ah, the Royal Crest," said Cyneric. "Of the oh-so-noble House of Aryssen."

Aren smiled. "Do you know what it means?"

"The dark red represents blood. The black represents the night, of course. And the Regal Standard, in blue and gold, stands for the defeat of the Old Federation," said Cyneric. He'd stopped right beneath the crest and had turned around to face Aren. "The Griffin stands for the bravery and the valour of the Zaldroni, and the bow and arrow represent the Fourteenth Deryz, your ancestor, and the Law of the Old Deryzi, which lives on in the queen's Justice." He drew a sharp breath before continuing. "Finally, of course, the fierce crowned skyvern stands for the ancient House Aryssen of Ayleris itself," he said smiling again. "That's right, I may just be a Panderer, but I've done my reading."

"It doesn't surprise me that you have. But you forgot about the stars, just behind the wings of the skyvern there."

Cyneric raised his eyebrows, looking at the little stars in the top right quarter of the crest. "The Stars of Hercan?"

"Originally, yes. But they aren't just the Hercanian Stars here. Each of them represents a great Weslin family of the Old Federation, the ones that defected to support the monarchy in its earliest days. Dresden, Hercan…and Ashcrest," said Aren, his voice trailing off. "It only took a dynasty lasting hundreds of years for House Ashcrest to change their minds, I suppose."

"Soren Ashcrest will suffer for what he is doing to your family. Fate is cruel."

Indeed, it is. "Cyneric, what exactly does the White Wing in the top left represent?" said Aren. "Of course, the blade it upholds is the Skyvernblood Dagger, but what about the wing itself?"

Cyneric narrowed his eyebrows. "Like I said, I am merely a Panderer, I cannot speak for such things," he laughed. "But I've heard quite a number of stories over the years."

"As have I," said Aren. "That it's from a dove, Jerton's Dove, to represent the Weslin, or maybe to stand for peace. Or perhaps that it represents the faith, and how it upholds the crown."

"Unfortunately, I cannot help you. Maybe this would be a conversation best suited to have with Her Majesty," said Cyneric. "But I wouldn't bet on that. Now come, we mustn't dwell for too long."

As they entered the royal quarters, the next set of steps led to a circular landing, opening into three different corridors. Aren walked to the corridor furthest to the right, decorated in the standard burgundy and gold of the Aryssen dynasty. Cyneric followed him in, stopping just outside the door to his room.

"I'm going to leave you here," said Cyneric. He bore little expression on his face, just a thin sincere smile. "Breakfast will be in the Sailor's Foyer. Your mother has quite a lot planned I hear."

"Thank you, Cyneric."

"I trust to find you in the Garden of Ysseria an hour after dawn," he said sternly. "*Before* breakfast."

Aren shivered at the thought, but he knew he had a lot of training to get done before the Recedon and he also knew that he had to make a lasting impression on the people of Sturrock, his future subjects. If he were ever going to ascend the throne one day, he would need to have secured their trust in him, like his mother had done, and her father before her. He had heard the stories of how the peasants from Berespids and the vendors from the market stalls of Hartyl Street had come together and waved banners in the name of King Derys II atop Azara's Peak for his coronation. His family's legacy was one which had never failed to deliver on expectations, it was daunting. Nonetheless, he smiled at Cyneric, who nodded back and turned to leave.

"Wait."

Cyneric turned back to face him. "Hmm yes?"

"Thank you for everything you've done for me, you know, in the Panderer's realm. For teaching me their ways, helping me fit in."

"This isn't the end, Aren, it's only the beginning." Cyneric's smile returned to his face. "You have nothing to thank me for. I did my duty by you, and by your mother and father. He would be immensely proud of you if he were here today," he said. "I am glad that you have been granted the chance to return home, though. I know what it can feel like, obviously, being stuck in a world that never truly feels like your own. I believe in you. I believe in your training and your efforts, and I am all but certain that you will perform immaculately."

Aren was lost for words, as it hit him. After the Recedon, he would see less and less of Cyneric – a man he considered to be as close to him as his own father. Certainly, a man that he knew better than his dead father. Cyneric took the silence as an opportunity to leave, he nodded and bowed, then turned away, closing the door behind him.

Aren dimmed his lights, and found himself sat on his bed, lost in thought. The moonlight glistened through his window, bouncing off his pale walls. The chill of the southern night had started to creep in through the glass, despite it being tightly shut. In the distance, he could hear what he could only presume to be trees, rustling in the wind against the tall walls of the Valecrest Palace. At one point, the muffled sounds of an aerodyne flying high above the city echoed through the trees, far beyond his window. Apart from that, a motionless silence, stirred only by the infrequent, distorted noises of Sturrock, drowned by the vast gardens of emptiness beyond the western walls.

Liars and Thieves
Rhedas

"Ferus?" the minister whined. The noise bothered Rhedas, but he kept his mouth shut. "FERUS!"

There was no response. Of course, why would there be? Kyril Sandaerzi hopped around like a small, fat goose looking for a man who clearly did not want to be found.

"He must be busy," said Rhedas.

"What did I tell you?" said Kyril, a cross look on his face. He walked over, his arms folded over his robe. "Never speak out of turn, it isn't a good habit."

"Yes, but –"

"No ifs and no buts," came another voice. Rhedas turned to face the man. It was Tamuz Sandaerzi. He hung from the marble steps leading down from the Hall of Worship. "Your place at the North Parydon hangs by a single thread, don't keep tugging at it. First, the lies, now this boorish behaviour…it is not the Sandaerian way. If you cannot keep up, there is nothing holding you here."

"Lies? I never told a lie!" said Rhedas Sandaerzi. "The dreams were real, very real. If you would just, please listen, I didn't mean to cause any offence, I promise!"

Kyril shook his head and tutted. "To say such a thing… about Her Eminence…"

"I saw it! I saw it, I swear! Great peril, in the shade of the aspen trees… It brought tears to my eyes, seeing her like that, a knife buried in her neck… I cried myself back to sleep…"

"Stop with the nonsense, Rhedas," said Tamuz. "I will not ask you again. There are no aspen trees between Nynnevor and Veytora."

Rhedas knew to stop. He couldn't be kicked out from the North Parydon, it was the only place he could call home.

"I am sorry, so sorry," he said. "If it may be, I can give my apologies to Her Eminence myself, in person?"

"It most certainly cannot be," said Kyril. "Her Eminence does not require your apologies, or anyone's for that matter."

"And you could never be trusted to go up to Veytora," said Tamuz. "We would never allow it."

Rhedas nodded woefully. At least they were honest, though. It could have been worse. They could have been liars and thieves like those that dwelled in the south. Those that wore the bluecoats. Those that wreaked havoc, painted the streets red. He'd seen it all, he'd never forget. The dreams kept him up at night.

Kyril Sandaerzi clicked his fingers. "Are you lost again, Rhedas?"

"No, no, I am not lost," he lied.

"Hmm. Why don't you come follow us," said Tamuz, striding down the steps. "You have much to learn here, as does that Ferus. Can you believe in five years he has never worked in the Hall of Answers?" he muttered. "It's a pity he isn't around now. Oh well, you can show him later."

"Where are we going?" said Rhedas.

"The Hall of Answers," said Tamuz sternly. "Keep up. Come, Kyril. You'll help him, won't you?"

"Hmm," grunted Kyril, nodding.

"And what's there? In the Hall of Answers?" said Rhedas.

Tamuz smiled. "All the answers. It is where we keep the books and scrolls that we receive from the Keep," he said. "To check them for lies and truths and to make adjustments wherever necessary. Kyril will show you how it is done."

"And what of it if we cannot say that it is a lie or a truth written in the book?" said Rhedas.

"Then we leave it. We return it to the deluge of books in that Keep until someday some poor minister receives it again...and the cycle repeats."

"Oh," said Rhedas, stumbling over a vase.

"Goodness, be careful, will you?" said Kyril, brushing past him.

"Tamuz, is it true?" he whispered. "The sightings?"

Tamuz Sandaerzi looked around him before nodding in silence. Rhedas trailed a few paces behind the pair. He wasn't sure if they thought he were deaf, or too stupid to care what they were talking about in such hushed tones, but he wasn't complaining. He'd gotten himself into so much trouble already, he'd ought to stay to himself.

"And have we told *her*?" said Kyril. "Her Eminence."

Tamuz nodded. "She was the first to know, she had to be. It is she, who will lead us out of this darkness… It has been prophesied since as early as the First Age of Shadows."

She wasn't even alive in the First Age of Shadows, Rhedas thought. What an absurd remark. The girl was barely in her nineteenth year. He fiddled with his thumbs as he tried to clear his mind of the dreams, they were getting more and more vivid.

"And what has the queen said?" said Kyril. "About the rot, I mean."

"The queen hasn't stepped foot in Fencliffe for years," said Tamuz. "She probably doesn't even know about the rot. Always sending that measly Means Counsel of hers… I do wonder what's going to happen now though, now that he's gone."

"He'll be replaced by another," said Kyril. "That is what always happens."

"It's a pity, this one seemed promising," muttered Tamuz, looking left and then right, as if deciding which path to take. "This one believed… or at least, he didn't treat the farmers as if they had no brain."

"Who? Lord Berywen?" said Kyril. Rhedas had heard the name… He'd heard it in his dreams. He'd heard it from those that wore the bluecoats.

Tamuz nodded. "He listened to the farmers, to what they said they had seen… the vile demons. It is the stuff of stories, but when a hundred men tell you what they have seen it is not to be taken lightly. Especially not when many of those men are mysteriously dropping dead."

"It is that man she keeps by her side," said Kyril, shaking his head in disdain. "That…Pennyn, he is the one poisoning her mind. I remember the days that Prince Weryn were still alive, she wasn't nearly as gullible."

"Perhaps King Aren will be of more use," said Rhedas, immediately wishing he hadn't. It had slipped out of his mouth as if he had no control. The pair stopped in their tracks and stared at him sternly.

"*Prince* Aren," said Tamuz, taking a step closer to him. "Were you eavesdropping? You insolent, disrespectful man." He slapped him across the cheek and Rhedas let out a small shriek, like that of a little child.

"I'm sorry, I am so–"

There was another stinging thump, this time from the back of Tamuz's hand. "Always sorry," said the minister. "Yet you never change. You never cease to disappoint us."

"And what makes you think that Prince Aren the Forgotten will be any better?" said Kyril. "The boy is never here, always far away in Asenia. They have done well to keep him hidden from his subjects."

They'd reached the courtyard, a small group of ministers that were stood under the shade of a tree turned to face them as Rhedas held his palms over his red cheeks.

"He might come up here," said Rhedas. "To Verenia… North Verenia."

"Why would he do that? When his own mother pays us no heed?" said Kyril.

"I just… I just think so," said Rhedas, keeping his dreams out of it. "Sorry."

"Tell you what, if the boy Prince comes up here, beyond the three rivers, we will take you to him ourselves," said Tamuz. "Maybe request an audience."

The pair burst out laughing, with no care for who may be around them. Rhedas decided he would spare himself any further humiliation and keep his mouth shut, for good this time.

The Crown's Sincerest Welcome

Aren

Aren sat alone on a bench in the Garden of Ysseria. It was a peaceful but eerie morning silence, broken only by the songs of birds in the trees of the palace. The night hadn't been easy, he'd felt restless of the days to come. And on top of everything, training with Cyneric before breakfast had really taken its toll on both his body and his mind. His muscles ached and his head was full of thoughts.

But still, he smiled. He smiled for he was going to see his friends again at breakfast. Friends that grew more and more distant from him. He knew that he hadn't been there for them. Not for Olivia when her father had decided to leave the Council, nor for Jaspyn when his sister had died. How could he have been? He'd been a world apart. At least those two knew his secret. But what would the others have thought of him? Lara, Chrysan. Even Eyan. He may be a traitor's son, but he'd been his friend once. They'd all have been fed the same lies as everyone else, of course. That the journey back from East Asenia was far too dangerous. But would that have been enough? What of Jaspyn's family? He buried his head in his hands. Would they ever truly forgive him? How could he have expected them to? To them, he was the Crown Prince of Landridge. The heir to a dynasty probably older than their family name.

He squinted as the morning sun rose past the tower opposite. He decided he'd better get a move on, or his mother wouldn't be too pleased.

Aren hadn't been to the Sailor's Foyer in years, he hadn't a clue how he'd navigate the labyrinth of courtyards and viaducts of the Northern Compound. It had a way of appearing foreign to even its most familiar residents, it had been designed in such a manner by the old bluecoats themselves, long before the reign of the Aryssen dynasty. They had been very clever with their construction of the Compound, making it almost impossible for invaders to find their way around. The old bluecoats had never allowed maps to be drawn up either and that tradition continued to this day. Aren's own ancestors had made certain of that, as they built the palace known today around the Compound that had once served as a great capital for the Old Federation. Aren couldn't help but marvel at just how much of a feat it was…the narrow corridors, the ancient wall hangings. He much preferred the rest of the Valecrest Palace, of course. From the freshly trimmed gardens and sunny courtyards to the tall, antique windows that the spring sun would dance through in the evenings; the finest of Verenic architecture.

A figure appeared in the corridor in front of him, a girl. He followed her quietly into the corridor, careful not to make a noise. The girl had silky black hair that he knew all too well and she wore a navy dress, tightened at the waist by a gilded sash. In her hand, she held a familiar small, leather pouch with the blue and gold crest of House Berywen. Three streams of gold which met atop a dark midnight blue field, three silver pairs of crossed swords between them. He walked up closer to Olivia Berywen, and gently tapped her on her right shoulder. She gasped loudly, clutching her arms in front of her.

"How have you been?" he asked.

The colour returned to her face as she turned around, and she just about managed a smile, the corners of her emerald eyes narrowing. "I'm so glad you're here. How have *you* been?"

"I'm well. Madness…six months feels like forever, doesn't it?"

Olivia plunged forward to wrap her arms around Aren, gripping him tightly. He could smell the rose scented oil in her hair, and her hands were cold. He looked at her closely when she pulled away, she looked quite thin, and her face seemed paler than ever before. It wasn't a surprise, this was Lord Berywen's doing.

"How's your family, Olivia? Keeping well, I hope?" he said.

She smiled at him thinly. "As well as can be, what with everything happening. Father almost didn't let me come today, said it might look bad."

"Oh," said Aren quietly.

"Yeah. Chrysan's pledged himself too, to Eyan's father. You know what he's like, once he's committed to something there's no getting him out of it," she muttered. "At least I'm seeing father more now, I suppose."

"Why? Because he's at home?"

She shook her head. "Because he's in Sturrock. Barely saw him when he was on the Council…God only knows why he spent all his time in Fencliffe and Jertonshield."

"Yeah, that's true," said Aren. "It'll be nice having him around." *Even if he is fighting for the wrong side.*

"Well, I'm sure it'll all blow over soon, and we can all go back to normal," said Olivia, with a sense of optimism that he'd missed. It was short-lived, though. She frowned at him. "I'm afraid this might be the new normal. I know I shouldn't be saying this to you, you've only just arrived, but they're gaining support by the day, you know."

These were the words of her father, not her.

"I just want you to know, no matter what happens with my father and the…bluecoats," she spat the last word as if it left a bitter taste in her mouth. "*I* will always be on your side, not theirs."

"I'm glad to hear it," said Aren. "I don't know how worried I should be about Soren Ashcrest."

"Well…I don't…"

"You can be honest."

"It isn't going to be easy," said Olivia. "But the queen has got plenty of support around her. Now come, let's not be late." She hugged him again, this time looking at him with a raised eyebrow. "Were you…lost?"

"No, of course not."

"It's just around the corner, the Sailor's Foyer."

"I know," Aren lied. "You seem to know the Compound well, don't you?"

Olivia laughed. "Only because I was here last month."

"What on earth were you doing all the way up here?"

"I was with Lara. For an audience," said Olivia. "With the Zaldroni merchants."

"Merchants? What merchants?"

"Of Arvendon and Wyntock End."

"Didn't know you were so interested in what Zaldroni merchants had to say," said Aren, chuckling.

"Not at all," said Olivia dryly. "But it wasn't a day wasted, at least. I found out a lot about the Compound, about the Foyer…it used to be the chamber of audience for sailors, you know, hence the name. Lord Fraston was telling me all about it," she explained, tracing back her steps.

"Lord Fraston? Fraston Spenler? What was he doing there?"

"You don't suppose Lara held an audience with fishermen and market stall owners all by herself, do you?" Olivia laughed. "He taught me how to find my way around the palace. Did you know the old bluecoats used to meet at least once a month with all the Asmoni fishermen? The best of the best were rewarded handsomely by the First Warden."

"No, I didn't know that actually."

"Yes. Apparently, the oil paintings of merlynfish on the back walls were a favourite of Oscon Hercan's. They were ordered to be put in by Sayax Aston himself."

"It's quite remarkable, I must admit," he said, not really paying too much attention to the thing. "I must ask Lara all about it later."

Olivia gave him a funny look. "You haven't yet heard?"

"Heard what?"

"Lara left, just a couple of days before you arrived actually."

"Left? Left for where?"

"For the North Falls," said Olivia. "I thought you'd already have known."

"I hadn't a clue," said Aren. "Why?"

"Well, her father moved up there a little while ago, perhaps last month? I can't say I know why."

"Oh," said Aren.

"I'm sure she'll come and visit once she hears you're back, though."

"I hope so," he muttered. "But she was here last week?"

"Yes," said Olivia, her eyebrows raised. "That was the last time I saw her. Why?"

"So, what exactly did you get up to in this… *audience*?" said Aren, ignoring her.

"Not a great deal, if I'm being honest. It was such a dull affair."

"Then why did you decide to attend?"

"Father wanted me to spend some more time with the good folk, said it'd do me some good," said Olivia. "What a load of rubbish."

Aren had to stop himself from rolling his eyes in front of her.

"I'm lucky I had those two with me, I don't know very much about the Zaldroni merchants and what they do. Saved me a bit of embarrassment having Lord Fraston by my side. I can't remember the last time I even went into Arvendon. It's always so incredibly crowded and smelly, I hate going there. The last time was probably when Jaspyn and I took —"

She stopped, but the sorrow that had swept over her face spoke volumes.

"Daria," he said.

"Yes." She cleared her throat. "I can't believe it's almost been a year. He's so strong."

Aren nodded silently, shuddering at the memory of the wretched day. Cyneric had been the one to tell him.

"It's a terrible, terrible disease, Glint's Dusk," said Olivia.

"I just wish I'd had a chance to say goodbye."

"We mustn't think like that," said Olivia. "Or else we'll never forgive ourselves."

He didn't know if he deserved forgiveness.

The Falls were so deep in the very heart of Verenia.

"It's so far, Nynnevor."

She looked puzzled. "Nynnevor?"

"It's the Verenic name," said Aren. "Forgotten already?"

"Ah, yes, it is," she said.

"It'd be nice to take a trip north someday," he said. "All of us. I know Jaspyn's always wanted to visit the Nevebaris too, he's never been."

"That sounds lovely," she said. The gentle strum of a harp grew louder. "We're here."

Around the turn of the corner stood a large wooden door, with small brass doorknobs in the shape of five-pointed stars. Even from outside the room, he could smell the freshly baked dough and hot buttered cocoa. Aren pushed the vast door open. The room was still largely empty; in one corner sat the Crown Chancellor, Pennyn Runeval, a dark-skinned man with dark hair. Next to the antique paintings, the harp player stopped as she saw Aren walk in, it was Valery Rennero, the Health Counsel. She combed through her silvery hair with her fingers, straightening out her bun. Her face and arms had more wrinkles than the last time he saw her, but the grace with which she smiled at him was the same.

He eyed the centre of the room, almost empty. His mother was certainly nowhere to be seen. Jaspyn, however, was sat at one of the long wooden tables in the middle. His fair skin was ever-so-slightly tanned, and his auburn hair looked lighter than usual, burning bright as it caught the morning sun. He was dressed in his smartest black tunic, neatly pressed.

Aren let the door shut behind him and Jaspyn's head turned, a wide grin on his face. He got up from the table and sped towards them, not a care for his surroundings.

"Aren! How have you been?" he said raucously.

Some of the others seated in the hall took turns to glance at all the commotion, whispering to one another.

"We should take our seats," said Aren.

So much had changed in the six months they'd been apart, yet much felt the same.

"It's funny, none of them have come up and kissed your ring yet, Aren," joked Jaspyn. "It's odd, by this time we're usually surrounded by your noble friends."

"Mother has specifically instructed for us to be left alone this breakfast," said Aren, in a lowered voice, looking around. "How are your parents?"

"They've been worse," said Jaspyn. "How was it there this time, you know...*East Asenia*?" he winked.

"It's been better," said Aren, still glancing around the room but nudging his leg sharply beneath the table.

"Ow! Sorry."

"How's Hartyl?" said Olivia suddenly. "Keeping well I hope."

Aren raised an eyebrow. "Who is Hartyl?"

Olivia nodded. "The stray cat he found by the markets."

"Don't call her a stray," said Jaspyn seriously. He struggled to keep a straight face though before erupting into laughter.

"I can't believe you called the poor thing Hartyl," said Aren.

"He found it down on Hartyl Street," said Olivia.

"Yes, that is where I found *her*," said Jaspyn. "What else was I to call her? Fluffy?" he shook his head. "Wouldn't be so accurate, you saw how thin and frail the poor thing was, didn't you?" he looked over at Olivia.

"Looked like she hadn't eaten in days," said Olivia. "Probably hadn't, to be honest, that's maybe why she followed you home.

There's so many of them that live there, in the shade of the Arvendon Bridge."

"I've heard there were thousands more during the days of the old bluecoats," said Jaspyn. "But as the city grew and more and more markets opened up there, they all died out."

"They were considered quite auspicious in the Anercusian faith," said Olivia. "That's why so many Weslin families still keep them around."

"Didn't know *you* were so close to your faith," said Jaspyn, chuckling.

Olivia's pale cheeks went red. "I'm – I'm not," she said. "I suppose on my Weslin side nobody really is. On my Zaldroni side, though, I've heard my great grandfather was a Verenian minister."

"Verenian?"

"Yes," said Olivia. "He led worship in the High Parydon once."

"I've always wanted to go there, to the Falls," said Jaspyn.

"That's the *North Parydon*," said Aren. "That's...*them*. The Sandaerians."

"Oh, of course," said Jaspyn. "They were one faith, once, weren't they? The Verenians and Sandaerians."

"In the time of the Deryzi," said Olivia. "Hundreds of years ago."

"Indeed," came a voice, startling Aren. "No, don't let me stop you," said Pennyn Runeval, looming over them.

"Right...well..." Olivia continued.

"Perhaps you'd be better suited to explaining it to me," said Jaspyn, looking up at him. Pennyn Runeval raised his brow and crossed his arms.

"Very well. All you need to know is that we were all Sandaerian once, in simpler times. Then war and disagreement came and changed that."

"And so..."

"And so that is how the High Parydon of Sturrock came to be. That is how our faith, as we know it, came to be," said Pennyn. "We call ourselves Verenians with pride, to set us apart from the barbaric Sandaerians that wreaked turmoil upon this land for hundreds of years."

"Thank you," said Jaspyn, and the chancellor nodded before turning to Aren.

"I've got some people for you to meet," he said. "So, stick around, will you."

"Oh," said Aren. "Who?"

"You'll see soon enough," said Pennyn. "Although, perhaps it'd be more fitting after the Recedon."

"Why?"

"So they have a better impression of you," said Pennyn, before glancing over at Aren's friends. "*It is high time you step up, my prince*," said Pennyn in Verenic. "*The waters are rough, and the winds are strong. I have made a list for you, a list of nobles.*"

"*A list?*" Aren replied. "For what?"

"*To talk to, to get to know,*" Pennyn added. "*We do need a Means Counsel, after all.*" And with that, he winked at him and disappeared just as quick as he'd snuck up on them.

"What was that all about?" said Jaspyn.

"Nothing, he just wanted a word."

"I hope you enjoyed the lesson," said Olivia, slapping Jaspyn on his back. "Plenty more if you have any further questions, I'm sure."

Jaspyn shrugged again. "I'm always getting muddled up with these things. Us lowborn folk aren't too particular about these things...faith, blood, name," he laughed. "Or what we name our cats." Suddenly his expressions darkened. "Daria loved them."

Olivia bowed her head. "She did."

"She loved going down to the markets with you," said Jaspyn. "She'd never stop talking about it."

"Some of my happiest memories," said Olivia. "She loved stroking all the cats as they scurried past us in the evenings, we spent so many afternoons by the pepper merchant's stall – when you'd go for your dual wielding training...at the University."

Jaspyn smiled sadly back at her. "I remember, she was always so excited when I'd tell her that you were going to take her into town."

Aren wished there was something he could say, anything at all, that would ease his friend's agony. Silence was kinder sometimes, though.

The doors creaked opened once more, this time the queen marched into the room, and she wasn't alone. The room fell to silence almost immediately, and Aren watched as nobles all around him rose up from their seats. She wore a sombre beige dress, golden flowers stitched into its sides. A long, dark burgundy scarf trailed over her right shoulder, pinned to her dress by a golden brooch.

"Please do take your seats," she said.

Just behind her was a tall man with curly brown hair. He looked familiar somehow, they all did. Beside him, two figures that didn't look too much older than Aren – a shorter and paler brunette girl, with piercing steely grey eyes and another man, taller than Aren, and not too much older either. His wavy chestnut hair was similar to Aren's too, though longer with lighter streaks. Aren recognised him almost immediately, from the night before. The three were very obviously related by blood, the boy and the girl in particular bore uniquely similar features. A sharp jaw, striking grey eyes, and even their attire…the pair wore the same long, charcoal robes, laced with dark red silk. He supposed they were brother and sister. The older man, on the other hand, wore a dark burgundy cloak, a white tunic neatly tucked underneath.

"That man," said Aren, "the one with the long hair, next to the girl. I've seen him before."

Olivia and Jaspyn shared a puzzled look. "Next to Éline? That's her brother."

Éline? It sounded vaguely familiar.

"Éline Nazeris," Olivia chimed in. "That's her brother, Ylor. Though I don't know if you have met him?"

Éline Nazeris?

"I thought it'd be pretty obvious, I mean, everyone in that damned family looks the same." said Jaspyn.

It dawned on him. He hadn't heard that name in years. *Eli.* Of course, how could he have forgotten? After all, he had been close to her once, before he'd been sent off to the Panderer's realm. The woman stood before him looked nothing like the jolly girl from his childhood, though.

"She's unrecognisable."

"Hmm?" said Jaspyn.

"She looks like her mother," said Olivia.

Her mother. Aren's earliest memories of his life at court were fading. Summers at the palace. Playing by the ponds in the west gardens. But this one, this one was clear.

"Her mother died, didn't she?" said Aren quietly. "During the Insurgency. That's when she came to court, Éline…when the violence broke out in Zaldron."

"Well," said Olivia, her eyes wandering over to the brown-haired girl. She brought her voice down to barely a breath. "She's missing. The body was never found. That's why Lord Nazeris never married anybody else," she whispered, looking around her. "Some say he refuses to believe it, that he thinks she'll come back somehow…like…like magic."

Aren eyed him, proudly stood at the front of the room. An older man, his hair greying. He certainly didn't look like a madman. "I don't think I've ever met Lord Nazeris," said Aren. "What's he like?"

The man was a mystery. High Lord of Zaldron, and a very important man indeed, that is all Aren knew of him. The Zaldroni banks had flourished under him, Pennyn had always said. His mother had always sung praises of him, more than any of the other High Lords of Landridge, yet Aren had never even seen a picture of the man, let alone met him. The Zaldroni tended to stay in Zaldron, after all.

"What is he…like?" said Olivia. "Well…he led the war against the Zaldroni Insurgency."

"Oh yes, I remember that actually," said Aren. "Well, what do you make of him?"

She gave him an odd expression. "You know what I think of that family, Aren. They're Zaldroni… *pure* blooded Zaldroni," she whispered.

He glared at her, more confused than ever.

"Never mind, the real question is, what are they doing here? In Sturrock?" she said.

"I suppose we'll all find out soon enough," said Jaspyn. "What I do know, though, is that Ylor sort of gives me the creeps, even that smile of his…thin and cruel."

"Did you ever meet him?" said Olivia.

"No," said Aren. "Just Éline." The memories flooded in. Playing with her in the Garden of Ysseria when he'd been a little boy, they'd spent hours chasing each other around the palace that day. The day that he'd found out that he was being sent away. Of course, he hadn't quite understood what it had meant. Maybe if he'd known, he'd have spent more time with her…with all of them.

Maybe he'd have said goodbye properly. Maybe he would have told her the truth. No, nobody could know the truth about the Panderer's realm. The first time he'd been back in town, she'd already left, and he'd never seen her since. He'd forgotten about her. Would she have forgotten about him? They'd both just been children after all.

"Aren?" said Olivia, waving an arm in front of his eyes.

"Huh?" he said. "Yes, what is it?"

"The Recedon – it's soon, isn't it? Are you ready?"

"More than ever."

Jaspyn slapped the table with his palms. "I know you've both explained this to me before, but what is the ceremony for? Is it…is it like a coronation?"

"Not a coronation," said Aren, looking up at his mother, his fingers tapping gently on the table in front of him. "It's…I don't really know how to explain it…"

"It's an ancient custom," Olivia chimed in. "From before even the Old Federation. From before there were kings and queens or wardens. From the time of the Old Deryzi."

"Yes, yes exactly," said Aren. "Couldn't have said it better myself."

"But what is it *for*?" said Jaspyn.

"I suppose these days it serves as a way to gain support from the people, put on a show for them. Historically it was more about coming of age, I think. To celebrate maturity. A way to forge or reinforce alliances, a way to show the people that the Crown Prince or Princess was ready to ascend the throne. But now…now it's more about tradition and about getting a chance to impress the nobles…and the good folk." His fingers struck harder and faster against the wood, there was no pattern to his tapping. Just a wild, constant patter.

"Right, of course, that makes sense," said Jaspyn, looking down at the feral hand. "So, the thing with the arrow then?" Olivia sighed loudly.

"What? We can't all be born noble," said Jaspyn, frowning. "Excuse *me* for not knowing the ins and outs of royal rituals."

"No, that's not why –"

"It's an old tradition now, more than anything," said Aren, interrupting her. "I'm just waiting for it to be done with, if I'm honest. I've laboured over it for hours, weeks on end, and if I'm not ready now then I don't know if I ever will be."

"An *old tradition?*" said Olivia. "I'd say there's more to it than just that. It arises from as early as the days of the Sandaerian Dues. I just find it so fascinating, and I'm not even Verenic. How the Fourteenth Deryz courageously took the Falls…I mean *Nynnevor*, I suppose, during the Hercanian Uprisings."

It *was* fascinating. His ancestor's courageous actions had directly put the Old Federation in power. That, in turn had led to the chain of events that had led to Aren's family being seated on the throne today. He wondered where he'd be if House Aryssen had never come into command. If the Old Federation remained the capital system of rule. If Sturrock was still just the summer capital, and Ayleris the winter capital. He'd probably be on some farm outside Ayleris, maybe Astonkirk.

"Why a bow and arrow?" said Jaspyn. "It's on your crest too, I've always wondered," he said, pointing towards the mounted plaque at the front of the room.

"Because that is what the Old Deryzi used," said Aren. "Just tradition." That was the answer to a lot of things, tradition.

"*My lords and ladies. Dearest friends. Elders.*" His mother's voice echoed and the room fell to complete silence. She commanded a respect from every single person in the room, a respect that Aren hoped he'd one day command.

"I will spare you the formalities, we are all aware of the dire circumstances of these times in which we live," said the queen, her eyes stern and lines stretching across her forehead. "But still, it is important to live a little from time to time. Celebrate our successes. That is why I have called this breakfast." She took a moment to smile coldly at nobody in particular. "I will also address some of the changes my council will be implementing with immediate effect. Changes that will support our battle against the transgressors."

Olivia was fidgeting with her hands, her head bowed. Aren gave her a gentle nudge and smiled. It must have been difficult for her, all this. The least he could do was comfort her. Sadly, that was also the most he could do.

"Mr. Runeval, if you will." His mother signalled to the Crown Chancellor with two fingers before walking over to her seat on the raised platform. It was an old wooden chair, glossed with polish and cushioned with a deep mauve velvet bearing her monogram, intertwined in a wreath of Aspen leaves.

"Greetings, all. I'd like to begin by echoing Her Majesty's sentiments in *complete* condemnation of the so-called Federalist movement. I would also like to reassure you that the Crown is in as stable a position as it has been for years. To strengthen the prosperity of our great kingdom, there will be some new additions to Her Majesty's Crown Council. Let me begin by introducing the new Crown Treasurer, Lord Arcadius Nazeris. Lord Nazeris has graciously accepted the call to Sturrock to oversee Her Majesty's Crown Treasury and the Royal Bank of Verenia."

There were surprised whispers around the room. Olivia looked away, fiddling with her hands.

"May I also extend the Crown's sincerest welcome to Lord Ylor Peryval Nazeris, the Earl of Portcarcern and Lady Éline Diaren Nazeris, the Countess of South Kestoryn, who will be accompanying their father to the capital."

Ylor Nazeris gave a slight bow of the head, turning to grin smugly at Pennyn while Éline gazed modestly at the small crowd. She stood with her fingers laced in front of her, rubbing her palms together. Her eyes wandered solemnly over the room, never meeting his. Her lips were tightly pressed together in a narrow smile and her thin eyebrows ever so slightly furrowed. He smiled eagerly but her gaze never fell in one place, her eyes constantly meandering across the room. She turned around to face her brother, who gave her a cold, thin smile.

"Lord Nazeris will keep his title as the High Lord of Zaldron but has announced of his intention to abdicate in favour of his son, as soon as Lord Ylor is ready," said Pennyn. "So, until then, we will share Arcadius." The Crown Chancellor laughed, but nobody else found it funny. The whispers had begun again.

"Thank you, Mr Runeval. I do hope there is enough of me to be shared," he chuckled awkwardly, rubbing his round belly, to quiet, scattered laughter from the nobles. "All jokes aside, I do look forward to working with you, Crown Chancellor, and with the rest of the council."

Aren's eyes shifted over from the Treasurer to his children. Ylor subtly motioned to his sister and slipped away, and she followed, her head bowed. They stood behind a small table neighbouring Aren's. Ylor looked over, staring at him. He didn't break eye contact as he pulled out a chair loudly, smiling through him all the while. He winked as he sat down. Éline's gaze was still lowered, her palms flat on the table.

The High Lord of Zaldron walked up to the queen and bowed down to her. "I vow to serve the Kingdom loyally in the name of Your Majesty from now, until the day my duty is complete."

Jaspyn yawned noisily and Olivia struck him hard on the back of his hand.

"I pledge myself to the Crown, the People, and the Kingdom as their Treasurer, under Her Majesty Elvira the Third of House Aryssen, Queen of Landridge and East Asenia."

The queen stood up, her long burgundy train draping behind her. Pennyn Runeval walked up to her side, holding out a bronze vessel in his cupped hands.

"I call upon you, my lord, to serve your Kingdom, and I assent to your vows. I ordain unto you, the mantles of the Treasury, and the mantles of the Royal Banks and put into you my trust and my faith. Hold out your arms in the name of the Crown." She dipped two of her fingers into the bronze vessel and reached out to the lord's forearms, smearing them slowly with the clear Waters of Léoree.

"*Lyn Dendrus Landrizio,*" Lord Nazeris muttered, looking up at the queen, who smiled back at him.

"What's he saying?" said Jaspyn.

"Shhh," said Olivia, flapping her hands in front of him.

"*In the name of the Crown of Landridge,*" said Aren, keeping his eyes on Arcadius Nazeris, who got up and took three steps backwards before bowing to the queen once more. He turned to face the nobles and smiled, laying his eyes on Aren. There were a few claps here and there as he walked in silence to join his children.

Pennyn Runeval cleared his throat as he stepped forward once again to address the nobles. "Thank you. With everything going on in these turbulent times, I'm certain some shared efforts lie ahead of us," said Pennyn, "I'd like to reassure you all that we are very close to announcing who shall take on the role of Means Counsel."

The murmurs echoed once more as a few of the older nobles glanced over at Aren's table…but it wasn't Aren that they were looking at. Olivia's pale cheeks reddened.

"Pay no attention to them, Olivia," said Jaspyn. "They only see one side of the coin. Don't let anyone make you feel bad about your name. You're born with it, there's nothing you can do to change it."

Pennyn Runeval cleared his throat again, much louder this time and the murmurs quietened. He clapped twice, beckoning the chefs to clamber onto their feet. Each carried two or three silver platters, still steaming. One approached their table, clad in white from head to toe except his collar, which was laced in gold, and his toque, which bore Queen Elvira's burgundy monogram. He was a large man with a round waist and he stumbled and limped as he walked. He laid out the silver dishes on the table, rich cream-filled pastries, traditional stone-baked cheese and chicken dira and fried scampi. The smell was overwhelming, and Aren could hear his stomach growl. It had been a long morning.

The Boy Prince
Laris

A young boy stood up on a bench, his eyes sparkling with excitement. Laris Hontren eyed the lad carefully. His brow looked as if it was heavy with sweat, probably after having had to journey on foot here for miles from the Arvendon markets. After all, Laris himself had dragged himself to the palace from the squalor of Hartyl Street. The boy's pale, grimy face gleamed and sparkled under the light of the grand chandelier which hung above them from the ceiling, intricately decorated all over with diamonds and garnets and gold. It dangled at the very centre of the room, shining over the masses gathered in the vast Crown Foyer, some dressed in their finest silks whilst others wore dirty rags.

A single mesh drape hung between the common folk and the nobles, propped up by tall metallic columns and manned at every post by officers of the Royal Guard. The hall itself was truly grand, in every sense of the word. On his side of the curtain, hundreds of common people, heaping on top of each other against the boundaries to try and get a good view of the platform at the front of the room. Laris thanked his laurels for his towering stature, he needn't worry about not being able to see what he'd come here for. Not for now at least. If somebody tried to push *him* out of the way today, there would be blood.

But the other side of the curtain was a different thing altogether. A much larger portion of the hall, filled with nobles, dressed in the richest of purples and blacks and reds. The majority of them were sat at long, rectangular tables, while others were stood around the hall, milling about in smaller groups.

There were cheers and catcalls from the back of the hall. Laris turned to see what was going on. A dark-haired woman stood on the other side of the net curtain; hands pressed against it. Behind the whistles, Laris could just about make out her sweet voice. She was a noblewoman, but Laris didn't recognise her. A noblewoman talking to the lowborn. Could her intentions be as noble as she'd have liked the peasants to believe? There weren't many nobles at all that even looked people like him in the eyes and if they ever did, there was always a motive… a hidden agenda. Perhaps this one wanted to win their hearts in the name of the Crown Prince. After all, that's why they were all gathered here today. Well, most of them, anyway. Laris, of course, had his own reasons.

"It's him! It's the Prince!" A voice came from in front of him. It was the lad stood on the bench, leaping up in joy. "Daddy, look!" he exclaimed.

Laris got closer to get a better look. Hurriedly, the boy rushed to hush his father and the others around him, pointing excitedly to the doorway.

"He's going to talk! Daddy…look! Shhhh."

Finally, a figure appeared from the doorway, a fairly short man, with bronzed skin and short, dark hair. Those around the father and son shuffled around to try and get glimpse, and a few children groaned forlornly, not tall enough to see what was going on. The boy's father looked confused.

"No, lad, it's not the prince," said Laris. He wasn't going to say anything at first, but something about the twinkle in the boy's eye told him that he should. "That's just the Chancellor, he's not royalty, he's just like the rest of us," Laris laughed.

The boy turned around, then looked at his father, bewildered.

"The Crown Chancellor, Donny, he takes care of things for the queen. His name is Mr. Runeval," the boy's father said. "Pennyn Runeval." The father smiled at Laris with narrowed eyes.

"What things?" said Donny.

"You know, all the things the queen deals with. The farmers, the shops, soldiers too! The chancellor helps keep 'em all in check," said the father. Laris looked back through the thin curtain to the nobles, pretending not to listen to the father and son.

"Then…then what does the queen do? And why can't Prince Aren do all that, why do we need Mr. Ru- … *Mr. Ruvenal?*"

"Mr. Runeval," his father corrected him. "He's there to set everyone straight, make sure everyone's following the rules, upholding her justice. And as for the prince, he doesn't–"

"The prince?" Laris couldn't take it anymore. He roared in laughter, leaving the boy in hysterics. "How often have you even seen the measly little git? *Bravery and valour,* is it? I'd bet he doesn't even–"

"Excuse me, sir!" The boy's father covered his son's ears. "If you don't care for the queen or her family, why are you even here? Why must you spread your poison, with that vile tongue of yours too. Let the children have someone they look up to, they've got years to learn and grow. Besides..." He lowered his voice and looked around. "They should know where the power is... Even more so these days."

"Why I'm here is my business and mine alone," said Laris gruffly. "Where the power is? The lad should see the truth while he's still young, no point feeding into childish fantasies of heroes and nobles and blue blood. The power is, and always has been, with the *people*. Now, if people like you keep empowering the bitch in her fancy glass dining halls and–"

"QUIET!! Damn you!" The father was seething. He took a step towards him, looking up at his face but just one glimpse of the scars just beneath his left ear and the man backed away. Laris smirked. Quietly ushering the boy off the bench, the father glared at him in disgust and walked away.

Laris sneered, making sure it was obvious that he was proud of himself. It was clear that that man was pretending to be someone he wasn't, half the common lot here were. He looked around at their pathetic attempts at trying to fit in, trying to live the life of a noble, even just for one day. Stained tunics made to look as if they were made of silk, but it was obvious to anyone with a pair of good eyes that they weren't. Burgundy scarves draped over the shoulder. Not enough to hide the dirty rags beneath. He had no such intentions. The curtain between him and the nobles was thin, but it was there. He wore a ragged brown vest, over his fraying grey shirt. Safely tucked in the top pocket of his shirt was the tattered old piece of paper that had brought him to this godforsaken place. He gently rubbed his hand over it as if to make sure it was still there, full well knowing that no one had dared come close enough to him to attempt picking his pockets. He didn't have to explain himself to anyone, he was here for his own reasons. He, of course, had no interest in watching their Verenic masters flail about with a bow and arrow. It was the cold chill of a previous life that drew him here, but he'd never admit that to anyone, and nor should he have to.

The crowds fell quiet as Pennyn Runeval walked forward to address the masses.

"It's *Mr Ruvenal!* He's about to speak, daddy!" Came little Donny's voice from a small distance as his father tried frantically to shush him. Laris chuckled to himself at the innocence of children. Knocking a rather round man out of the way, he walked up as close to the mesh curtain as he could without falling through it entirely or getting stopped by one of the royal guards. He wondered where the queen was, or the prince, for that matter. Oh well, he didn't care. He wasn't here for them.

He combed through the noble crowds between himself and the chancellor. Through the doorway in the distance, he caught a quick glimpse of a tall, young man with bright red hair, dressed in dark red. Not one of the royals, it was clear. Perhaps one of the nobles' children? The lad disappeared behind the wall before he could get a second look. He cast his eyes over the rest of them. But the search was futile. She wasn't there. He could only see nobles that he had no interest in acquainting with. So incredibly pompous, sat miles apart from each other whilst the rest of them on *this* side of the curtain struggled to catch sight of what was going on, pushing and shoving each other. There were several long tables, all leading towards the chancellor, near where a small ensemble was sat, tuning their instruments. Some tables were sparser than others, with maybe two or three lords or ladies sat along them. Others seated a handful of nobles, all pretending to listen to the Crown Chancellor's dull speech.

For the most part, they seemed as if they'd been moulded from the same clay. The same proud silks to match their proud faces. Most were careful to avoid looking towards the common folk altogether, consciously tilting their heads to face the opposite side of the hall. Some stood out, though. On one table, a young copper-skinned woman with curly black hair. She wore a lilac dress bearing a white orchid, a silver bracelet on her left wrist. She didn't look like she belonged there, but she smiled thinly into nothing just the same. Across the table, a swarthy man, wearing a charcoal silk tunic and tightly bound light fawn slacks. Something about him too seemed peculiar, different from the other aristocrats. He made less of an effort to appear interested in the mundane affair. He looked as if he'd rather be elsewhere.

Laris looked at the crest woven into his tunic. It must have been one of the Verenic noble houses. There were so few Weslin noble families left that he recognised each and every one of their marks. Hercan, Ashcrest, Banlin...Dresden. He knew them all. This one, though...it was something else. He racked his brains trying to figure out where he'd seen the three blades before. *The Purple Blades*. She'd shown him in a book, once. Of course. This was the crest of House Escos.

There was an eerie sense of calm about him, the Escosi, that could not quite be placed. An emptiness upon his face, as if he had even less reason to be here than Laris Hontren himself. The Escosi was sat next to the famous Lord Nazeris of Zaldron, and despite the fact that Laris knew neither of the men, he couldn't bring himself to trust either of them. Luckily, he had no need to.

A woman with dark hair appeared next to the pair. His heart stopped for a moment. Could it have been her? Alas, just some other Weslin woman he didn't recognise. *Wait*. He did recognise her. It was the woman from earlier, the one that had been talking to the common folk. The only one that had given them more than an ounce of attention this whole afternoon.

She whispered in the Escosi's ear as she hugged him and ran her hand over the top of the man's chest, before smiling politely and quickly walking away. Particularly handsy, for a noblewoman. Except, she hadn't just fondled him, *had she?* It almost looked as if...*had she slid something into his pocket?* He couldn't see it clearly; he was too far away. He also didn't care enough to strain his eyes any longer. The bizarre lives of nobles, he mused. Wasting so much gold on this unnecessary gathering and all of the luxury that came with it to satisfy the desires of richer men, for what? To what end? The tables were all adorned with glistening bronze dove ornaments at their centre. He wondered how many days of bread even *one* of these pieces could afford him. All this for the prince who never showed, he thought. Where was he anyway?

The Crown Chancellor finally reached the end of his tedious speech. "My Lords, Ladies, Good folk and Elders," he announced, "I now call upon Her Majesty, Queen Elvira of Landridge and East Asenia. Please rise."

As the queen finally emerged onto the platform, the band at the front of the hall began playing the Skyvern's March. *Dreadful sound*. Laris had never much enjoyed it. The lords and ladies rose from their seats. Behind him, a blaring cheer stirred amongst the common folk, a few bellows and whistles trailing after the rest of the applause had stopped.

"My Lords, Ladies, Good-folk and Elders," her voice boomed across the room.

He cared little for what she had to say, though more than he'd cared for Pennyn Runeval, granted. While she spoke, a large trunk, covered in a white and golden sleeve was being slowly and carefully lowered just above the platform by a thick, white rope. Some of the common children gasped and turned to look at it, some even cheering and pointing loudly. The queen ignored them all and carried on.

"And it is with great happiness that I now call upon my son, His Highness Aren of the noble House Aryssen, Crown Prince of Landridge and East Asenia. *Lyn Dendrus Landrizio.*"

Laris had endured enough. He just wanted them to get on with it. The drummers in the small orchestra played heartily as the boy prince finally walked out onto the stage. Noble and commoner alike, the hall roared in applause as he made his way to the front of the platform, stone-faced as ever. He wore a simple dark burgundy tunic, tight charcoal slacks underneath. In his right hand he carried an old, black-plated bow. A quiver had been placed on a small stool near the left of the stage. In it, a set of arrows, each with a dark red arrowhead.

Pennyn Runeval and Elvira stood at the back of the stage, next to some other Verenic man. He was older, much older, his thick beard grey and his hair balding. He was dressed in long beige robes. Perhaps the High Minister, by the looks of things at least. Behind them, two members of the First Guard. They looked as if they wouldn't be able to defend the queen from a swarm of butterflies, let alone a real threat. Such delicate uniforms, a pompous burgundy cape trailing behind them – they'd be useless in combat, those silly frocks. He shuddered at the thought that these men were considered the fiercest and most feared warriors in the kingdom. Fierce and feared was found under the shade of the Arvendon Bridge, or amongst the smiths of Astonkirk, not sat pompously in some palace built on the blood of innocents.

A large podium was being carried out at the opposite end of the platform. It was black in colour, bearing the crest of House Aryssen. It must have been at least partially hollow from the top, from what Laris could see, with a large bronze chalice peering out from within it. The ugly thing towered well over the boy, tall enough to cast a shadow over half of the crowd of nobles.

With long, powerful strides, the boy prince walked to the edge of the stage, picking up the quiver. He looked shaky. Who wouldn't be? Anyone's heart would be in their mouth, for sure. After all, the lad was barely nineteen years. Laris thought back to when he himself was nineteen years old. The world was different then. Well, then again, Laris wasn't a Crown Prince, was he? This boy was…he wasn't just a petty commoner. He had great power, great riches – there was a price to pay for all that. There had to be. He watched Aren Aryssen trying his best to embody confidence and strength as he looked out at the crowds and bowed. The prince then uttered a few words in Old Verenic. A sullen tongue, certainly, but it did have its own beauty.

"Eno Deryz Teceziar, Lyn Dendrus Landrizio y pyrzun tilaria pero dalto se benora ten herorzia hin pyrio."

Laris hadn't a clue what it meant. Some whimsical lie, he was sure. Something of crowns and blood and faith. The podium opposite the prince suddenly let out immense flames from the top of the chalice, reaching up much, much higher than the lad himself. The flames burned tall between the boy at one end and the old trunk that hung from the ceiling at the opposite end.

The prince took his first step forward, his bow under his right arm. It was a different walk now. A more rehearsed one, veiled thinly by poise and composure. Until he stumbled. He'd gotten his boot caught in a crack in the stage. It was small, but everybody had seen it. Dispersed laughter erupted from the common crowds around Laris as the boy prince regained his balance and continued forward. He saw some of the nobles covering their faces and looking away as they sneered, too.

"Geddonwithit ya toff!" someone bellowed loudly from behind Laris, to a roar of jeers and laughter. Laris sniggered but was sure the prince had heard it too. The poor boy looked tense as ever but kept his face stern and hard as he continued marching on.

He lifted a red-tipped arrow from the quiver, muttering something quietly to himself. Maybe a prayer. They seemed at one with their faith, the royal family. How much of it was real, and how much just for show?

"Louder!" shouted somebody from the crowd. It was the same voice from before. Laris no longer found it amusing, he was waiting for the affair to be done with. From the looks of his face, it seemed that the Crown Prince thought the same. At least they had *that* in common.

Very carefully, the boy nocked his arrow, raising the bow and aiming it at the flames rising high above the podium. He waited, breathing slowly until the tremble of his hands had all but stopped. He lowered his hand again. Even from a fair distance, Laris could see clearly how unsteady the lad was. He waited patiently, breathing slower and deeper. The hall fell to near silence again as every noble and commoner alike waited with bated breath to see if their future king was worthy of his crown.

Laris knew what the prince was doing. He was waiting for gaps in the flame, seeing if he could glimpse the trunk hanging from the ceiling behind the fiery podium. It had only been a few moments, but it had felt a lot longer. Laris knew that a bow, especially a big one like that, got heavier the longer you held it. The boy had to act quickly if he didn't want to make a joke of it.

And that was when the prince quickly jolted his bow up higher, aiming at the thick rope holding the trunk. The lad must have caught site of it. He was patient. Wasting not a second more than necessary, he drew back the string, pulling his arm so far back that his right hand brushed his right cheek. He let go. The arrow soared through the flames, its head catching fire almost instantly – then went on towards the rope, missing it. Laris' heart skipped a beat. He looked away. He didn't care for the boy prince nor this silly ritual, but he'd become caught up in the moment.

There were cheers from the nobles, and he looked back. It was done. The arrow had skimmed past the rope, but that had been enough. The flames licked the rope and the rope quickly set ablaze too. Slowly but surely, strand by strand the rope charred and turned to dust until the weight of the trunk hanging below it was too much to bear. Down fell the trunk, with a loud thud that echoed ferociously throughout the hall, making some of the younger children around him gasp. The prince stepped forward and turned to face the crowds, who had all started cheering and clapping. He was ushered back by Pennyn Runeval to the old, robed man stood beside the queen.

"I now call upon His Eminence Myril Hernelis, the Minister of the High Parydon, to ordain the Crown Prince as the next King of Landridge and East Asenia, as well as the next great Deryz of the Verenian faith."

The tall, kindly-looking man smiled and nodded at Elvira Aryssen, walking up to the podium where the fire had been put out and the chalice was being removed by two gloved men dressed in beige tunics. He held out his hands, and the men offered him the chalice, smeared with ashes and oil. The minister walked back to Aren, chalice in his left hand. He got out a small piece of white cloth from inside the pocket of his robes, and rubbed it against the inside of the cup, before lifting it up to Aren's forehead and gently dabbing it against his forehead. He muttered a prayer in Verenic, loudly. Laris could hear the words clearly but had no idea what they meant. The old man repeated the ritual, dabbing the cloth gently against the boy's skin, at the bottom of first his right eye, and then his left. An incredibly bizarre way to ordain a future king, Laris would never be able to understand these people. One by one, the minister repeated the rite, doing the same with both of Aren's arms and finally both of his palms.

"Lyn Dendrus Landrizio."

The crowds erupted in applause as the prince bowed before them. Laris remained silent, watching solemnly from behind the curtain. The nobles all rose up in respect and the prince smiled, for the first time that afternoon. It looked almost like a genuine smile. He walked forth, almost to the edge of the raised platform, and waved at the crowds looking up at him. In that moment, he looked no more a prince than little Donny. The same innocence, the same pride. It was a pity that Aren Aryssen's fate had much more in store for him though.

Two men, dressed in the familiar beige tunics walked out onto the stage and lifted the old trunk, carrying it back out of the hall into another room, a smaller one. A chef walked out of the room and held the doors for them. Must be the kitchens. It made sense, too. Laris knew what the trunk held inside it. Heaps and heaps of Asenian cherries, ready to be made into a Red Pudding by the finest chefs of Sturrock. Indulgence was part of the reason he was here, after all.

Some of the commoners towards the back roared louder and louder as the trunk was carried away from them. The chef holding the doors was a large, round man. Fitting, Laris had to admit. He slipped into the hall quietly while the crowds cheered for their Crown Prince. Something about him was suspicious though…Laris had an eye for that sort of thing. He watched the chef closely as he slid past the nobles, smiling and nodding awkwardly at a couple of them along the way. The fat man's eyes were fixed though, on one table in particular. He made for it. It was the table with the beautiful dark-skinned woman, the one in the lilac dress. He looked straight past her though, at another noble. The one dressed in black. The Escosi nobleman. The chef nodded at him, and the nobleman got up from his seat quietly. To Laris' surprise, the chef suddenly smiled from ear to ear and spread out his great fat arms and hugged the nobleman tightly. The men embraced for a moment, before the chef suddenly withdrew, nodded and slipped away again as quickly as he'd came.

"Oi!"

Laris turned around.

"What you playing at?" said a deep voice. It was a large, well-built man, similar in stature to Laris himself. He was stood beside a round boy, with dusty brown hair.

"What do you want?" barked Laris.

"Geddout of the way!" he shouted, and some of the peasants around him jeered and scoffed at Laris.

Laris stood his ground, turning back around to face the stage. He ignored the shouting behind him.

"You bloomin' idiot!" shouted the man. "I saw how awful you were to that poor man and his son earlier. I saw you push people outta the way to get to that curtain, and you just all but kicked my son over to stay there. What ya playing at? Maybe I'll kick *you* outta the way," he hissed.

The threat didn't scare Laris. He turned back around and smiled maliciously at the man. "Maybe if your fat son had eaten less pies in his younger days there'd have been a little more space for both of us."

The man charged at Laris fist-first, knocking him back into the curtain and causing a roar of sneers from the commoners around him. His chest stung from where the man had punched him. He worked up the power to strike back and swung hard. It was too late.

He was on his knees, his stomach in agony from where the man had kicked him. He punched the man right in his balls. The man yelled out in pain and Laris punched him in the face, clambering to his feet and pushing him back into his son.

There was a loud noise. He felt an extreme pain in the back of his leg and suddenly he was on the floor. He rolled over, wincing quietly to see two Royal Guards stood over him, their rifles pointed at his head.

The List

Aren

Aren looked to see where all the noise coming from. The crowds behind the curtain, they were jeering and milling around one of the benches. A circle of royal guards pushed the commoners away as the cheers turned feral. Aren didn't care. He felt free, liberated. He took in a deep breath and smiled. Most of the burden that had plagued him for weeks was finally gone.

Looking at the crowds before him, he knew in his heart it had all been worth it. Behind the curtain, little children sat on their fathers' and mothers' shoulders to try and get a better look at him. Closer, dozens of smiling nobles' faces looked up at him, gleaming with pride. Amongst the smiling faces was one that he recognised, though he couldn't quite figure out where from. She'd stood up and was clapping frantically even after many of the other nobles had stopped. An older woman, she had light brown hair, a kindly face, only slightly wrinkled by her years though he supposed that she must have been around his mother's age. The woman was sat by herself on a table across from the Crown Council.

As the nobles all sat down once more and the noise died down, he took a step back to stand beside his mother while the chancellor began to say some words. Aren's mind wasn't fixed on the speech though, it was wandering.

He considered the importance of the conversations he'd have tonight. He eyed each member sat along the central table. Lord Nazeris, then Lord Gavyn Escos, the Arms Counsel. An influential voice at court, years of experience in matters of war and defence behind him. An extremely important man for the family – one whose heart Aren knew he had to win. Opposite him, Aren's uncle Skander, the Crown Envoy. Everyone had always marvelled at how remarkably similar Aren looked to him, though Aren had

54

never really been able to see it himself. The man had an incredibly innocent face, like that of a child.

He glanced over the rest of the table. Devis Kennard, the Lord of Clandestine Affairs. Aren had only met him once, a shrewd man with a constant frown on his face but polite enough where it mattered most. Next to him, Valery Rennero, the Health Counsel. He knew her probably the best. She was an incredibly kind lady, one of the best. She had had long blonde locks when he'd first met her. Those blonde locks had long since been tied neatly into a silver bun. She always did look so immaculate, especially for somebody who worked as hard as she did.

Finally, right at the end of the table was the Justice Counsel, Lord Oscon Spenler. Probably the biggest mystery on that table as far as Aren was concerned. He knew little about the man, except that he was very good at what he did. He'd taught the Laws of the Old Federation at the University of Ayleris for seven years before he took his seat in Council. Quite a remarkable feat for a man of his age. Strangely though, Aren was less conscious of meeting Oscon tonight than he was of meeting his sister Linara. Pennyn had said she'd be important. He had no idea how he'd go about it; he'd heard from Olivia that she was a rather discourteous woman...that her brother Fraston was far more amicable. It was a pity that *he* was not a priority to Pennyn Runeval. Aren eyed the empty cushioned seat between Valery and Oscon, the one meant for the Means Counsel, and he went through each of the names of the nobles before him today in his head. So many names, but so few that he knew well.

Aren noticed the empty table right at the back of the hall, brushing up against the meshed curtain. It appeared that despite the Crown's numerous invitations to the Fenwern family, they had not been able to make it after all. He had thought that it might've been too soon to invite them to something like this, a celebration of sorts, but his mother had been adamant. A mistake, clearly. He wondered why Jaspyn hadn't told him earlier, he'd had plenty of opportunities.

Pennyn Runeval finished his speech and suddenly it was time. Time to make his mark. The nobles busied themselves, straightening their tunics, putting down their wine glasses, all desperately eager to welcome their prince. Well, nearly all of them.

He stepped forth and the queen followed, placing her hand gently on his shoulder.

"Just a moment," she said to her First Guard, shooing them away. She took him aside where they wouldn't be heard. "It's time, Aren."

"I know," he replied, a bead of sweat trickling down the side of his face. His mouth was dry, and he leant to the side, stretching out his arm for a glass of water but she stopped him.

"I won't take long," she whispered. "Let me be frank. This is an opportunity for you to make a name for yourself at court, and not just the name you were lucky enough to have been born with. An arrow was never going to make that name for you, my boy. How the people see you today – noble or otherwise – that is how you will make your name."

He felt at odds with what she'd said, if he was honest. It was as if all the hard work he'd put into the Recedon, all the training, it had been for nothing. For months he'd been constantly reminded how important it was, for months he'd laboured over it and just like that, she'd brushed it off as if it were a piece of pie.

"But you did incredibly well. Look at them, look at their faces… They love you. They're eager to hear from you, which is a good sign. You'll always have plenty of time to spend with your friends, my boy, but this is going to be your best chance at spending time with your people."

"Yes, I told them, Jaspyn and Olivia. That I won't be able to see them until after I've met each and every one of the nobles, especially the ones Pennyn would like for me to meet."

She smiled at him. "Don't treat it like a chore. You'll look back on this night and wish you'd spent more time just talking to your subjects, getting to know them. I know I do."

"What was your Recedon like?" he asked.

She laughed. "There will be plenty of time for those stories later," she held out her hand and a steward reached forward from behind a table and handed her a glass of clear water. She passed it to Aren, its touch was icy. It felt calming against his blistered, sweaty palms.

"Here, drink up so you are ready for whatever the evening throws your way," she said. He nodded and gulped the water.

It was as if she'd appeared out of thin air when Aren saw her, behind his mother, he recognised her straight away. The woman that had been sat amongst the nobles, by the Crown Council. She stretched forward her hand and tapped the queen on the shoulder, hard. His mother turned around, but it was too late. A First Guard had his left hand wrapped tightly around the woman's arm, his other reaching towards his weapon.

"Stand down, Sir Ysser, this is no foe," said Elvira, laughing softly. "I mean it, now, unhand her."

"You heard her," said the woman, shaking her hand free. "Don't do that again."

His mother leapt forward into a warm embrace, leaving almost no time for Sir Ysser to pull away.

"Aren, you know Lady Rayne," said his mother.

"I don't expect he does," the woman chuckled, raising her thick eyebrows at Aren. "Been hiding from me for so many years, haven't you?" She lowered her spectacles down from the bridge of her slightly crooked nose. Her face was kind, and he felt a sense of safety and warmth in her company, but if he was being honest, he had no idea who she was.

"Of Jertonshield, my lady?" said Aren.

She laughed hysterically. "No, no, of course not. Of Lyndan, I suppose."

Suddenly Aren felt very embarrassed. "Lady Rayne Dresden, of course," he said. He knew her only by name, had he ever met her before? Probably not. He'd heard great stories about the High Lady of Medlanta, though. The fierce mare of the peninsula. She'd built up quite a reputation at court, for someone who had spent no time there. Something he shared with her, he supposed. Some had gone as far as describing her as a recluse. He couldn't blame them either, she never visited Sturrock anymore, not even with her own sister at the Valecrest. Lord only knew when his aunt Wynter had last seen her.

She looked at him oddly, a soft smile on her face. "Good lord, you're a spitting image of him."

"Uncle Skander?" he said. He'd heard that enough, he didn't need it coming from his uncle's sister-in-law as well.

Rayne laughed raucously again. "No, silly boy. Weryn."

"Oh," he said awkwardly. "Of-of course," he added sheepishly. He'd heard that she had been close to his father.

She gently ruffled his hair, much like his mother sometimes did. "You've been feeding him well, I see," she said, turning to face the queen. Rayne's face suddenly darkened. "Or I should say, *they've* been feeding him well, up in Asenia."

"Indeed… they have," said his mother, laughing it off. Rayne wasn't laughing anymore, though. She had a peculiar knowing expression on her face which sort of gave Aren the chills.

"Say, have you seen Wynter?" she said suddenly. "Lord, she's always frolicking about. I saw poor old Skander sat by himself while your chancellor was giving his never-ending speech. How she can just leave her husband to his wits like that is beyond me."

"I think I saw her with Lady Linara earlier on. Before the speech," said his mother.

"The Spenler girl?" said Rayne. She shook her head. "Wynter would never go near the plebs. The Spenler girl was right up in their faces, I saw her. How she can mingle so freely with them like that I'll never understand. Did you hear of the arrest your lovely guards made earlier? An oaf of a man."

"Ah, is that so?" said the queen, subtly looking over her shoulder to see if anybody was within earshot. She glanced over at her brother, Skander, who was still sat at the Council's table with the other nobles.

"Well, Inigo's not with his father," said the queen.

"And he's not with his sisters either is he?" said Rayne. "I saw them by the kitchens, with the Berywen girl and that red-haired lad."

"Vidalia and Cyera? Yes, they're both with Olivia," said Aren.

"Olivia, eh?" said Rayne, her eyes narrowed. "Well Olivia looks like she would get along well with the girls."

"So, I imagine he was getting quite tired," the queen continued. "Inigo. He was probably fussing, he does that a lot. She might have taken him out into the courtyard, he does love it out there."

"Ah, that sounds about right," said Rayne solemnly.

It suddenly dawned on Aren that she had probably never even met her nephew. The littlest Aryssen wasn't even two – he'd been born long after Rayne had turned her back on Sturrock for the last time. Inigo had rarely seen outside of the palace walls, let alone outside of Sturrock, Uncle Skander had made sure of that. So, aside from the odd picture of him, Rayne had probably had very little to go on.

"Well, *Your Majesty*," said Rayne, almost mockingly. "I really must take my leave now. I sense if I keep you and the prince from your eager subjects any longer, I might lose my head." She looked over at the First Guard, Ysser. "If *he* doesn't take it first. I'm watching you, lad."

His mother laughed as if she'd forgotten where she was stood for a brief moment before quickly composing herself again.

"I suppose I should pay them some attention," said the queen. "Some of them have made longer journeys than you." She laughed out loud again and this time some heads turned from near the Crown Council. Aren had rarely, if ever, heard a joke come out of his mother's mouth, let alone in front of nobles. He was even more shocked, however, when Lady Rayne pulled a silly face at his mother, sticking her tongue out at her like he might have expected from his little cousin Cyera.

"See you when I see you," Rayne said to the queen. "Bye bye now, little one," she said to Aren, smiling. He wasn't sure he'd ever met anybody like her, not in this world nor in the other. Quite the personality, to put it lightly, and the flamboyance to go with it too, her hands flailing about while she spoke.

He cast his eyes over the nobles again. A pair of wide eyes stared back. A woman's…a woman who he didn't know. She didn't look like she was from around here, dark skin and thick, curly black hair. She wore a flowery purple dress, something from a faraway land. His mother was quick to note his gaze.

"Zenara Itris," she said. "She's a former Asmoni dignitary. She's lived here for nearly all her life, though, her mother was Landridgian. From Astonkirk."

Aren had heard the name somewhere. Not from his mother, certainly, but it sounded familiar.

"Her father was quite an important man in Asmon," his mother continued. "You'd do well to drop by and say hello."

He quickly realised where he'd heard the name – from Olivia. It had been quite a scandal amongst the bluecoats. This woman had been involved with Soren Ashcrest, if the rumours were to be believed. While Lady Ashcrest was still alive. A mistress. She looked a lot younger than Eyan's mother, now that Aren had actually seen her.

"Why was *she* invited?" asked Aren. "I've heard rumours she'd been involved with the bluecoats."

"Allegedly. And briefly."

"Would it send the best message, having her here?" said Aren in hushed tones. "After all, Asmon itself is a republic."

"Yes," said his mother. "In fact, her father was the Premier."

"What?" said Aren, in awe. "A Premier?! *Quite* an important man then." He looked at the Asmoni woman again, sat amidst a small crowd yet lonelier than ever, judging by the look on her face. Gavyn Escos on one side, Fraston Spenler on the other, both with their backs turned to her. "And you trust this…Zenara?" he asked.

"She's a sympathiser, at best, Aren… she *herself* has brought us no harm. Like I said, her father was indeed a very important man – that makes her a very important woman," said his mother. "I invited her here today to help build some bridges, perhaps win over an Asmoni influence. Her alleged association with the bluecoats, however brief, is a stroke of luck for us if anything. Having someone like that endorse the Crown? That's an asset."

Aren quietly nodded but he was far from convinced. Someone so deeply involved with Ashcrest himself? But there was no way she'd change her mind and he wasn't going to embarrass himself trying to talk her into it.

"Right, I shall leave you to it, then," said his mother, clapping her hands together. "You know what you're here to do."

Easy for her to say. Before he'd had time to answer, she'd turned around and she was gone.

She was stood next to the kitchen doors by herself when Aren finally found her. He was scared, in some ways, she didn't seem like she was happy. But then again from what he'd heard, Linara Spenler rarely ever did look like she was happy. He'd just have to get over it. He anxiously walked over, rehearsing in his head what he'd say, how he'd say it, again and again until he was sick of it. He was just grateful she was alone.

A rather large man emerged from the kitchen doors, it was the chef. He knew Chef Roy, though admittedly not as well as his predecessor. Roy had only joined the palace staff within the last year. Him and Chef Herssel didn't really get along, and if Aren was being honest, he much preferred the company of Herssel, his warm smile and friendly chats. Chef Roy was a proud man, he was less pleasant to be around at times. Luckily, he usually kept to himself.

To his surprise, the chef made right for Linara. Unlucky for Aren, he'd hoped to catch her alone. Her eyes met the chefs from a distance and neither said a word. The chef merely slowed down, shook his head like a dog, then walked away. *How bizarre.* Linara suddenly caught notice of Aren, though. The woman turned and smiled at him thinly, tucking a braid of her long brown hair behind her right ear.

"Your Highness," she said, attempting a curtsy – one of the least polished ones Aren had seen. "What can I do for you?"

"My lady, I was wondering if I could perhaps have a short word with you, maybe out in the Central Courtyard?"

Linara looked around and then shrugged nonchalantly, "If you wish. It's up to you, Your Highness." She toyed with her watch, waiting for him to say something. It seemed as if this were the last place she'd have liked to be.

"I suppose we could stay here," said Aren, pulling up his sleeves and crossing his arms. "You're from Fencliffe, right?"

"Yes. Well, originally. Spent the last few years in the capital, of course," she said.

"And what brought you to Sturrock?"

She raised her brow. "What brings anyone here?" she said. "Work, sir. My brother works with the merchants of Wyntock End, I've been helping him."

"Lord Fraston?" said Aren, then cursed himself under his breath. She'd probably think he was stupid now. It was hardly going to be Oscon, was it? What business would the Justice Counsel have with the merchants of Wyntock End?

"Yes, Fraston," she said. "He's been working with some of the traders to help with the shortages back home. I'm sure you've heard of the droughts. In Fencliffe?"

"Yes," said Aren, though he knew little about them. "And I suppose with Lord Oscon here too, the three of you in the same city, you must all be quite close?"

"Well, I don't really see Oscon very often," she said, fidgeting with the lace on her collar. "What with his fancy seat at the Council. I saw him today after months."

She was a difficult person to speak to. "Is that so? A shame," he said. "I suppose, then, that you'd relish a role that allowed you to see your brother more often? Maybe one here at court?"

"With all due respect, you can stop, Your Highness." The woman smiled at him in pity. "I know what you are trying to do."

Aren looked at her in confusion. "And what am I trying to do?"

"You're trying to find a new Means Counsel."

He hadn't been expecting that. "Well, say if that was my agenda here, what would you say to that?"

"Well, I mean no disrespect, Your Highness," she said, lowering her gaze. "And I stress on that, I truly don't mean *any* disrespect. But I know that I'm not the only one being considered, am I? And if I'm being quite honest…I think there are probably others much more suited to the role than I."

"On the contrary, I think that the work you've done here proves that you might actually be the perfect person for it. Besides, your history in Fencliffe precedes you. The work you've done at the wheat farms, it's quite remarkable," said Aren, shuffling on his feet. "And you know Fencliffe inside and out. Frankly, you would be an incredibly valuable asset to the Crown. One that we can work with to uphold the peace and prosperity this kingdom has seen for so many years."

It was a well-rehearsed speech. He'd been practicing, picking up bits and pieces from Pennyn who was probably the most articulate man he knew, aside from Uncle Skander.

"*So* many years?" said Linara curiously, raising her eyebrows slightly. "I beg your pardon, sir, but I think I must get on with the dinner. Do convey my regards to Her Majesty, just in case I don't get the chance to speak with her personally," she said frantically, and with another quick curtsy, she was on her way.

What a rude woman. Never once in his life had a noble or commoner had the audacity to speak to him like that. At least, not in this world. Would she have acted the same way if it was his mother that she had been addressing and not him? It was difficult to say.

"Aren!" came a voice. It was odd, he wasn't used to hearing his own name. Not in a place like this. He spotted Lady Rayne bearing a wide grin at him.

"Aren! Don't make me run all that way," she groaned, waving her hands about maniacally.

"Greetings, my lady," said Aren, as some of the nobles beside him murmured.

The woman looked to her left and then her right, then winked at him. "You can stop with the wishy-washy *greetings* nonsense, lad."

Aren suppressed a laugh. He felt quite comfortable around her now – as if they'd known each other for quite a while. They *had* known each other for quite a while, he supposed, but never properly.

"Where are you lost, lad?" she said, clicking in front of his face. "What are you doing here? I've just been with your friends over there, they're by the photographer," she pointed at a small table near the front of the hall, "Olivia Berywen," she said, looking up as if thinking deeply. "And the common boy, the redhead, I forget–"

"Jaspyn."

"Yes, yes, Jaspyn," she said. She looked at him closely, her eyes narrowed. "Well, what is it?" she said.

"Your pardon?"

"Your face," she continued, tutting. "You look awfully tense. Such wrinkles won't do you so good, not at your age. So…what is it? What is it you are trying to do here, lurking by yourself in the corner by the kitchens?"

How was he going to get out of this? "I'm not trying to, I… I suppose I just got a tad overwhelmed by everything. Thought I'd take a moment to myself, is all."

She stared at him a bit, her eyes still narrowed. "A bad liar," she said. She smiled then, lowering her voice to just above a whisper, "I'm only pulling your leg – your mam's told me all about your agenda for the evening."

Why would she do that?

"Trust," said Rayne suddenly. "It's an immensely beautiful thing, isn't it? Your mother wants to teach *you* all about trust, and how to spend it." She lowered her round glasses to the bridge of her nose and looked at him curiously. "And make no mistake, it *is* something you spend, trust. You must be wise with how you do so," she chuckled. "Yes, the pursuit of a new member of council is always a tedious one," she said, tutting. "Let alone the role that nobody wants, in a time that challenges the best of us. And I mean, even if someone did want the role, the offer coming from you? Hmm. Might just prove a slight hindrance."

"Why would I be a hindrance?" said Aren, eyebrows furrowed.

Rayne laughed. "I mean no offence, Aren, I really don't, but how often do your subjects catch glimpses of you?" she said. "How often do you meet with the Council? Any of the other countless nobles in this city? How much do you suppose that they actually *see* the heir to their throne? This…this gathering here is probably the longest appearance that you've made in one place in *years*. How can you then so simply expect them to take you seriously?"

What she was saying was fair, but had he been given the opportunity to change that? How was he supposed to prove himself to his people if he couldn't even prove himself to the nobles? And how was he supposed to prove himself to the nobles if they wouldn't even give him the chance? If they wouldn't…*trust* him.

"So, how can I get them to trust me?" said Aren.

"Another quick learner. You take after your father in that regard," she said. "Trust will come with time."

"That is something I don't have," said Aren. "The queen and Mr. Runeval wish to speak to me soon after this whole thing. If I had to guess, they will ask me lots of questions about today, about each of the nobles I met. Maybe even about who should fill the seat of Means Counsel."

"The queen? Is that what you call your mam?" she said, raising her eyebrows. "Ah, and Mr. Runeval, of course…" she added, her upper lip curled up almost in disgust. "Well, Aren, how did I get *you* to trust me? Upon our first real encounter, no less."

"How do you even know that I trust you?"

"Oh, sweet boy. We're beyond such petty lies, wouldn't you say? I think we both know that you do trust me, it's all in your eyes. To which extent, I cannot say, but you want to open up to me…you believe I'm a good person at heart."

"You opened up to me, you were honest and reassuring," said Aren, tired of the whole thing. "That is why I trust you." This lesson was taking a lot longer than he'd have liked.

"Yes, yes. But of course, *honest and reassuring* can only get you so far," she said. "I showed all my cards. Or at least, I let you think I showed you all my cards, that's all that matters. I told you of my agenda from the very beginning, leaving us no room to go back and forth on what I want from the conversation."

"So, then I need to tell them exactly what I'm doing while I'm doing it?" said Aren, in disbelief. He wasn't quite sure what to make of it.

She nodded. "Tell them what you're up to before they themselves tell you what you're up to. Because believe me, they *all* know what you're doing, so you may as well win back some trust by showing them all your cards from the beginning. Sheer honesty."

Could she have been on to something? Or perhaps she was as mad as she sounded. "My lady, *the role that nobody wants*, that is what you called it. Why?"

"Maybe you need to ask yourself why your friend's father fled in the first place."

"Lord Berywen? He left because he was a Federalist."

"Oh, you are an innocent one, aren't you?" she said, smiling. "Of course, you aren't entirely *wrong* – but there are other forces at play here, don't you see? Why do you suppose he put on that bluecoat? What drove him to Ashcrest's cause?"

Aren hesitated to answer, not fully understanding the politics of it all. Olivia and Cyneric had both taken turns explaining it all to him before, even Lara had had a go once, but he'd never fully grasped it. It was a complicated subject, something for others to worry about.

"Well?" she said, toying with the frame of her glasses.

"Because he started to believe that power shouldn't belong to any *one* person from blood or birth," he said. "He undermined the law of the birthright. He thought it should be for the subjects to decide, that is what the bluecoats think, no?"

"Well… yes, but think deeper, Aren." Deeper? There wasn't any more to it. He stared back at her blankly.

"The farmers' strikes in Jertonshield? The droughts of Fencliffe?" she said.

How could farmers and crops hundreds of miles away have driven Lord Berywen to follow Soren Ashcrest?

"Somebody was getting in the way of the good man doing his job," said Rayne.

Getting in the way? "Do you mean to say there was some sort of…sabotage involved?" said Aren.

Lady Rayne laughed again. "No, my child. Not quite in the literal sense, anyway. I mean to say that Lord Berywen was not always in complete agreement with the other members of the Council about how to handle things in the west. And though he wasn't…perfect by any means, far from it, maybe not *all* of his ideas were that outrageous."

"I'm sorry…I still don't understand," said Aren. "The whole point of a Crown Council is so that people can disagree with one another, so that discussion can be had on how the country shall be run."

"That is a nice theory," said Rayne. "But in practice, perhaps not as nice. Lord Berywen could not bear any longer to be a part of an institution that stood by and watched as countless farmers hung themselves, not able to help them in any way," she said, her bright face now dark and serious. "Most of his ideas were ignored. Maybe if they had been taken seriously, so many children wouldn't have been orphaned. Maybe he'd still be sitting over there," she said, pointing at the table of the Council, far across in the centre of the hall. The empty seat of the Means Counsel stared back at him, and Aren was left open mouthed.

"And why wasn't he listened to? Did my mother not see to reason? Or was –"

"Your mother is an incredibly honourable woman. I admire her in every way. She is a good queen, and she treats every matter that reaches her, no matter how small, with utmost importance. Every matter that *reaches* her," said Rayne. "And this, as you well know, was no small matter."

He shuffled on his feet, restless. "So, you're saying that most of Lord Berywen's ideas never actually came to my mother?"

"Precisely so. Now, who do you think on the Council has that sort of power? Who handles all the important decisions?"

"Mr Runeval?"

The High Lady said nothing, but the crinkle of her smile in the corner of her eyes spoke volumes. Aren suddenly felt cold all over, his skin tingling and his arms and legs stiff.

"Trouble is though, the chancellor isn't the queen, is he? *She* is. Your mother. But sweet, sweet Elvira, she forgets that sometimes. Can you imagine old Pennyn in a crown?" she laughed again.

"But Lord Berywen could have spoken to my mother himself, if he was worried about Mr. Runeval. Why didn't he?"

"Now, from what I make of it – he did try to, on several different occasions, but it was no use," she said, shaking her head and tutting again. "*Blind faith*. She has blind faith in that man, in Pennyn. That's what trust does to a person. That's the dark side of trust. Now I ask you again, who will *you* place your trust in, Aren?"

It had given him a lot to think about. He nodded politely at Rayne and cleared his throat. "I will definitely be careful."

"I hear an unlikely noble might be the fairest choice of them all, have you spoken to her yet?" she said.

"Linara Spenler? I managed a quick word, but she made it quite clear she wasn't interested."

A look of disgust swept across Rayne's face, and she made no effort in concealing it. "Could it have killed Pennyn to come up with some better names for this bloody list? No, no. I would strongly advise you catch hold of Zenara Itris before the night is done. Or perhaps Tylus Banlin, he'd be a fair choice too, I suppose, if he didn't let his tongue run so free. Lord Hercan, now he'd probably have made a fine Means Counsel – maybe even the best choice, it's a pity the Crown had other plans for him."

"And what exactly were those…plans?" said Aren. This was his chance, to find out the truth once and for all.

"That, my dear, is a conversation you'd ought to have with the queen."

A Promise of Peace
Jaspyn

It was dark in Aren's private study. Jaspyn had always found it a tad eerie in here. Well, he'd always found it a tad eerie in most of the palace.

"So, that's all your father said on the matter?" said Aren. "Olivia, answer my question."

"Hmm?"

"That Lord Hercan's move wasn't a personal decision. Is that all he said?"

"Yes, yes that's all he said," said Olivia, taking a sip from her glass of cherry juice. "But a part of me believes he knows more."

Jaspyn was sat beside her, listening attentively. He hadn't said much the whole afternoon. Ever since the Recedon his friends hadn't talked about anything else. In truth, he had nothing to say on the matter, so he kept his mouth shut.

"And these *whispers* he heard…a pretender Deryz? Have we heard from the ministers of the North Parydon themselves? Or is this all just hearsay?" said Aren.

"All just rumours, really," said Olivia.

"And what are the rumours?" said Aren, though Jaspyn had now heard Olivia tell the story what seemed like a million times.

"You know the rumours. From Veytora. Some fanatic claiming to be holy. Claiming to be the True Deryz."

Jaspyn grew tired. They were going around in circles. A man claiming, he was the True Deryz, the Last Deryz Returned, to lead his people to victory…it was a grim thought. Prophecies were dangerous. His own family paid them no heed. It's a pity that Aren's people weren't the same. This…stranger, this *fanatic*…he could bring the royal family a lot of trouble. Long gone were the days when they held power up in Verenia, the Sandaerian ministers were not to be taken lightly, even today. They had influence. That's what faith did to people. They had been large supporters of the monarchy once, helping fight against the Old Federation when Aren's ancestors first forged the Crown. Those days were over though. These days, it seemed people simply needed an excuse to align themselves with anybody who opposed the Crown...a pretender Deryz? Might just prove the most dangerous foe of them all. Once more, Jaspyn decided he would keep his mouth tightly shut, no matter how much it frustrated him.

Olivia pulled out a tattered old book out of her sack, blowing the dust off of it. She placed it on the central glass table between the two leather settees. The smell of musty old pages quelled the scent of the three candles burning on the wooden window ledge beside them.

"Where did you get it from?" asked Aren.

"Legacy Hall," she said. "It's a wonder just how much I can still get away with in this palace."

The Sandaerian Promise, its front cover read. She opened the dusty thing up, frantically flipping through the fraying pages like a madwoman.

"Trouble is, I don't know what exactly I'm looking for..." she said, her brows furrowed.

"Wise bat, aren't you?" said Jaspyn. Truly, she was. She'd surrounded herself with books growing up, she knew the value of words, of ink and paper. He wished he could say the same of himself, but there was a lot he didn't know about the world that she'd easily be able to tell him.

"Well, thanks," said Olivia, slamming the book shut and sitting back in her chair, her arms crossed.

"I didn't mean to...Obviously, you are –"

"It's alright, Jaspyn."

"No, really, I'm sorry–"

"It has nothing to do with you."

"Right then, what's the matter?" said Aren.

"I just don't always feel like I belong here."

"Who's making you feel like that?" said Aren.

"Nobody," said Olivia. "And everybody. Maybe not in front of you, but I see the way they whisper when I enter a room. They hate me, they hate that I'm different...all of them. Just on the way back from Legacy Hall, the whispers, I could hear them all! Even during the audience with Lara – I'm not blind. Not a peep out of anyone when she walked in. Me, on the other hand…" she stopped. "Sometimes, I wonder…who has it worse off? Eyan or I? Maybe it'd have been better if my father had completely cut all ties to the Crown like Soren Ashcrest, including me. He keeps me around for diplomacy, I know he does – why is he trying to keep a foot in two boats? Two boats headed in the opposite direction too. I'm treated like a traitor at court and a sympathiser at home. Our family is constantly ridiculed on both sides of the river. I mean, you can't blame them entirely, when the son is pledging allegiance to the First Warden while the daughter spends her afternoons at the Valecrest…it's…just so stupid…"

Olivia looked as if she'd forgotten where she was. Her usually calm composure had turned into something else entirely, her fists tightly clenched and her face red. Jaspyn couldn't help but ponder though, maybe in some ways she wasn't wrong. Maybe Olivia's life *would* have been easier without Aren in it. A terrible thought.

"Sorry," said Olivia. "I didn't mean to go on and on."

"Olivia no one would dare treat you like a traitor here," said Aren. "They'd have me to answer to, and my mother. Next time something like that happens, even a small, petty thing, you let me know."

She nodded. "The day of the breakfast, I saw the way the chancellor was looking at me," she said. "I saw the side glances and I heard him, when he was speaking to you in your tongue."

"You heard him say what?" Aren laughed.

"I heard him say *Means Counsel*," she said. "And then he laughed, and he winked at you. I might not understand your tongue but even I can piece together what he was playing at."

Aren burst out laughing and Jaspyn glared at him until he controlled himself.

"Sorry," said Aren. "I didn't mean to. But you've completely misunderstood the thing. The conversation Pennyn was having with me had nothing to do with you."

"Then what on earth was he talking about?" said Olivia.

"He was telling me the importance of getting to know the nobles," said Aren. "Because we need a new Means Counsel."

Olivia uncrossed her arms, and her face loosened. "That's all?"
"Yes."
"Then why didn't you just tell us," said Olivia.
"Didn't seem relevant at the time," said Aren.

"Well, have you thought about it?" said Jaspyn.

The pair turned to face him.

"About the Means Counsel?" Aren asked.

Jaspyn nodded.

"Fraston, or maybe Linara though she didn't at all seem keen on it," said Aren. "Or Zenara Itris."

"Who the hell is Zenara Itris?"

"The Asmoni," said Olivia. "Can she be trusted?"

"Truth is I never got the chance to speak to her anyway," said Aren. "But some seem to be convinced by her."

"Who else is there?" said Olivia. "You can't tell me that's all, surely?"

Jaspyn knew little in the way of politics, but he'd learnt a fair bit more about the newest guests of the palace since he'd laid eyes on them. "What about Ylor?"

Aren turned to face him. "Ylor Nazeris?" he said. "Isn't he a little too young for that sort of thing?"

"He's young enough to forge a lasting effect on the kingdom's wealth, one that won't just be washed over by his successor. But he's also old enough, with the right sort of guidance, to have had a fair bit of experience – granted not a great deal – but a fair bit, under his father. He saw the rise of Kestoryn first-hand, let's not forget," said Jaspyn. These were scarcely his own words, but he gave the pair a smug glance just the same. The Zaldroni merchants of the Arvendon markets where he lived would not stop singing their praises of the Nazeris family, so he'd made it a point to stop and ask some questions about the peculiar bunch and why they were so loved in Zaldron.

Olivia raised one eyebrow. She opened her mouth as if to say something but closed it again.

"Think about it, him and Arcadius already have a bond – not just of court, but of blood…they could work hand-in-hand as Crown Treasurer and Means Counsel," said Jaspyn. "The banks, the farms and the pantries all need to understand each other well, after all."

"I haven't even spoken to Ylor yet, I have no idea what he's like as a person," said Aren.

"You haven't really spoken to Lord Fraston either," Jaspyn reminded him. "Hearing about him is not the same as speaking to the man himself. Just a little thought, anyway, in case it was worth considering what your subjects think." He folded his arms and looked away, towards the pile of books by the window. He tried to make out the title of each one, squinting hard, but it wasn't of any use. His eyes had never been particularly brilliant, it was probably the smoke and soot of the old town, his mother had always said.

Olivia had clearly had quite enough. "Not Ylor," she said shakily. "It's…it's b-bad enough that Lord Nazeris is the Treasurer, doesn't it trouble you in the slightest?"

"Why would it trouble me?" said Aren.

Jaspyn rolled his eyes, took in a deep breath and prepared for the worst.

"They are not like us, Aren."

"Who?"

"House Nazeris, the Old Zaldroni, all of them. The rumours, Aren."

"And why is that?" said Aren, bewildered. But Jaspyn knew the rumours she was talking about. He'd spent plenty of time with the Zaldroni merchants down in the old town.

"They aren't like us. We don't bleed the same," said Olivia. "They're from the shadows, they descend from the very first creatures of the night – the ones from the stories."

"Come on, Olivia. You don't truly believe that do you? Any of it," said Jaspyn. He'd always heard the stories too, of course, but his mother had raised him to place little importance on such myths. Legends and tales of old, that's all they were. He'd bet anything that Aren's mother had done the same – and Cyneric too, he would probably laugh even at the slightest mention of such an absurd thing. But Olivia, her father, they weren't like the rest. Nor was her brother.

"It's not about what I believe," she said. "It's not…there's a reason they're so mysterious, so… peculiar. Ylor especially. You said it yourself that day, he gives you the creeps. Éline too, did you see how empty she looked? Completely vacant…" she paused. "I believe legends and myths all come from somewhere. There's some truth to nearly all of them."

"Dwellers, Olivia? Have you any idea how ridiculous you sound?" Jaspyn burst out laughing, he could help himself no longer. "Isn't House Berywen itself half Zaldroni? When are *your* fangs coming in? Bloody ridiculous."

Olivia's jaw was tightly clenched and the lines along her forehead ran deeper than ever. "You find it funny but trust me on this one – sometimes we just…we shouldn't question these things, stories that have been passed down to us over a thousand years, generation after generation… It isn't as simple as you'd think it to be."

"You haven't answered my question," said Jaspyn.

"YES. My family is half Zaldroni but that isn't how it works, you know it isn't."

"And how does it work, exactly then? Whatever *it* is?" said Aren.

Olivia grew visibly impatient of the conversation. "Never you mind, the both of you. It's beyond your understanding."

"Well, make us understand," said Jaspyn. "The old wives' tales. Suppose we *did* believe every story passed down in our families…"

"Some of those stories you talk about? The old wives' tales? They speak of another realm. You know, the realm of the Panderer – a world that exists beside our own. A world where all magic and morality were lost. A world that was made to punish the First Ones. The ones from before the Old Deryzi. There are hundreds of thousands whose belief in that old story doesn't extend much farther beyond just that – an old wives' tale. But that isn't entirely the case, is it?" she turned to face Aren directly. Suddenly Aren's face was white and his eyes wide. But Aren was shocked easily, he'd been brought up that way. Jaspyn, on the other hand, wouldn't back down so easily.

"Aren't we being punished enough in *this* realm?" said Jaspyn. "Doesn't this realm itself have a distinct lack of *magic and morality*, not sure if you have been paying attention." He stood up from his seat furiously, scoffing. "Besides, the two stories aren't quite the same thing though, are they Olivia? The Panderer and the Dweller, they…they can't be compared. You speak as if the Zaldroni Exile was justified." He'd heard a lot about it down in the markets, all the grim details. The details they probably spared when the stories were repeated amongst noble children. How Zaldroni men and women were dragged out of their houses into the streets, many killed or worse. The end of House Asellar. All for what? Rumours? Myths? The red of Olivia's pale cheeks had told him he'd won, and that was enough for him. So long as she understood the power of her words. He drew a deep breath and sat back down.

"The Asellars were far from innocent," said Olivia. "The most wicked, the most cruel, out of all the Old Deryzi." She shook her head fiercely, her mouth screwed up in the ugliest of frowns.

"A pity isn't it, that an entire noble house is judged on the actions of two bad apples?" said Aren. He sounded surprisingly calm, Jaspyn hadn't a clue how he did it.

"The Asellar brothers were cruel, there isn't any denying that, but there was more to House Asellar than just the two Deryzi they're now known for," Aren continued, his voice louder now. "There was more to the Sandaerians than simply cruelty and punishment, they're not so different from us. Can you honestly say that each life that was taken…each merchant that was brutally murdered, each innocent that was slaughtered or shipped back to Zaldron hundreds of years afterwards deserved it? For what? For being Zaldroni? In a time when it wasn't popular?"

"To heck with all of the Old Deryzi, I say," said Jaspyn suddenly, crossing his arms again. Though the startled look on the young prince's face staring back at him made him curse his loose tongue yet again. Suddenly the calm had left Aren's face, suddenly his brow was raised, his eyes narrow. "I just – I mean, from what I've heard, the whole system was corrupt, or had turned stale by the end anyway," said Jaspyn. "Darsyn, Asellar, Malysor…the lot of them. I never remember the other one –"

"Salyver," said Olivia. "And Aryssen, of course, let's not forget." She looked over at Jaspyn in disdain. She then turned back to Aren, the corners of her mouth curling into a gentle smile. "The Wind Riders. The Masters of the Sky."

Masters of the Sky. That was one way to put it, Jaspyn supposed. He himself hadn't seen any man or woman take to the skies in all of his years, of course, and he wasn't one to believe without seeing. The only skyverns he'd seen were in the paintings and tapestries that hung in the great halls of the palace.

"Okay, let us not dwell," said Aren, breaking the cold silence between them. "The world hasn't seen a single skyvern for centuries so I'm not sure those words even bear any meaning anymore. What is more relevant right now is the matter of the Means Counsel." He faced Jaspyn, his glare for once icy and rigid.

"I don't care that Ylor is Zaldroni. The thought never even once occurred to me," said Aren. Jaspyn held back his smile as Olivia rolled her eyes.

"I'd rule out Ylor regardless of his blood – simply because I don't know him, at all," said Aren. "Nor do I have the time to get to it."

"Fair," said Jaspyn. "So that leaves you with Fraston." He wasn't going to spend any longer than he had to on matters of court. He figured he'd leave that to the courtmen and courtwomen.

"Sounds promising," said Olivia, not looking up from the old dusty book she'd opened up again. She'd busied herself flicking through the stained pages.

"Found anything in that old thing yet?" said Aren.

She shook her head and tutted. "Do you know why I'm more worried about this so-called Deryz in the far north than I am about Soren Ashcrest?"

"I would guess…because the Sandaerians have a lot of power," said Aren.

"On the contrary, the Sandaerians have little power," said Olivia, half chuckling for once. "In comparison with the rest of the Verenic, anyway. They're influential, yes, but nothing compared to you and your family. The people don't trust the North Parydon, they haven't forgotten…" her voice trailed off as she licked her finger and turned another page. "But the biggest issue with the Sandaerians…what sets apart your faith from theirs? The main thing?" she asked.

"They believe that the Fifth Deryz was the last," said Aren.

"Whereas the Verenian faith, the true Verenian faith, denounces this claim," said Olivia, finally looking up, smiling at Aren. "Right?"

Aren nodded. "We believe that the Blood of the Old Deryzi ran through their children's veins. All the way to the Fourteenth Deryz, my direct ancestor."

This much was clear to Jaspyn. Beyond that, he knew little of the matters of Verenia, the matters of Ayleris and the North Falls and beyond. His family was of no faith…he knew little of Parydons and Aneglins and so forth, so he'd never gotten to learn *anything* about the Sandaerians or Verenians or Anercusians or otherwise. He scarcely knew the difference and a part of him felt he was better off that way.

"Exactly," said Olivia, still looking down at the dusty pages, turning through them one by one. "The bloodline can't be ignored. And *you* believe that an Aryssen king or queen is chosen by the Lord, anointed by chance or by destiny; you believe the Sovereign to be the true Deryz of the Faith," said Olivia.

"But the Sandaerians have never accepted that claim," said Aren, shaking his head. "They kneeled to us all those years ago as kings and queens to govern the lands of men, not as a Deryz to lead the faith, it is only the Verenians who believe so. That hasn't changed, so why would it matter now? Why should we worry about a pretender from a faraway land?"

This time it was Aren who got up from his seat, striding over to the window. He looked out towards the city, his face golden from the touch of the sun. Jaspyn glanced out too. Even from where he was sat, he could see the towers of the High Parydon across the waters of Merlynshore Bay. Much of the rest of the city was covered in a haze though, far below.

"The monarchy isn't so fragile as to rest completely on the Faith," said Aren. "The Crown fell to my family because people were fed up with the Old Federation. Verenic, Zaldroni, Weslin alike. It didn't matter what your blood was, or what your father named you. It didn't matter what your faith was…we had Prentuish priests lay carpets of daffodils when we arrived in Sturrock. The Old Aneglin waved our banner with pride up in Ayleris."

It was almost as if Aren had been there himself by the sounds of it, Jaspyn couldn't help but think. He bit his tongue to stop himself from smiling at the thought.

"Yes, Aren, but think back. The Old Federation itself had only risen to power because people were fed up with the Deryzi. People were fed up with the Sandaerian Dues. The power and where it lies is always changing," she said, letting out a great sigh. "The Sandaerians believed that the Last Deryz would return, at a time of great peril. That is what their scriptures and scrolls say. He'd return to lead his people to victory, to triumph against those who would do them harm. I don't believe that this usurper in the north is the Last Deryz Returned for even a moment, but even if a handful of people take his claim seriously, that could make for a grave threat to the Crown."

"She's right," said Jaspyn, half reluctantly. When Olivia wanted to be, she could be wiser than them all. "Especially these days when you're already facing so many adversaries in the south," he added. Jaspyn had had the privilege of being of common blood, so people weren't constantly terrified of speaking the truth around him. He'd lived in Arvendon forever, he knew what the people *really* thought. What would never be repeated amongst the nobles.

"When the Hercanian Uprisings happened, there was a reason for the people to rally behind Oscon Hercan and his Old Federation," said Aren. "People were dying. Families were going hungry. The Sandaerian Dues had divided people on their faith for years, and the Federation brought a promise – the abolition of the Dues and a message of hope: that the *people* will have the power," he added. He took a few paces across the room before looking out of the window once again, his back to Jaspyn. "And then when the Aryssen Dynasty rose to power, it was because – again – people were dying. Hundreds lost their lives in the Exile, if not thousands. The whole system was crooked, top to bottom. The people finally realised that the power had never belonged to them at all, it was simply an illusion. A lie," he shook his head fiercely. "My family brought them a promise of our own, a promise of peace, and of fair rule. And so far, we've given them no reason to betray our cause."

Olivia smiled towards the prince's back with almost as much admiration as she did his face. Clearly, the speech had worked on one of them at least. It *was* an inspiring thought, but not strictly true. Jaspyn kept his mouth shut, though. He'd said enough today.

The Northern Shore
Elvira

The queen's study was warm, the evening sun peering in through the windows. Hundreds of books lined the shelves around Elvira. She sat slumped in a chair by the fireplace, examining her collection. Each one had a story behind it. She'd always loved books, even as a child. Both her sisters never had, they'd always busied themselves with menial things, constantly worrying about making themselves look pretty. Skander was the only one who'd ever sit beside her and read while they were growing up.

Her heart suddenly felt heavy with guilt, a lump in her throat. After all, her sisters *had* to make themselves look pretty, they weren't ever going to be queen. Not unless something awful had happened to her. They had to attract suitors some other way. Skander though, he'd always breeze through the books after she'd given them to him. An Aryssen Prince, there was no need for *him* to make himself pretty. In fact, fifty odd years ago, the Crown would have fallen to him before her, even though she was the older of the pair. Still, he'd grown to be a sincere man, almost as sincere as Pennyn. In fact, Skander might have been one of the humblest men she knew. She was proud to have been able to choose her own brother as the Envoy, it was not a privilege shared by many kings and queens of the years gone by.

Footsteps in the corridor outside interrupted her thoughts. Cyneric Porter's deep but muffled voice trailed soon after, getting louder and louder as he approached her door. Then came the knock. They'd taken long enough; she'd been waiting for some time now.

"Enter," Elvira said firmly, and the doors swung open.

Her son stood beside Cyneric in the doorway, rather sheepishly. Cyneric was holding a small box in his hands, wrapped in brown paper. He must have noticed her stare at it as he took it as an excuse to break the silence.

"Oh, it's nothing," he said. "It was for the Fenwern boy, but he didn't want it."

"Jaspyn? Why not?" she said, raising her eyebrows. "Is he still here? Was he with you, Aren? I didn't intrude by calling you here, did I?"

"He was leaving anyway," muttered her son.

Cyneric shrugged his shoulders. "The real question is, what was that – that *fool* doing? What's his name…Ferian, is it? Stood outside pretending he's important. I marched straight past him with this in my hands," said Cyneric, lifting the box up in front of him as if it were a severed head. "It could have been anything. A weapon. Poison. The fool didn't bat an eyelid. If it wasn't for the other one stood there, the Banlin chap, I would've just walked in, no questions asked."

"It's like I said before, the First Guard all know you," said Aren, looking down at the floor. "They're not going to ask you any questions any more than they'd ask me."

"I say they should ask *everyone* questions," said Cyneric, his eyes narrowed. "Trust nobody."

Elvira laughed. "Maybe they smelt the Red Pudding inside that thing," she said, pointing to the box. "I can smell it from here. It's no wonder they let you pass. Why didn't Jaspyn want it anyway?"

Cyneric shared a look with her son.

"I don't really know," said Aren, shuffling on his feet. "Mother, I'm assuming you've called me here about the Means Counsel."

"Can't a mother just spend some time with her son?" said Elvira, ruffling his soft hair. She knew the boy was right, though.

"A mother can," said Aren. "A queen may not always have the time for it, though."

He was so wise for his age. So soft-spoken. She saw more and more of Weryn in him these days, the Weryn she knew years and years ago. The Weryn she knew when they'd fallen in love.

"I will always have time for you," Elvira lied, pinching his cheek. He brushed her hand away and smiled thinly. The cold space between them was telling…they both knew the truth. They hadn't seen each other since the night of the Recedon, she'd been busy. She felt a certain guilt, but she had to focus on the bigger picture. It was for the good of the country. She knew he'd understand, but there would come a time when his faith would falter. When he'd lose hope. She prayed he'd see it through. "But since we have landed on the subject, have you thought about it?" she asked. "Means Counsel."

Her son nodded. "Lord Fraston Spenler."

It wasn't the name she'd hoped for. In fact, the boy couldn't have chosen more poorly. But she smiled back at him thinly. "Very well." He needed to know she had faith in him. He needed to know he was ready. "Perfect, I'll invite Fraston to tea sometime this week."

"Mother," said Aren weakly. "I had a question."

Her heart raced. "Go on."

"This isn't about the Council, it's just something that's been on my mind these past few days…Something that…Something I've been wondering for some time now, I haven't been able to ask you, I didn't know *how* to ask you."

Her mouth was dry, but she forced a smile. "You can ask me anything at all, dear," she croaked. She prepared herself, though. She prepared herself for the lies to come. She didn't like lying to him, not one bit, but one day he'd understand.

"I was wondering, when…when Daria was ill, did we do everything we could've done to help?"

It hit her like a dagger straight through the heart. She'd rather have taken the dagger, in fact. She had to tread carefully; it was tragic what happened to the Fenwern girl…every parent's worst nightmare.

"I've told you before, Aren. Of course…we did all that we could. Circumstances were such, that even the most that we could do was simply not enough." She looked at him sadly, and then down at the floor. She hoped that that would have been good enough for him. It had been good enough for her, most days. She tried not to think back to the nights that she'd been sleepless, the nights she'd wake up screaming, seeing Jaspyn's little sister's lifeless body…seeing his mother bawl her eyes out, screaming that the Crown was a lie. Cursing at her. Screaming that she had all the wealth in the country but stood by and did nothing as the Dusk took away Daria's last breaths. It was a terrible, terrible thing.

"I know," said Aren. "It's just, I know Jaspyn's parents were… I'm not sure how to–"

"They'd just had their daughter taken from them, Aren. Their daughter of five years. You couldn't have expected them to act any differently." She spoke sternly. She fought back the nightmares she'd grown so used to. She fought back the dreams of Aren dying, being taken from her. She fought back the tears.

"Sorry," said Aren, looking down sullenly at the carpet. It was obvious that he was upset, it always was, but she knew it was better this way. She turned her head to look at the darkening window, blinking away the tears in her eyes.

"Your Majesty, there was something else," said Cyneric Porter, clearing his throat. "When we left the Panderer's realm, we left quite a few of Aren's things behind since we were in such a rush. Menial things, but I know you said–"

"Still?" said Elvira, her heart racing once more. "I thought you brought back those things days ago." Cyneric couldn't have been this incompetent, even for a Panderer. He was one of the cleverest men she knew. Why hadn't he just done as she'd asked?

"No, Your Majesty. There was no time."

"I asked you to *make time*," she said, maintaining her stern tone. "The pendant too? How could you let this happen," she said, suddenly realising how hot her ears were. Cyneric Porter and her son looked back at her, bewildered. "The pendant that I gave you with your father's watch," she said to Aren, grabbing him tightly by the arms.

"It's with the rest of my things," said Aren. "In the Panderer's realm."

"Well, bring them back as soon as possible," she said quietly, shuffling around where she was stood. "They carry a lot of sentiment, some of those things." She was conscious not to worry her son too much, he didn't understand yet, he couldn't. Maybe one day he'd see. Maybe one day, when it was too late.

Cyneric waited a moment before opening his mouth. "Your Majesty, if I could be excused. I have arrangements to make for the prince's training tomorrow."

She glared at him, then nodded, even if reluctantly. The Panderer left swiftly, nodding gently at Aren on his way out. She could tell her son was anxious, unsettled. He looked like he wanted to say something, like he was waiting for the right moment.

Finally, the boy cleared his throat. "Your pardon, mother. I just wondered, was there a reason you didn't choose Lady Rayne to be your Means Counsel."

Elvira narrowed her eyes.

"It's just, I saw how close you both are, and I've heard all about what she has done in Medlanta, and I've been thinking about it ever since. She wasn't even on the list."

Elvira shook her head. "She wouldn't agree to it. Truth be told, I hardly expected Rayne to show up even at the Recedon. The invitation I sent out was a mere formality," said Elvira. "In fact, she's on her way back to Lyndan as we speak."

"What? Why?"

"She doesn't leave Lyndan, she's rooted to it. We haven't seen much of her down here since the Insurgency," said Elvira, sitting down in her chair again and taking a deep breath. "You remember Lord Irvin?"

"No, I don't, actually."

"Rayne's brother. He fell in the Insurgency, of course, why would you remember him..." she muttered. "Rayne lived at the palace then. You might not remember, you were a little boy. After he died, Rayne vowed she'd never marry, never bear any children. I think she blamed herself, somehow. They say she promised herself she'd never turn her back on her home again. That she'd carry out her brother's duties till her last day. All I know is she packed up her things and within a week she was gone."

"She sounds like a really strong woman," said Aren. "A loyal one. I enjoyed our conversations the night of the Recedon, I did hope we'd be able to speak some more, there was a lot that was left unclear..."

"Her resilience is unmatched, as is her loyalty. But she is devoted to Lyndan, to House Dresden," said Elvira. "I've asked her many, many times to take a position on my Council. I don't think there's anyone that I can trust who would better lead the Department of Clandestine Affairs. But each time the answer's been the same."

"I see," said Aren. He was looking right through her, at the bookshelves to her back. He didn't look like all of him was there. "What about Lord Hercan?" he said.

"What about him?" Elvira fidgeted with her bracelet. What would the boy know of Perwell?

"Would you say he's loyal?" said her son. "Why isn't he on the Council?"

"One of the most loyal!" snapped Elvira. "He'd be on the Council too if it wasn't for…" she stopped. She didn't know if it was time. Aren would find out when it was time.

"If it wasn't for what?" he asked.

She smiled at him, wringing her hands together. "Lord Hercan didn't want to be on the Council," she lied.

"Mother," said Aren. His tone grew more and more serious. "You never once mentioned in any of your notes or messages for me that Lara and her family had left. Lara's one of my closest friends, I keep thinking… why would Lord Hercan suddenly up and leave? I hope I'm not too presumptuous to think it might have been because he wanted a role on the Council? Or… maybe because he didn't like how the Council was doing things? Perhaps there was a disagreement of some sort… between him and someone on the Council?"

What was he playing at? Maybe it *was* time he knew. She sighed out loud. "No, Aren. That isn't why he left."

"No?" he said. "I was under the impression he left on his own accord… is this not true?" Her son had a suspicious tone about him, and she hated it.

"Speak plainly, Aren. There's obviously something on your mind."

"Nothing," he said dryly. "All I want to know is if there were some bigger reasons that Lord Hercan and his family moved, to the North Falls of all places."

"To *Nynnevor*," Elvira corrected him. "You've been spending too much time with your Weslin friends," she added sternly. She was careful not to give too much away with her eyes. In truth, she didn't want to tell him. Not now. But she knew she didn't have much in the way of choice. "In the spirit of honesty, I feel I do owe you an explanation. Something you should know about this life is that ofttimes, the decisions we take are precautionary – a means to defend the Crown. There isn't always a definitive reason for an action to be taken; the act itself may fruit no real benefit to the Crown – but it's all part of a bigger picture, see. Had it *not* been taken, perhaps we'd all have suffered harsher consequences. Perhaps catastrophe. Or… perhaps nothing would change at all. Perhaps the action itself was pointless. To rule justly is to know the ins and outs of where to draw the line. When does the potential of consequence outweigh the desire for normalcy?"

"Mother, you're speaking in riddles again," he said, his tone now confronting. "Are you saying it was *your* doing?"

She wasn't ready. "Well…yes, and no," she said. "The idea came from Perwell himself. I would never command a man to uproot his life, his family…he saw what was happening down here, with the bluecoats. We had reason to fear the same sort of thing was happening in the depths of North Verenia, with the Sandaerians. Whispers and murmurs, nothing more. But it was enough for us to believe it could turn into something more."

"The Sandaerians? Aren't they loyal to the Crown, though? Was there risk of a rebellion?"

"There's always risk of a rebellion," she said. "But Lord Hercan graciously offered to move up to Nynnevor, to be our eyes and ears. To make sure everything stays as it should."

"These whispers," said Aren, ignoring her. "What exactly did they speak of?"

"It really isn't anything to worry about," she said. "They're just whispers. Of a healer. From the northern shore."

"From Veytora?" said her son, making her raise her brow.

"Yes," she said.

"And you're worried that the Sandaerians might bow to him? Because of the prophecy of the Last Deryz."

She laughed. "Prophecies don't frighten me. But you're right, I do fear the *people*. The Sandaerians put us on the throne reluctantly, they bow to us reluctantly. And as for bowing to *her*, I don't know yet if the things they claim about her are even close to being true."

"*Her?*" said Aren. "A woman? Do we know her name?"

"A girl, more than a woman," she said. "Like I said we've only heard whispers, but if they are to be believed… Her name…" she trailed off. For the first time she felt a chill on the back of her neck. "Her name is Develyn Asellar. Or so, that is what she is claiming."

Aren stared at her, wide-eyed and open-mouthed. "Asellar? How is that possible? I thought, I thought all of… She has to be lying, surely. She has to!"

"Best not to concern yourself with this Sandaerian nonsense, my boy. Without a Deryz to place their faith in, they're a lost folk. They long for someone like her to come along and wave her hands about to give them a sense of purpose. It was why our faith split from theirs, it's why we're proud to call ourselves Verenian. If they want to believe that a saviour has risen to guide them, let them have their fables, we don't need the North Parydon. They've never considered the People's Sovereign their Deryz, and we have never needed them to."

Her son hadn't been paying much attention, though. "House Asellar has been gone for generations. For hundreds of years, it has been driven to extinction... Even before the Exile, most were humiliated to bear its name, with everything that the Asellar Deryzi did in their time. That's what you'd always told me, isn't it?"

"Yes..."

"Yes? Then that would mean... That would mean this usurper, if they believe her, she'll have a claim to the throne! A stronger claim, in fact. She could gain support!"

"Yes... but they were *Verenian* Deryzi, the Asellars. Not one of theirs. The Sandaerians never recognised a Deryz beyond the Fifth, remember. Why should they start now?" said the queen. "And the Verenians...we do not believe in such nonsense."

"But...but the Sandaerians...they believe their Last Deryz will return, mother. We were the last of the blood of the Deryzi...that's what made our claim. Malysor, Darsyn, Salyver, Asellar... They were all long gone. I fear we'll lose more than the Sandaerians if word gets out..."

Elvira shook her head. "Not a single soul in the kingdom talks fondly of the Asellar brothers. There was no peace under their Derzine rule. The kingdom suffered at the greatest cost while they fought each other blindly, wreaking havoc over cities from coast to coast, from the mountains in the south to the *Nevebaris*. Even today, ask anybody, common or noble blood, and they'll gladly tell you what they think. Why do you think that is?"

"Because they were the only Zaldroni Deryzi."

She shook her head again. "It had little to do with their blood, or the pale colour of their skin, I can tell you that. They were horrible, horrible men. Even the worst of the Malysors who were said to kill their wives with blood magic when they grew tired of them were a considerable step up. Why would any sane man or woman bow to an Asellar now?" She'd rehearsed this conversation in her head countless times, by now it was a fluent performance.

She'd spent so many nights laying there in bed, reasoning with herself. Putting it all together.

"Because..." Her son just stood there in silence, blinking. "I don't know," he muttered, looking down again.

"A healer from the backwaters of Veytora is no threat to us. To the High Parydon, maybe, if they cared about that sort of thing. But I say live and let live. The North Parydon can do what they want, so long as they bow only to the Crown. The Anercusians and the Faithless have done so too, for hundreds of years."

An Unrivalled Honour
Eyan

Eyan stood in silence, careful not to make the slightest noise. Gently, he leaned in towards the door, his ears pricked. The rain pattered down on the skylight above him, but still he managed to make out the voices behind the door to the dining room.

"It didn't work," the man said. "The dumb lad couldn't do it. Fat dunce."

"Mind that tongue of yours, Gav."

"I don't know why *she* couldn't do it herself," the vulgar voice replied. "Root and stem, both."

"No more than why you couldn't," came a third voice – a woman. "Now stop with your senseless accusations and get back to the matter at hand. The next time can't be a failure."

"Indeed, root and stem both. But take the root out and the stem won't be able to hold its own. The boy is weak, we've all seen it. He isn't..."

That was all he heard, when he felt the dreaded tap on his hip.

"M-master Eyan," came Renut's sickly voice. "Is everything alright?"

"Yes, yes." Eyan Ashcrest cleared his throat. Damn Renut. He looked at the steward stood sheepishly before him, tray in hand. "I'm just waiting for the First Warden to be done."

"Have y-you knocked?" said the little man, daftly. "Your father shouldn't be too long now, he had me bring these d-down," he said, lifting up the tray of biscuits.

"Yes of course I've knocked!" said Eyan, lying through gritted teeth. "But if you *must* insist on bearing witness to every little thing I do, then by all means..."

He knocked loudly on the wooden door. There was a momentary silence before his father's voice came from the other side. "Renut?"

"I'm with Master Eyan, s-sir," said the steward.

"I can speak for myself, thank you very much," said Eyan loudly, glaring at the little man. "I can wait until you're done," he said at the closed door, this time a little less loudly.

"Yes actually, could you?" said his father. Whispers followed but he couldn't make them out. There were all sorts of noises coming from behind the door whilst he waited; rustling, clicking sounds…he hadn't the slightest clue where they were coming from. Renut stood next to him the whole while, tray still in hands, his arms trembling.

"You can put that on the ground, you know," he said to the steward.

"No, it's food," said Renut. "We do not put food on the ground."

Of course he doesn't. Eyan folded up his arms and looked down at him as menacingly as he could. "We're Anercusian too, you do know that I hope? We don't care about petty things like that, though. The First Warden won't care if you've put a tray on the floor for a few moments."

The steward was shaking. Of course, Eyan knew deep down that in truth, his family was as Anercusian as they were Verenian, Sandaerian or Prentuish. In other words, not at all. They'd go to the Aneglin once, maybe twice a year – and usually it was for the sake of appearances more than anything else.

"Here," said Eyan and snatched the tray from the steward's hands.

"Master! No, what will they say… the son of the First Warden cannot be seen like this."

"I don't think they'll care," said Eyan. "They have bigger things to worry about these days."

The big brass doorknobs suddenly turned, and the door creaked open. Behind it, two figures, fully hooded and cloaked, head to toe. He could see just their mouths, which weren't covered by the hood. The woman had bright red lips. The rest of their faces were completely hidden, and he recognised neither the man nor the woman. His father was sat at the round table behind them, in front of the window. His greying hair glistened as it caught the light. The rain hadn't stopped, it made an awful sound as it pattered against the window.

"Off you go," said his father to the two cloaked figures who were stood staring at Eyan. They swiftly left, leaving the door open behind them. "Close that, will you," Soren Ashcrest said to the steward. Renut wobbled to the door and gently pushed it shut. Eyan was stood silently, tray in hand. His father fingered at him to put it down on the table and Eyan obliged.

"We were just talking about you," said Soren.

Sure they were, Eyan thought, but no words came out of his mouth.

"About your training."

"What about my training?" said Eyan.

"We'll talk about it soon," said Soren, reaching over for the tray. He gestured at the little man who trotted over and slid it towards the First Warden. He picked up a biscuit and put it into his mouth whole.

"Who were those people?" said Eyan. "Were they… you know, *them*?"

His father stopped chewing and looked at him dead in the eyes. "We'll talk about it soon. Come, take a seat," he said, mouth full.

Eyan sat himself down on one of the wooden chairs. "Any more news from the far north?"

His father nodded. "A little. Nothing of importance." He looked over at a shivering Renut. "You are excused." The steward wasted no time in getting out of the room, shutting the door behind him.

"Bless him," said Soren. "Those people, they're our associates. They're helping our cause."

Associates or masters? Eyan couldn't help but wonder silently, though he knew his father would never tell him if it were the latter.

"Good turnout this morning, down in Treaty Commons. Despite the downpour, that is. You should've been there, Eyan, hundreds of bluecoats. Hundreds of banners."

"That close to the Royal Quarter?"

Soren nodded again. "We could see the palace guards across the water. They can't touch us. They have to keep the image of the Crown pristine, see."

"Doesn't mean the queen can't order an assassin," said Eyan. "It's been happening for centuries."

His father's expressions changed. His brows drew together, and his jaw clenched. "What did I just hear you call her?"

Eyan panicked. It was an honest mistake. "Elvira Aryssen," he corrected himself.

"The Crown forces cannot do anything to us. Those were different times, when cutthroats could take a man's life for speaking out against atrocities without a soul batting an eye. If anything were to happen to me now, to any of us, it would do the Federation more good than harm, actually. More would flock to our cause, probably in the thousands."

He had an odd sense of pride in his voice. Eyan wasn't quite sure what to make of it. He nodded reluctantly.

"Are you listening, boy?"

"Yes, sir."

"Good. You remember that thing I discussed with you?"

It was a vague and hazy statement. His father discussed a lot of *things* with him yet managed to keep from him so much more.

"About the good Lord Berywen?" said the First Warden.

"Right, yes. Did he agree?"

Soren shook his head. "Sadly not. A real pity, truly."

"So, what does that mean?" said Eyan, fearing the worst. He fought against the lump in his throat, thinking of what would happen to those he'd once loved.

"Nothing yet," said his father. "But one thing I can tell you for sure – our friends from Éterin are a little more conflicted than is ideal. Chrysan, bless the lad, he's alright. He's constantly trying, doing his part. His father, though…something needs to change," he said darkly, with a shake of the head. "He has to show his complete loyalty to us, to our cause. And the girl, don't even get me started… how were you ever friends with her? Have you seen her muck about in the palace as if she means something there? One of our associates was telling me actually, speaking to the Zaldroni merchants in an *audience,* Eyan. As if she's more than a plaything for that boy prince."

"Olivia wasn't like that back then."

"No? Hmm I guess not. She might learn a thing or two from the Hercan girl. Studying at the University of Ayleris now, we hear. Verenic history and language, granted, a worthless field, but at least the lass is doing something important with her time."

"Lara's at the University now?"

Soren nodded. "You'd be there now too, if it weren't for your training."

Indeed, he would. He'd been looking forward to it since he was a boy. Going off to study in some other city, in the depths of the Verenic Riviera, or amid the mountains of the Medlantan front. Maybe even in the lush green forests of Zaldron. Whether it was the scorching north or the grey south, he'd always told himself he'd go as far from his father as possible.

"Yeah, if it weren't for my training…" he muttered under his breath.

"You are to up your training by another two hours per day."

It was worse than a tight slap to the face. *Two. More. Hours.* "Yes, sir," he said quietly.

"You don't want to know why?"

He didn't, really. "Why?"

"You know our plans for the Aryssens went awry," said Soren. "You do know that don't you?"

"I've heard some things," muttered Eyan.

"Well, there are new plans in place. Bigger plans. They won't see us coming. More importantly though, they won't see *you* coming."

Eyan's heart all but stopped.

"Relax, boy. I'm not asking you to commit murder," said his father, chuckling.

Murder would've been easier. That wasn't the problem. If his father was suggesting what Eyan had in his mind, he'd be more than happy taking someone's life instead.

"You will lead a squadron into the palace. It's all happening sooner than you think. This time, there will be no margin for error. Nobody will stand in your way. Your biggest issues will be already taken care of, you needn't worry. We've bought the Wyversens."

The Wyversens. It was looking more and more serious. If the Wyversens were for sale, the Crown really stood no chance…did they?

"Why me?" Eyan gulped. He had no soft spot for Aren, nor Olivia, Jaspyn or anyone at court. Not anymore. He didn't care. Or did he? It was hard to believe that they'd been such good friends, not that long ago either. He didn't, however, want to be immortalised as a traitor. His memory was never going to be as flowery and pure as the others. He'd lost the right to be remembered for his loyalty long ago, but at the very least, he'd have liked to be remembered as brave. As a renegade. A deserter. A fighter. Not a snake.

"It has to be you. You're our best shot. You'll do me proud – you'll do the Federation proud. Make no mistake, this is an unrivalled honour."

"When is it going to happen?" said Eyan, not certain whether he even wanted a truthful answer.

His father smiled at him. "You'll have a few days. We have other plans before then, plans to ensure that your endeavours are successful."

"But *why. Why me?*" He'd rarely taken that tone with the First Warden, but in the heat of it all, he'd lost his senses. He didn't care.

Soren's face went dark again. "Because it's *their* will. We cannot say no."

Of course. His masters.

Sentry Hall

Ysser

H e stood by the fire, stiff and steady. He could feel the sweat trickling down from his brow. The queen was cold, so the fire burnt. He wished now that he'd taken the post at the door, but in all fairness, it had been a chilly night so the thought of the fire had been welcoming. Unfortunately, he'd underestimated the bulkiness of the heavy First Guard uniform. That damn Ferian. He could have warned him. After all, Ysser Banlin had had very little experience wearing the queen's colours. Nothing like Ferian – the Wyversens had produced generation after generation of the First Guard. He looked over at Ferian stood at his post by the door, perfectly stone-faced, pompous and proper. His skin was golden, not blotchy and pink like Ysser's had become, standing in his heavy coat, the cumbersome cape dragging him down. Damn Ferian.

Ysser looked over at Prince Aren, pushing around the roast chicken and Fencliffian salad on his plate. He reckoned the Crown Prince could do with a bit of nourishment. Every appearance he'd made in public since coming back from Asenia, he'd looked sicklier, paler than before. Every single one.

He looked over at the queen, sat opposite her son. Her mind was somewhere else. Did she even want to be there? This was the first dinner the two had shared in a while. In fact, now that he thought of it, he'd barely seen them spend *any* real time together ever since the good prince had come home. And even now, they sat opposite each other in silence, playing with the food on their plates. What a peculiar family. He'd spent a lot of time with her, of late, since him and Ferian had been posted to her personal detail. She was nothing like the rumours. Nowhere near as ruthless, but also nowhere near as remarkable. By no means average, though. Quite odd all around.

There was a knock at the door. The queen flinched at the sound of it, laying down her fork and sighing loudly. Rightly so, who would disturb her during a private dinner with the Crown Prince? Let alone when she'd given specific instructions to be left undisturbed. Ysser hoped that whoever was on the other side of the door had a *very* good reason to be there. He feared for them, in fact. There was a second, louder and more frantic knock. The queen looked up to the door, placing her knife gently on the plate in front of her too. She then gave a nod to Ferian.

"What is it?" Ferian said loudly at the closed door.

"Your Majesty, may I come in?" came a rather distraught voice. Ysser recognised it, it was the voice of Deric Serrano, the First Guard.

"Enter," said the queen, stone-faced as ever.

Ferian pulled the door open, and Deric clambered in impatiently, looking anxious as ever.

"Your Majesty, there's been an incident, a terrible incident. Your Majesty and the prince are being summoned to Sentry Hall urgently by Lord Escos. The chancellor has already arrived."

He sort of shuffled around on his feet, fiddling with the buttons on his coat. "It's a matter of urgency, madam, the Arvendon bridge, they've –"

She put a hand up to stop him. "Stop babbling, Deric. Tell me slowly and clearly what is happening."

"Sturrock is falling, Your Majesty," he said. "They've taken the bridge, the bluecoats. They've taken Treaty Commons and infiltrated the Royal Quarter. We've received word the palace could be under siege within the hour and that it's vital that you and the Crown Prince join us at Sentry Hall, each second is crucial."

She rapidly got out of her seat, spilling over her juice in the process. "It's alright, Aren. You can finish your dinner, I'll get a handle on this."

"Your Majesty," said Deric. "Lord Escos was quite particular about His Highness joining us too. For his safety, more than anything. Sentry Hall is the safest place to be if the palace should be taken."

"Is that so?" she said, in a mocking voice. She shook her head. "No, Aren, you stay here. In fact, I'll send for Cyneric so he can wait with you. Ysser, you stay here with Aren. Protect him."

He hadn't been expecting it. She hadn't even looked him in the eyes when she'd given the damned order.

"No," said Deric. He was pale faced in fear of what she might say, but he stood his ground. "The First Guard is an ancient guild, Your Majesty. Our duty is first and foremost to protect you, the People's Sovereign. As First Commander, I cannot allow putting your life in danger by letting an officer stay here."

"Your *duty* is also to *serve* the People's Sovereign," said the queen flatly. "Like you said, we don't have time to go back on forth on this, allegedly. I'm not budging until I know that the prince is safe. In fact, I'm less and less convinced that *this one* is capable of protecting my son," she turned around to scowl at a silent Ysser Banlin. He gulped. "So, I'm not leaving here unless *you* or Ferian stay," she said, looking at Deric again.

"I'll escort you to the hall," said Ferian suddenly, breaking his silence. "Nobody swings a sword better than I; this you can ask the commander. Not even he can triumph against me."

Deric looked as if he'd seen a spirit. "Very well. *I* will stay here with Prince Aren. Ferian, Ysser, take the rest of the lot and escort the queen. Immediately! Go!"

Ysser gave the slightest of nods to his commander, his left eye twitching. Was it true? If so, he couldn't help but feel he'd much rather be cosy with the prince in this dining room than be traversing the northern compound with the queen. He stopped himself. To die for his sovereign would be an honour. To defend her in her time of need, this was what he'd taken the oath for.

"Today would be lovely lads, go!" barked Deric, and they set off, Ferian leading the way. They strode quickly and with purpose, taking pauses at every corner, at every bend in the narrow corridors. Suddenly the familiar corridors of the palace were a labyrinth, anything could be waiting for them at any turn. Ferian and Ysser took turns scouting the corridors ahead to see if they were in the clear. A dangerous game. Someone had to play it, though. Through it all, the queen bore little more expression than the officers. Whether it was resilience or stupidity, he couldn't help but admire her a little.

"Has Skander been notified?"

"The prince's family is being isolated in the Western Quarters," said Urten. "They should be safe there." It was like nothing Ysser had ever seen during his two years serving. The First Guard were to be seen and not heard, yet today each one of them had a voice.

"And Lord Nazeris?" said the queen.

"He isn't in the palace tonight."

"I know he isn't in the palace," said the queen. "But what of his children?"

"Lord Ylor and Lady Éline are beneath Lyndan House," said Deryl.

"Perfect, we can get word to them from Sentry Hall," said Urten. "Ferian, are the twins still posted at Lyndan House?"

"Yes," said Ferian. Ysser had always avoided the twins. The palace guards usually knew their place, respected the First Guard, but the twins…they'd always had the audacity to talk back. Ysser wondered if they were perhaps a bit slow.

"Perfect," said the queen. "Aren's friend lives in the shadow of that bridge…" she muttered.

"Your pardon, Your Majesty?" said Urten.

"Jaspyn Fenwern. I fear for his family, if they've taken Arvendon – the bluecoats – I just…"

Ysser had rarely heard the queen's voice break. Whenever she spoke of the Fenwern boy though, she went soft. After all, that family had been through a lot, he'd heard all about it. He wasn't sure if she felt responsible for their pain, he certainly didn't think she had any reason to. Hundreds of children died everyday of disease, of hunger. The Crown owed little to the Fenwerns, the queen had already done so much more than could be expected. If the girl's death was fated, then it was fated. There was nothing anyone could do to change that now.

"Have we sent scouts up Aston's Watch?" said the queen.

"Yes," said Urten. "Mr. Runeval and Lord Escos are dealing with them."

Ysser glanced over at his peers. He realised soon that he was the only officer not to have yet uttered a word. Incompetent indeed, he thought. "And Aerial Command?" said Ysser, gulping. Suddenly, all eyes were on him. He had to say something, he'd been trained just as well as they had. Besides, he had thought up a very good point, after all.

"No," said Ferian. "It's too soon for that."

Ysser nodded in acknowledgement. Too soon? He scoffed, but not before they'd all turned their faces away.

"The Sentry will be the first port of call," said Ferian. "They'll end them. It's just a matter of time."

Indeed, the Sturrock Sentry was not a force to be reckoned with. He had served too, of course, they all had. Those days were behind them, though. They'd been a dull affair.

They turned into the West Parydon Pass and Urten suddenly held out his hand, silencing them. They stopped in their tracks, eager and ready. Ysser caught a flash of bright silvery yellow hair. He'd seen the man's face. What was his name? Joten. He'd just joined the palace guards, a former man of the Sentry. One of the youngest in their regiment. Ysser had served beside him once, a true patriot.

"You can calm down," said the queen loudly. "That's just a guard. Joten, is it?"

Urten looked at her as if she'd asked for his first-born.

The fair-haired gentleman turned to look at them down the corridor, bewildered by all the fuss.

"Where are you headed, son?" she said.

He looked at them all suspiciously for a moment before he opened his mouth. "The Parydon," he said. Strange, thought Ysser. He'd never realised the lad was Verenian.

"Off you pop," said the queen. "Go on now, don't stick around for too long."

Urten's expressions changed. He waited until Joten was out of earshot "Your Majesty, what if he's a turncoat? What if he's gone into there now to tell his masters exactly where we are?"

The queen remained silent, though. Urten may as well not have spoken a word, Ysser supposed.

There was a sudden thud. Ysser turned around to see Deryl on the floor, his head rested against the wall and crimson blood flowing down the pale wall behind him. Ferian Wyversen stood over him, rifle in hand. The butt was red with blood. Ysser's heart stopped. Ferian charged forward at Ysser, pushing him backward and causing his sling to come loose. Ysser turned to see the rest of the First Guard assembled around their queen. Suddenly, he was frozen. In one smooth motion, Ferian let his own gun go, it hung from his sling. He swung his sword out instead, plunging it sharply ahead of him, reaching for his pocket with his other hand. Ysser dove in front of the queen and her men, but it wasn't her that the traitor had swung the sword at. The blade struck straight up. It tore through the white plaster of the ceiling, splitting it right open. A powdery substance trickled out, first slowly, then all at once upon the lot of them. Ysser gasped for breath. He covered his mouth. He'd seen it before. He knew immediately from its dark purple glow.

"ASTER'S PINE!" he bellowed to his comrades but it was too late. He turned to see them coughing uncontrollably, spasming and firing their rifles without a care for where the shots landed. Ferian screamed as a stray bullet hit his arm. The air seemed to be sucked from the corridor, as Ysser felt his own lungs shrivel. He gasped loudly, clenching his fists tightly, desperate for a shred of air. He felt his throat closing, he gagged and sputtered. The queen was on her knees, frantically trying to keep her mouth and nose covered with her hands but it didn't seem to work.

"Cloth!" he screamed to the queen. "C-cloth!! Cover yourself!" He pulled up his own heavy cape and held it firmly over his nose and mouth to show her.

He turned around, he couldn't put his back to the traitor. Ferian Wyversen had been prepared. He was charging straight at the pair of them, a dagger in his hand and a white scarf wrapped tightly around his nose and mouth. Ysser looked around for Urten, or Deryl or the others. No one was there. *Shit*. He kicked the traitor hard and fast in his shins, causing him to cry out in pain and fall to his knees. He cut the traitor's sling with a sharp stroke of his dagger, and the rifle fell to the ground. He looked for help but it was no use. The purple poison had had its effect. His comrades' lifeless bodies lay all around him, their faces pale, eyes still open – blood red. Dark blood trickled out of their noses. There was a fiery rage in Ysser's chest. He got up, fist tightened and made for the traitor's face, but he swerved, and Ysser fell to the floor. He looked back to the queen. She was on the floor too, tears in her eyes. She was using the mantle of a dead Urten Barriser to cover her face, her face resting just above the guard's bloody corpse.

"Why?" she said, muffled through the cloth. The traitor moved toward her, dagger in hand. Ysser slid over, putting himself between the two. He made his peace with this world, and he drew a shallow breath.

"Why?!" the queen shouted once more.

Ferian said no words. The traitor smiled thinly with his menacing eyes as he edged towards her. Closer still. He stopped.

Ysser looked up at him, tightening his grip on his own dagger. The traitor suddenly drove his blade towards him and Ysser struck back, slicing the side of his arm. The traitor had the advantage, with two free hands. Ysser jabbed him again, in his gut, but he kicked ferociously and stepped back. Ysser readied his blade again, keeping his other hand firmly on the cloth that stood between his face and a most painful death. He scrambled around for a rifle, shuffling corpses over.

There was a sharp sting on his forehead as he was thrusted backward into the wall and his skull smacked against it. The back of his hair felt warm and wet. His forehead throbbed where the traitor had thumped him. Through hazy, bloody eyes, he watched the turncoat edge closer still towards the queen, as he sat slumped against the wall, his eyelids heavy. The will to defend her was gone.

"Ferian, I implore you. There is still time. Stop this," said the queen.

The traitor didn't bat an eyelid, his gaze remained fixed as he walked closer and closer. Ysser's eyes were closing. He held on, just about. He had to keep one hand on the cloth. He had to hold on. *Not like this*.

"You've already committed treason, but regicide, Ferian. Regicide's another thing," she said. "They will find you; they always do. You'll be dead before trial."

Ferian's expressions didn't change. Through squinted eyes, Ysser could just about make out his face. He was dead set on her. The queen glared right back, as if staring right into his soul. The shock and fear had left her eyes, and all that was left was pure hatred. Disgust.

"Why don't you just take thing off, Your Majesty?" said Ferian, breaking the cold silence. "Just open your mouth and nose and *breathe*. Be free."

"I want you to look me in the eyes when you do it, traitor," said the queen. "To let your enemy siege the city, attack the very citizens you vowed to protect…"

"Don't you get it, you hag?!" shouted Ferian. "There was never a siege."

"But…" Her eyes went wide and then really small all of a sudden.

Ysser had to act fast. The dead guards' rifles were too far out of reach. Even if he could get to one, Ferian had the upper hand. Ferian had proven himself to be faster, stronger. There was something extraordinary about the way he moved. Something he'd never seen before. Could the queen stall for time? Surely the noise would have alerted someone? Surely someone was on the way? If Ferian was going to shoot her, he would have done it already instead of approaching her so slowly and cautiously with his sword.

Ysser eyed the rifle on the blood-stained carpet. He didn't know if it was a risk worth taking. But he had to do something…it was up to him now. He'd die knowing the oath he'd taken wasn't just empty words.

He got up quietly, as quietly as he could, avoiding the traitor's gaze. Ferian's eyes were so firmly set that he was oblivious. As quickly as he could, Ysser reached forward with his free arm, stretching his back as quietly as he could, biting his lip so he didn't scream. The rifle was almost within reach, just sitting on the floor. He held his breath and pushed forward. The cold touch of the bloodied gun was a welcome sensation. He pulled it up. He didn't know whose it was. He didn't know how many bullets he had. He had one shot. One shot at taking down the traitor before he could realise what was happening. He struck fast. He pulled the trigger as many times as he could, pointing it directly at the traitor's back. There were six loud bangs. The back of Ferian's coat stained red. The traitor stopped in his tracks and fell to his knees. The shock made him lurch backward, and loosened the scarf wrapped around his face, but he kept his hand firmly pressed on it. To Ysser's horror, Ferian stood up again, as if nothing had happened and darted straight for the queen.

The gunshots had given her time to pick up a sword and she swung it hard and fast at the traitor. There was a muffled cry of agony. Blood dripped from Ferian's right arm. Ysser spun him and pushed him forward, presenting the queen with another opportunity to kill him – but Ferian had been too fast – kicking his right leg up, he knocked the sword out of her arm, causing it to fly far back behind her. She clambered to her knees to try and pick up a rifle, but it was out of reach. The body attached to the cloak covering her face was weighing her down. Instead, she pulled the corpse's dagger. She twisted back around, ready to kick the traitor hard in the gut but Ysser had made it easier for her. He'd leapt up behind Ferian, the corridor spinning around him, and grabbed his neck tightly in a headlock. He hadn't the strength to strangle him. Ferian was far too strong. But this would do. The traitor's sword flailed around erratically, but he was trapped…for now. Ysser hoped. He hoped that the queen would seize the opportunity to end him, but she was too far. His eyes were getting mistier and mistier, and his forehead stung like anything. He didn't know how much time he had left.

He pulled the traitor closer to the queen, as they wrestled each other tirelessly. He could see her waving her dagger in his direction. She was so close now. Now was the time. He swung around and punched the traitor in the face. Once. Then twice. Then the third time, he grabbed the cloak on Ferian's mouth and yanked as hard as he could. But the traitor had wrestled free of the hold, and he jabbed the sword blindly forward. His eyes went redder than ever as the purple poison took over his lungs. He coughed and choked on empty air and fell to his knees at Ysser's feet, but it was too late. Far too late. Catastrophically late. Ferian's last strike had been a fatal one. Not for Ysser Banlin though, as fate would have it. The traitor had driven the sword deep through the heart of Queen Elvira Aryssen. She gasped loudly, choking on her own blood. The burgundy cloak over her mouth went dark with her blood, as it gushed out, seemingly endlessly. Ferian rolled at Ysser's feet, laughing wildly as he took his last breaths. He'd served his purpose. He was dying happily. It wasn't fair. Ysser's heart stopped. He watched, mortified, as she rolled over on the ground. He rushed to his queen's side. He held his hand firmly over the deep wound in her chest, hoping there was a way he could save her. Her left hand twitched, then rose up to touch his bloody shoulder. She was trying to say something. He brought his ear closer to her paling face. He tried to make out the muffled words she was saying, through the bloodied cloak.

"Rain," she said, gasping for breath. "Trust… Rain…." Or at least that's what he could make of it. She choked on the third word, Ysser couldn't figure it out. He nodded at his dying Queen and tried his best to listen. *Pan? Pen?*

"Pen?"

She softly shook her head in despair, her eyes sadder than ever. "Pand…" she gasped. "Pen..dan…"

What could it possibly be? "Pennyn? Panderer?"

She didn't shake her head this time. She'd taken her last breaths.

As he gently placed her head on the bloody carpet below, closing her eyes and covering the rest of her face with the cloak, he heard thundering, heavy footsteps behind him, just outside the corridor from where they had entered. There was noise opposite too. Before he'd had time to react, the palace guard Joten walked out of the Crown Parydon into the corridor, immediately unsheathing his dagger at first sight of the blood-stained walls.

As Ysser rose up, his hands painted with the blood of his queen, the blood of the crown itself, he heard the heavy footsteps approach nearer and nearer behind him.

"Cover your faces!" he shouted, weaker than ever.

He turned around to see the Crown Chancellor Pennyn Runeval stood in horror, Cyneric Porter by his side, and King Aren Aryssen just behind them.

Trust…Rayne.

The Whole Truth

Aren

Grey clouds loomed over the city, casting their shadow through the large glass windows. The stars hanging from the ceiling of the Hall of Krelis dangled still, lifeless. The balcony hanging above the large tapestries on the wall had been closed off, all corridors blocked to the rest of the palace, except of course to a very select few. Aren sat at the centre of it all, as still and lifeless as the stars which hung from above him.

"I'm sure you can appreciate, Mr. Banlin, that you were found in the middle of it all, alive and well," said Pennyn. He was sat to Aren's right, whilst Cyneric sat to the left. At one end of the long, wooden table was Lady Rayne, her eyes red and swollen and her cheeks pale. The guard Joten sat opposite her, on the other side of the table.

Aren had stayed largely silent throughout. He didn't have any more within him. Aside from a crushing ache in his chest, he felt nothing at all. His palms were sweaty and cold and occasionally he'd feel a shiver run down his spine.

"Sir, I have no reason to lie. I know how it must look, but you must believe me. We've been at this for two whole days now," said the traitor Ysser Banlin, his hands and feet bound to the table. "If my intentions had been malicious as you say, why would I have warned you all from afar? T-to stay back and to cover your faces? I'd have let the Aster's Pine do its trick, would've…would've made life so much easier for me, if that were what I'd set out to do."

Joten raised his voice from the corner of the table. "It's true. I was the first to arrive, just before you," he said to Pennyn, in his thick Pyburrock accent. "Sir Ysser was quick to surrender. He could've easily taken me, I've seen him train countless times."

Pennyn raised his brow. "And do describe to us again what *you* were doing in the Parydon at such an hour? I hope you don't take this the wrong way, but it strikes me as odd, someone with your… well, someone of your…background, within a stone's throw from *any* Parydon, let alone at a time that no prayers were taking place," said the Crown Chancellor.

"What are you trying to say?" said Joten. "I don't have to be Verenic to be a servant of the Faith. My blood means nothing, plenty of Weslin out there that believe in the One."

"Well…not the *same* One, surely," said Lady Rayne.

Joten slapped his hands on the table and then took a deep breath. "I've told you before, I'm Sandaerian. I don't know what else you could possibly want to know about my beliefs."

"Then why were you in the *Crown Parydon*? No Sandaerians down here, is there?" said Cyneric.

"Sandaerians respect *all* Parydons of worship, not just those with our own ministers at the head. A House of Worship is a House of Worship, I would have even prayed in the Aneglin if it wasn't all the way up in the Northern Compound, that doesn't make me Anercusian does it? The highest Lord is One, he cares not for such petty things."

"Okay, granted," said Lady Rayne, though her face said otherwise. "Do tell us though, what possessed you to seek worship in *precisely* that very moment, the exact moment that the queen walked past with her guards," she said. "I haven't travelled all this way to hear you blabber about the awakening of your faith. I'm here for the truth. For a just trial, should the situation require one – though it's sounding to me more and more like it mightn't even come to it."

"My lady…" began Joten.

"No, I'm not done. I'm here because Elvira was my friend before she was my queen," said Rayne interrupting him. "It has been two days since the assassination and all you fools have offered us, I could probably have gotten from an outspoken priest, Sandaerian or otherwise."

"I shouldn't need to justify my faith," said Joten, shuffling on his chair, his arms crossed. "I would remind you, sirs, and madam, that this is not my hearing. I am not the one who will face trial, and all I can do is offer my honest outlook on what has happened. I cannot help more than that, I wish I could."

For the first time, Aren spoke. "You're right, it won't be your trial." He rose up from his seat, looking the traitor Ysser in his eyes. "It was *you* that was caught with your hands tainted with my mother's blood. It was you who conveniently survived, while your brothers in the First Guard fell," he said. "So speak, Sir Ysser."

"Mr. Banlin," said Pennyn, correcting him.

"Right. Mr. Banlin, then."

Ysser just looked back at him, quiet and weary. It must have been the look that traitors gave when they knew they had nothing more to say. Nothing more with which to defend themselves.

"It was you who was found next to the wounded body of Ferian Wyversen. The son of one of my mother's oldest allies, might I add. And you dare have the audacity to accuse *him* of treachery? How am I to trust *anything* you have to say?"

Aren turned around to face the wall behind him. He wanted to cry. He wanted so badly to let loose and let the tears flow. But he couldn't do that, not now. Not in front of these people. Not in front of his mother's cold-blooded murderer. He wasn't just a prince anymore, he wasn't an heir. His mother would have wanted him to show strength, to show courage.

"Your Majesty," croaked Ysser finally. Aren had his back to the traitor's face, but his meek voice was trembling. It was almost a convincing performance. "If you want to take my life for hers, take it. She was my queen, and I failed my First duty to her and to the kingdom," he said. "But I am no traitor, and nor shall I die with my people believing that I am one."

"That is for a trial to determine," said Pennyn.

Ysser turned to face Lady Rayne. "You say we've given you nothing. You say we're talking in circles. But it was my *own* testimony that brought you here, my lady. I'm the one who heard her last words. '*Trust Rayne*'. I do not know you, why would I give such a testimony if I was lying? What would I have to gain?"

"We'll find out, one way or another," said Cyneric.

"Actually, I'd like to speak with His Majesty alone, if I may," said Ysser.

"And what gives you the impression that you have the right to demands here?" said Pennyn.

"I really do think the king will want to hear this."

"If you are withholding information, Mr. Banlin, I need not remind you of the consequences, on top of what you are already facing, of course," said Lady Rayne.

"It's imminent. You have nothing to lose, keep my shackles on. I've given you no real reason not to trust me."

Aren thought about it. What could the turncoat have to say? Maybe he would try to cut a deal – maybe he'd lead them to his masters. Maybe he could tell them more about Soren Ashcrest's plans. Was it worth it? He wanted the traitor to suffer, but he was just a puppet in it all. The prospect of bringing his *masters* to justice…it was tempting. He didn't know which he wanted more. He didn't know if it was even justice on his mind, after all. Maybe it was vengeance. Whatever it was, it grew like a wildfire, raging crimson inside his head.

"Actually, that isn't strictly true, Ysser." Pennyn's voice came from beside Aren. The Crown Chancellor glanced at Cyneric, and then Aren. "You've given us nothing but reasons not to trust you."

Ysser's eyes narrowed. "What the hell are you talking about?" He was tired now, he looked it. And the tiredness had clearly brought with it bouts of frustration. It was good, Aren supposed. Maybe they'd break him. Maybe they'd finally get the truth.

"We all heard the gunshots from down the corridor. Six loud shots. You told us you shot Ferian in the back, you told us he was about to kill the queen and you had to shoot him in the back six times to stop him. They weren't fatal blows, for some reason, but you did shoot him in the back six times…yes?"

"Indeed… I don't know wh–"

"There wasn't a single gunshot wound on his body. We had Valery Rennero thoroughly examine it herself, not a single one anywhere."

"Like I said, the shots didn't kill him – they just stopped him a little, I don't know what armour he was wearing that –"

"He wasn't wearing any armour. Not even his First Guard armour. Ysser, there wasn't a scratch on his body, apart from the places where you'd stabbed him."

Ysser's jaw dropped. The whites of his eyes widened, and his pale face went paler still. Then, a look of utter disbelief. A look of confusion.

"But…but, he wasn't only shot on his back," said Ysser, his eyebrows skewed and his fingers clutching at the few blonde hairs on his head. "He was shot on his arm. Yes, on his right arm – when the guards were dying, bullets flew like mad. One of them got him, I saw. There was definitely no armour on his arm, this I am sure of…how…how can you tell me that there weren't any bullet wounds on his body?"

"Because there weren't. We were thorough. We checked every inch of the corpse, and like I said, the only wounds were inflicted by your blade," said Pennyn. "So, the question is, why would you lie about that? You knew we heard the gunshots – you could have told us anything – you could have told us that he tried to shoot at the queen, or even that he'd tried to shoot *you*. The only reason you'd lie, is if perhaps the truth itself was uglier."

"What are you suggesting?" said Ysser.

"*You* tried to shoot the queen. Your silent assassination attempt was a failure, with all hope lost you gave it up and fired your weapon at her–"

"To even suggest such a thing is a travesty," said Ysser, slapping his hands against the table, rattling his shackles in the process. "A mockery of my guild and a dishonour to the queen's memory. Besides, if I *had* taken six shots at the queen I would not have missed."

"So, you expect us to believe you missed Ferian, who was closer to you?" said Rayne.

Ysser sighed out loud. He then looked Aren in the eyes. "Your Majesty, sir, I *need* to speak to you, alone. I don't know how these wounds suddenly disappeared from the traitor's body, but I *swear on my own mother's life*. I shot him. He fell to his knees. I couldn't have missed. Please let me speak to you alone. I beg you, it is the last thing I will ask of you."

Aren glared at him. "Anything you have to say to me, you can say in front of these people."

Ysser looked nervously back. "Your Majesty, I beg it of you. I think you would want to hear this in private."

Aren wouldn't be swayed, not by a criminal. He shook his head sternly. "Anything you have to say," he said, looking the cruel man dead in his eyes, "now is the only time you'll be given until your trial, should we feel generous enough to give you one."

"Alright, sir," said Ysser wryly. "I will be transparent, I suppose," he muttered. "I believe in her last moments Her Majesty was trying to tell me something. Something important."

"Yes, yes we've all heard your story about trusting Lady Rayne," said Pennyn.

Ysser glared at the Crown Chancellor, his eyes full of contempt. "No, this is something else. I couldn't make much sense of it at the time, but maybe, *hopefully*, it means something to you," said Ysser, turning his head to Aren. "Then perhaps you might be able to trust me."

"Out with it then, don't blabber," said Rayne.

"It sounded like she was…well, I could be wrong about this, but it was as if she was trying to say 'Pennyn' maybe," he looked at the Crown Chancellor. "I thought maybe she had a message for you, sir, but then it began to sound like something else altogether."

Pennyn. It was curious. What if it was not a message for the Crown Chancellor, but rather a warning to her Council? Aren hadn't forgotten everything he'd heard about the chancellor the night of the Recedon, from Lady Rayne herself.

"And what did it begin to sound like to you then?" said Pennyn, rather sarcastically.

"*Panderer*," said Ysser. Suddenly, Aren's core was weak, icy cold. He clenched his jaw tightly and took a deep breath in, then out. Those around him did better to conceal their emotions, a toughened exterior built up over years of lying, probably. It was the way of the court, after all. But for Aren it was difficult, immensely difficult to hold it all back. Cyneric gave him a gentle nudge with his knee below the table and cleared his throat.

"What exactly do you mean?" said Cyneric.

"It sounds absolutely ludicrous, I know, that's why I didn't want to mention anything because I thought maybe I'd misheard it but maybe…" he stopped, eyeing Aren, gazing down at his hands, fidgeting with a loose nail in the table, and then up at Aren's sweaty forehead. "Maybe, I wasn't wrong," said Ysser. "Does it mean anything to you, Your Majesty? I dismissed it, I suppose it means nothing to me except for the stories we've all heard as children. But maybe…*maybe* Her Majesty meant something by it."

Of course, the word meant a great deal to Aren, and to Cyneric. He looked over but his aide's eyes were fixed elsewhere, on Rayne who was looking sheepishly back at him.

"You're sure that's what it was?" said Pennyn. "Not another one of your lies to try and convince us that you aren't guilty?"

"Well, sir, no," said Ysser. "I cannot be sure of what she said…but that's certainly what it sounded like. It was quite muffled, through the…"

"That will be all," said Cyneric. "Unless there is something else?"

"No, sir, that is all."

"Thank you, Mr. Banlin," said Rayne. "I suspect we will know soon whether you will get a trial."

Ysser nodded quietly.

With that, she summoned two officers of the Sentry, who undid his chains from the table, and walked him out of the room. A dark fate awaited him, this much Aren could be sure of. He'd be taken to the cellars where he was being held, beneath the Hall of Krelis. There was no need for a trial, Aren would convince the Council not to waste time on one. The man needed to be punished…didn't he? But what if…what if he wasn't lying? After all, how could he have possibly known to say *Panderer*. Or how could he have known of the bond between his mother and Rayne. That's when Aren remembered the first time that he'd met her. The night of the Recedon, when his mother and Rayne had shared a hug. When they'd made silly faces at each other. *Stand down, Sir Ysser.* The traitor had been there. He'd seen it all. He'd known of how close the two had been. He'd have known to mention Rayne, to prove his innocence. The man was crafty, that was for sure, he was more than capable of it.

"May I be excused as well?" said Joten. "I don't have anything further to say."

Rayne frowned and shook her head. "We have some more questions, just not for you. But perhaps you should stay, as you said, you were the first there when it…when it happened." She turned to face the Crown Chancellor. "Our witness, where is he being held?"

"Just down the corridor, my lady."

"Well, why don't you go and get him?" she said. Joten sank wearily into the bench, head in hands.

"Now, now don't be so thoughtless," said Rayne. "I hope you can appreciate, we wanted to question this witness separately to Mr. Banlin, he came forward after the queen's death."

"Of course, my lady. Who is he?"

"Well, your guess is as good as mine," she said, shrugging her shoulders. "I suppose we'll both find out soon enough, won't we?"

"He swears he has information that could be worth something, but he says he'll only speak directly with the king," said Cyneric. "That's all we know. He came forward as soon as word of the assassination had gotten out."

"But that wasn't so long ago," said Aren. "How did he get a word into the palace so quickly?"

"Well, actually he was already within the palace grounds," said Cyneric. "In a cell. He was arrested the night of the Recedon, most likely wants a pardon, or maybe something else, a reward of some kind, who knows."

"And if the information he provides is of use to us, he shall indeed be rewarded," said Aren. "Especially if it helps implicate that traitor." Aren had no sympathy for treachery. He'd see to it that his mother's killer would be brought to justice.

Cyneric nodded silently, a solemn look of despair on his face. It was an expression he'd rarely worn in all the years Aren had known him, something he kept buried even through some of his darkest days.

The doors finally opened again and Pennyn arrived with their witness. A tall, scruffy looking man with short, unkempt brown hair. He looked as if he hadn't showered in days, and he had three scars stretching below his left ear, one reaching just beneath his dirty chin. Pennyn sat the man down and there was a brief silence before the man cleared his throat to speak.

"So, I hear you have some information for us," said Lady Rayne, interrupting him.

The man scoffed. "Not even a dash of courtesy, I've been waiting in that godforsaken cave for some time, you know." He turned to look at Joten, as if inspecting him. With his neatly pressed guard's uniform and his well-kept fair hair, smartly parted to one side, they were stark opposites of one another, as different as two men from the same city could be. "Who's this, then?" said the scruffy man.

Rayne scowled at him, then her expression softened into an empathetic smile, her eyebrows slightly raised, and the corners of her mouth curled downwards. "My apologies, how has your day been? I hope we've kept you comfortable. Are there any other graces the Crown can extend to accommodate you better?" she said.

The man looked confused. "Well, actually, it wouldn't hurt–"

"Shut your mouth," she said sharply, her lips pursed tightly together again. She crossed her arms and looked down at him as if she'd stumbled across some rubbish on the side of the road. "Now, out with it. Is it *good* information that you have for us or are you just…looking for a bone, as it were?" she said. "We've had quite enough of ravenous dogs in here."

Aren raised his hand politely to stop her. This man hadn't done anything wrong. In fact, he'd gone out of his way to come forward to help them. If he *did* know something, Rayne's constant berating and belittling wasn't going to get anything out of him.

"Good day to you, sir," he said calmly. "Now, may I ask what your name is?"

"Laris Hontren," the man said.

"Laris? Quite unique, I hope you don't mind me asking where you're from? It doesn't sound like it's from down here."

"Arvendon," he said. "Born and raised in Sturrock. Will probably die here too. Never seen further than Astonkirk, to be honest." There was something endearing about the way he spoke, despite how rough he looked. Maybe it was the Arvendon accent he'd grown up hearing around Jaspyn. "Me grandmam though, she worked for the Old Aneglin up in Ayleris, she were a missionary. She'd a knack for this lad, an orphan she'd helped raise, name was Laris. Named me after him."

"Your Majesty," said Pennyn, giving the witness a condescending glare.

"You what?" said Laris.

"You're speaking to the king."

"It's alright, Mr. Runeval. This man is here as a friend of the Crown," said Aren. "You have my word you will be released, friend." He was desperate to get something out of this commoner, something of use.

"Now now, let's not jump bridges," said Laris. "I ain't a friend of the Crown, but I *am* here to tell you summat I think you'd wanna hear."

"Right, will you get on with it then?" said Cyneric.

"Before I do, what I said about the dosh…"

Pennyn glared at him. "Now is not the time for negotiations, Laris."

Rayne laughed raucously. "Of course, the peasant wants a bone. What did I tell you, Aren?" she said, before setting her suddenly cruel eyes on the witness again. "How much are you looking for? Enough to get you out of Arvendon, I'd bet."

Laris looked carefully at the High Lady of Medlanta, inspecting her face, her eyes as carefully as he'd done Joten. So carefully, in fact, that she shuffled in her seat, folding her arms and passing her eyes around the room.

"What did you say your name was, my lady?" said Laris.

"What's it to you?" she said, frowning. "Rayne. Rayne of Lyndan. Now, what's it to you?"

Laris smiled, but it was a rather unkind smile. Almost as menacing as had been Rayne's eyes, just moments ago.

"I knew I'd heard that ratty voice before," he said. "Rayne Dresden. I can't believe—"

"You will not take that tone with the lady," said Pennyn, slamming his palms down hard on the table and making Joten jump.

Aren remained quiet though, curious to see what would come of it. Rayne looked shocked, and for the first time in all the time Aren had known her, was left unable to speak.

"I will take whatever tone I damn well please, I'm here for your benefit and not the other way around. *You* need *me*," said Laris, pointing his grimy finger in Aren's face. "Now come on now, Dresden, why don't you tell your friends how long we've been old pals eh?"

Rayne's expressions changed. "We aren't. We haven't ever been, stop embarrassing yourself," she shook her head and scowled at him. "I never even met you. We aren't old friends, don't pretend we are. I didn't even remember your *name*. Think about that, that's how little you mattered to her."

"You shut your mouth."

Cyneric and Pennyn both rose from their seats in fury.

"Now, now, lads. That isn't necessary," said Rayne. "He knows his place. Don't you, Laris?"

Laris Hontren's cracked lips narrowed, and his eyebrows drew closer together until they were almost one. He turned to face Aren. "I have a new proposal, Your Majesty."

"We will make no deals with you. We honour you with the offer of a reward, and you treat us like this?" said Pennyn. "You speak to a noble lady, a High Lady, like she is some common peasant?"

"I wasn't talking to you," said Laris, turning to Pennyn. "Besides, aren't *you* some common peasant?"

"You-"

"I wasn't talking to you," Laris repeated himself. "Next time, be quiet." He turned to face Aren again.

"Go on," said Aren reluctantly, not knowing what else he could say.

"I will spare you any lies, the reason I came forward was…well, the reason anyone like me would come forward. An easy earning," said Laris. "And freedom."

"Not surprising in the slightest," said Cyneric.

"That ain't to say that my information is of any less value, though," said the witness, scowling. "In any case, I've changed my mind. No sum of money'll open my mouth now, I don't care. Throw me into the bay, torture me."

Aren felt a growing rage inside him, and he made no effort to conceal it. His precious time was being wasted and his mother's murderer still breathed. He clenched his fists tightly and slammed them on the wooden table, his head throbbing and his legs trembling.

"Your Majesty," said Laris, chuckling insolently. "I didn't expect-"

"I'm presuming there's a point you're getting to," said Rayne. "We all grow impatient of your incessant rambling."

"Indeed. No money will open my mouth, but there is one thing that I will settle on. Just one thing, that can get you the information you're looking for. I want to meet with *her* sister," he said pointing to Rayne Dresden, though not shifting his gaze from Aren's face. "Wynter."

"I won't have it," said Pennyn, slapping his hands down on the table once more. "How dare you?"

"Again, I didn't ask you," replied Laris before turning to Aren again. "It doesn't have to be in private, it can be on her terms."

It was a strange request. Lady Wynter was a married woman. A royal too, by vow. Why *her* out of all people?

The look of horror on Rayne's face had spoken volumes, though. How *had* they known each other? There was definitely bad blood, Rayne had made it clear. But a meeting... Uncle Skander and Aunt Wynter *could* understand...couldn't they? To avenge the queen? It was just a meeting, after all... Was it too much to ask?

"No," said Aren. "Keep your information. Mr. Runeval, get this man out of here." It was tempting, but Aren was determined not to let anyone push him or his family around.

"No, Your Majesty," said Rayne, smiling thinly. "I will make it happen. He wants a meeting, that is all. I will see to it myself. If he wishes to be turned down by the same noble twice in his lifetime, I will see to that if it means justice for the queen."

"Are you sure?" said Aren.

"I'll see to it, you don't worry about that."

"For at *least* an hour," said Laris, clearly dubious.

"Yes, yes, no need to keep blabbering," replied Rayne. "You will get what you have asked for, on the Crown's word. Now, will you finally be of some use to us?"

He did not respond to her. His eyes remained fixed on Aren. "A tall, dark man, rather on the large side. That's one of the people I saw."

"On the night of the Recedon? Would you be able to point him out from a picture?" said Aren.

Laris nodded. "Him and a woman. I was there, among the common folk. They were suspicious-like, more so than the nobles usually are. She slipped him something. Something quite small, like an ampule. It was dark blue, maybe purple."

Purple.

"What did this woman look like?" said Aren.

"Paler than him, with dark, silky hair, kind of long. She was probably Weslin, maybe Zaldroni?"

"And what were *you* doing at the Recedon?" said Rayne.

He finally turned to face the woman again. "What do you think would've brought me here? All the way up to the Royal Quarter? The icy chills of Wynter, of course." He gave her a sinister grin and she responded with a look of utter revolt.

"Mr. Runeval, can you arrange for the pictures to be brought in?" said Aren.

"Already here," said Pennyn. "Here we go," he pulled out from his brown hide bag a collection of small, blurry pictures of the many prominent nobles that were present at the night of the Recedon, the royal family, the Crown Council, the High Lords and

Ladies and the loyal households. The pile was thick, scattered in disarray across the table. Pennyn took his time to meticulously arrange them one by one, separating them into neat columns.

"Any popping out at you?" said Cyneric.

"There, him," said Laris, pointing to a faded picture of Lord Gavyn Escos. "That's the man I was talking about."

Gavyn. Bizarre, very bizarre.

"And the woman?" said Pennyn.

Laris frantically combed through the pile, looking at each picture carefully. Finally, he tapped on the table with his large knuckles.

"Her," he said pointing at the picture. "She's the one who handed him the ampule."

Aren's stared at the picture in horror and the room fell to silence. Everyone sat on the table went still. Even Joten, who'd quietly been listening, clearly eagerly waiting for it all to be over, was sat in awe. *Linara Spenler.* Why? *Gavyn Escos…*his mother's own Arms Counsel.

It came back to him all at once…the night she'd been killed, the night he'd had dinner with her. His last dinner with her. Deric Serrano had said it was *Lord Escos* that had wanted his mother there. And Aren too. He had been quite persistent on that, it was why they'd kept him behind bars right next to Ysser Banlin. They'd perhaps gotten the wrong man locked up below the Hall, after all. Perhaps it wasn't Deric that had lied about the siege at all. Perhaps it had been Gavyn Escos who had conspired with Ysser. Well, Deric was in their custody for now, they'd bring him back in for questioning. The guard had been pretty useless so far, but perhaps they'd be able to jog his memory. *But Linara?*

Aren could gather his thoughts no more. They were blurry, misty even, and the world around him was no better. He felt weak, he hadn't the will to sit up straight and the stars hanging from above seemed so distant now…so hazy. The sound of the trees swaying outside of the window faded, and suddenly Aren felt lost. More lost than he'd ever felt in the Panderer's realm. More lost than he'd ever felt in any realm.

Why? What had they to gain? *Something quite small, like an ampule.* How did an ampule of Aster's Pine take out almost the entire First Guard? Surely, it wasn't possible. And if it were more than that, as the traitor Ysser had claimed, how on earth had they gotten that much of the purple poison into the palace in the first place?

"Are you certain, Laris?" said Pennyn. "This is a grave accusation – a more serious one than you might think."

"Unmistakeable, those eyes of hers. Even from a distance."

The initial shock of it all had turned into anger. *How could she?* Aren couldn't believe he'd spoken to her that same night, he'd have done well to take her life. Maybe his mother would be alive now if he had. To think, he'd asked the traitor to be on his mother's council. She was probably plotting the assassination even then, when he'd been speaking to her. She was probably planning his own assassination. Aren had stopped listening to the conversation between Pennyn and Laris completely. How could he focus? He was lost, somewhere else, alone.

Perhaps her brothers had been a part of it all too. Lord Fraston and Lord Oscon…they'd been quite suspicious too, hadn't they? Or was it his mind playing tricks on him now? Oscon was on the Crown Council too…he'd certainly have been of use to the bluecoats, wouldn't he? Aren felt empty. Who could he trust? His mother's Crown Council was compromised…people from within the palace itself had wanted him dead.

"Alright, thank you. Is there anything else you can tell us about the night?" said Pennyn. "Anything else suspicious?"

"Now hold on, where's Wynter and when will I get to see her?" said Laris.

"Hold your horses, she isn't going anywhere. Let all of this be dealt with first, we have a long way to go from here," said Rayne. "You have my word, and you have the king's word. You will get your little parley with Wynter."

"This is the exact sort of thing I was trying to avoid," said Laris, spitting on the ground. "I acted in good faith, now I can't be sure you'll ever act on your…*word*. You toffs and your word mean little to me."

Rayne smiled mockingly. "I suppose you can't be sure of that, can you? You'll just have to have faith."

"But, for fuck's sake I've had a –"

"Come on now, Mr. Runeval. Would you please escort our guest back to whichever dark cellar he came from," said Rayne. "Don't worry Laris, you'll be back before you know it," she winked.

Laris Hontren looked infuriated, but he didn't say anything as he walked out of the room with Pennyn because he knew it was out of his hands now.

"Wait, wait there's more!" He suddenly waved his arms around like a lunatic.

Aren turned around to look at him. "Go on."

"The chef. The fat one. Him and the Escosi were being all kindly-like. They'd hugged or summat. I just thought it was a bit strange, you know…the Escosi being a nobleman and all."

Aren nodded. Pennyn grabbed the witness' arm and walked him out of the room in silence, Laris muttering under his breath all the while.

"What a vexatious little twat," said Lady Rayne, as soon as the doors had shut behind him.

Aren said nothing, he was drained.

"The Spenler bitch, I saw her at the Recedon too. Aren, she was with the common folk. She spent a little too much time talking through that curtain if you ask me."

"We can't be sure he's telling us the truth," said Aren.

"I don't like him any more than you – this much I think is obvious – but I *do not* think that he was lying. Not about what he saw. I saw Gavyn with the chef too."

Aren nodded. He knew that he'd seen the chef with Linara too, but he said nothing. It had all started to make sense. Maybe a part of him refused to believe it, no matter how much sense it made.

"Your Majesty, I think you should get some rest," said Cyneric.

"No, I think I'm doing just fine."

"You need to sleep, Aren. Take care of yourself before you let this consume you."

"Joten, you're free to leave now. I'm sorry we wasted your time, you may as well have left. Ah, well, you live and you learn," said Lady Rayne. "We'll be in touch if we need any more from you." She accompanied the confused guard out of the room before closing the door behind him.

"I'm going to have to agree with Cyneric here, Elvira wouldn't have wanted to lose you to them like this, don't let them win," said Rayne, sitting down once again.

Aren nodded meekly. "I don't think I can sleep right now, but I'll try to get some rest in the study. I just wish Olivia and Jaspyn were here, when will they be allowed back into the palace?"

"Not too long now," said Rayne. "They will be allowed back for the funeral."

"Okay, thank you," he said glumly, getting up out of his seat. Both Cyneric and Rayne rose up out of their seats as well, but he stopped them.

"I'd prefer to walk alone," he said.

The pair shared a glance.

"It would make us all a lot more comfortable if someone you trust was with you at all times, Aren," said Cyneric. "At least until you appoint your First Guard."

"It's a very short walk. I'd much prefer to be alone, there's barely anyone in the palace anyway."

"Aren, I really think you–"

"The decision is his," said Lady Rayne sharply. "Let us not forget *he* is the People's Sovereign, now."

Cyneric conceded, bowing to his king as Aren got up. "We will meet with Pennyn, perhaps discuss the Crown Council and figure out if there's anyone on it that we can actually trust."

Aren nodded and wondered if he could trust anyone at all. He smiled weakly at the pair of them and shut the door to the Hall of Krelis quickly behind him. He wasted no time and walked straight down the corridor, as brisk as his legs would take him. He had so many things on his mind. He wished he could rest, but he couldn't bring himself to it. Vengeance. Justice. Duty. Honour. The agitating words echoed in and out of his thoughts, leaving his body tense, cold. He shook himself free of them, turning into the long, narrow corridor that bordered the Garden of Ysseria. The last time he'd been here, his biggest worries were to impress the nobles at the Recedon…how stupid he'd been. He could smell the Waters of Léoree, the sweet familiar fragrance of a warm, kind embrace. He could feel his eyes well up, but he kept on walking. He looked out through the large glass panes, thinking back to the mornings he had trained there with Cyneric. Not too long ago, but such simpler times. Had he known he would have had such little time with his mother, he would have spent it very differently.

He stopped at the sound of a sharp crack. Had it come from behind him? There was nobody there. A branch rustling in the wind, or hitting against the glass of the windows next to him, perhaps? He wiped the sweat from his brow and frantically reached for his dagger, his palms slippery as he unsheathed it. He spun around, placing his back against the wall and slowly edged towards the corner. He slowly and carefully peered around it, his dagger in his trembling hand. Of course, nobody was there, but Aren could feel his heart pounding in his head all the same. Suddenly the longing to spend some time alone was gone, suddenly he felt sick to his stomach. More frightened than ever…more frightened than he'd felt in the Panderer's realm. This was supposed to be his home.

He wondered if he should just swallow his pride and go back to the hall. Cyneric wouldn't think any less of him, would he? Wouldn't that be what a king would do? Fear was a normal thing, after all. He trusted Cyneric and he wished, more than anything now, that he wasn't alone. Maybe it would do him some good. He cautiously crept back down the old corridor towards the Hall of Krelis, hoping Cyneric and Rayne hadn't yet left, his heart racing. He kept his dagger gripped tightly in his sweaty palm, right up until he had reached the large wooden doors to the hall.

To his relief, he'd left the door ever so slightly ajar, and he could hear a deep voice from behind it. It certainly sounded like Cyneric. He reached for the brass knob when suddenly he stopped in his tracks and snatched his hands away just as quick…what if it wasn't him? He couldn't remember if he'd left the door open or closed when he'd left, he'd been in such a rush to get out of there. What if it was someone else? Why would Cyneric still be here? He said he was going to see Pennyn, after all. He waited to see if he could make out the muffled sounds of a second voice. It took no more than a few seconds for him to hear Rayne's familiar Medlantan accent and he sighed in relief once more. The voices suddenly quietened though, falling to near silence. He pressed his ear against the gap between the two doors, just about able to make out the soft whispers. He decided to open the door very carefully with a gentle push, ever so slowly, just enough for him to be able to hear more. Unsurprisingly, it was Cyneric Porter's voice that emerged. He recognised it in an instant, even at a whisper. He pushed the door slightly further, praying that it wouldn't creak.

"But they haven't yet, have they?" Rayne whispered.

"It was the same with Ethan," whispered Cyneric.

"He has more support now than ever before, I just hope it's all hearsay, all of this nonsense," whispered Rayne. "If it does come down to it, he's got two legs to stand on, I reckon. They can't change that unless…unless it gets out, somehow."

"And you believe they'd cast her aside? And are we sure about the sightings, where I'm from these things are usually down to paranoia and –"

"It's not what I believe, it's what I've seen. Where you're from is a different world entirely, Cyneric. The whispers alone aren't a great worry, but what I saw with my own two eyes… it is not deniable. On a train, of all places…"

"He wasn't lying then, Ysser," Cyneric whispered. "About the Wyversen lad."

More secrets. He felt incredibly frustrated. Why were they whispering? Behind his back…after everything that'd happened. Who was Ethan? It was a name he had only heard in the Panderer's realm. He had to hear more. He hastily pushed the door further, but it had been a mistake. The door loudly squeaked as he pushed it, and the whispers immediately stopped. He knew he could not stop there now. He swung it open fully and trudged in, sheepishly.

"Your Majesty," they both said in unison, with a slight bow of the head.

"You're back – is there a problem?" said Cyneric.

Before Aren could get a word out Pennyn Runeval came barging into the room from behind him. He all but pushed Aren out of the way as he clambered into the hall.

"Deric Serrano is dead."

A Dream is Just a Dream
Rhedas

Rhedas wiped the sweat from his forehead and went straight back into it. He reached for the bucket he'd thrown into the deep, dark, seemingly bottomless well, but it was pointless, far too deep for him to grasp. Kyril wouldn't be happy at all. He cursed himself for his clumsy fingers. He cursed himself for his awful dreams. They had never picked a good time; they always came to him when he was the least bit ready. He missed when it was just sleepless nights, when his dreams didn't bother him while the sun was up…at least he wasn't always getting into trouble then. The visions were getting clearer now, far more vivid, getting in the way of him doing what he was here to do.

He picked up the rope and swung it blindly in, hoping that by some mercy of the One, it would strike the bucket's handle so he could reel it up. His faith let him down and the empty echoes of the rope hitting the brick walls of the well were all that fruited from it.

"Having a little trouble, are you?" came Kyril's cruel voice from behind him. "Are you sure you're fit to be a minister? Of the Sandaerian faith, no less. It isn't a joke, you know."

"I'm – I'm fine."

"Are you?" said Kyril, grabbing him by the shoulder and pulling him sharply away from the well. He looked down into it and tutted. "A simple task. Such a simple task, and yet you have made it into a…" he sighed. "Tamuz will not be pleased. I will speak to him at earliest convenience, and I will see to it that you are disciplined accordingly."

"You aren't senior to me," said Rhedas, trembling. "You cannot *see* to anything." It was so unlike him; he hadn't wanted to say it but yet he had. He felt a sharp stinging pain on the skin of his cheek as Kyril Sandaerzi swung him a tight slap across the face. He unclenched his aching jaw as the warm, tingling sensation on the side of his face subsided, fighting back the tears.

"Say that again. I dare you."

"Sorry-"

"I came here to tell you something, something of utmost importance, and this is how you treat me?" said Kyril, tutting again. It was an irritating sound, his constant tutting. The fat priest swung his silk scarf over his shoulder and shook his head. "This is a time for us to be united, as brothers of the North Parydon. Not a time for you to be finding reasons for us to cast you out."

He wouldn't like that at all, being cast out. Rhedas was at home here, more at home than anywhere he'd ever before been. He shuddered at the thought and shook his head. "I'm sorry, I'm sorry."

Kyril smiled. "That's what we like to hear," he said. "Now listen, I came to you because we've received word of... strange happenings, let us say. Very strange. All over Verenia and even in the faithless south. I know that you seem to be a master of strange happenings, so I suppose..." He looked around him to make sure the other ministers weren't nearby.

"I... I don't... What is it?"

"Danger lurks outside these walls. All over the damned country. Enemies that we don't share blood with, those that we have been fighting since the First Age of Shadows itself."

"Are you talking about dwellers?" said Rhedas.

"Shhh. Don't use that word, not here," said Kyril in a panic. "But yes, the ones from your dreams."

They weren't the only ones from his dreams, thought Rhedas. The ones who wore the coats stained blue, the boy with the flame-kissed hair, the lynx and the skyvern...great peril.

"The sightings... they've been happening for weeks, months even. But now..." said Kyril. "Now one of our own has been attacked."

"What?" said Rhedas. "Who?"

"Ferus," said Kyril, sighing. "He is fine now, healthy. But it was terrifying. A test of his faith."

"The dwe-" he stopped himself. He didn't want another slap, his cheek still hurt from the last one. "The creatures of the night, how do we stop them?"

Kyril frowned. "Well, you know how we stop them. You've read about it haven't you? The Key. Forged by blood, blood of the Old Deryzi."

"Well… yes, but…" He didn't know how to say it. "My dreams, they're…"

Kyril looked at him expectantly. "Well? Your dreams what?"

"We cannot use the Key of Blood."

"Of course, we cannot. It has been lost for centuries, but it is the only way we can stop them."

Rhedas didn't want to admit the harsh truth he knew. The truth of its whereabouts. That it was not lost after all, at least not in the sense they imagined it to be. He left the truth unsaid, for he knew the bitter future that lay ahead, he knew what needed to happen.

"I was hoping, well, *we* were hoping that your dreams might be of some use after all," said Kyril. "Master Tamuz and I."

"How so?" What had changed? Why did they now trust his word? After weeks and months of being constantly ridiculed, the fat priest was now coming to *him* about his dreams? Before, they'd thought him mad, or stupid, or perhaps both.

"To figure out what to do about these…sightings. To protect our people, the people of Verenia."

"I'm afraid I do not know anything about that," Rhedas lied. "My dreams are difficult to piece together. One thing I can tell you is that it is of utmost importance we head south."

Kyril stared at him blankly. "Why so?"

"Because there are people we need to speak to. We must talk to the queen."

Kyril sighed. "The king," he said. "King Aren."

So that is what had changed. That is why he'd come. "Her Majesty is dead?" asked Rhedas. "She…"

"Yes," said Kyril. "Killed by one of her own, we hear. Ashcrest's doing, no doubt. Faithless man. Vile, vile creature."

He didn't know the half of it, thought Rhedas. There was so much more to come, oh so much. He wished it didn't have to be the case, enough blood had been spilled already, but it was what needed to happen. The dreams had been clear.

"And Her Eminence?" said Rhedas.

Kyril frowned again. "How dare you?" he said. "Just because one of your dreams came to be needn't mean they all will. Sometimes a dream is just a dream."

He wished that were the case, but his dreams were different, he knew it. "Sorry," he said. "I just thought…"

"Yes, well, you thought wrong. Perhaps it wasn't Her Eminence you saw in the dream, perhaps it was the queen."

Rhedas shook his head. "Pale skin, emerald eyes. Long dark black hair, the darkest. Young, beautiful. The dream was clear."

Kyril sighed. "Don't repeat this nonsense in here again, Tamuz won't be happy. I'm only saying it for your own benefit, you want to stay here, don't you?"

"Yes," said Rhedas. "But first, like I said, we must go south."

"I suppose it couldn't hurt, an audience with the king. It is just that…Sturrock is so far."

"Not Sturrock," said Rhedas. "We head to Ayleris."

Kyril glared at him in annoyance. "What do you want to go there for?"

"Just trust me," said Rhedas, knowing that his comrade wouldn't. "We need to warn them, the king, Her Eminence, we need to tell them all."

"Her Eminence knows," said Kyril. "And as for the king, I will send word down to Sturrock."

"No," said Rhedas. "We will not tell them of our arrival. We do not want to be turned away."

"But it will take *time* for us all to travel down to Sturrock," said Kyril. "We need to tell them; it is as you said. Perhaps King Aren will be a little more receptive."

"Don't tell them," said Rhedas. "Please. They will let us in, have faith. And then we can tell them about the threat they face." Ayleris wasn't too far. It would be a short trip down.

Unbroken Vows
Aren

It was a warmer day than usual. The grey water in Inigo's Pool shimmered in the sunlight. Aren was stood on the neatly trimmed grass next to Aleryc's Memorial, his family's mausoleum. Olivia was stood right next to him, Jaspyn a few paces away. He couldn't tell if it were tears or sweat trickling down her cheek, though Aren's own face felt cold and numb, even in the unusual heat. The other nobles all stood under the shade of the High Parydon a short distance away, nearly everyone dressed in the most sombre beige.

"It was a beautiful ceremony, Aren," said Jaspyn.

"Yes, it was ni- nice. The High Minister was very kind," said Olivia, who hadn't been able to stop sniffling.

"Come on, Aren. I think it'd be wise to go back to the others now," said Jaspyn.

"Half of them cry false tears," said Aren. "I'm not going to go over there to appease them. I won't spend a moment longer than necessary making small talk with them about what a wonderful person my mother was. They aren't innocent. Some of them may as well have been complicit themselves in her murder."

"Still, Aren. Don't you want to be there for the ones who actually need you? Lady Rayne, Pennyn, Valery, to say the least," said Jaspyn. "Their tears aren't false. You and I both know this."

"When is she g-going to be moved?" said Olivia.

"This afternoon," said Aren.

"What do you mean *moved*?" said Jaspyn.

"The body… it will be taken to the Valecrest. There will be a private service in the Crown Parydon, and she'll be laid to rest in the West Cemetery," said Aren, a tear rolling down his cheek. He wiped it away quickly with his hand.

"Through…through *that?*" said Jaspyn, pointing at the masses heaping on top of each other outside the tall black gates of the Parydon.

"Well, no," said Aren, blinking away another tear. He looked around to make sure nobody was in earshot. "The tunnels," he said. "Beneath the Parydon…they lead straight to Lyndan House. They'll move her this evening, once all the nobles have left."

"Oh," said Jaspyn.

Maybe they were right. Maybe he needed to be there for the ones who'd been on her mother's side till the end. "I'll see to them."

"Hold on, we'll come with you," said Olivia. "You aren't alone in this."

The crowds of nobles were sweaty. Maybe even sweatier than the peasants beyond the gates, some in tears, others climbing pillars to try and get a better view. Barely any of them were dressed in beige, a few were even in filthy rags. Some of them cheered, whilst others jeered and mocked wildly as Aren walked past. Some younger children clapped and shouted as their parents struggled to hush them.

"The Absent King returns!" shouted a man from behind the walls. Aren searched to see where the voice had come from. He wasn't going to take any of it, not today. He strode towards them, but Jaspyn's clammy hand grasped at his as he tugged him back.

"Just get Cyneric to sort them out," said Jaspyn.

"And be known as a coward?"

"You don't have a First Guard, you refuse to have the Sentry protect you…what are you going to do? Something tells me they aren't going to change their minds after a polite telling off."

"I don't care."

The gates rattled and roared.

"The hag is dead! How you gonna hide now?"

This time he could see where the voice had come from. A fairly short man with long greasy hair. He was probably very poor; he'd dressed himself in a dirty shirt with grease marks all the way up the sleeves. Poor or rich, Aren was furious. He yanked his hand free from Jaspyn's grip and made for the gate, but some of his subjects had already begun heckling at the man who had made the remark. A woman gasped as another man wrapped his hands around the long-haired fellow, strangling him.

126

"Stop this!" Aren shouted. It was enough to draw attention from several nobles too. His throat was dry, and he struggled to find the words, but he knew that his mother wouldn't have wanted him to watch in silence. Especially not on a day like this. *Act justly but with mercy.* That is what she'd always said. A part of him wished he could just turn away, let the common folk brawl and leave them to themselves, but he couldn't in good conscience let this man pay for his dreadful words with his life, no matter how dreadful his words had been. They'd kill him for sure.

"Your queen wouldn't have wanted this," he said. "The ignorant will never learn. Let him say whatever filth he wants to say, killing him won't solve anything." He looked carefully at the man's collar. Jerton's Dove hung from his shirt. The mark of the bluecoats, of Soren Ashcrest. "Another will just take his place, it'll drive further divisions between us at a time when we need to come together."

"And just how far are you gonna keep forgiving, son?" shouted a woman from among the crowd.

"That's *Your Majesty*, miss," said Olivia Berywen. "Address your king properly."

"Before a king, he is a son! A son of Verenia!" she shouted. "He'd ought to learn to punish his subjects! This stupidity is what took his mother and soon enough it will take him, and then the rest of us too."

Us?

The cheers suddenly darkened, turning to heckling and cursing.

"Give us back our land then!" someone yelled, a younger Weslin lad. "The pathetic son of Verenia should bloody well *stay* in Verenia!"

Jaspyn pulled Aren away, holding him by his shoulders. "Ignore them. Olivia, go and get someone to deal with all of this." He walked Aren back towards the High Parydon, where the nobles stared in horror.

"Don't even think about looking back at them."

Aren was mortified, left speechless. More than anything though, his heart ached. Soon enough, all eyes were on him. Some whispered amongst each other, glancing at him sideways. Aren tried his very hardest to maintain a firm face, holding back his tears, fighting the urge to break down. He didn't know how. He walked glumly, his head down, hoping that nobody would see his face. But before he'd made it to the shade of the tower, he felt a gentle tap on his shoulder.

It was Éline Nazeris. Her brother and her father were stood behind her. After all that had happened, he felt a gentle warmth seeing their familiar faces. Even Ylor, with all his dubious expressions.

"Ignore it all, Aren," she said. "Sorry – I suppose I mean *Your Majesty*." She smiled at him emptily.

"Hello," said Jaspyn quietly.

"Oh hello, Jaspyn," said Éline. "It's been far too long, hasn't it?"

"Ylor Nazeris," her brother's cold voice came from behind her, as he extended his hand to the king. "Nice to meet you, Your Majesty. And Mr. Fenwern, of course," he nodded at Jaspyn, who nodded back silently.

The nobles' attention had since been diverted back to the commoners stood outside the walls of the Parydon, as Cyneric struggled to bring some order to the crowd.

"I'm so sorry," said Lord Nazeris. "About Elvira, I truly am. It burdens my soul that we've been fated to meet in these circumstances. Everything has been so incredibly rushed, I couldn't even get a word with you at the Recedon. We arrived quite late, you see."

"Thank you," said Aren. "My mother spoke very highly of you and your family. And I've got very fond memories of Lady Éline…from her time in the capital."

Arcadius looked unsettled. "Oh yes of course, I suspect the two of you'll have a lot to catch up on. I think you'll get on quite well with Ylor too, he's very much like you," Lord Nazeris smiled at his son who looked lost in deep thought, much like he always did. Aren struggled to see the similarities at all. But before he could respond, Pennyn Runeval appeared from beside him.

"Lord Nazeris, a word please," he said, before turning to Aren. "Pardon me, Your Majesty."

"I shall speak with you very soon, I hope," said Lord Nazeris, and he was gone.

A touch of sadness swept across Éline's face. "I really am sorry about your mother. She was so kind to me in some of the most difficult times of my life… I always felt welcome here at court. It saddens me that I wasn't able to spend more time with her."

"I appreciate that," he said. He noticed her brother's watchful gaze, as if he were carefully examining Aren and Jaspyn. Ylor caught Aren's stare and broke away, looking to his sister instead. He wore a very thin smile, similar to his father's, it was distinct from his sister's vacant, lost one.

"Where's Olivia? I've been meaning to catch up with her as well. She's rarely at court anymore," said Éline.

"She is just dealing with…well, the people outside," said Aren.

"Oh, I see," she said, lowering her head and looking at the ground in front of her. "It's so incredibly hot, isn't it? We thought we'd escape the sun down here. Sturrock isn't much known for her summers-" Her brother gave her a peculiar glance and she stopped. It might have been his imagination, but Aren could have sworn he saw Ylor tighten his grasp on her shoulder.

"Isn't it colder in Zaldron?" said Jaspyn.

"Well, yes, but quite a summer we've been having," said Éline. "Suppose I thought we'd have left it behind. Guess not." This time it was unmistakeable; her brother patted his hand on her shoulder and suddenly her smile was gone.

"Suppose you'd know all about the heat though, from Asenia?" said Ylor, looking at Aren. Suddenly Aren felt his own smile tighten, clenching his fists.

"Indeed, especially in those awful barracks," said Aren almost naturally. "I do feel so much pride for our troops that are still out there, I've seen it first-hand, it isn't easy at all." It was a well-rehearsed lie, one that Aren had spun in many flavours over the years. By this point, it had almost seemed like the truth.

"What was it like up there?" said Éline. "Is it true what they say about the Keepers of the Border and the bartering of ale in the dead of night? Or is it all just as ruthless as it sounds? You know, with all the fighting going on? You know, my brother actually knew someone from –"

Ylor cleared his throat loudly and she turned to face him and then turned away again, her gaze sinking to the ground.

"It was definitely not how most imagine it to be, it's quite special up there. It's far from the pressures of court, the Asenians are mostly a very friendly folk, but yes, the fighting is all very real."

"What about you?" said Jaspyn to Éline. "How was life at home after you went back?"

There were no emotions on Éline's face. "It took a bit of getting used to, mother not being there anymore. Ylor and father helped me through it, though," she said softly. "I don't resent her for it at all anymore. I did at the beginning, but I'm sure she had her own reasons for leaving the way that she did," she sighed. "It's gotten a lot better, though. The fighting stopped. The banks are doing better than ever before. Kestoryn has never seen greener days according to my father. Zaldron's doing better than any other of our country's lands, I hear, you know, if it wasn't for the –"

"Come on, Éline," said Ylor. "There's no reason to show off to our neighbours in the capital. Sturrock's been treating us very well too, hasn't it?"

She smiled at him. "Yes, I suppose it has."

Olivia emerged from behind Jaspyn. "Good afternoon, Éline. Lord Ylor," she said flatly, nodding at the two of them.

Ylor smiled thinly again. "*Lord Ylor*? No need for all that. Besides, there aren't commoners around."

"I beg your pardon?" said Olivia, her eyebrows raised.

"The commoners. They aren't within earshot. You needn't address me with such formalities."

"The *good folk*," said Olivia, a shocked expression on her face.

"Yes exactly, them. There's not any nearby."

"Well apart from me, I suppose," said Jaspyn.

Éline glanced over at her brother, who was stood open-mouthed. "I'm so sorry Jaspyn, he didn't mean to be rude," she said. Aren wasn't quite sure that he didn't. It wasn't exactly a palace secret that Jaspyn was of common blood. Ylor knew exactly what he was saying, he wasn't innocent. He was cruel, or he was stupid.

"Don't worry about it," said Jaspyn. "I am what I am, and I'm proud of it. We can't all be noble, can we?" he chuckled.

Éline looked blankly over at Ylor who had his head bowed.

"Yes…very well… Ylor, then," said Olivia awkwardly. "I take it the both of you will be eating at the palace tonight? With Lord Nazeris?" said Olivia.

Éline and Ylor shared yet another silent look with one another. She looked as if she were about to open her mouth to say something but she kept quiet. Ylor, though, was quick to open his.

"No, actually we won't be there tonight," he said. "We're so very sorry...we'd love to make it, but father needs us to do something. It can't be changed."

"The Asmoni traders?" said Aren. He'd heard a rumour that Lord Nazeris had put his children to work.

Ylor nodded. "Yes, they arrive this afternoon. I'm so sorry we can't be there to..."

"Oh, don't worry," said Aren. He was somewhat relieved, maybe even a bit jealous. He wished that he himself didn't have to go. He couldn't stop wondering why custom forbade him from grieving by himself, behind closed doors. Perhaps with those closest to him. Why did it have to be such a public affair, every step of the way?

"If you don't mind, I must excuse myself – I think it's time I see to some of the nobles," said Aren.

"Of course, Your Majesty," said Ylor.

Rayne was stood by herself beside Aleryc's Memorial, her back to the crowd. She looked as if she was reading the inscriptions engraved in gold on the side of the column. He walked up behind her, not really knowing what he'd say.

"My lady," he said. That was always a good start.

Lady Rayne turned around to face him. "My boy, how are you?" Her voice wavered. Her tongue didn't carry its usual venomous bite, she spoke plainly, weakly even.

"As well as I can possibly be. And you?"

She just nodded in response, turning away from him again.

"My lady, I've got something I'd like to ask of you."

"Oh?" she said. "Do go on."

"I know that you have duties, duties that are dear to you, outside of court. Outside of Sturrock, in fact," he said. "I know that you're only here out of sheer respect for my mother. Yet, I'd like you to stay for longer."

It wasn't the response he'd anticipated. A dry silence. He couldn't quite tell what she was thinking by her face alone, it was as plain as her voice. For someone as flamboyant as she, Rayne either did surprisingly well to hide her emotions, or perhaps she simply felt nothing at all.

"I remember what you said to me the night of the Recedon. About trust. I need everyone I can trust right now, and I look around myself and see so few," he said. "I feel unsafe in my own home. Gavyn Escos and Linara Spenler are *still* nowhere to be found and frankly – I don't trust my mother's council. *My* council. It's looking more and more likely that Ysser Banlin spoke the truth. Deric Serrano is dead... I don't know what to make of it all. But what I do know, is that my mother's dying words were that I should trust you."

"And the Spenler girl's brothers?" said Rayne, finally opening her mouth.

Aren brought his voice down to a whisper. "Fraston is missing, and Oscon is in custody. We aren't taking chances this time so he's being kept beneath Sentry Hall itself."

"That must be quite the debacle, mustn't it? A member of the Crown Council in the wind, another locked up..."

"Word won't get out about him," said Aren. "Pennyn, Cyneric and I are the only ones to know."

"Son, if you believe that to be true, then you may be more credulous than I'd anticipated."

Aren raised an eyebrow. "Nobody knows that he is there...not even Jaspyn or Olivia. I don't see how anybody could find out."

"Those who do you harm have their ways," she muttered. She paused for a moment, looking at him curiously. "Son, is this your command? Or are you *asking* me?"

"I beg your pardon?"

She sighed. "This...*thing*. About wanting me here, is this a command as my sovereign king? Or is it a request? Do I have any say in the matter, as it stands?"

"A request," he said. "A humble one. I'm asking you because I don't know where else to go. The threat of the bluecoats isn't over. They wanted me dead too, let's not forget. Besides, from what I hear about you, your years of experience with these things, and all the people that are loyal to you, to House Dresden, I can't think of a better ally to have here at court."

"Not too many years of experience," she chuckled softly. She looked out to the water, deep in thought. "After Irvin died, there were certain things that I swore I'd change about my life. One of them was that I would devote myself, all of myself, to carrying his legacy – House Dresden's legacy – on my own two shoulders. After Wynter married your uncle, I was the last Dresden left in Lyndan. The last one that mattered anyway."

Aren nodded at her. "My mother did always say you were rooted to Lyndan's soil, but I suppose I thought I may have been able to change your mind." He toyed with the button on his tunic. He hadn't the slightest clue *why* he'd had that impression, his mother had never managed it. "I know I can't keep you here forever…All I do ask is that you stay just a few more days at the least and let me know what you think, then you can take the first train up to Lyndan if that's what you still want."

She nodded. "I owe it to Elvira. I'll stay for a few more days," she said. "But let me be frank. Please don't get your hopes too high about me moving here. I have very, very few good memories of this place."

"That's all I can ask," he smiled at her. He knew if it had come to her as a command, she'd have had to stay, but that wasn't how he'd wanted to start his reign. He was desperate. He longed for somebody he could put his faith in. He looked around at the other nobles. Lord Nazeris, smiling thinly at nobody in particular. Tylus Banlin, as unjust as they get. Pennyn hadn't even wanted him here at the funeral, he thought the lord wasn't to be trusted. Too close to the enemy. Perhaps he was right. Or perhaps Ysser Banlin had been innocent in it all. Could Pennyn himself be trusted? He eyed the Crown Chancellor, stood next to the fountain, his arm around Valery Rennero. She was sobbing. In fact, since the night of his mother's death, he hadn't once seen her without tears in her eyes. Her silvery hair was more dishevelled than he'd ever seen before. Her tears were genuine at least, but Aren couldn't help but wonder how many of the other nobles were feigning theirs.

The World We Want to Build
Eyan

The Spenlers irritated him most of all. Any time Eyan could avoid spending with them, he was most grateful for. Taking them into his own home, it had been a hellish nightmare.

"Now, we mustn't be soft, remember that," the pompous bastard said. "Do you understand?"

"Yes Fraston," Eyan replied.

"Good." Fraston Spenler rolled up the piece of paper and handed it to him. "In case you forget."

"How do you know it so well?" said Eyan. "The Northern Compound, so few know its ins and outs."

"You leave that with me," he said smiling as he tapped him on the shoulder.

Renut cleared his throat, tray in hand. His little hands were trembling once more, and his face was drowning in sweat.

"You…you idiot!" Fraston shrieked.

"I-I j-just have some f-food," the little man replied. "F-from the k-kitchen."

With one quick swing of the hand Fraston smacked his arms hard and the tray toppled over, biscuits and sandwiches scattered all over the marble floor.

The little man let out a loud gasp. "S-sir! The f-food!"

"Did your mother never teach you not to interrupt your betters when they are talking about serious matters, strategy and such?" Fraston scowled. "You should wait outside quietly."

"I d-did," said Renut. "The d-door was open so I thought…"

"You thought foolishly," said Fraston.

"I'm s-sorry," said Renut. "I am." He knelt down and began to pick up the pieces. Eyan folded up the piece of paper and placed it in his pocket, kneeling beside him.

"Here," said Eyan. "Just put it all back onto the tray."

134

He felt Fraston's cold grip on the back of his neck and was jolted upwards.

"Are you stupid?"

"I'm not," said Eyan, his jaw clenched.

"Let the help earn their share. Don't go soft, Eyan, I've heard what you're like."

"I'm sorry," he replied. "I won't."

"Out!" Fraston shouted and the little man scurried out of the door, not turning back even once. "You need to surround yourself with stronger people, soldiers."

"Understood," said Eyan, tired.

"Let's go over it again. Remember, the stem cannot sustain itself without any roots."

"Hmm?"

"The *boy*," said Fraston impatiently. "We have made your life easier. His roots are gone, he will be easy to remove."

Easy wasn't the word he'd have chosen but he kept his mouth shut before he too received a smack.

"You need to be wise once you're in, stick to the corridors I've highlighted in that thing," he pointed to Eyan's pocket. "And remember, if you *can*, spare the ones I've listed."

"And if I can't?"

"What do you think?" Fraston spat out. "If you can't, then don't. You know what your priority is tomorrow, you mustn't stray from it. This time we shall leave no stone unturned."

We. It was a big word for someone who'd be sat miles away across the bay when it all happened.

"The ones you've listed," Eyan said, pulling out the piece of paper again. "Olivia Berywen."

Fraston groaned. "Her father won't have it any other way, and her father is important for what is to come."

"Right, of course," said Eyan, his heart beating faster. "Rayne Dresden? Éline Nazeris?"

Fraston's eyes widened slightly. "Many of the names on that list come from your father," he said. "I don't know what reason he might have to spare your old friends."

Eyan nodded quietly and cast his eyes further down on the tattered piece of paper. "And what of this one? Roy, is it?"

"Yes, yes, spare the idiot chef too," said Fraston. "Our man on the inside."

"He was the one who failed last time?" said Eyan.

Fraston nodded. "My sister practically served the purple poison to him on a silver platter, but the fool said it'd been too much of a risk. Ah, well. He might be important to us in the weeks to come."

"Of course," said Eyan. "And those that I…need not spare?"

"The ones you shall kill?" said Fraston, chuckling. "Say it as it is."

"Yes," said Eyan. "Have you made a list for that too?"

Fraston's eyes narrowed. "Every last one who serves that false king."

"Hmm?" Eyan gulped.

"Every cook, every guard, and most of all everyone who sits on that deceitful Council."

"*Every* noble?" said Eyan.

"You can start with my traitorous brother Oscon."

Eyan took a step back, leaning against the windowpane.

"Bloody pathetic, that man. He should be embarrassed to bear that name. *Oscon*." Fraston shook his head. "*Every* noble you find, I mean that. Don't go soft."

"I…"

"You know how they are, that's why you mustn't spare anyone. Not even the child, what is his name?"

"Inigo?" Eyan felt sick to his stomach.

"Yes, even the children. *Root and stem*. If you spare any, the crown will fall to them. That is how their twisted perversion of power works."

"My father didn't tell me I had to murder anybody in cold blood," said Eyan, crossing his arms. "That is not what his movement is about."

"Your father isn't here is he?" said Fraston, crossing his own arms. "He's asked me to see to this so that we do not fail. And this is the only way we can make certain of that."

Eyan pulled a chair and slumped in it.

"The world we want to live in, the world we want to *build*. Where power lies in the hands of normal people like you and me. Where the poor are not forgotten, where the farmers are not ignored but *celebrated*. That world cannot exist beside this one. It cannot exist unless the Aryssen family and all who support the tyrants are ended."

"Or until they surrender," said Eyan.

Fraston shook his head. "There is no surrender, not for them." He stood beside Eyan and gently placed his hand on his shoulder. "Just remember, this is the day you have been training for. You are prepared, there is no force that can stop you."

Eyan nodded.

"Just stay with your people," said Fraston. "And don't get lost."

"Understood."

"The palace guards, they're going to be more on edge after, well, you know," said Fraston. "So be careful and shoot first, think later."

"Yes," said Eyan.

"And keep our...*friends* closest to you," said Fraston, looking over his shoulder. "They don't bleed like you or me. They are stronger, the palace guards' bullets won't do anything to them."

"And I should take a sword," said Eyan.

Fraston nodded. "And a dagger and perhaps bow, if you think you'll need it. You know, just in case things turn sour."

"And they won't mind?" said Eyan. "Our...*friends*."

"Let them. What difference does it make?"

Words of a Charlatan
Aren

"*King Aren the Absent*," the headline read. Aren held the paper out in front of Pennyn Runeval, hoping that he was making himself clear.

"How am I supposed to win over their trust? The Verenic think I'm not strong enough, the Weslin doubt my right to rule over them, and on top of all that, nobody seems to think I've been around enough to know how to be a good king!" he shouted.

"Not *all* of the Verenic," said Pennyn, glancing out at the courtyard through his window. "And indeed, not all of the Weslin."

"My point stands. Look at this," he pointed to the paper. "They spared no detail. Look. *Son of Verenia*. What sort of message do you think that that gives? I thought we had our own people over at the Press. How could they let this happen?"

Pennyn shrugged his shoulders. "*Had* our own people over at the Press. Lord Berywen used to deal with them, so it wouldn't surprise me if his departure might have swayed their loyalties."

Aren picked up another paper. The Dove's headline was perhaps the most painful. '*Peasants and Princes*' was plastered across the top. Below it, '*the hag is dead.*' It was even more painful reading it now than when that wretched man had bellowed it at the funeral with no respect nor shame.

"They're twisting my words. I've never called anyone a peasant, I never would. I had just buried my mother, don't they see that?" he said, all in one breath. He sighed loudly, trying to keep his voice strong. "The *hag*, Mr. Runeval? Who allowed this to be printed?"

Pennyn looked tired. "If I can tell you one thing about your duty, it's that they'll never make it easy for you, Your Majesty. We can't stop them from printing things like we once did, the world is a different place now. It would just add to the fire. These days,

138

more and more monarchies are being overthrown, more and more kingdoms burnt to ash. A Verenic sovereign and a Verenic chancellor leading an ancient dynasty in which the majority are Weslin and Zaldroni people, it's never been easy," he said, with a gentle shake of the head. "It never will be. There's awful, awful people out there. That is what led to the Zaldroni Insurgency, let us not forget."

"But the Old Federation was no better, was it? What they did to us…to the Verenic, to the Zaldroni. Corrupt system, corrupt people."

"The Federation was no better, granted. But at the time, it was the best way forward, was it not?" said the chancellor. "The people are stupid, understand this. They have no memory, none at all. At the time, a union between the Weslin and the Zaldroni was best for them. It was a way to topple years of austere, cruel Sandaerian rule. A way to abolish that godforsaken tax. In truth, we – the Verenians – were blood traitors. For years we'd lived as one people, as the Verenic. We turned our backs on our Sandaerian brothers when it suited us, and we played our part quietly in the Hercanian uprisings. It was the lesser evil at the time. The Asellar brothers had done enough to leave a sour taste in the minds of every commoner when he heard the word 'Deryz'. They'd had enough, all of them. To *survive*, we fought for the side that would win. It was a time for the Weslin, Your Majesty. Oscon Hercan, Sayax Aston, Tilas Jerton – they were all heroes. Jerton's sacrifice still rings in the heart of every man or woman alive today – the Verenic too, even if it *was* all bullshit."

"Why are you telling me all this?" said Aren. He didn't appreciate spontaneous sermons on years long gone, history couldn't be changed after all. What he needed was an explanation for what he should do next, how to stop this from happening again.

"Because in truth I fear that in many ways not much has changed at all. The people – the good-folk, the nobles, all of them – they look for the best possible way forward for them, they want to *survive*. These days, the bluecoat threat grows stronger. I fear Soren Ashcrest brings them assurances. Of power, wealth, you name it. You have to see that as of now, whilst we hold the power, their promise grows stronger, day by day. Every loss we take is a gain for their cause, whether or not they've earnt it. The Fencliffe droughts, the disappearances, and of course…" he took a sharp pause. "The queen's death."

Aren had had enough. Pennyn's job was to find solutions and for all the talking he could do, he could find none. "So, what would you have us do? Sit back and let it all happen? Pardon me, but I don't see the crux of the matter. They're justified in what they print about my mother? We should let them do it?"

Pennyn sighed. "No, Your Majesty, of course not…"

"Then what?" said Aren, making no effort to hide his outrage.

"I'm just saying…if we were to do anything to stop them, the people printing these awful things, it would work against you. It might stop them for now, but I can promise you that in the long run it will work to tear down everything your family has built. The people adore the illusion of freedom, taking that away from them will give the bluecoats the upper hand, more will rally to their cause."

"So, nothing," said Aren. "We sit and wait. A pity."

"If you desire a change, perhaps it would be worth having a conversation with Lady Olivia," said Pennyn, his eyebrows wrinkled together. There was something dark and serious about his voice and Aren didn't appreciate what he was implying. "She's back, perhaps you could have a word now. She's in the dining hall up in the Western Quarter."

"I will do no such thing," said Aren, shuddering at the prospect of that conversation. "Olivia has no say in the matters of her family, or of the Ashcrests."

Pennyn nodded but said nothing, his eyebrows still pulled together and deep lines running down the middle of his forehead.

"How have we ended up here, Pennyn? How have the bluecoats suddenly gotten so much more support? How were they able to get the Spenlers? And Lord Escos? The Escosi are Verenic!"

"That means little these days," said Pennyn. "And at the same time, it means a great deal. This has been a long time coming. Nothing about the rise of the bluecoats is sudden. I told you that people rally to the cause that will benefit them the most."

"Why? How would it be any better?" said Aren. "The Federation, I mean."

"Power," he said. "It is all about appearances, like I said. They paint the illusion that the power will reside in the hands of common men, when in reality it won't…it never did."

Aren sat down, resting his arms against the wooden table of the Crown Chancellor's office in the Council Foyer. He had a nice view of the night through Pennyn's window, stars dotted across the clear black sky.

"I'm drained of all this. I'm losing sleep over it. Maybe we should have just put that Ysser Banlin on trial and handed the masses a bone. Now they don't know who to blame and the bluecoats are using that too. My weakness is their strength," said Aren.

"Your Majesty, it is not your weakness," said Pennyn. "All the evidence pointed to Ysser's innocence in the end, and Laris Hontren's testament corroborated it. Putting an innocent man on trial is not a feat of strength. It might not seem like it now, but your decision was a wise and selfless one. The nobles know you; they know your family, they'd know that you wouldn't rest until your mother has justice."

Aren got up from his seat again. "*Know* me? They've barely even seen me. '*Aren the Absent*', they aren't entirely wrong. Lady Rayne's been just about the only one to be completely honest with me, why couldn't you have done the same?" His voice was more raised than he'd intended, and he regretted it straight away.

"Sir, I've known you for a very long time, and your mother for even longer," said the chancellor, taking a step closer to him. "For that reason, I will be completely honest with you. I always am. Perhaps though, my politeness impedes the honesty. Maybe I've been too nice to you, especially while your mother was still with us." His voice started to tremble. He took a deep breath before continuing. "That's not to say I was being at all untruthful when I told you it *was* the right decision to let Ysser go. Trust me on this, Your Majesty. The nobles know you, they *owe* you."

"I'm sorry, Pennyn," said Aren, and he genuinely was. The man looked vulnerable now, as if Aren's words had torn through his heart. "I didn't mean to..." He didn't know how to finish the sentence.

"If I have ever been anything less than completely honest to you it has been out of unwavering respect to your mother, and nothing else."

The truth was, perhaps Aren had been too harsh. Possibly because of what he'd heard about the chancellor. Speaking to him today though, the rumours weren't easy to believe. It was strange thinking about what Rayne had told him. Perhaps his mother *had* been blinded by the chancellor, but from what he'd seen today, Pennyn's heart was in the right place.

"Pennyn," said Aren anxiously. "Have we heard from Lady Rayne?" She'd not yet sought him, and with every hour that passed, the little hope he had left faltered.

"No, I don't believe so, but Cyneric did mention that he'd been in touch with her again this morning," he said.

Aren thought back to what he'd overheard the other day, behind closed doors. The look of horror on the faces of Cyneric and Rayne as he'd walked in. It made him nervous. He felt so lost in this new world…it felt hard to breathe, as if there were a massive weight on his chest.

"I'd like to speak with Cyneric," said Aren. "Olivia will have to wait a while."

"Of course, I'll send for him right now."

"No," said Aren. "He should be in his lounge?"

"Yes, sir."

Curse Cyneric's quarters for being so far. They weren't far at all of course, but the journey seemed longer than ever. Aren kept his wits about him, gripping his sheathed dagger tightly as he turned the dark corners of the palace. He buried his fears deep within himself, he couldn't let them overcome him, not today. His hands trembled as he reached the Garden of Ysseria. There was a soft thud. Once again, his heart raced but this time he didn't let it stop him. Obviously, nobody was there. He pretended he was the strongest of all the kings to ever walk the corridors of Valecrest Palace, no force could stop him.

He held his breath as he knocked twice, loudly, on the door to Cyneric's lounge.

"Yes? Identify yourself," Cyneric's voice emerged from the room.

"It's me," he said.

"Aren?" He opened the door, holding a sparring baton in his right hand. "What are you doing here? Why didn't you bring a guard with you?"

"Doesn't matter," said Aren, as he made himself comfortable at Cyneric's dining table. "Have you heard from Lady Rayne?"

Cyneric's eyes swayed to the left, away from Aren's. "Yes, I have."

"What has she decided?" said Aren. "About staying here, at the palace. Just a little bit longer, maybe a month or two."

Cyneric lowered his gaze, and then raised it again to speak. "It's still a no."

Aren's heart sank. He was disappointed in her decision, but knew he had to respect it. If Rayne hadn't changed her mind for his mother, why would she ever change it for him? It wasn't fair, but he couldn't blame her.

"What did she say?" said Aren.

"Just that she couldn't break her vows, nothing new," said Cyneric. He was chewing through his words, rushing. It wasn't like him in the slightest. "Is there anything else?"

"No," said Aren. "But why did she come to you and not to me?"

Cyneric smiled sardonically. "Is this what it's come to? Questioning your oldest friend, like this?" He shook his head, chuckling. "She didn't come to you because she'd already told you the same thing over and over again, there was no point."

"Sad thought, isn't it? You being my oldest friend. All for you to evade my questions like this."

Cyneric stood in silence. For the first time in all the years Aren had known him, he looked unsure of himself. Hesitant. There was a distant thud in the woods outside the window, then the rustling of trees. He ignored it.

"What was that?" said Cyneric, using the opportunity to turn around, but Aren wasn't going to let him avoid this so easily. It was time.

"Cyneric…"

"What is it?"

"The day of Ysser Banlin's hearing, when we heard from that man, Laris Hontren. I overheard something you said."

Cyneric raised his brow. "Heard *what*?"

"You were talking to Lady Rayne after I'd left the room, I'm not sure what about…but I heard something, a name. A name that I'm certain I've only heard in the Panderer's realm."

His mentor looked even more unsure still, dubiously crossing his arms and tilting his head to one side.

"*Ethan*," said Aren. "Is that your name? Your Panderer name? The one you were born with?"

Cyneric stared blankly back. "I beg your pardon?"

"It's a Panderer name. I've only heard it in that realm, and as far as I'm aware, Rayne wouldn't know of an Ethan, so I'm at a loss." It was strange to consider that in all the years since he'd met his aide, there was a whole part of him that Aren had never known. "I know you changed your name when you were first brought to this realm, I know *Cyneric* isn't the name you were born with, but I've never known your *real* name."

"And you still don't," said Cyneric scornfully. "My name here was only given to me so there were no questions about my heritage. Just a lowborn Weslin lad who worked hard for his place at court."

"And what of your Panderer name?"

"I've known no name other than Cyneric for years. Nobody here, let alone Lady Rayne, knows my Panderer name – and they never will. I don't know what you think you heard, Aren."

"I know what I heard!" Aren shouted. "I spent years in that land, I think I would know."

Cyneric stood in silence.

"You're one of the few people I'm left with that I still trust," said Aren. "And Rayne, but only because my mother trusted her. So, if the two of you are hiding something from me, I want to know what it is."

"You can trust Pennyn just as much as you trust me. He's a good man, a genuine man. He's misguided at times, but–"

"Can I?" Aren muttered, interrupting him. There was another clanging sound outside, probably a distant fox down in the woods. They'd always manage to find their way through the outer walls into the palace lawns. Cyneric turned towards the window and Aren grabbed him by the arm, tugging him back. He wasn't going to allow anything to hold him back, let alone a pest. "Can I really trust him? Pennyn?"

"Well why wouldn't you?"

"The last thing my mother said to Ysser when she died was his name. Why would she? What if she'd figured out who had betrayed her? What if Pennyn was working with Linara and Gavyn and–"

"She didn't say Pennyn." Cyneric sighed out loud.

"How do you know that?"

"She said *Panderer*."

"Why? I know you're hiding something from me." Aren raised his voice now.

144

"Alright. I'll tell you everything. Just know that this has been kept from you for your own wellbeing and for nothing else."

Aren wasn't sure how to feel. He could do nothing except brace himself for what was to come. After all that had happened since he'd come home, he wasn't sure that much else could surprise him if he was being honest.

"There's a lot to say. I'm…I'm not quite sure where to begin. Well, I suppose we could start with your upbringing. Why do you think you were brought up in the Panderer's realm?"

"Because my mother wanted it."

"Yes, but *why?* What do you know of the reason?"

"To protect me. From the Insurgency, from everything else that was going on. Then there was something about a prophecy too. About my survival, my health or something like that."

"You aren't wrong," said Cyneric. He moved around the room, turning his back to Aren for a moment, then turning to face him again. "But that isn't the sole reason. What else do you know of the prophecy?"

"Nothing."

"You know where it came from?" said Cyneric.

"I know that my mother had been told she might not be able to bear a child, that she'd been trying for some time. The prophecy was of my birth. Something a healer told her? I don't think my mother or father took much notice of prophecies; my mother hated talking about them."

Cyneric drew a deep breath and raised his hands to his temples, running his fingers through his thick, greasy hair. "There was a healer, yes. Your parents saw healers, doctors, alleged foreseers and the like from all over Landridge. This particular healer was different, though. She claimed she prophesied your birth. That she *foresaw* your life. An Heir to the Crown. She said that it could only happen with blood magic, that there would be a condition – a stark condition – to your birth."

"Blood magic?"

Cyneric nodded. "I don't know the details of what it is she claimed to have done, I don't think anybody does. Nor do I know if she truly used any blood magic, all I know is that you were born within the year."

"Coincidences happen," said Aren. But it had gotten him to think. "You said that there would be a condition to my birth. What do you mean?"

Cyneric sighed again. "Yes, a condition – a prophecy. A few prophecies, actually. One of them foretold of a great waste across the land, a massive famine that would rip through the country in the first few years of your life. Another told of a stone – a stone of sacrifice and how it would bring the dawn when the beholder needed it the most. A lot of nonsense, to this day nobody knows of such a stone nor why we might need the dawn, but one, one prophecy stayed with your parents for months. It was a graver one. That your mother's firstborn would never be able to live beside her. That he'd never be able to breathe the same air she breathed. That he could never walk upon the land she walked, never would your footprints tread over hers. Ultimately, your birth would mean the queen's death." Cyneric took a pause. "The healer said a great many other things – many were rubbish, all lost now…"

Aren took a moment to take it in. Then, his eyes narrowed. "But…but my mother didn't die giving birth to me," he said. "My mother lived almost twenty years after my birth."

"That is not what the prophecy said," said Cyneric, looking down glumly. "Besides, your parents did not believe her. So, Prince Weryn gave the healer sanction to use her purported blood magic, so long as it brought nobody any harm. Soon after, of course, the queen was pregnant with you."

Cyneric paused for a bit, pacing around the room again, slowly, his arms crossed once more. "They still did not believe though, in her prophecy. They put it down to mere coincidence, as would any sane man. Then you were born, and of course both you and your mother survived the birth. They all but forgot about the old healer's prophecy. They were sure that the woman was lying or mad, perhaps both. Eventually, the scrolls she'd scribed were thrown from the palace never to be seen again. Then a little before your third birthday, your father died."

"Right," said Aren, not quite sure where this was going.

"The queen was so overwhelmed that she'd completely forgotten all about the prophecies. The scrolls were lost, they were never again talked about within the walls of this palace. In those times though, Lady Rayne was here at court. She's quite a firm believer of such things. The mystical, if you will. She reminded the queen of the healer's prophecy, of the devastation that was said to befall us all. But your mother, she still paid it no heed – after all, the prophecy hadn't said anything about your father's death."

"Exactly, it did not," said Aren. "So why…"

Cyneric raised his hand to silence him. "A few short days afterwards though, the first flickers of the Zaldroni Insurgency rose up against the Crown. A great waste across the kingdom. In almost every city in the south, every village between Sturrock and Pyburrock." Cyneric took another moment to himself, clutching his empty hands as if he were grasping at air. "An ambush happened at Wyntock End, in the very early days when it all began. The queen almost died at the hands of Zaldroni Insurgents, *you* almost died. Your mother began to see things in a different light from then on. She feared for the safety of her family, of you. She began to consider if perhaps there was some truth to the healer's prophecy."

Aren clenched his jaw tightly. "So, she exiled me to the Panderer's realm? Over a prophecy?"

"Yes. And she sent me with you. But it had never been her idea, it was something your father had thought up when you were born, because of the prophecy. In case there were any truth to it. There, in the Panderer's realm, you wouldn't breathe the same air as your mother. You wouldn't live beside her. You wouldn't walk the land she walked on."

"Over some healer's words? I spent my entire life away from my home, away from my family, over a prophecy?!" He breathed out heavily and placed his hands on his head, grasping at his hair.

"It wasn't mindless trust. There was more truth to what that healer had said, Aren. Incredibly specific things. The Insurgency, for one…the healer had talked of its ruin, a great waste across the land."

He thought about the years he could have spent here, with his mother. He thought about how safe he'd felt when she'd held him in her arms.

"Your mother invited that old healer back to the Valecrest and asked for counsel, she felt desperate in that moment, knowing that your life might be in danger. The healer never came, only a letter arrived from the far north in her stead. The letter had only three lines written on it, but very specific. Things that nobody outside these walls knows about. Things that nobody *can* know about."

"What were these *things*?" He was losing his patience with every moment that passed. His heart felt as if it might burst, and his body suddenly felt very weak, on the brink of collapse at any moment. How much worse could it get?

"The first, that skyverns will fly above this palace once more."

"Utter nonsense," said Aren. "What else did the charlatan have to say?"

"The second was that the brother would rise from within the shadows themselves."

"Brother? I don't have a brother."

"The prophecies were in Verenic, I do not know if they translate well."

"And what was the third?"

Cyneric paused and drew another deep breath. "I do not remember the exact words, but she knew of your father's true heritage."

"Doesn't everybody?" said Aren. "Everyone knows that the Jeffyrs are a mix, there are so few Verenic families alive today that are pure of blood. Everyone knows my father had Weslin blood in him."

"No," said Cyneric. "Weryn Jeffyrs had no Weslin blood in him."

"Huh? You're lying. He couldn't have been Zaldroni, my grandparents would never allow it."

"He had no Zaldroni blood in him either. Nor Verenic."

He stared back emptily.

"Your father was a Panderer, Aren."

His eyes widened and his body could hold him up no longer. He sunk into the armchair beside him. "No," he said. "What does that mean?" He shook his head. The noises of the palace drowned out and his heart pounded in his chest, slowly and loudly. "Stop lying to me. My father…my father was Prince Weryn Jeffyrs. He was born here, his family has always lived *here*. In the south. In this world."

Cyneric just looked back at him in silence. The room spun into a blur, and Aren's head pounded. Throbbed.

"Cyneric, I've met my father's family. I've met my grandfather. My uncle Mentos. My father was Weryn Jeffyrs. My father…"

"No, Aren. Your father *was* a son of the Jeffyrs, but he was a Panderer, just like I am," said Cyneric.

"How is that…how is that possible?" Aren shook his head as if he were mad yet again. "No, I don't – I can't understand."

Cyneric knelt down beside him, placing his cold hand on Aren's shoulder.

"When your grandparents, the Lord and Lady Jeffyrs, got married all those years ago, they'd had no children. No heirs. They had a large fortune with nobody to inherit it, nobody to carry their legacy. And when Lady Jeffyrs did give birth to a girl, the baby didn't make it through the night. It was a dark time, a time your uncle would never talk to you about. Your grandfather was obsessed, fixated on an heir to the fortune. An heir to bear the Jeffyrs name." He paused again. "Are you alright, Aren? I didn't want to have to tell you like this."

"I'm fine. Continue." There wasn't much else he could manage to say.

"Alright, well, if you're sure," he said. "They were close friends of the Crown, of the royal family. Your mother's parents, King Derys and Princess Zaylee, they decided they'd strike a deal with the Jeffyrs family. They wanted to help." He stopped for a moment again, looking out into the starry night, raising his right hand to Aren as if to silence him. Aren had no patience for Cyneric's paranoia today.

"What was the deal? What does this have to do with my father?" Aren shuffled around, restless.

"Wait, Aren, just a moment," said Cyneric as he walked to the window.

"No! I need to know this. Enough lies. Enough secrets and prophecies. Tell me the whole truth."

Cyneric sat down beside him. "You know of the Panderer's bloodgate, in the cellar beneath the palace. You know that only the Aryssen family knows of it. Where it is. How to open it. Your dynasty has kept this secret for hundreds of years, the truth of the Panderer's realm. Only an Aryssen possessing the Skyvernblood Dagger can open it. It's a *perfectly kept secret*. Been that way for centuries. Until King Derys' deal." He grew more serious, his eyes fixed on Aren. "The king offered Lord Jeffyrs a son, so long as he asked no questions. The condition was a marriage – between the Jeffyrs boy and the king's daughter, should he have one. Not long after of course, your mother, Princess Elvira was born. And so, one of the richest families in the south would align itself forever with those ruling over them. It was known to nobody, except the king and his wife, where the Jeffyrs boy had come from. His true heritage."

It was unfathomable. Aren refused to believe it, he couldn't. Cyneric was lying for some reason, a cruel, horrible lie. But Cyneric had never lied to him, had he? He felt the urge to vomit, but he kept it together as well as he could.

"Aren, are you sure you are fine?"

He couldn't bring himself to speak, or even nod in response.

"Aren?" Cyneric placed his hand on his shoulder and gently shook him.

"Lord Jeffyrs had no questions? About where this child had come from?" croaked Aren finally.

"He knew better than to ask. King Derys had had a reputation, as you very well know."

Aren wasn't sure what exactly he knew. His entire life had been lies after lies. As he grew older, the lies ran deeper. "Cyneric, how could they? Just take a baby from its mother? A Panderer, no less. Nobody batted an eye in the Panderer's realm?" He couldn't piece it all together.

"He had a poor mother," said Cyneric. "You know that poor mothers don't do too well in the Panderer's realm," he said sadly. "There was no way she could afford to feed one child, let alone two. Derys offered her gold for her silence. Enough gold to feed her daughter, enough to change her life even, and start anew."

"Two children?"

"Yes. Your father was a twin," said Cyneric. "He had a sister. He was little over two weeks old when Derys took him, so he'd never known her, or anyone in that realm, not even his own mother."

"She's still alive?" said Aren.

Cyneric sighed and shook his head. "I don't know. We don't know anything about where your father comes from, anybody who knew that is dead. All we know of it all is that his name was Ethan. Not even a family name."

"My father's name was Ethan?" For some reason, in that moment, that is all Aren could say.

Cyneric looked back at him, confused. "Well, yes."

"And how do you know about all this?" said Aren. "Who else knows?"

150

"Very few that are alive today. Lady Rayne and I are the last. I only know because she told me, your mother."

"And how does Rayne know that his name was Ethan?"

"You know that they were always close, Weryn and Rayne?" said Cyneric. "Your father told her about it, all of it. He only knew his name because his mother had told him, in her final days, when she'd started to lose her mind."

"So that day, in the Hall of Krelis…"

"We were talking about him, your father. We didn't want his name to fall upon some curious ears, especially not in times like these. So, we used his other name, one that nobody knows."

"And who else?" said Aren, barely able to grasp what was coming out of Cyneric's mouth. "Aside from Derys and Zaylee, who else knew?" His mind was racing. The traitors…they couldn't know. No one could know. He could feel his heart pound and throb in his head again.

Cyneric looked at him curiously. "Artemis Escos," he said. "And Qila Wyversen. Both dead."

"Both of traitor blood."

"There is no such thing as *traitor blood*," said Cyneric.

"And nobody else?" said Aren.

"Not as far as I'm aware."

Aren stared at the dull wall opposite him. "I'm of mixed blood, then. A *Half Panderer*," he said.

"And what difference does that make?"

Aren got up again, walking to the window. He looked outside, watching the trees brush against each other in the night's autumn wind, partly because he needed a way to avert Cyneric's piercing eyes.

"I suppose we have a lot more in common than we thought," said Aren to his mentor. "Why did she never tell me?"

"It was not her secret to tell, for one thing," said Cyneric. "For another, you were much, much safer not knowing."

"And she told *you*?" he said, with no regard for how spiteful it sounded. Immediately, he regretted it and looked over at Cyneric with his eyes wide and his heart heavy with guilt. Cyneric merely smiled at him as if to tell him not to worry, as he often did.

"I expect she knew I'd be having this conversation with you one day," said Cyneric. "She told me I was only to tell you when she died."

"*When* she died? So…so she knew she was going to die? I don't understand. Why did…" He stopped in the middle of his sentence. "By bringing me back here, she knew she'd be ending her own life. She knew what was going to happen. That's why she died, because I came back home. That's what the prophecies said, isn't that right?"

"No, Aren. She died because Ferian Wyversen drove a sword through her heart. Prophecies are funny things. We can't have blind faith in them. She knew she was going to die one day, we all are."

Aren wasn't listening though. "Why did she decide to bring me back? Why now? After so many years, what changed?" he sobbed, unable to stop himself. After years of longing to return, years of begging his mother, spending nights crying to himself, he suddenly wished he'd never come home. He suddenly cursed himself for ever wishing otherwise.

"Because you are ready, Aren," said Cyneric.

Aren wiped a single tear from his cheek, suddenly realising the truth of it all. "How did you know his name?" he said. "My father's name. How did you know it?"

"Your mother told me."

"Yes, and how did she know?"
Cyneric shrugged. "I imagine your father did, just as he did with Rayne."

Aren wasn't done. "And…and…what were you talking about that day? With Rayne?"

Cyneric took a moment. "There's a stormy wind taking flight, Aren. I wish I could continue to ignore it, I wish I didn't have to admit to myself that it might just be true…The droughts in Fencliffe. The missing people. The dead. The suicides. There's a reason for it all. A real threat, the strongest threat – not just to your reign, but to humanity itself–"

Cyneric couldn't finish his sentence. There was a deafening bang. Aren turned around to see the door had been blown open, a cloaked man stood behind it, rifle still pointed. There was a second thunderous sound. Before Aren could realise what was going on, Cyneric dove at him, grabbing him with one arm and plunging to the ground behind them. The armchair tipped back and gave them cover, if just for a moment. Aren peered around the corner. Two men, the first with his gun in hand, while the other carried a dagger.

Cyneric sprung up, launching his own dagger at the first man's neck. It hit him dead in his throat, he fired his gun at the wall as he stumbled to his knees, choking on his blood, the blade still buried in his neck. As his head hit the ground, he stopped struggling for breath, and his eyes rolled back. Cyneric reached to disarm the second man, but he'd already disappeared.

"AREN!"

The man had landed right in front of Aren, looking him dead in the eyes, a disgusting grin on his pale, wasted face. Aren unsheathed his own dagger, jumped up and drove his hand forward towards the man's chest. He missed. He struck again, this time knocking the blade out of the man's hand. Aren went for a third blow. The man blocked the attack, holding Aren by his wrist, he bent to reach his blade, but it was too late for him. Cyneric lunged up behind him, cleanly splitting his throat open as blood gushed out.

"We've got to run," said Cyneric. He grabbed the dead man's rifle in his right hand, holding Aren by the wrist with his left and they rushed out of the room. They bolted out into the narrow corridor, its walls stained red.

"Help! Guards! The king is under attack!" shouted Cyneric. They looked left and right frantically, not a living soul in sight. The palace guards' corpses lay against the walls, their necks sliced open and their tunics red.

"We can't wait," said Aren. "I hear more."

"This way, quick!"

Cyneric pulled Aren to his side, and they headed out into the courtyard, climbing through the window into the darkness of the night. The stone sculptures in the Garden of Ysseria lay shattered and bloody. The water in the fountains murky and red.

"We've got to get to the rest of the Council," said Cyneric.

"No," said Aren, grabbing him by the wrist. "We can't trust the Council."

"Fine. But Lyndan House or the Council Foyer are probably still our best chance at getting out of this alive," said Cyneric. "Follow me."

Much of the palace was lined by the dead. Aren stumbled and tripped, using a wall for support. He looked up, the doors to the Parydon were broken, bloody handprints plastered all over it. He quickly found his balance and turned around; his hands wet with the warm blood that was smeared on the wall. He'd tripped over an arm. The guard's body lay face down, the back of his head split open. The guard had fair hair, his white skin bloody and grey. Aren felt dizzy. He gently turned the body over.

"It's him!" Aren sobbed, as Joten's dead face looked up emptily at him.

Cyneric whisked him away, dragging him by the wrists. "There's nothing we can do for him," he said, now panting.

A shrill sound pierced Aren's ear. It was a sound he'd never heard before, it sounded almost like a cry. It stopped, then rung again, and then again. *Three long sounds*. Overbearing sounds. Aren knew what they were. It didn't come as a surprise to him, if only they'd rung sooner.

"The three bells of siege," said Cyneric.

Aren nodded. "What is the point of those bells if they were able to get to us before they were sounded?"

"No idea," said Cyneric. "Here, come over."

"Where do we go from here?" He turned the corner, almost expecting an army of bluecoat invaders. He was anxious to get out before the corridors were overrun with them.

"If we cut across the central courtyard and make a run for it, we can climb through the bottom windows and get into the Council Foyer. That should be safe."

"So should the Western Wing. That's why the royal residences were built there, but that didn't stop them, did it?"

Cyneric nodded. "It is entirely your call. We can still try to get to Lyndan House, the tunnels might be a safer bet."

"The Foyer is closer," said Aren. "Let's not take the risk."

Cyneric nodded and hurried ahead.

"Wait a minute, Olivia!" said Aren. "She's in the dining hall, we need to get to her!"

"It isn't safe. The best thing we can do is find the rest of the Council and secure the palace."

"I don't care, we need to help her."

"AREN!" he shouted, grabbing him by his shoulders and shaking him like a sack of potatoes. "It's like I said. It's not safe here. There are bound to be more. We're here already, as soon as we cross the courtyard and get into the Council Foyer, we can send Olivia some help straight away. That's her best chance."

Aren didn't say anything. He had nothing he *could* say, so he traipsed behind Cyneric towards the courtyard.

"Cyneric, wait!" Aren hissed.

He grabbed Cyneric and hid behind the bend of a wall with some ivy hanging down it. Footsteps approached from across the viaduct.

"I just saw more of them," said Aren and Cyneric nodded. They waited in silence as the noises drew closer and closer. Aren held his breath and clutched his blade tightly.

"Sounds like a group of them, three at the very least," whispered Cyneric.

The men appeared around the corner. There were four of them. Two had brown hair, one was bald and the last of them had black hair. Aren and Cyneric crouched, their backs tightly pressed against the wall. They'd hide here until all the men had passed. They wouldn't be spotted here. Everything would be fine, Aren assured himself. They wouldn't be spotted. They couldn't be.

The men walked past, oblivious. To Aren's horror though, two more appeared further down the corridor, coming from the opposite end. But they weren't cloaked at all. In fact, they were clad in white. They were from the kitchen. They drew closer, and the four men surrounded them from all sides, forming a circle around them. Aren's golden monogram emblazoned the chefs' toques. Aren's heart sank as he realised who they were. It was Chef Roy and Chef Herssel. His core filled with terror when he quickly realised that they'd probably have been coming from the dining hall, where Olivia was. The bald man grabbed Chef Herssel by the throat, while another – the dark-haired one – ripped off the toque from the chef's head.

"You kneel to the tyrant, do you?" said the dark-haired man, his back to Aren, who watched in silence from a few paces away, hidden. The chef whimpered, sweat trickling from his brow. Chef Roy knelt beside him, a terrified look on his face. "DO YOU?!" said the man again, much louder this time. Aren had heard the voice somewhere before. He knew it well. Very well. He couldn't place it. Cyneric and Aren watched as one of the other men spat at the royal monogram on the chef's toque and threw it onto the floor.

"Answer him, then," said the bald man.

The chef sobbed and cried as the man with black hair unsheathed his dagger. "Please…Please…I don't…I'm just… I just make a living here, I kneel to nobody…"

"Making a living? On the blood of innocents?" said the bald man.

"Please…" the chef sobbed. "I haven't done anything…I haven't–"

He couldn't finish his sentence. His sobs suddenly stopped as the black-haired man plunged his dagger into the chef's chest and twisted hard before pulling it out. The chef fell to the floor, his blood smearing Chef Roy's untainted white trousers on the way down. Aren clutched at his mouth, wanting to be sick. He almost screamed, the tears flowed down his cheeks, but he tried his best to stay quiet. He couldn't afford to make a noise. Not as much as a sniffle. The bald man nodded at Chef Roy, and the fat chef got up and darted down the corridor. As the men turned to go up the stairs at the end of the corridor, Aren caught a glimpse of the man with the black hair. They say a person's voice is one of the first things you forget, that's what Aren had always heard. It was true. But his face…it was unmistakeable. The face of a murderer.

"Eyan…" whispered Aren, after the men were out of sight.

"What?" said Cyneric.

"Eyan Ashcrest. That… that was Eyan. My… my old friend." The words were bitter and ugly.

"That butcher was never your friend. Your friend died when he chose that life. Now come on, before they come back."

They clambered out of the viaduct, carefully climbing over the ledge and dropping into a bush just below.

"Ow!" shouted Aren, grasping his left wrist and Cyneric slapped his hand on Aren's mouth, stopping him in his tracks. A drop of blood trickled down Aren's arm from where it had scraped against a branch.

"We have to be quiet," whispered Cyneric. "There must be more, we aren't safe yet."

Aren nodded, and Cyneric pointed forward with his finger. He set off quick, Aren following him closely. Before they could reach the other side though, the doors to the Crown Foyer on the left swung open with a thud. Another man appeared from behind them, soaring towards them with a sword in his hand. By the time Cyneric had loaded his rifle and pointed it at the attacker, it was too late. He was directly in front of them. Aren kicked forwards, knocking the man's hand and successfully disarming him but the man pushed through, clasping his cold bare hands around Aren's throat. As Aren gasped for breath, the man's pale, ugly face was inches from Aren's. His sapphire eyes were all he could see, bloodshot and dirty. Suddenly his tight grip loosened slightly, and his gaze shifted down. He eyed the wound on Aren's left wrist, almost dazed, his eyes glassy and his mind somewhere else.

Aren used the opportunity to bury his dagger into the man's chest. The man's hands unclasped, and he fell away from Aren to the grass below. There was a loud noise, then another, as Cyneric shot the corpse twice.

"Can never be too certain," he said.

Aren took a step back, clambering over the edge of the fountain. He breathed sharply and deeply, putting his hand to his chest.

"Aren!"

"I'm-I'm fine," he gasped. But it wasn't easy, watching the life leave his eyes, the murderer.

"Are you sure?"

"The Crown Foyer is compromised. Lyndan House isn't too far from there. Are you sure the Council Foyer will be safe?" said Aren.

"Of course not. How can I be? But I still think it's our best chance," said Cyneric. "We can climb underneath the Assembly Viaduct from there and flee the palace if need be."

"And that's where the tunnels are?"

"Yes, and beneath Lyndan House."

"Then let's not stay here for long."

"I think our best chance is to climb through those windows, over there," said Cyneric, pointing at the smaller frames at the bottom of the vast wall opposite them. Aren nodded. They edged carefully towards the wall, but before they could reach the windows, a loud shattering noise stopped them dead in their tracks. It was accompanied by a bloodcurdling scream. One of the windows higher up had shattered, a body flying out of it and landing hard on the ground below. It sounded as ugly as it looked. There was a large cracking sound, as well as the spatter, as bones, flesh and blood all hit the stones below. She lay dead on the floor, her eyes closed as peacefully as if she were asleep, but her mouth wide open and her face disfigured, bloody. The back of her skull was completely smashed from the fall. Her familiar silvery hair was painted red, the dark blood had pooled all around where she'd landed. Her skinny left arm was twisted around her side, broken in the middle, the bone showing. Aren recognised the woman, of course, but he wished he didn't. He was numb. He didn't care anymore, he cried out loud in agony. He sobbed and sobbed, but nothing could bring her back. The last piece of willpower he had, shattered, dragging him down to the ground. The shattered glass and stones cut and tore at his knees, but he didn't care. He was still, almost as still as the body before him.

"Aren, we can't do anything, she's gone now. Come on, this isn't safe, we've got to get to the Foyer…"

Aren sobbed loudly, on his knees. He couldn't hear Cyneric, not really. He was far from here, somewhere else.

"Valery…" he said. It was all he could get out. Valery Rennero's dress was bloody, torn from the fall, and her skinny trunk lay twisted and lifeless before him.

"Aren –" said Cyneric quickly, drawing his rifle.

Aren felt the cold grip of a pair of hands on his shoulder, but he didn't care.

Cyneric scowled. "What do *you* want?" he said to the assailant.

Aren turned around.

"I know a way out," said Ysser Banlin, his left-hand half shackled. "Shhh."

"What?" said Aren.

"The twins," said Ysser. "They're stationed at Lyndan House. They're alive, they're well. We can get you out of the Valecrest through the tunnels."

Ayleris
Laris

There was a distant thud. Laris clambered out through the bushes clumsily, knocking the pail over. He didn't care much, soon he wouldn't need to work for the gatherers anymore, soon he could leave it all behind, leave Arvendon behind. Maybe they'd deliver on their promises. Maybe *she'd* take him back. He spat out. Why did he find himself yearning to trust the very people that had cast him aside? That had treated him like something they'd stepped in, rather than like a real person. It was no use counting on their empty words. But still…Wynter had been different, always. No matter what the bitch Rayne had to say.

The clatter and clanging grew louder still, louder than it'd been all night. He'd been able to hear it for much of his hunt, even in the depths of the forest. It was a good thing he hadn't been trying to sleep that night, or else somebody would have to pay. He kicked the pail aside with his boot and slipped through the trees, climbing onto a boulder to see what the hell was going on. He'd never heard the bustle of the city quite like this at the crack of dawn, let alone with the constant clanging and thuds and bangs, as if they were on the battlefields of East Asenia.

The sun was high enough in the ochre morning sky now for him to see the city in the distance, the markets of Arvendon, the shadow of the bridge, the towers of the Parydon. There was something different about it all. The little people buzzed around on the streets, like ants scrawling to their nests. There was a certain panic, one he couldn't place. Thick black smoke rising from behind the silhouette of the Valecrest, across the water. This was a different city altogether.

He jumped off, swinging his pelts over his shoulder. He shoved the skinned rabbits into his rucksack, held his bow tightly in his arm and set off. He'd have to get closer to get a better look, closer to the fires, closer to the ants scrambling through the markets, closer to the city he'd called home his entire life. The noises hadn't stopped, in fact they'd only gotten louder. Screams too, now. Of men, women, children…bloodcurdling, piercing screams. Unlike anything he'd ever heard before. He held tightly onto his bow and felt around him for his quiver. It was still there, thankfully. He wished though that he'd taken a rifle instead today, cursing himself under his breath.

The water was just ahead of him now, the smell of ash rising from behind it. He struggled to get a clear view of the Royal Quarter, with the trees and smoke and haze all in the way. He sighed and dropped his rucksack, making for an old oak beside him. He hung his bow on his back, just in case – couldn't risk leaving it behind. He gripped onto the branch just above him tightly, pulling it down just a smidge. It snapped, falling to the mud below. He tried another, thicker and stronger-looking branch, pulling himself up this time, using the trunk for support. It worked, he hoisted himself all the way up, gripping onto the trunk tightly, clambering from branch to branch until he was finally high enough.

The view was breathtakingly terrifying. The fires burnt from within the markets themselves, from houses, all over the city. There were men marching up and down Assembly Way, right in front of the Royal Quarter. They didn't look like the king's men. Bodies hung from the Arvendon Bridge, he couldn't see their faces. He gulped. The ants crawling through the veins of the town were screaming, crying, carrying bits and pieces and bags in a frenzy. The roads themselves were bloody. He looked up to the Valecrest, looming over the fallen city. The majesty and elegance of the palace was gone, only sorrow and anguish left behind. The flag atop it was not that of the kingdom, nor was it the Royal Standard. He recognised the blue banner almost straight away, with Jerton's Dove plastered proudly across it. Soren Ashcrest had won.

He wasted no time, sliding down the old tree as quickly as he'd climbed it, even quicker still. His palms burnt and stung but he carried on, there was no time. He crumpled his knees as he hit the muddy grass below, tumbling over to break the fall. He picked up his bag and made for the opening to the woods, moving quickly and carefully. Suddenly, he found himself worrying. Worrying not just for himself, not just for Wynter either, but for those that he cared little about. He found himself wondering if Rayne had gotten out, if the king had. He couldn't quite tell why.

"And where are you off to?" came a voice from behind him.

He reached for his dagger.

"No, don't move now," said the voice. "I asked you a question." It was the voice of a woman, probably a young woman. "Turn around, slowly please."

He obliged. Indeed, a young woman, a young woman pointing a shotgun at his head. She didn't look like she was from around here, a Uressi perhaps, maybe an Asmoni.

"Well, what is it?" he said.

"What is what?" she scowled. "I asked you a question, I'm not going to ask you again. *Where* are you *headed*?"

He groaned. "Where the fuck does it look like I'm headed? The city."

She laughed. "*That* city? The one under siege?" she pointed her gun at the smoke rising from within it.

"Yes, *that* city."

"Why?" she said.

"What's it to you? Who are you anyway? Where are *you* headed?"

She smiled. "Azara Urisci," she said.

"The hell is an Azara Urisci?" he grumbled.

She frowned. "My name," she said. "Funnily enough I'm headed there too. What is your name? Are you familiar with Sturrock? I can't say I am." She lowered her shotgun.

"If you're looking for a travelling companion, look elsewhere," said Laris, irritated. If she were going to shoot him, she should just get on with it.

Azara scowled again, and then reached into her pocket. Laris wondered if it would leave him enough time to reach into his own and pull out his dagger. Or if it was enough to nock an arrow onto his bow and aim at her throat. It wasn't. Her hand came out and she held a tattered, folded up piece of paper inside it.

"Arvendon," she said. "Do you know it well?"

He half wanted to lie, but at the same time if she had business in that part of the city, he wanted to know why. She wasn't a bluecoat, not from the looks of her, beige tunic, brown leather belt and a dark brown fur coat around her. She was from the north, probably the far north, or some foreign land where it was always summer. She wasn't used to the southern cold. Judging by the state of her, she wasn't one of the king's either. No finery, not like the pampered guards he'd seen down in the Valecrest.

She pointed up her shotgun at him again. "You know you have an incredibly rude habit of avoiding my questions unless I take up arms against you. So, I'll ask you again, like this."

"Aye, I know Arvendon," grunted Laris. "What's it to you? What is your business there?"

She lowered her shotgun again, tedious affair. She held out her piece of crumpled paper, opening it up. "Do you know this boy?" she said.

Was she foolish? "It isn't a neighbourhood where everybody knows everybody," he said.

"Well, maybe you could take me to Arvendon," she said. "Where I can find him."

He looked carefully at the piece of paper. The picture wasn't too clear, but against all odds, he did recognise the lad. Pale, red-haired boy, unmistakeable.

"Never seen 'im," said Laris. "Like I said, it's a big city. A big, big city." And he'd seen the boy right in the heart of it, but he wasn't about to tell her that.

"Very well," she put the piece of paper back into her pocket. "You could still show me to Arvendon, yes?"

"It isn't the best time to go to the markets," said Laris, sarcastically. "Can you not see?"

"And yet we both find ourselves venturing into the thick of it. Why?"

"I'll tell you mine if you tell me yours," said Laris.

"I'm afraid I feel as if I'm at a bit of a loss," said Azara. "I've just showed you why I'm going into the city. I'm yet to hear why you are."

"None of your business," said Laris. "Now if you'll let me, I'll be going thank you."

She scowled at him once more. "You are not going to help me?" she scoffed.

"Shouldn't help strangers in times like this," said Laris. "You'd do well to learn that down 'ere. Shouldn't ask strangers for directions either. Now, will you be shooting me, or can I get going?"

She ducked all of a sudden, hiding behind a large rock. "Shhh. Get down!" she whispered.

He saw why. The bluecoats were marching, horses and motorcars behind them.

"The fuck are they doing all the way up here?" whispered Laris.

"Looking for Aren Aryssen, I would assume," said Azara.

"Up here?" he said. "They're coming up from Assembly Way. They're headed *out* of Sturrock. Well, some of them at least."

She looked at him oddly. "Yes? Why wouldn't they?"

He looked at her, confused.

"The king, his family, they've escaped," whispered Azara. "Didn't you hear? That is why the city looks the way it does. That is why they're headed out of Sturrock."

Laris found himself sighing in relief. "I need to get closer," he said.

"Are you mad? Or stupid?" said Azara.

He ignored her and crawled a few steps forward. Two bluecoat generals were stood at the edge of the old road, talking angrily to each other.

"Pssst!" Azara's irritating voice came from behind him. She waved at him to get back. "There's too many of them!" she whispered.

"And?"

"Aren't you going to help me?" she said.

"Why would I do that?" he whispered back, and he turned his back and set off. He ignored her hisses, crawling from boulder to boulder, using the trees for cover. He turned around to see her slip away. He was glad she'd finally got the hint; he wasn't interested in whatever she had planned and if she wanted to hurt that lad, he'd have no part in it.

He edged closer yet to the bluecoat armies, treading ever so carefully on the rustling leaves and twigs below. He didn't want to think about the fate that awaited him if he'd be caught.

"In the dead of night," said one man. "Like cowards."

"And the boy saw it happen? Soren's son?"

The first man tutted, shaking his head. "They took the tunnels. Eyan just watched it happen, like always. I always had my doubts about the lad, weak one he is. Still soft when it comes to his old pals from the Valecrest."

"Do you think we'll catch up to them?" said the second man. "They can't have gotten far, could they?"

"I ain't too sure," said the other. "Oi, faster!" he yelled at an infantryman. These men looked about ready for war. It was obvious that a siege hadn't been enough for them. They looked as if they were out for blood, it sent a shiver down Laris' spine.

"Where could they go from here?" said the second man. "Can't have gotten far, where is there to go?"

"The First Warden has his doubts. Suspicions. Astonkirk, probably, but they wouldn't stay there for long, it wouldn't be safe for 'em. New Castisa, it's more of the same. They wouldn't risk going up to the Falls, not if they want to keep them Sandaerians on their side… which itself is doubtful, of course. No, there's only one place they could go, really… Where it all began, where the Deryzi ruled from hundreds of years ago. Won't stop us though, we'll march right up there, they ain't got a lot of time on their side. Their sanctuary, it won't be a sanctuary for long."

"Yeah? Where's that then?"

"Ayleris."

Nine Long Nights
Aren

Aren woke up with worn out, stinging eyes. His head was pounding as it had been for so many days and his mouth was completely dry. This was the first shred of sound sleep he'd had for a week, and it hadn't helped him at all, he felt worse than ever.

The nights were the worst, he could never bring himself to close his eyes. Flashes of that night flooded in at every chance. The night of the siege. The night it had all changed. He got up out of the chair he'd been slumped in, groaning as he stretched his aching neck and walked to the window. He was drenched in sweat, his hair greasy and his tunic dirty. The heat was hard to bear. The air was thick, even inside the castle's walls. He looked out, squinting at the blinding light outside, the sun was hung fairly high in the sky, it must have been almost the middle of the day. The river glistened and shimmered in its light. He rubbed his eyes, grimacing as the white light pierced in, bouncing off of the pale, beige and brick red rooftops of the Old District of Ayleris.

He watched over the city below quietly. He liked watching the boats docking in the river, and the merchants carrying crates of fish into their markets on the bank. It was good for thinking. He'd spent a lot of time up here thinking about a lot of things as the city below him fortified its ancient walls. It had been nine nights since he'd fled his home. Nine long nights since he'd ran away in the cover of darkness. Like a coward. He'd spent each one plotting how he'd fight back. Planning how he'd take it all from them, everything. He had lost so much along the way.

There was a knock at the door.

"Your Majesty?" came a familiar voice. "Are you up?"

"Yes, Ysser. Has Pennyn been?" croaked Aren, opening the door.

"Yes, sir. I told him I'd send for him as soon as you're up," said Ysser Banlin. "He's been waiting for some time, he didn't want to wake you up."

"No need, I'll go myself," grumbled Aren. "Come with me."

The corridors of the Malysor Castle were hot and stuffy, light peering in through the tall stained-glass windows on either side. Aren had never been up here before. It was remarkably different to the Valecrest, strange and foreign to his eyes. What it lacked in grandeur and size though, it more than made up for in age and antiquity. Its battlements were stronger, more fortified, and its ancient walls and towers cast their shadow over the old town below. It was designed to be a lot easier to defend, more of a fortress than a royal residence, by all means. The narrow corridors were largely bare, and the windows looked out to the river or over to the Halls of Femoren Deryz. The mark that the rule of the Old Deryzi had left behind could still be seen… not only all over the castle, but all around it too. The ruins of the old city walls still stood proudly behind it, patches along it built up with new dark red bricks. How they'd ruled with faith rather than fear, over much of Verenia and beyond, it was a thought Aren couldn't get out of his head. A dynasty older than any King, Queen, Warden or Lord – a dynasty as old as time. They were strong once, brought to their knees only by the bluecoats. Aren had let it happen again.

"It's hot isn't it, Your Majesty?" said Ysser.

"Yes, it always is this far north. The Verenic summer isn't one to be reckoned with."

"Wow…Was it like this up in Asenia?"

"Worse."

"I can barely fathom… I suppose because it's even further north, across the sea," said Ysser. "Are the winters colder?"

"Did Pennyn say what he wanted to discuss with me?" Aren had no time to spare for small, pointless conversations.

"No, just that I should send for him when you're awake."

"I see," said Aren glumly. He hadn't seen much of the chancellor since their arrival. Pennyn had been busy, almost as busy as Aren. He spent all of his time figuring out how it could have happened. Who had betrayed the Crown? It drove him into a sort of madness, something that Aren shared with him. They couldn't rest. They couldn't carry on. The bluecoats had won, plain and simple. Half of the Council had committed treason, the other half was dead, or missing. "Do you know if we've heard anything from Sturrock? Anything at all?"

Ysser shook his head silently. "I'm really sorry, sir."

"And Éterin? Have we heard from Lord Berywen?"

Ysser sighed. "Yes. He wants her back, he's not willing to discuss terms. Any terms."

"A pity. Did Pennyn try to get in touch with Chrysan?" said Aren. "I told him to do that, perhaps her brother might prove more useful, more understanding."

"Yes, and unfortunately the response was the same."

"Wonderful," said Aren dolefully. "It baffles me why we can't have Olivia talk to them herself, tell them she is happy here, that she's safe. Why won't Pennyn allow it?"

Ysser remained silent as he held the old, battered door open for Aren, all the while looking at the stone wall, avoiding his eyes.

"She isn't a prisoner here," said Aren. "Olivia. She doesn't want to go back down there, it frightens her. They should understand that it is much safer for her here." It was easy for him to say, but deep down he wasn't so sure if it *was* the safest place for her. At the surface, as he watched the old fishermen and merchants down below, it almost seemed as if nothing had happened at all. As if they were completely safe here, far from any trouble. At this point though, he didn't know any place that was safe. Perhaps Asenia, despite the war raging through it. If they hated anything more than the Crown, it was bluecoats.

Ysser cleared his throat loudly as they arrived at what was now the Council Chamber, a barren old hall filled with books from a different time. A lone guard stood outside in front of the door to the room.

"Seypor, Deryz hen pyrio," he said, nodding at them.

"Er, very well, hello," said Ysser, awkwardly and the guard chuckled softly.

"'Ello is…is not for you…is for Deryz, for king," said the guard and Ysser's face reddened.

"Seypor," replied Aren and the guard smiled, bowing his head slightly.

"De…chancellor awaits," he said in an incredibly thick Verenic accent.

Aren nodded and brushed straight past him, opened the door himself and left Ysser to wait outside. Pennyn Runeval was sat at the head of a long, rectangular wooden table with old, cushioned chairs lining it on either side. He stood up as soon as Aren walked in.

"Good afternoon, Your Majesty," said Pennyn. "You needn't have come all this way."

"It was no trouble, I didn't really get much rest anyway," said Aren. "I hear we have matters to discuss."

"Yes. Soren Ashcrest has made yet another speech," said Pennyn. "The fourth one just this week. The air's ripe with talk of the Crown's inability to defend Sturrock. I think it's time to lay our claims firmly, Your Majesty, we've waited so long already. We must clamp down hard and fast, or this will only get worse."

"No."

"Your Majesty, whilst we speak, the Federation flies its banner in the south and in the west," said Pennyn. "A banner laced with blood, cruelty and treason. it's important we quell their treachery and that we do it immediately, before they have more time to gain support from the good folk. This is how it begins."

Aren stared numbly at the Crown Chancellor, stood stiffly beside the table.

"They've got a new name for us now, you know," Pennyn carried on. "The Kingdom of Verenia, that is what he calls us. Denies our rule in any of the lands south from Éterin. They've extended their borders further in from the east in Jertonshield. The rot will spread. Soon they'll push us out from here too. The *monarchy will fall*, Aren. We've seen it happen, we've seen great kingdoms burn as tyrants poison the minds of those that are loyal."

"Why won't you let Olivia talk to her father?" said Aren. Pennyn's words meant scarcely anything to him, his mind was elsewhere. "In fact, when will she be allowed out? Allowed to be free here? Why is she under lock and key?"

"She isn't actually under lock and key, Aren, she is as free as anyone is in this castle. She is down there for her *own* safety," said the Crown Chancellor. "And we have discussed this at length. The risks of a face-to-face encounter with Harvus Berywen could be disastrous! Not just for us, Olivia could get hurt. The man is sworn to Ashcrest, that hasn't changed."

"So, we keep her down in the dungeons, hidden away? For how long?" said Aren. "If she is truly here of her own free will, which she *is*, why can we not allow her to speak to her father herself? Lord Berywen will see for himself that she is safe."

Pennyn placed his palms firmly on the table, leaning forward and his expressions darkened. "And why is it that you still call him *Lord* Berywen?" he said, spitting out the name. "He's as much of a traitor as Soren Ashcrest, they're equally complicit. Truth be told, he might perhaps be the worse of the two if he knew what was going to happen that night and let it pass. Put his own daughter in harm's way for the good of whom? The traitor Ashcrest?"

"He wouldn't do that," said Aren. "He would never harm Olivia."

"Don't be so foolish as to presume you know everybody's intentions. Not your enemies, nor your allies," said Pennyn, making no effort to try to hide his frustration.

"As the king, I *command* you to arrange a meeting with Lord Berywen."

Pennyn sighed. "Aren, you know as well as I do that if that is truly your command, I will arrange for it," he said, sitting himself back down in the seat and leaning back, his arms crossed. "I won't be happy, but I'll do it. But you must realise the risks, you *must* see to reason. Or else, you are no better than the rest."

"I do realise the risks," he said. He sighed, deciding maybe it was time to have a conversation that was long overdue. He had nothing to lose now, after all…it was better to be out with it. "Pennyn, I was once told something about you, something which has plagued my mind ever since."

The chancellor stretched his arms back, crossing them behind his head. "What?"

"That you were not to be trusted," said Aren.

Pennyn frowned at him. "If you honestly believe I'd–"

"I know that you wouldn't have had anything to gain from treason. You hate the bluecoats just as much as I do," said Aren. "But the more I think about it, about you, I can't help but wonder, you had an incredible influence on my mother. She trusted you blindly, didn't she?"

Pennyn narrowed his eyes. "And you believe that that trust was misplaced?"

Aren held his left arm with his right hand, looking down solemnly to the ground. "It's best we unravel this now, if we are to continue fighting this war. Out of respect for my mother, I've given you the benefit of the doubt, but I know about your history with Lord Berywen. I know that you played a hand in his departure from court, whether or not that was your intention. You therefore pushed him further to Soren Ashcrest's cause, where perhaps his voice might be heard – again, whether or not that was your intention."

"What exactly do you think you know?" said Pennyn, seething.

"Fencliffe, the droughts there," said Aren. "The rot. Lord Berywen had ideas, warnings, he told the Council of what might happen, and he was right. You undermined him though, didn't you?"

Pennyn said nothing, his brows furrowed and his jaw tightly clenched.

"I *do* trust you, despite all of it. Without Cyneric, I have few to turn to for advice." He unfolded his arms and looked the chancellor in his eyes. "Even my friends, I can't talk to them. I'm alone, completely alone. Jaspyn is missing, or worse, and Olivia isn't allowed out of the dungeons. So, we need to be able to be honest with one another."

"Then I will be honest," said the chancellor. "As I have always been. It is my duty to the people to be completely truthful. If I thought that his ideas were mad, foolish even, then it would be dishonest of me to say otherwise."

"And is that all you did? Remain *honest* to the Council?" said Aren. "What about my mother? Were you always just *honest* with her? Or would it be fair to say that you perhaps overstepped your bounds as chancellor from time to time, maybe tried to sway her, change her mind if things weren't going your way…"

"Stop it," said Pennyn. "Please, just stop it."

"I am not angry with you," said Aren. "Like I said, I have always given you the benefit of the doubt and I know that you have the country's best interests at heart. But I would warn you though, that this is the final straw. Your ego cannot get in the way of your duty. My mother might have had a soft spot for you, but I won't allow it, I can't afford to. Not now."

Pennyn nodded almost cynically.

"We can start afresh," said Aren, his arms crossed again. "I'll forget the accusations against you, all of them, but if I so much as hear whispers of you not listening to reason, or neglecting the opinions of my Council, I will find myself another chancellor."

"I have never done anything that wasn't in the best interest of the Crown, and I won't start now," said Pennyn flatly.

"Good," said Aren. "Now, where is Lord Nazeris? Have we heard anything at all from Zaldron? If not, I'll find someone else to manage the Crown's gold."

The chancellor fiddled with his cup on the table. "He sent us word that his family have made it safely to Portcarcern," said Pennyn. "The journey was far from easy, they had to sail around the bay to avoid any bluecoats. They'll be leaving for Ayleris at the break of dawn tomorrow."

"Is it really safe to be docking in occupied territory? Can't imagine Pyburrock would be an easy road."

"No, Your Majesty, they'll be flown straight into New Castisa by an aerodyne. A motorcar will bring them from there to Ayleris, it has all been worked out to avoid the bluecoats altogether."

"I see," said Aren. "And I don't suppose we've heard from Cyneric?"

"No."

Aren slumped deep into the chair in front of him, leaning on its armrests. He cradled his head into his hands and sighed. The thought of losing Cyneric too...he couldn't bear it. For now, though, there was no time for all that. Grief was a privilege the king didn't have, not in the same ways as everyone else, he knew that now. He cleared his throat. "And the funerals? For the fallen?"

"Which ones?"

"Oscon, Devis, Syndon, Valery, all of them. Every single one. I want it to be grand, as grand as my mother's."

"Aren, I'm really not sure that that is the best idea, such grand processions... for *all* of them?"

"They died because of me, defenceless, doing their duty. I saw Valery's lifeless body on the ground, twisted and shattered...and...and for what? What had she ever done to harm a soul?" Aren took a deep breath and closed his eyes, they still stung as if he'd been punched in the face. "And Syndon – he died protecting his son." said Aren, looking up at the chancellor. "What had Syndon done that was deserving of his fate? Dead. Just like that. At the hands of traitors. His brother couldn't even say goodbye to him. Do you know why? Because Perwell was all the way up in the Falls, keeping a watch on the far north for us." He sighed and buried his head in his hands on the table. "All on my mother's orders. *Your* orders." He shook his head. "We must honour those that gave their lives so that we can be sat here together now, unscathed, for the most part," he rubbed over the deep gash in the side of his forearm, the stitches coming loose.

"While I completely agree with the sentiment, Oscon Spenler *was* the brother of a traitor," said Pennyn. "We cannot ignore that, especially now that the truth of Linara and Gavyn's conspiracy has gotten out."

"I don't care. We will honour the dead. *All* of the dead."

"The North Parydon will never allow empty burial, it's disrespectful to the fallen."

"Who said anything about a burial?" said Aren. "A vigil. A vigil for the fallen. We'll observe the southern customs, they *were* all from the south, weren't they?"

"Fine, Your Majesty," said Pennyn. "If that is your wish."

"Oh, and Pennyn, I'd like to speak to Olivia as soon as I can. We can't keep her holed up in the deepest reaches of the castle forever, she doesn't deserve it."

"It's for her own safety. There's a strong sentiment against her people up here these days. For good reason, some might argue."

"It scares me that *that* is what it's come to," said Aren. "I don't care. She'll be happier up here. Nobody is going to hurt here in my presence."

"I cannot stop you, then, can I, Your Majesty?" He emphasised on the last word, as if to mock him.

"Definitely not," said Aren. "There is also one final thing I'd like to address."

"What is it?" said Pennyn, a tired look on his face.

Aren got up from the table and walked up to the door. "I need as many allies, true allies as I can possibly gain," he said to Pennyn, opening the door.

"Ysser, come in." He smiled at the former First Guard, stood in the doorway. Ysser Banlin walked into the room, nervous and awkward.

"I'm going to relieve you of your pledge to the Crown," said Aren. "You've done plenty of it now. Defending two sovereigns single-handedly, it's got to have been exhausting."

"But I'm happy serving the Crown, Your Majesty. I don't know what else I'd do, this is the only life I've ever known, really."

"Hmm." Aren raised his eyebrows. "I know what else you could do."

"What?"

"Protect this city, defend us from harm."

"But…I'm sworn to the First Guard," Ysser shuffled on his feet. "It's a glorious guild, one I'm proud to uphold. I failed my duty once, I will never fail again."

"You didn't fail, the odds against you made it impossible," said Aren.

"I took an *oath*. That I would uphold the First Guard till my last breath."

"There is no First Guard anymore, Ysser. There hasn't been for a while. We've got the castle guards, I think I'll manage. What's more important to me is that the *city* defend itself against those that would do us harm, we cannot allow another siege."

"But…how?" said Pennyn. "We don't have the Sentry here. We don't even have any barracks within the old town."

"As Lord of Ayleris Command," said Aren, patting Ysser on his back. "I want you to take your pick of the best, as many as you think you need. Whether it's the castle guards or the Crown forces. You know them well, yes? You trained amongst them? You know who to trust, who to keep at arm's length."

Ysser barely managed to hide his grin. "But am I worthy? I have barely been on the First Guard for two years, most of your mother's generals and commanders had served her for most of their lives before they were given such an honour."

"Accept it as a show of my gratitude, for the valour you've shown us these past few weeks. For what you did that night, when all hope was lost. When both Cyneric and I thought that death might be the only way out."

Pennyn scowled and looked away, gazing out into the city below.

"Understood?" said Aren.

Ysser cleared his throat and nodded. "If that is your command, I will not fail you, sir," he said, bowing. "You said there are no barracks here. Where shall I work from? It would be unwise to set up camps here, at the castle itself. Perhaps somewhere close by, close to the river, but not on the castle's grounds."

Aren thought for a while. "Use the Halls of Femoren Deryz, it'll be big enough there, much bigger than Sentry Hall back at the palace."

Pennyn stood by in silence. His jaw was clenched again and his eyes narrow, but he managed a feeble smile.

"Is there something you wish to add, Crown Chancellor?" Aren said.

"Nothing," said Pennyn, hesitating. "It's just...the Halls, they are a sacred place, Your Majesty. To our culture, to our faith, they hold an important place in our hearts...to have forces train there, to fight..."

"Yes, the Halls do have an important place in our culture, but that place is in the past," said Aren. "For now, they serve a greater purpose. If anyone wishes to raise any concerns about that, please let them know to speak with me."

Pennyn could do nothing but nod, if reluctantly. He got up out of his seat and walked to the window, turning his back to Aren. Aren missed being able to rely on Cyneric, on his honesty. He wished he hadn't left.

"Have any of our spies in the south spotted him?" he said.

"Hmm?" Pennyn grumbled, back still turned to Aren.

"Cyneric, has he been spotted?"

"No, Your Majesty," said Pennyn, finally turning around. "Did he mention *at all* where he might have been headed? Why he couldn't have come with us?"

"No," said Aren, his eyes misty again. "Just that I should stick by Ysser's side and not to think about him or anyone else that I'd left behind." He turned to face Lord Ysser. "Could you send for Olivia?"

"It isn't safe for her up here," said Pennyn. "Perhaps we should go down to see her–"

"She isn't going to live in fear forever. She deserves better. That'll be the last I hear of it. Lord Ysser, please send for her." The guard nodded and bowed before leaving.

"And will the Aerial Command be moved here? To Ayleris?" Aren asked Pennyn.

The chancellor shook his head. "The *dynes* are far safer in New Castisa, for now. They can be in the air within the hour, the fields here are too small, they aren't built for that sort of thing. Besides, it is important we have them there in case the bluecoats try to move in from the west instead of from the capital…"

"The capital?" said Aren. "The capital is Ayleris now."

"You are right," said Pennyn. There was a short, cold moment of silence before Pennyn cleared his throat.

"I never thought I'd see the day," he said, looking up at Aren. "The day it'd finally happen, the day our great country would be torn into two. It's been a long time coming, for as long as I can remember, but I never thought I'd live to see it."

"There's a lot I never thought I'd see – things I'd have never wanted to see, things I wouldn't pray upon my enemies. I've witnessed many of them over the last few weeks," said Aren. Suddenly, he was back there, in that palace courtyard. The horrors flashed in and out of his mind, he was powerless. He could see her plummet towards the cold hard ground, helpless, screaming. He could see his people bleed around him, the cobbled pathways and grass in the gardens stained red with their blood. The dead chef, the dead guard. He could see it all.

"Aren?"

"Yes?"

"Are you alright?"

"Of course."

He wasn't. He couldn't be, not until he knew his people were safe. So many had died for him, countless.

"Pennyn, my family, are they safe here?" he said. The chancellor gave him a puzzled look.

"Safer than in the south."

"But can we truly say they are safe here? That nothing would bring them harm?"

"We can never know that for certain," said Pennyn. "Ashcrest knows we would have come here, this I can tell you."

"Syndon died protecting his son," said Aren. "But we cannot even be sure that Jeryn is safe here? It's as if he died in vain."

"Jeryn is a strong young lad," said Pennyn.

"That isn't what I asked, I asked if he is safe here. What about Cyera? Vidalia? She's not far down the line of ascension. Inigo's barely crawling, what about him? Or any of my uncles and aunties?"

"They're as safe here as the rest of us, as safe as they would be anywhere," said Pennyn.

"Anywhere?" said Aren. "What about East Asenia?"

Pennyn crossed his arms and frowned. "What of it?"

"I think we should send them all there. Grecia, Sierra, Skander, Wynter, and all the children. At least until this all settles down."

Pennyn raised his eyebrows. "You think sending them away, from one country torn by war to another country torn by war, would make them any safer?"

"The Union doesn't love us, but we share a common enemy in Soren Ashcrest. We have the upper hand up there, for now at least. Perhaps we could strike a deal, let them extend their borders past Seviria. My family will be far safer there, in hiding, than they would be anywhere in Landridge."

Pennyn looked far from convinced and opened his mouth to speak before a knock at the door interrupted him.

"Lady Olivia Berywen, Your Majesty," said Ysser.

"Enter."

The door opened and in came Olivia, skinnier than ever, though her skin wasn't nearly as pale. Aren wondered how it had bronzed even in the darkest depths of the castle. The journey up, perhaps. It had been a long and treacherous one and the Verenic sun was far from forgiving.

"I've been waiting to see you, Aren." Her voice was feeble. "Have they heard from Jaspyn?"

Aren bowed his head. "No, Olivia."

She let out a small sniffle and turned her bony face away.

"We'll find him," said Aren. "I know we will."

"Hmm."

"Take a seat," he said, pulling out a cushioned chair and dusting it off with his hands before sitting down beside her. "Olivia, I want you to know that we're doing everything we can – absolutely everything – to tell your family that you're safe here."

She nodded, a sullen look on her face.

"If there's anything else we can do to make you more comfortable, please let me know," said Pennyn, but his tone was cold and distant. He sat back in his chair, arms crossed behind his head. She nodded at him then looked down to the stone floor.

"Olivia, there's something else. I know it isn't much, but I've invited Lara down from Nynnevor."

Olivia looked up, her face suddenly a tad brighter. "Really? Lord Hercan is letting it happen? Her term doesn't start for another couple of months."

"Perwell was most happy to oblige," said Pennyn, before Aren had a chance to answer. "He knows how close you all are."

"Thank you," she said. She wrapped her thin arms around him, gripping him in a tight hug. She smelt awful. Damp and dirty. "Really, thank you. I don't...I don't have words. You are always putting others before yourself."

"I just wish I was able to help everyone we left behind," said Aren. "I don't even want to begin to think about what Jaspyn must have gone through."

"That isn't your fault," she said, her voice breaking. "As long as he stayed out of trouble, laid low after the siege, I'm sure–"

"He hasn't responded to anything that we sent. None of the spies we sent to Arvendon, none of the letters. His parents haven't seen him either. They were already so broken over Daria...I... I ruined everything didn't I?"

"You did nothing," said Olivia.

"But maybe that's the problem," said Aren.

"Your Majesty," a knock came at the door. "There's a message from the Gory Gate. Somebody's here and is asking for you. They've both been taken down to the cellars."

"Thank you, Ysser," said Aren, his heart full of hope and fear. "Did you say *both*?"

Ysser nodded. "There were two, apparently."

The guards opened the doors and two shadowy figures stood in the darkness. Aren got closer to get a better look. He smiled jubilantly as their faces became visible.

"Hello Aren," Cyneric grinned at him. He squinted to see the face of the other, it was Lady Rayne. Suddenly he could feel tears well up in his eyes.

"I've decided to finally take you up on that offer, *Your Majesty*," said Rayne. "That is, if it still stands."

"Yes... yes, of c-course it does," he said. She smiled warmly and hugged him tight, ruffling his hair as he hugged her back.

"Cyneric found me," she said. "After the siege. Smuggled into Lyndan in the darkness of night! Heaven only knows how he managed, through the mountains, through Astonkirk. But boy was I glad to see his sullen face at the manor gates."

Cyneric chuckled softly. "Not as glad as I was to finally get some real food and water, mind you."

"He told me that you'd made it out alive, all of you. He convinced me that this is the only right choice, the only important one."

"But…"

"Lyndan is safe from the bluecoats for now, the peninsula is patrolled by half of the Dresden troops," said Rayne. "We have the mountains in the south and the Strait in the north, we will be fine. It is far more crucial that I am here, to help you, to be of service to you."

Aren leapt forward for another hug, this time wrapping his arms around the both of them. "You have no idea how happy I am to see you both."

"Likewise," said Cyneric, grinning. "Now there's a lot we need to talk about and I'm not sure it can wait."

"Yes, of course," said Aren. "Do you want me to call Pennyn in? He'd love to see you both."

Rayne eyed him curiously, over the top of her eyeglasses. "Yes, of course," she said. "Firstly though, have you formed your Council?"

"I am waiting for Lord Nazeris, he's arriving tomorrow. As for the rest of them, I haven't given it much thought."

Rayne smiled. "That will change. Now, onto the next, when are you planning to declare war? And lay your claims?"

"Is that necessary?" said Aren. "Everyone knows we're at war."

Rayne rolled her eyes and Cyneric glanced over at her.

"I'm surprised you haven't done so already," said Cyneric. "Every moment we waste is a precious one. It's vile, what's happening in the streets down there. I'll never forget the horrendous things I've seen… things no man should ever see." He took a deep breath. "Speaking of which, Aren, we were having a conversation just before the siege. A rather important one too."

"Yes, I remember it all too well," said Aren. He'd tried to brush it aside; he'd tried not to think about it too much over the last few days. There were far bigger problems at hand, worrying aimlessly was good for nothing.

"I wanted to talk to you," said Cyneric. "*We* wanted to talk to you, about the dangers that surround us here. It is what you heard us speaking about that day…in the Hall of Krelis. It's important that you know, now that…" he stopped. "Now that some things are clearer."

Aren nodded.

"The droughts in Fencliffe," said Cyneric. "The killings, the rest of it, we think we know the cause," he said, turning to Rayne, who nodded back at him frantically.

"Aren, you've heard the stories, I'm sure. The men of the shadows. Creatures of the night," said Rayne.

"Dwellers," said Cyneric.

Aren gave them a sceptical glance. "Yes, I've heard the stories. But I struggle to see the relevance."

Cyneric gave him a worried look. "Well, they are not just stories," he said.

"Indeed, far from it," said Rayne. "The threat of these creatures has loomed over us for thousands of years."

"Stories," said Aren. "Stories have loomed over us."

Rayne glared at him. "No, Aren. More than just stories."

"There were sightings," said Cyneric. "In Fencliffe. In fact, Lady Rayne has seen one herself, with her own eyes."

"Hold on," said Rayne. "Before I continue, maybe it is best you do bring in the chancellor, dear."

Cyneric glanced over at her. "Are you sure?"

"Yes," said Rayne. "Because he was warned. The Sandaerians warned him, Lord Berywen warned him. He chose to do nothing."

"Then I will ask him why myself," said Aren.

The room was silent when Pennyn Runeval finally walked in. The pleasantries were brief, this time there were no endearing embraces.

"Dwellers?" said the chancellor. As ridiculous as it sounded, the look on his face spoke volumes. "We knew of the sightings," said Pennyn. "Elvira and I, we knew. Dwellers exist only in legends and myths, same as skyverns and phoenixes. People have been purporting to see them for as long as time itself. People will see what they choose to… Just last month we heard of skyverns being spotted in the north. All lies. Lies or madness."

"Of course," said Rayne in a condescending voice. "I should have known it was you."

"So, you are saying that dwellers, skyverns, elves and witches, they all exist, do they?" said Pennyn, scoffing. "Don't be absurd."

"Chancellor, please do shut up," said Cyneric. Pennyn looked at the Panderer in horror. "Let the lady continue, please. This is important."

Rayne turned to look at Aren. "Horrible things. Their eyes... they thirst for blood, you can see it in their empty gazes. Their wasting faces, pale and dreary. Faster than us, stronger too."

Aren supposed that Lady Rayne and Cyneric had both gone mad. "My lady, I don't suppose you could tell us *where* you've seen these...dwellers...or creatures, whatever you would call them."

"Just the two," said Rayne. "Two dwellers. And I'm not the only one either."

"You are not?"

She nodded.

"And where did you see them?" said Aren.

"On the train down to Sturrock," she said. "Just out of Astonkirk. We suddenly stopped, it was the middle of the night. I wanted to see where all the commotion was coming from. And then I saw him. Outside. In the valley. Pale face, dark eyes. Greasy hair down to his shoulders. Fast as lightning, fastest man I'd ever seen. He climbed up the rocks next to the tracks and that was that. I didn't see him again, until a half hour later, when the train was already moving."

"That doesn't mean–" said Aren but Cyneric was quick to interrupt him too.

"Please Aren, let her finish."

"The second time, I saw him in the nobles' carriage. He'd dressed himself differently, but it was definitely him. The thirst in his eyes," she said, shaking her head. "I didn't say anything to anyone because I wasn't going to pick a fight that I would undoubtedly lose. I kept thinking to myself...there are always impostors trying to smuggle themselves onto nobles' carriages, so I didn't make much of it. I was like you, I *chose* not to believe. It wasn't until Elvira told me about the sightings in Fencliffe that I started to think about it, really. And then of course, after Elvira's death..."

"What happened?" said Aren.

"The day of the hearing. I saw a woman, she had that same empty gaze. Madness in her eyes. I saw her go into the kitchens, and...I swear my eyes weren't deceiving me, I swear it, I really do."

"What is it, my lady?" said Aren. She was frantic. A fear in her eyes that he'd never before seen.

"I saw her bear a smile. A horrid, ugly thing. Two thin fangs, much like those of a snake. For a moment I thought I'd finally lost it, but then–"

"Then she told me," said Cyneric. "And I will admit, I wasn't convinced at first. I thought she'd gone mad too," he said. "But then, as Rayne told you, she isn't the only one who has seen a dweller with her own eyes."

"Have you?" said Aren.

"Yes, as have you," said Cyneric. Aren didn't know what to make of it. "The night of the siege." Suddenly, Aren's heart pounded faster and he breathed heavier. He could see it again, all of it.

"The one with the sword?" said Aren. "In the courtyard?" He ran his fingers over his wound again, it stung more than usual.

Cyneric nodded. "He was so much faster than me. Stronger too."

"That doesn't mean that he was a dweller," said Aren. "Maybe he was just stronger than you."

"Took the words right of my mouth, Your Majesty," said Pennyn.

Cyneric sighed. "I've fought many men in my life. Many faster than me. Many stronger than me. Vile, cruel men who have no sense of remorse, no guilt. This one was different, Aren."

Rayne nodded. "They're real. Very real. We had our warnings," she said, looking at Pennyn. "But we took Lord Berywen for a fool."

"Now, I never said I took Lord Berywen for a fool," said Pennyn. "But he was delusional, he thought of everything as a conspiracy, he wasn't–"

"That's enough," said Aren. "What's in the past cannot be changed."

"Indeed," said Cyneric. "Well, we now believe that Lord Berywen may have been right. All of the missing people. The missing cattle. The farmers' suicides. The droughts, the rot."

"What has it got to do with the rot?" said Aren.

Pennyn sighed. "We had letters, from the North Parydon. From a man who calls himself Tamuz Sandaerzi."

"And what did these letters say?"

"That these… creatures… they cause the rot where they feed, where they spill blood," said Pennyn. "Your Majesty, forgive me, Aren, it was all nonsense to us–"

Aren raised his hand to stop the chancellor.

"So, the missing people…they're dead?" said Aren.

"Maybe," said Cyneric. "Or maybe worse."

"Worse?"

"Well, they probably fed on the cattle. That's why they raided the farms. The men and women though, I don't think they'd have killed them all," said Rayne. "Not without reason."

"Then what…" Aren didn't need to finish his sentence. "Oh."

"What was the dweller doing in the palace's kitchens on the day of the hearing?" said Cyneric. "Or in the siege? Why was he there?"

"You think they're working for Ashcrest," said Aren. It sounded absolutely senseless, irrational even and yet there was a part of him that wondered…could it be true? He wasn't a stranger to the impossible, after all. He had seen things in his life, senseless and irrational things.

"I definitely believe they played a big part in the siege," said Cyneric. "That is how they were able to get past our men with such ease. Maybe even in the queen's assassination, maybe that is how they got the Aster's Pine in without anybody asking questions." He crossed his arms and drew his eyebrows close together. "Worse yet, I think they may be raising an army."

"And that's why so many are missing," said Aren. Even the thought was a terrible nightmare. "Is that even possible?" said Aren.

"I don't know," said Cyneric. He glanced over to Rayne, and she shrugged her shoulders.

"All I know about them comes from stories and legends," said Rayne. "That they feed on blood. That they can't be killed easily."

"Why would they be working for Ashcrest? If they're faster and stronger than us, why would they kneel to any man? Whether a King or Warden. Why would they need to?" said Aren. The thought was still wild and hard to believe but Aren was determined not to make the same mistakes as his chancellor. "Not to mention, the Old Federation instigated the Exile. The old bluecoats, they killed hundreds and thousands of innocents just on suspicion of them having the blood of the dweller. They all but erased the Zaldroni from existence, banished them to their island. Then why would the dwellers join forces with *them*?"

"That's a good question," said Rayne, squinting. "And why haven't they hurt us before? What has changed now?"

"That is for us to figure out," said Cyneric.

"Well, let us begin, then," said Aren.

The People's Sovereign
Olivia

The flag of Landridge was lowered to half-mast. The crowds stood behind her and the nobles gathered on the balconies of the Old Aneglin all fell to near silence as the first beat of the drum echoed around her. The quartet at the bottom of the steps beside Olivia played the Skyvern's March solemnly as three children emerged from the doors of the Old Aneglin, all clad in white, a basket of flowers in each pair of hands. They walked straight past Olivia to the priest stood atop the steps, dressed in a most pristine white cloak. Olivia watched him bless each basket, using three fingers to touch each one before kissing his hand, his eyes closed.

But far beneath, the commoners jested and jeered, cursing and spitting at the sight of it all. It was disgusting. But then, she couldn't blame them really, could she? After all, they were northerners…they had seen first-hand the hostilities of the southerners that had ruled them hundreds of years ago. The Old Aneglin itself was a monument to all of the awful things the old bluecoats had done. The majestic building hadn't always been an Aneglin – it had once stood as a Parydon, a place for the followers of the Old Deryzi to gather at night's end. A place as sacred as any. They'd spared nothing, the Weslin, they'd taken it all. It was only natural that the Verenic, at least some of them, still had no room in their hearts for southerners or their ways. The faces in the crowds below her suddenly sung a different song, one of frustration, of struggle.

She watched as some of the commoners tried to clamber over each other, reaching over the barriers. It looked less like a vigil and more and more like a riot. Over to the left, four men had marched past her to almost the top of the marble steps. By their uniforms, she could tell that that they were guards of the Malysor Castle, each with a rifle on his arm. Aren was stood behind them all, at the very top. He looked over at Olivia, giving her a thin smile, then looked away again, to the crowds, a lost look about him.

"Our brothers, our sisters, our elders," shouted Aren, louder than she'd ever heard him. Many of the crowds went quiet as the guards pointed their rifles up to the skies for their salute. They fired all at once, a deafening crack. The crowds roared louder than ever before. She looked to the commoners, the closest ones to the barriers. The loathing in their eyes as they caught sight of her. Why wouldn't they loathe her? She was the daughter of a traitor. A traitor of the south.

The bells of the Aneglin rang and she was suddenly scurried away by Cyneric, his giant palm placed firmly around her shoulder. She followed him up the steps to the grand black doors of the Old Aneglin. She turned her head back, catching a glimpse of Aren and Pennyn following behind her, but Cyneric pushed it right back around.

"Don't look at them, the good folk," said Cyneric. Olivia nodded. "Hopefully Ashcrest receives our message loud and clear."

Olivia couldn't take it anymore. "Your Majesty, a word?"

"Of course," said Aren. She slipped him far away from the rest, heading to the south-facing balcony, well out of earshot.

"Well?" he said, a proud smile plastered across his face.

She stared at him emptily. "You do know some of the Verenic out there are calling you a weak king?"

"Why? Who?" His smile disappeared. "Most of the nobles thought it was brave."

"You don't rule over only the nobles," said Olivia.

"And what problem do the commoners have with me then?"

Olivia raised her brow, clenching her fists tightly. "The vigil. Some would say you are bending to the will of the enemy."

"I will say it however many times it needs to be said. The Weslin of the south are not my enemy. The bluecoats are my enemy. There's no honour in disrespecting the fallen, I stand by it."

"I agree," said Olivia. "It's a pity though, that some of your subjects will simply never see through the same eyes as you or I. They don't know of war, nor politics or the honour of soldiers…most of them know only of famine, of hunger. Famine and hunger imposed on them by the war that, to them at least, the southerners wage on you. The war many of their sons and daughters will probably die for."

The king said nothing, but his eyes frightened her all the same.

"Your Majesty," came Pennyn's voice. "Dinner will be served soon."

"Thank you," said Aren. He held out his arm to stop the chancellor. "Actually, whilst you're here, I wanted to find out where we stand, with our borders in the south and the west."

Pennyn took a step back and looked over at Olivia, and then back at Aren. "Is now truly the time, Your Majesty?"

"Yes, a better time than any."

"They are as secure as can be. We've still got New Castisa and Astonkirk, both crucial parts of our plan."

"Really?" said Aren cynically. "And what plan is this?"

"Our plan to win the war," said Pennyn coldly.

"How so?" said the king.

"New Castisa gives us way to Éterin by river," said Pennyn, turning to Olivia. "Where the three rivers meet. And of course, Astonkirk gives us a path to Sturrock from behind the mountains, if it comes to it."

"And what good does the river to Éterin give us?" said Aren. "Éterin still flies our banner."

"Aren," said Pennyn in hushed tones which made Olivia squirm. "We can talk about this later."

"Olivia is one of us. She can hear anything you've got to say."

"Very well. Éterin is the ancestral home of Lord Berywen, Aren. If ever we wanted to negotiate with the turncoat, it'd be easy to send a fleet down the river to knock on his family's doors."

It didn't much shock her, if she was being honest with herself. Pennyn had never liked her, nor her family.

"Chancellor, we are not attacking Éterin. Not without good reason. You do realise this is Olivia's family?"

"My apologies, Your Majesty," said Pennyn. "I was under the impression that I might be able to speak freely," he said. "But of course, we would not lay waste to Éterin just like that. Not without good reason. Of course not. But if it did come to it…"

"And what is happening in the south?" said Olivia. She thought she'd better change the course of the conversation before her king and chancellor thought to plot her own assassination right before her eyes. "In Sturrock. Have we heard from Jaspyn?"

"No," said Pennyn. He shook his head sadly, but it was a false kind of sadness. "And as far as the borders are concerned," he lowered his voice to no more than a loud whisper. "Lady Rayne has heard from her spies in Sturrock. What remained of the Sentry, they were able to secure a border, though a weak one. North of the city. They've set up camps between the foothills of the mountains and caused a lot of the bluecoats to retreat. Our armies fought off the remaining rebels. We're close to cutting them off entirely, it won't be long until they're forced to make a hasty move."

"I'm glad," said Aren. "Let's hope that day comes soon. And what about the Strait of Zaldron? Is it patrolled?"

"Yes. We've got most of the Nazeris army down there."

"Speaking of the Nazeris army, where is Lord Nazeris? said Aren. "I haven't seen any of them yet."

"He was on the balcony," said Olivia. "I saw him." Crafty lunatic. She wasn't sure which one of his cunning children scared her the most.

"Ah, well." Aren seemed to take a moment to think about it. "And Medlanta?" he said. "Is Lyndan safe? Without Rayne, I mean." He had a frantic, obsessed look about him.

"Perfectly safe," said Pennyn. "Do you really think she'd agree to leave without making the necessary arrangements?"

"We should send in more men, don't you think?" said Aren. "My understanding is limited, I admit, but we stand a fair natural advantage over Ashcrest in the south, don't we? With the cover of the mountains, but as for the east…"

"It's a peninsula," said Pennyn. "They've got Verenia on the other side of the water in the north, and the mountains to the south, so if the bluecoats were to take it, they'd have to traipse straight in from the west. We've got hundreds at the City Guard in the west. They've set up camps, same as Sturrock, to hold the border. Lyndan can withstand almost any siege that comes her way."

"Understood," said Aren, seeming half-convinced.

Olivia had to admit, it was all very cleverly thought out. The chancellor clearly wasn't taking any chances. For good reason, of course.

The hall had only gotten more crowded, as more nobles milled in from the outside. Olivia was stood beside Aren quietly, to be seen and not heard. She was waiting for him to finish speaking to Tylus Banlin, a conversation in which she had no interest. She wanted to go and find Lara, but Aren had been clear in his instructions. She was to stay by his side. Like a dog.

"Your Majesty! The queen would have been proud!" a voice said. It was a noble. Olivia didn't even know her name, she wondered if Aren did.

"A true Son of Landridge!" said another.

Aren smiled and thanked them both before excusing himself and slipping away to the corner of the hall, gesturing for Olivia to follow.

"Guess I should start calling you *Your Majesty*, then?" came Lara Hercan's poised voice, a beaming smile across her face. "That was such a good speech, Aren. My father would have loved it."

"Thank you," said Aren, unable to hold back his own smile. "You're very kind."

"Definitely," said Olivia. "A King of Landridge, indeed." She swallowed her pride and set aside her worries, putting on the widest smile she could manage for the both of them. It was particularly difficult. Luckily, she was put right out of her misery when Lady Rayne appeared from behind them, as she often did.

"Been avoiding me, have you?"

"You have a habit of beginning your conversations by sneaking up behind me, don't you, my lady?" said Aren, turning around to face her.

"I suppose I do," she said, chuckling. "It was beautiful, your speech. *Lyn Dendrus Landrizio.*"

Lara inspected Lady Rayne, deep in thought. Suddenly her face lit up with pride. "In the name of the Crown of Landridge," she said.

"Yes." Rayne smiled. "*Se benora.* Very good," she said. Olivia wasn't sure that it was. Even *she* knew that much Verenic. Aren, on the other hand, looked at her in admiration as if she'd recited a poem from the time of the Old Deryzi.

"Of course, you study at the University, don't you?" he said. "You must know this place better than I do."

"Well, barely," said Lara. "I've scarcely been here, when father learnt what'd happened in the south, he brought me home at once.

So, I don't suppose I know the city too well… not as well as I know Nynnevor."

"And what is it that you study?" said Rayne.

Lara's eyes began to wander again, as if she'd lost herself in thought. *"Nyralis ten lytor Verenzi"* she said, a proud smile on her face.

Olivia couldn't help the envy that poisoned her thoughts, but she wore a polite smile. Lara *should* be proud of herself. A southern girl like her, a Hercan no less, spitting out Verenic like that. The impressed smile on Aren's face made it that much worse, but why shouldn't he be impressed, after all? Olivia found herself suddenly wanting to be excused.

"Not shabby at all," said Rayne. "Unfortunately beyond the capacity of my own abilities in the tongue."

"Verenic History and Language," said Aren. "That sounds really difficult."

It couldn't have been that difficult, thought Olivia. Lara's own mother spoke Verenic. Still, she wore her smile. "I'm very proud of you, Lara." Perhaps in another life, one where Olivia's father hadn't chosen to break faith, she *too* would be at the University. Perhaps.

"Thank you," said Lara, smiling sweetly. "Thank you all, really."

"What's it been like?" said Aren. "I'd always thought I'd study at Ayleris, if it were possible. It's a pity I will never be able to now… now that, well…"

"Now that you're king?" said Olivia, and Aren went red.

"It's been delightful," said Lara, changing the subject. "A real pleasure, it is the most enchanting tongue I know of."

"I can imagine," said Olivia. "History…what was the word for that again? You said it earlier…*Zytora* was it?"

Lara and Aren laughed. "No, *zytora* means *time*. I said *nyralis ten lytor Verenzi.*"

"I'll bet you're the centre of everyone's attention," said Olivia. "A Hercan like yourself, studying Verenic history." She laughed, but this time nobody else did. Aren just glared at her. Lara was still smiling though, thankfully.

"No, actually, it's quite the opposite. Everyone is really very nice and there are far fewer eyes on me than I'd have thought, what with a foreign dignitary in the hall."

Aren gave her a sideways glance. "Which foreign dignitary?"

"Oh, you don't know?" she said. "Zenara Itris. The Asmoni."

Zenara Itris. Where had Olivia heard the name before? The Asmoni…*Zenara*…In Ayleris. The odds of that weren't great. Aren gave Lady Rayne an odd glance, and she in turn responded with a gentle nod. It wouldn't have surprised Olivia if Rayne had known of this already, she seemed to know everything there was to know about anything important. Or at least, her spies did. That much was clear. That's when it dawned upon her. She suddenly felt sheepish for not asking earlier.

"My lady," said Olivia suddenly. "Might I have a word?"

Lady Rayne turned to face her. "Mhmm?"

"Just – just a quick word, if it's possible," said Olivia.

Rayne smiled her thin smile and followed her out. "What is it dear? I must confess, if this is to do with your father, I'm afraid I might not be of much help…"

Olivia smiled politely. "No, my lady. Actually, I have something to ask of you," she said. "And of your spies."

Rayne drew her eyes together. "The *Crown's* spies, dear," she said. "The Department of Clandestine Affairs. What is it?"

"Well, yes," said Olivia. "But also…*your* spies," she said. She knew there was a difference between the two and she was going to make that much clear.

"Very well," she said. "How may *they* be of use to you?"

"I was wondering if they may be able to get some information. From the south."

"That is generally what spies are used for, Olivia dear," said Rayne. "Why don't you tell me what it is exactly that you wish to find out. Don't hold back." She took a short pause. "Oh, and do be sure you make it clear why you are asking it of me in the king's absence," she added, raising her eyebrows.

"It's silly," said Olivia, going red. "A petty thing, especially for Aren, what with the war and all… But still, it is incredibly important to me. More important than I could put into words," she added. She drew a sharp breath. "Could your spies find out what happened to Jaspyn? Jaspyn Fenwern."

"Jaspyn…" she muttered. "The commoner, dear? Pale of face, sharp jaw, red hair?"

"Yes," said Olivia. "He's been missing since the night of the siege. His family hasn't heard from him, neither have we. We don't know where he was that night, he wasn't in the palace. His sister died last year…I can't imagine how his parents must be feeling." Saying it all out loud right now put a lump in her throat, and she struggled to hold back the tears in her eyes.

Rayne looked at her sadly. "If he wasn't in the palace, and we don't know where he was, I'm not sure how much help my spies might be."

"But still," said Olivia. "They're our last hope."

"Fine," said Rayne. "I have but one thing to ask of you. Why couldn't you have just asked the king?"

"I have," said Olivia. "More than once. I realise he has a lot on his mind though, so I thought I would come to you myself…"

Rayne nodded. "A lot indeed."

Olivia stopped herself for a moment, looking up at the woman's critical gaze. "And of course, your spies report directly to you, not to the king."

Rayne raised her eyebrows once more.

"If Jaspyn *is* dead, I fear that he'll keep it from me, they all will. I would rather know."

"Very well," said Rayne. "But don't make it a habit of going behind his back. It would not do you so much good in the long run."

"Don't worry, you can tell him I asked you," said Olivia. "This isn't a secret matter. I wouldn't dream of keeping anything from him. Nothing at all." The king was the People's Sovereign after all, no matter how Olivia felt about it. She clenched her fists and marched off, before she said anything else she wouldn't be able to take back.

The Royal Family
Lara

The smell of old, dusty books was in the air. It wasn't a smell that Lara was particularly fond of. She was sat in the Regent's Study with Olivia, who was brewing a cup of tea. The air between them was cold and thin, though the Ayleris heat hadn't dwindled in the slightest. Cold and thin with worry. With anguish.

"So, his family haven't heard from him either?" said Lara.

"They haven't, but they could be lying."

"Why would they be lying?"

Olivia sighed. "I don't know."

"After what happened to Daria…" muttered Lara. "I can't fathom what they're going through. To lose a second child…"

"We don't know that he's dead," said Olivia sternly. "He can't be dead."

Lara sighed and placed a hand on her friend's shoulder. She'd heard horrible tales of what was going on in the south, though. She knew that if Jaspyn's own parents hadn't heard from him, it wasn't looking good at all. But still, she found herself nodding in assurance. "He'll be fine."

Olivia pulled out an old book with tainted, creased pages. It had no title on its leather cover. She opened it up to reveal an intricate pattern sprawled across two pages. A detailed map, spreading from one edge of the book to the other. Dust flew up out of it and onto Olivia's face as the heavy covers hit the wooden surface. Lara wafted away the dust with her hands, sickened by the stink. Olivia shook her head disapprovingly and flipped the page to reveal another large, complicated map, the ink fading from it. *Nevebaris Verenzi* was scrawled across the top right of the page. Lara recognised the words immediately.

"Ayleris," said Olivia loudly, pointing to the word at the top of the page. "Do you understand any of this?"

"Only little more than you," said Lara, looking at the Old Verenic words etched all over the page. "There are few in our country who would."

"What do you mean?" said Olivia, slightly irritated. "You study Verenic. You go to the University to learn...all this!"

"This isn't the Verenic they speak here," said Lara patiently. "I cannot understand most of this, it's archaic."

"Asenian Verenic, then?" said Olivia.

"No, Olivia. It's *Old Verenic*," said Lara, shaking her head. "The kind that Aren and his family speak."

Olivia looked even more disappointed. "I see. Well, you can still pick out words, right? Places? Rivers? Those words haven't changed. You can understand those?"

Lara didn't know how to respond. "Well, yes, about as much as you," she said. "What are you thinking?"

"More than me, I'm sure," said Olivia nodding in a frenzy, ignoring her latter question. "*Nynnevor* – the North Falls, right? What does this one mean?" she said, pointing to the words scrawled across the top right of the page. "*Nevebaris Verenzi*."

Lara nodded. "The Verenic Riviera," she said. "This is an ancient map of Verenia, from a completely different time. What are you doing with it?"

Olivia frantically turned the page to what appeared to be a map of Old Sturrock. "There could be something new here. Something we don't know about... Perhaps something from the days of the Old Federation. Do you see anything? Anything at all?" she said. "Something about the covered approaches? The mountain passes?"

Lara frowned. It had suddenly gone too far. "Olivia, I'm not sure that this is good for you."

Olivia looked at her scornfully. "What do you mean? What isn't good for me?"

"The covered approaches? The mountain passes?" said Lara. "And just what will you and I accomplish with that information? We'll get Jaspyn back on our own, will we?"

"Well, I..."

"Two noble girls like us? Orchestrate a breach into Arvendon under Soren Ashcrest's rule? Do you hear how ridiculous you sound?!"

"Don't mock me. Many girls have been warriors, many of the greatest warriors of the Old Deryzi were women–"

"That is *not* the discussion we are having," said Lara. "Many girls have been warriors – many girls *are* warriors. But *we* are not warriors," she crossed her arms. "That isn't to say they don't exist. That Zenara Itris, the one from the University – she has a friend. A Uressi friend. I've heard she's tougher, faster, and stronger than most men she's faced. Of course, women are–"

"Maybe we could ask her then," said Olivia mockingly.

Lara wasn't going to have it. "Tell me, what were you looking to gain from this?" she said, seriously, pointing at the old book. "Even if we *were* to happen upon something that the sharpest minds in the Crown's forces may have missed – and we're talking about soldiers that have probably spent half their lives fighting in those very mountains – what would you have us do with it?"

"We could get Jaspyn back. We could win the war. We could tell Aren, or Mr. Runeval, or someone. We could–"

"Why aren't you having this conversation with Aren, then?" said Lara. "This old, tattered map," she said, toying with the fraying edge of the page. "He can read it better than you or I."

"He won't do anything. None of them will do anything. We need to take control of things – we need to – we need to give them a plan. A reason to do something."

Her eyes were filled with madness. It was a madness that Lara had scarcely seen before, she couldn't help but feel sad about it. Guilty, somehow. "I understand your pain. But obsessing over Jaspyn won't help us," she said. "What can the two of us do alone? Olivia… they'll announce an attack, any minute now, I know they will. Aren, the Council, we should wait for them. My father reckons it'll be coming any day now, and he's got *years* of experience."

"I've waited for long enough!" said Olivia, now raising her voice. She looked absolutely unhinged. "What do you think he's going to do? Nothing. It took him days to even let me out of the bloody dungeons."

"And don't you think that was for your own good?" Lara began raising her own voice. "Do you know how dangerous it is for us to simply exist up here? Two Weslin girls like us – and not just any Weslin girls, either. To bear Berywen or Hercan as a family name? Let alone to be the daughter of a bluecoat general? Because that's what you are, Olivia, you do see that, don't you? That's what they see you as, the king's subjects." She stopped herself from saying anymore.

"I suppose," said Olivia, somewhat calmer now, though a bitter scowl remained on her face. "I just wish there was more we could do, you and me. I… I feel so helpless. I just thought that if we found something – anything – maybe they'd have no choice but to listen to us. To do something. I know it was a silly idea, but I just can't stop thinking about how much pain Jaspyn must be in."

Well, at least Olivia wasn't entirely delusional, thought Lara. It certainly was a silly idea. One of the silliest she'd ever heard from her. But still, she didn't want to think about the very likely possibility that Jaspyn's fate may have brought him far worse than mere pain. Had Olivia not heard of what was happening in the south? Had Olivia not understood what it all meant? For her sake though, Lara managed a gentle nod just before a knock at the door startled her.

"Come in," said Olivia and Lord Ysser Banlin walked through the door, clearing his throat as if waiting for a more proper greeting of some sort, but Lara just stared at him until he finally opened his mouth to speak.

"Lady Olivia, Lady Lara, the king summons you for the audience," he said. "It's quite urgent."

"An audience?" said Olivia. "With whom?"

"The king's family – the…err…royal family," said Ysser. "They are saying their goodbyes."

"Oh," said Lara. Her mind began to wander. "*All* of the royal family?"

Ysser lowered his head and didn't say anything. "Would you follow me, my ladies?"

Aren's audience was in the Throne Hall, an underwhelming room for its purpose. Much smaller than the vast, daunting one at Valecrest Palace, Lara supposed. The walls seemed colder and more lifeless than ever. Aren was sat on the throne, a large wooden chair, its head bearing the insignia of the Crown of Landridge. Ugly, Lara thought, much uglier than the one down in Sturrock. Then again, the Old Deryzi weren't exactly known for their grandiosity. It was simple. Wooden. She looked up to the king who sat upon it, his face sterner than she'd ever known, untouched by even a speck of emotion. Gathered around him were the more solemn faces of the royal family. Prince Skander, his wife Lady Wynter, and all three of their children. Beside them, Princess Sierra and Princess Grecia. A face was missing though, of course, and in this moment, Lara missed her Uncle Syndon more than anything. She wished she'd been able to see him one last time before the night of the siege, she wished she'd had the chance to say her goodbyes to him just as she'd come to do now, but life hadn't been so kind.

Her eyes wandered to the far left of the hall. Jeryn was stood by himself, his hands in his pockets, his face turned away from the king. Even from the back of him, she could tell he was growing up to be quite the spitting image of his father. If only Syndon were here to see it. His boy was looking more and more a Hercan every time she saw him. The light, sandy hair. The middle parting. The broad shoulders. She wondered if he'd changed his mind. She *hoped* with all her heart that he had. Or if his mind was still made up… if he was about to make the biggest mistake of his life.

"Your Majesty," said Olivia, clearing her throat. Aren stood up from his seat and the room fell silent. Each face wore a slightly different expression, each a distinct melancholy flavour. Not just the royal family either…Lady Rayne, Lord Nazeris, even the commoner Cyneric Porter.

"Come here," said Aren, gesturing to the pair of them. Lara waited until Olivia had made a move before she too obliged. His stone face wasn't nearly as stern now, up close. Lara could see cracks in the tough facade. She could tell he was holding back his feelings, trying his best to embody the king that he had to be – for his people, for his family. She'd seen it, that same look. In Jeryn's eyes. In Syndon's eyes. In her own father's eyes. She wondered if he'd live up to all those expectations. She curtsied before the king, looking him dead in the eyes as she bent her knees unlike Olivia beside her, whose gaze was lowered.

"When are they leaving?" said Olivia, her eyes still fixed on the ground rather than on the king himself.

"In a few hours or so," said Aren. "From New Castisa."

"I suppose we'd better say our goodbyes then," said Lara.

"I'd agree," the king replied.

Wynter frantically reached her arms out towards Olivia and swept her aside. "My sweet sister. Don't pay heed to the vile things they're saying on this side of the border. None of it. We've always taken you in and you're safe here, you'll continue to be safe here under my nephew's rule."

"Sister?" said Rayne from behind her, laughing. "She's about half your age."

Wynter's cheeks went rosy. "I just mean, she's a sister to us all. Don't let anyone change that, Olivia. Promise me?"

Lara didn't wait around to hear her friend's response. She quietly slipped away to the other side of the room, careful not to draw too much attention to herself. She had far more important matters to tend to. She knew she wouldn't be missed anyway, she had to be honest with herself. At the end of the day, she wasn't a royal. She wasn't the king's best friend, like Olivia. Her father wasn't on the Council. No, she wouldn't be missed.

There he was. His innocent face had a touch of arrogance she'd never seen before. She knew as soon as his eyes met hers that this wasn't going to be a pleasant conversation. His jaw was clenched, his gaze fixed. He drew in a deep breath as she approached.

"You're making a big, big mistake. Frankly, I'd never thought you to be this stupid," she said.

Jeryn Hercan's unapologetic gaze sent chills down her spine. "I have nothing further to discuss with you. Let us bid our family farewell."

Your family, she thought, but she stopped herself. "You've made up your mind then?" she said. "Do you think you're being brave? Clever? Because you aren't. The king would feel far better if you were safe.

"Don't make this about the king."

"Fine. *I* would feel far better," said Lara. "Father would feel better. I don't think you understand the position you're in. I don't think you see what being the last of the Hercans truly means for us all. Uncle Syndon didn't lay down his own life for you to go and martyr yourself, you – you inconsiderate fool. He made the ultimate sacrifice so you could live on, so you could live a long and happy life. So your children may one day bear the Hercan name. How can you – how can you be so stupid?"

"Don't tell me what my father died for, nor what he would have wanted," said Jeryn, through gritted teeth. "Where was *your father* anyway? The night of the siege? Where were you?"

"Jeryn…we've talked about this so many times now, your–"

"Then leave it be," said Jeryn. "If we've talked about it *so* many times, my mind will remain unchanged, and you can perhaps put your efforts to some better use."

"Your life will be in an immense amount of danger here! Go to Asenia with the others, you'll be safer there. If not for yourself then for your father, for his noble house. For his lineage." It was as if she were speaking to a wall. No, she'd have gotten more of a response from the wall.

"My choice to stay here *is* for my father, don't you see that? I'm not staying here for myself, nor for the king, I'm doing what my father taught me was right," he said proudly. "And as for the Hercan family, I'm not the last Hercan am I? You're alive and you're well, and close to marriage too by the sounds of it so there'll be lots of little Hercans for Uncle Perwell to play with," said Jeryn. "How can you expect me to run away across the seas with the rest of them whilst *you're* still here?"

"Because I'm not a member of the bloody royal family! We cannot *all* be royals, can we?" she said, lowering her voice to a whisper. "You're much, much more of a target than I am for that reason alone. Besides, you're a boy. Well, a man now. And as the last male Hercan heir, it's your duty to continue our legacy." He looked at her as if she'd gone mad, but she continued. "You know well that the day that I'm married off will be the last day that I'm a Hercan. You know how hard it was for my parents when I was born, and you also know that there's no way my mother can bear children now, not after the last time. And now that your father–"

"Is dead?" said Jeryn. "That's what you wanted to say, is it not?"

"That isn't…no…that…" she struggled to find the words. "I just…your father would have…"

"I don't want to discuss it any further."

"Do you not care about your legacy at all? Your heritage? Oscon Hercan once ruled this land, brought peace to it. Our ancestors built Sturrock. Heroes have come and gone generation after generation in our lineage," said Lara. "In our name."

"I care about my legacy and my name as much as my father did in his life," said Jeryn. "Names mean little, actions mean a lot more."

"Your name does not mean little."

Jeryn shrugged his shoulders. "I don't care."

"You're a fool for doing this," said Lara. She respected him, but in this moment, she was being completely honest. He really was being utterly mindless.

"I suppose I am," he said. "But at least I'm not a foolish coward."

She scoffed and turned away. To her surprise though, Olivia was stood right behind her, fiddling with her belt.

"You sound like you've got a lot on your hands," muttered Olivia.

"Not on my hands," said Lara, rolling her eyes. "I don't care. Why should I? It isn't my life he's playing with."

"Have you spoken to the others yet? Grecia?" asked Olivia.

She hadn't. "Well, we just got here."

"She was quite worried about Jeryn," said Olivia. "He's not seeing eye to eye with Aren, and he's convinced he should fight if it comes to it."

"Like I said, I don't care."

There was a stir in the corner of the room. A guard cleared his throat and the bustling farewells suddenly faded. He walked briskly up to Cyneric Porter, brushing past the rest of them as if they weren't there, and whispered something into his ear. Cyneric nodded and whispered something back. The nobles looked at each other, anxious and tired. Lara imagined the worst. Finally, Cyneric broke the silence.

"We have guests," he said to the king. Lara was rather taken aback by his directness. She didn't know him well, though, so there was that. All that time he'd spent with Aren in Asenia, perhaps they were too close for formalities. But still, it struck her as very odd indeed.

"Who?" said the king. "Guests?" He sounded almost daft. Lost for words though she couldn't imagine why.

Cyneric opened his mouth to speak, then stopped himself. "Perhaps it is more pertinent that we make sure the royal family sets off in good time," he said. He stayed incredibly silent after that, speaking only in hushed tones with the Crown Chancellor as Aren said his final goodbyes to his family. It wasn't until they had all left that Cyneric spoke out loud again, for all to hear.

"Lord Ysser," he said. "Would you escort Lady Olivia and Lady Lara to the study?"

"No," said Aren. "Let them stay. Now, who are these visitors?"

Cyneric was hesitant. "Sandaerian Ministers, from the North Parydon."

Sandaerian Ministers? At the Malysor? Lara thought she'd heard it wrong.

"What do they want?" said Aren.

"An audience."

"Why?" said Lord Ysser, seemingly out of nowhere. There was a cold air between him and Cyneric and Pennyn Runeval, though again, Lara wasn't quite sure why.

"I'm not too sure," said Cyneric. "But it can't be good eh, can it?"

"We should bring them in," said Pennyn. Lara wasn't looking at him, though. Her eyes were fixed on Ysser, whose face was stern, and his brows drawn close together. His fists were clenched but the rest of the nobles paid him no attention.

"I do agree," said Cyneric. "Would be best to hear what they have to say, perhaps make some things clear to them too."

"Why not?" said Aren. "Bring them in. But Olivia and Lara can stay."

"Of course," said Cyneric, getting up from his seat, but this time Pennyn was the one who looked hesitant. But what could he say if the king had said his piece?

In any case, Lara had no interest in hearing the word of zealots, she'd heard enough at university. She had more important matters to deal with. "Actually, I will take my leave now, if that is fine with Your Majesty?" she said.

A Pity, Indeed
Olivia

Cyneric and Pennyn walked into the room with three men, a peculiar looking bunch indeed. Olivia looked at the state of them as they trailed behind the Crown Chancellor, dirty and burnt from the northern sun. Two of them were most definitely Verenic, they had the same golden skin and brown eyes as Pennyn. Both were fairly tall, perhaps as tall as Cyneric. The third though, he was paler, stouter and had longer hair and a thick beard. He definitely didn't look like he belonged with the others, an interesting story that must be.

As they came closer, she caught a stare from one of the men – the tall one – or had it been in her head? It definitely wasn't the one with the very short hair, that was for sure. He seemed lost and angry somehow. She glanced to his side, to the tall Verenic man with curly, sleek, black hair. He was quite handsome, now that he was nearer, even if he was in tatters. He had a sharp, narrow face and kind eyes. It wasn't until she'd caught a closer look at him that she noticed that his eyes were of two different colours. The left one was brown, whilst the right was a steely grey. How incredibly bizarre? But she thought it rude to stare, she'd been taught better than that, so she broke away and let her eyes wander elsewhere.

"You stand before King Aren Aryssen the Fifth, of Landridge and East Asenia," said Pennyn Runeval. "Your Majesty, I present Kyril Sandaerzi," he said, referring to the man with the stern expression. "He comes on behalf of the North Parydon. With him are Rhedas Sandaerzi," he said, pointing to the handsome one, "and Ferus Sandaerzi," he pointed to the paler, more round man.

"Your Majesty," said Kyril Sandaerzi, bowing before the king. His hard face turned into a sly smile, much like that of a fox. He then looked Olivia right in her eyes and it made the hairs on her neck stand up. "My lady," he said softly.

"The Crown is pleased to welcome you to Ayleris, Your Eminence, what can we do for you?" said Aren.

Kyril shook his head. "None of that, Your Majesty, please. Not necessary, no. Ministers of the North Parydon are merely *servants* of the Lord. Titles and names are all given up when we devote ourselves."

"I apologise," said Aren. "That is how it is said in the High Parydon, I was just being polite. Offending you wasn't my intention, good sir."

"The Parydon of the *South*," Kyril corrected him, smiling slyly once more. "In *our* faith, we reserve *Your Eminence* for the Deryzi of Old. Only the Last Deryz Returned shall retain the rights to such. The True Deryz," he said proudly. "Ministers are merely emissaries to the realm, slaves to the Almighty."

"Again, I do apologise," said Aren. Olivia noticed that he had begun to look the slightest bit nervous. It wasn't a surprise; she'd be nervous too. She knew that the Sandaerians were now integral to the king's control in the far north, what with the bluecoats having taken half of his country. Aren had to tread carefully, very carefully. After all, to a Sandaerian, the king himself was in some ways a traitor of the faith, usurping the title Deryz. The Sandaerians were incredibly particular about little things like that, she'd read all about it in that book from Legacy Hall – *The Sandaerian Promise*. She remembered it well, but then again, she remembered all the books she'd read well.

"No need for apologies," said a different man. This time it was Rhedas Sandaerzi who had spoken. His brown and grey eyes grew wide as he took a step closer. Ysser Banlin's hand slid straight to the sheathed dagger on his side. It was clear that Rhedas saw him, but the minister continued as if nothing had happened. "Your lack of familiarity with our culture does not cause any transgression to our faith, Your Majesty."

"Yes, indeed," said Kyril. "After all, it's not every day that Your Majesty graces us with his presence this far north into Verenia."

Olivia noticed Aren raise his eyebrows. "I am of Old Verenia. My mother's heart had deep roots in the soil and sand of the Riviera, we used to come up here all the time."

"Sorry sir, I meant to cause no offence," said Kyril, looking less sorry than ever. "In any case, since you *are* in Verenia now, I thought it best if we perhaps discuss a few...a few *important* matters. What with so many months and years of being ignored by the Crown…the matters have gathered," he chuckled. "Since so many cries for help had never seemed to reach as far as the walls of Sturrock… Oh well, at least you are here now."

"Go on," said Aren, ignoring him.

"Alas, it truly is a pity. If only we hadn't lost so much before being listened to. Even now, who's to say you will listen? Who's to say you'll act on the word of some mad men from Nynnevor?"

"The past is the past," said Pennyn abruptly. "You wanted an audience with King Aren, and you have one, so use it wisely."

Olivia had not yet opened her mouth and was very happy remaining silent. She felt rather uncomfortable in the room and wished she'd left when Lara had. Perhaps she'd be able to use her time to talk some sense into Jeryn, convince him to leave. Another incredibly uncomfortable situation but one she'd have picked in a heartbeat over this one.

"Right, Lord Chancellor," said Kyril. "Ferus, tell the king what you've seen with your own eyes."

Ferus Sandaerzi started moving his hands wildly, signalling and gesturing all over like a madman. Olivia was lost, and judging by the faces around her, so were they.

"Does he not speak?" said Aren patiently.

"He is on a fast, he will not speak for another three years," said Kyril.

"Three whole years? How does he know he will not lose his voice by the time he is done with this nonsense?" said Lord Ysser, speaking for the first time since the ministers had entered the room. He sounded grumpier than usual, and that was saying something.

"Faith and devotion," said Kyril. "If he is not meant to speak again, it was the will of the Lord. He will accept it with grace."

"And he's completed two years already," muttered Rhedas. Kyril turned around to face him, as if he had spoken out of turn. "Just thought I'd point it out, the fast was of five years, he has but three left."

What a barbaric faith. Olivia didn't let her face give it away though, she didn't want to cause any disrespect to the devout men, especially as Rhedas had turned once more to look her in the eyes.

"My lady, what did you say your name was?" he said suddenly. It was chilling. She suddenly forgot her own name, staring blankly back at the minister.

"Lady Olivia Berywen," said Aren, before Olivia could open her mouth. "Will that be a problem?'

"No, sir," said Rhedas. He turned to face her again, "I just feel as if we've met each other before, but it is only because my lady looks like an old friend. A very good friend." He started shuffling on his feet where he was stood, fidgeting with his thumbs.

"Come on Ferus, carry on," said Kyril, interrupting Rhedas. "Tell the king about it, what has come to pass." Ferus continued waving and flapping his arms around frantically.

"Enough, stop this!" said Cyneric. "The rest of you aren't on this fast, so why don't *you* tell us what exactly happened? Do you honestly believe this man's hand-flapping will be of any use to the king? Explain what he has seen and why you wanted an audience."

Kyril raised his hand to Ferus, who stopped motioning and took a step back. "Right sir, of course. I know you must have heard the whispers, the stories. I will waste no time as I know there is nothing I can do or say to convince you we speak the truth. If you think we are mad, so be it. Are you familiar with Sandaerian beliefs?" said Kyril in a dark, serious tone.

Olivia looked around her. Aren nodded silently. Lord Ysser's eyebrows narrowed. Cyneric gave nothing away with his face, but Pennyn was the one who broke the silence.

"Yes, a fair amount," said the chancellor.

"*Ristezi*," said Kyril. Olivia wasn't sure what it meant. "The bridge. There was a tribe, an ancient, wicked tribe, in our faith," he added. "An ultimate evil, the essence of death, of famine, corruption and sin. Creatures that dwell in the night, those that prey on us in our sleep. We've all heard the stories, I'm sure. The Faith tells us that this tribe was banished, culled, by the banding together of saviours of all creeds; martyrs, warriors and those of truest heart – from every tribe, every tongue. It was a test that the Lord had rained down on us all, and it was only when the bridge was built – the bridge between life and death, between good and evil, Verenic and Weslin, man and woman, whomsoever. Only then, were our people able to triumph over that wickedness."

"I have heard the stories," said Pennyn. "It's similar in the Verenian faith of course."

"Dwellers?" said Aren.

Suddenly it all began to take shape in her mind.

204

"That is what you wish to speak to me about?" He sounded almost sarcastic. She wished he wasn't so dismissive, not to these men.

"The Faith tells us that one day, when we've descended into our darkest ages, the tribe will return once more," said Kyril. "Much, much more powerful than the last time. They will slowly consume us all, destroying us from the inside, burning down our homes and spilling our blood out in the streets…"

"And what would make them so strong this time?" said Cyneric. He looked worried, which was frightening because Cyneric Porter never looked worried, let alone when speaking about a matter so trivial to him as faith. He was about as far from Parydons and Aneglins as one could get.

"One will emerge," said Kyril. "One to bring us all down in flames. There will rise a leader, a commander for the forces of evil, who – if not stopped, will devastate everything we have worked for, and bring an end to life as we know it. We believe that the day has come and that it is up to us, the Verenic – the *Old Verenic* – to stop the spread of this madness before it destroys us."

Aren's face was white in horror. Somehow, Kyril seemed pleased with himself.

"And you believe Soren Ashcrest to be this leader? This …this commander of evil?" said the king.

It wasn't at all what Olivia had expected Aren to say. Though to be frank, she didn't quite know what to expect at all. This was all very strange. To Olivia's surprise, Kyril Sandaerzi let out a small laugh.

"Heavens, no!"

"I'm not sure I understand," said Aren, suddenly very annoyed, his tired eyes small and his mouth screwed up.

"The real threat does not loom over us from the blue and gold banners flying in Sturrock or Jertonshield. The real war isn't for fancy palaces in the south, nor is it for power over cities and rivers and seas…the real threat runs deeper than that. The threat to man comes from the work of demons. Creatures of the night. Bloodthirsty men. Beasts of sin," said Kyril. "They see no borders. They make no empty promises. Their army follows them out of thirst, a necessity, not out of loyalty or love for country. Soren Ashcrest may be a lot of things but warm blood runs through his veins."

Olivia's mind went foggy, and her palms were icy cold. She took a deep breath and stretched her arms down her sides, clenching her fists.

"Hold on," said Aren. "What exactly are you here to tell us? You warn us of dwellers yet give us no proof. You tell us that a leader will emerge yet tell us nothing about him."

"The perversion of death they wish to spread," said Kyril. "It is happening already. *From the shadows they will rise to instil their malevolent destiny*. It is in the scrolls. It is in the scriptures. Ferus has seen these beasts, haven't you Ferus?" He turned to look at his silent accomplice, who remained still. "He has. He's seen them with his own eyes, and he's bound by the Parydon to speak only the truth. They're causing the rot in Fencliffe, and it won't stop there. They won't–"

"This *leader*, that is prophesied to bring us death," said Aren. "Who is he? You must have some idea."

Olivia noticed Cyneric's glances over at Aren, but they fell empty. The king's gaze was fixed on the minister.

"And what do you mean *they're causing the rot?* How?" Aren had an expectant look on his face. As if he knew the answer already, he just wanted to hear it from them. But the ministers did not oblige. They remained still and silent, their heads bowed.

"We've heard quite enough," said Pennyn Runeval. "I'm not too sure the king is keen on hearing more."

"Well, actually I –" said Aren.

"No," said Kyril, looking up at the king. "Let us waste no more of His Majesty's time. I have conveyed our message; my role is fulfilled. The rest is in the hands of the Lord himself; I cannot say or do anything else to change your minds."

"The Crown has heard your worries," said Aren. "Make no mistake, we take the Sandaerian word very seriously and I will act on what you've said."

"Of course you will," said Kyril. "As your people always have," he said scathingly.

"I ask only one thing, though," said Aren. "Is the North Parydon pledged to the Crown, as it has been for generations past?"

Kyril smiled thinly. "What a question to ask, Your Majesty. Well, does the North Parydon have reason to break faith with the Crown? It really has me wondering who you've been speaking to."

"Those that I trust," said Aren bluntly. "I have no reason to believe you would betray us. Whispers, is all." His candour shocked her. "I need to know if Verenia is united if we are to win this fight. If I am to rule *all* of Landridge under one banner."

"It was our combined efforts and joined forces that abolished the wretched Federation in the past, and we need to come together as one to fight that evil, or indeed any evil, again," said Pennyn Runeval. "If what you are saying about dwellers is true, to defeat them we will need to come together. It is just as your prophecy says."

Kyril shuffled on his feet. "There is no doubt in my mind that we will work well together, Your Majesty."

"Develyn Asellar," said Aren callously and the air went cold as ice. Kyril Sandaerzi's face went grey, and he turned to look at his accomplice Rhedas, whose eyes were wider than ever. "What do you know of her?" said the king.

"A healer, Your Majesty. From Veytora. I am all but certain we all know her."

"Just a healer?" said Aren, making Olivia shudder. "And what of her threat to my rule?"

"I will not lie to you," said Kyril. "There are some who do believe that the Last Deryz has returned. More than some, actually. Many have faith in the girl, but none can be sure."

Aren took in a sharp deep breath. "By the oath the North Parydon swore to my ancestor after we fought together to defeat the Old Federation, the only Deryz for the Verenian is the one that sits on the Throne of Landridge," said the king.

"It's a pity we aren't Verenian," said Kyril Sandaerzi, equally irritated. "For generations you drove us out of our homes, severing the ties between the North Parydon and the so-called *High* Parydon…cutting deeper the divisions that separated the Sandaerians from the rest of Verenia – and now – now when it suits you best, you would happily do the opposite? Don't tell me that my brothers and I are Verenian when you have spent centuries trying to prove to us otherwise. And as for the Asellar girl, if some would believe their Saviour has returned, let them believe. What threat does she pose to you or your rule? These dark times call for a return to faith, a return to how things used to be…"

"Well, I suppose…" came a feeble voice. It was Rhedas Sandaerzi, his gaze lowered. Olivia couldn't help but think that he must have been mad, madder than the other two. Sort of like an old dog she'd had once who'd started going blind and begun to chase rabbits around wildly. Rhedas suddenly looked up at her for some reason and it made her shiver once more.

"Do you have something to say?" said Aren.

"Well, no, just… well, her threat. I wouldn't say she isn't…"

"That's enough, Rhedas," said Kyril.

"What? It is true, I know it is. I've seen it. She brings the winds, the earth itself trembles when –"

"I said that is enough," said Kyril again, now livid.

But Rhedas didn't stop. "She brings the winds, she does," he said and to Olivia's astonishment, his piercing gaze once again fell on her. "And the storm, it follows. The *key*," he said. "You need the key." She felt her heart race as the mad priest's eyes widened, and the blacks grew.

"A great peril!" he shouted. His voice echoed around the room and Kyril's face went white with fear. Even Ferus looked as if he'd seen a ghost.

"A dynasty in ruin. What a pity, indeed," Rhedas continued, glaring at Olivia the whole time. She tried to look away from him, but her eyes wouldn't move. She felt stuck, frozen in time. Her heart beat faster and faster as he took another step closer to her. "Neither the winds, nor the free. Peril."

Olivia finally worked up the courage to speak for the first time. "What do you want?" Her voice was shaky, and she knew she must have sounded frightened, but it was all she could manage.

"Under the stars, yes," he said. "And the Aspen trees too." His face was absolutely vacant, his eyes completely empty. "You will face a great peril under the stars of deceit, it is written that way. But it is only then, only then can it happen. Only then can it *begin*. Blood of the free, blood of the winds, blood of the shadows. The lynxes will fight till the dawn. One will rally the pale-faced demons as the Skyvern flies once more. Great peril below, great peril all around…"

"RHEDAS!" shouted Kyril. His deep voice made Olivia jump. She wished it had come earlier though, before the mad priest had lashed out. She tried not to piece together what he'd said, the little respect she'd had for him was gone now that she'd realised that he truly was mad. A pity, indeed.

"Right, I've had just about enough of all this!" shouted Ysser Banlin. Olivia turned to look at the man, he was seething, his face pink and his forehead sweaty. "Come on," he said to the Sandaerian Ministers. "Out with you. The lot of you." He didn't give them a chance to speak and ushered them like sheep, slamming the door behind them.

"I'm sorry, Your Majesty," said Ysser to the king. "I don't think you should distract yourself with the petty, distorted beliefs of fanatics. I tried to be respectful, I tried to listen to reason, but see, this is what happens. Always." He turned to face Olivia, who felt the tears coming but she held them tightly in. It wasn't sadness, it wasn't even fear, really. She just felt overwhelmed with it all.

"Are you alright, my lady?" asked Ysser.

She nodded.

The Beggar
Laris

It was dark in the streets. It always was in the evenings, these days. The idiot king and his idiot family had cut off the south, left them with no means of getting any oil or any other goods for that matter. His stomach rumbled and Laris groaned. Food was scarce too, of course. He'd bet it wasn't in the far north where the idiot king sat, though.

"Mercy, please."

He felt a sudden grip around his right leg and shook it wildly.

"Mercy!" the girl looked up at him. She was skinny, clearly hadn't eaten in days.

"What do you want?"

For a moment or two, the lass just looked up at him, tears in her eyes.

"Well?"

"Mercy, sir. Spare change?"

"No, I don't have any change to spare," he said coldly. "Do you?"

And the girl let loose, wailing with no regard for where she was, in the midst of the Arvendon market. Well, it was barely a market now.

"Geddoffme!" he yelled, shaking his leg free of her. "Where are your parents? Your family?"

"All dead."

"Then who's at home?"

"No home, sir. Home burnt down. Please sir…a loaf of bread? A cob of corn?"

"Do I look like a farm hand to you?"

"I can't go hungry another night," she said. "Me stomach hurts and I feel sick all the time. I fainted this morning, hit me head on the cobblestones." She showed him the scar on her forehead.

"We're all hungry, girl. I can't help you." He started walking away from her. He didn't really know where he was going but he trotted on. Behind him, little footsteps followed.

"Mercy."

"I thought I told you I can't help you, girl. Fuck off!"

There were two gunshots and then the little girl let out a bloodcurdling shriek, covering her ears with her little hands.

"Is the girl bothering you?" came a dark and serious voice. It was a damned bluecoat mounting his damned rifle on his shoulder. The one next to him slapped him across the face.

"Henrut, I thought I told you we are to waste no bullets."

"Aye, but it wasn't a waste," said the one called Henrut.

"Not a waste?" the other scowled. "Using precious ammunition to scare little girls is precisely what the First Warden's men would call a waste." He turned to face Laris before eyeing the girl beside him.

"What business do you have with this man?" he said to the girl. She said nothing, simply shook her head and cried. "Well?" Nothing. He turned back to Laris. "What business have you with this girl?"

"No business, sir. No business."

"Is she bothering you then?" Henrut said once more, a menacing glare in his eyes. He lifted his weapon and pointed it at the lass.

"No," said Laris. "No bother."

"Aye, well keep it moving will you," said Henrut. "You're sure you don't want us to take care of her?"

"No," said Laris. "I was just about to take her to the shop."

The girl's eyes sparkled as she smiled up at him. The innocence of children, it always made him marvel.

The bluecoats nodded and left them. Laris all but sighed in relief. Another day alive in the wretched city was a day he could celebrate as a win in his books.

"Where are we going?" said the girl.

He scowled at her. "Nowhere. I only said that to get them to leave, else you'd be off with them to who knows where, or worse dead."

The girl looked at him sadly. "The way things are, perhaps dead wouldn't be worse at all."

Dammit. "Right, follow me then."

She smiled again. "Follow you where?"

It was a good question. He hadn't any money to give her, he hadn't lied about that. He hadn't any food, not really. Even the woods were sparse now, the bluecoats had already taken care of many of the rabbits and deer. His own last meal had been a chicken he'd stolen from one of the Zaldroni merchants at Wyntock End. A chicken that was to be sold to a bluecoat and his family, he'd later found out. He'd roasted it, the chicken, in a fire that he burnt far from the city, deep in the woods where the bluecoats scarcely went. He'd been lucky. That Zaldroni merchant, however, did not share his luck. He was dead on the street this morning, and his shop burnt to a crisp. Laris shuddered at the memory of it. But he looked back to her, the lass, and felt heavy.

"Just follow me."

He knew the markets beneath the bridge would be emptier now. Or at least, the ones left behind were the weaker ones. Sons and daughters and old, frail men and women looking after their families' stalls. He felt inside his jacket pocket to see if the knife were still there, it was.

"I thought you said you had no money," said the girl.

"Aye, I don't," he said.

"Then how…" her eyes widened, and she grabbed onto his arm tightly. "You…you are going to steal!"

"Yes," he said blankly. "I am."

"You shouldn't steal," the girl said.

"Perhaps if you'd have stolen a little more you wouldn't be begging today."

"I'd rather be a beggar than a thief." She snatched her hand away from his arm. "You're just like them, the looters."

"Girl, don't be daft. You know you need food and if this is the only way you are going to get it, there's little you can do about it."

"I can beg some more," she said, almost proudly.

"And how far has that gotten you?" he smirked. "You just stand here and keep a look out. You see, hear or smell any of those bluecoats and you come and find me. Understand? And don't make a noise."

"I will not help you steal."

"Fine, then stay hungry and die." He turned away and crossed under the bridge.

It was darker than ever in the shade of the Arvendon Bridge, just perfect. There was a gentle rhythmic patter of the water dripping from the broken pipes above, but other than that, almost silence. Nothing like the bustling centre it once was, it was a shell of its former glory. There was a foul smell too, a smell he'd come to know very well. The smell of decaying flesh. Round the corner, there it was. A pile of bodies, lifeless and still. There was a dark pool of blood under them too, some were fresh.

There was a crackle from behind him, he'd barely heard it. He continued forward, slowly. He knew better than to turn around. Perhaps it was a cat, this place had been full of them once. There it was again, a gentle rustle.

Then there was a loud crash.

"Fuck!" It was a lad's voice.

"Get him, he's over there!" The bluecoats emerged, four of them. They hadn't seen Laris yet, he had time. He ran for cover behind a stall, gripping tightly to his dagger.

The lad running held a loaf of bread in the one arm, a sword in another. It was a heavy-looking sword, not the kind you'd find in the slums of the city. Its shine was unmatched, its hilt encrusted with precious stones and polished wood.

"Don't just stand there!" One of the men fired his rifle three times.

"Aaaarrgghhh!" the lad yelled, the bread falling out of his arm. The men chasing him held spears and swords and daggers, except the one with the rifle. Was that how poor they'd truly become? He'd never know.

The rifleman fired once more and the lad dove to the ground, rolling over the puddle of blood. He rose up, covered in it. His side was red with his own blood. The boy looked familiar, Laris had seen his bright red hair before.

"Seize him! Now!" The rest of the men started to form a bit of a circle around him. The boy clambered backwards, stumbling over a dead man's arm. He had the fear in his eyes, the fear Laris had seen all over the city. But this boy's fear, it was different.

The boy swung his sword hard and jabbed it forward, just about slicing a bluecoat's arm. It was pathetic, the bluecoat swung his own sword forward and cut the boy's thigh right down the middle. The boy screamed in agony, clutching for dear life at his thigh, blood spurting between his fingers.

It was none of Laris' business. He should just let them settle their quarrels and be on his merry way. But the fear in the boy's eyes, *it was different.*

Laris took a deep breath. Without thinking much of it he launched himself forward, at the rifleman first, grabbing him by his collar and swinging him around. The swordsman lunged forward at him, but Laris was quicker, he pushed the rifleman out and the sword went cleanly through his chest. The swordsman watched in horror as his commander keeled over, his chest bloody.

"Arrgghh!" the man shouted wildly, pulling his sword out and jabbing it forward once more.

The boy jumped up, swinging his sword again, faster. This time, he didn't miss. He struck the sword through the man's neck and kicked himself free, grabbing the other sword.

"Look out!"

Laris turned but the other two had already gotten too close, he swerved as the spear came forward sharply, but it landed in his shoulder.

"Fuck!" he fell to his knees, grabbing his shoulder. It was not the worst pain he'd ever had, far from it, but it stung like hell.

The lad pounced at once, swinging both his swords as if he were dancing. The other two were faster, but he sliced the side of one's face all the same.

Laris leapt to his feet and threw his fist forward, but the grimy man grabbed it, pulling him closer. Laris used his other hand to drive his dagger forward, but he was too late. He was thrown back, far back. His spine felt as if it'd shattered as it hit the cobblestones below and his shoulder stung worse than ever. He tried to clamber to his feet. The lad wielded both swords seamlessly, backing away from the mad men. But the one with the spear was too quick. He drove it in his belly and twisted it around. The lad wailed, it was agonising to the ear. Dammit. Laris looked around for an escape else he'd be next. His dagger was nowhere near him, he had nothing to use for a weapon. And these men, these men were stronger than him, and that was saying something.

The lad fell to the ground and the one with the dagger stepped towards him, ready to drive it through his chest. Then there was a twang of a bowstring and the man fell. Another twang and the one beside him fell too. Two arrows stuck out of the dead mens' chests as they lay beside the dying lad.

Where had the arrows come from?

"Fuck, what's happened?!" it was a woman, a foreign woman. She cursed loudly, waving her hands around and saying something in a tongue Laris did not know at all. "What have you done?"

Laris couldn't get any words out.

"Jaspyn," the woman tutted as she approached the dying lad. "What have they done to you?" She shook her head. That is when Laris recognised her, Azara. Azara Urisci who'd met him in the woods.

The boy croaked. He couldn't get his words out either.

"Shhh," said Azara. "Try to stay quiet." She cursed some more and muttered to herself in her tongue.

"The...the b-bluecoats..." said the boy. "They...they kept...following me."

"Hmm?" said Laris, half-crawling towards the lad. Azara hushed the boy some more, but he went on.

"Th-they wouldn't let me go...they...they..." His eyes were closing.

Azara waved her hands around some more. "This boy, this boy is going to die unless we do something."

That much was obvious. "I'm not a healer, I don't know if you are?"

"This is no time for joking," Azara slapped him. "This boy has lost too much blood, his end is near."

"What do you want me to do?" Perhaps he could take the bread and run. He should never have revealed himself. This was not his war, not his battle.

"I might have a way, to...to save him," said Azara. "But it doesn't end there."

"What do you mean it doesn't end there?" Laris was pretty certain it had already ended.

"What I mean," she snapped. "Is that they are after him and they won't stop." Why was a lad from Arvendon so important to Aschrest's men? Why was he so important to the Uressi woman? So important that she'd carried a photograph of him that day in the woods.

"Hmm." Laris grumbled.

"So, we will need to fake his death," said Azara. "Dead boy means bluecoats will stop searching. Will stop following.'

It sounded absolutely mad, and he'd play no part in it. He'd take the bread and he'd run.

"I need to…" she started muttering to herself in her tongue again. "I need to take him into the woods."

The woman was madder than the men who'd come to kill him. "The boy is dead," said Laris. "I don't know how you will save him."

"He isn't yet dead."

"He will be by the time you get to the woods."

"Well, that is the only way I can save him," she snapped. "Now hold this while I lift him," she handed him her bow.

"Now, hold on. I can hold him," he said. "The lad looks heavy, we can carry him together."

But Azara had already swung the lad over her shoulder. "Hmm?"

Night had fallen and there wasn't a bluecoat in sight. Laris had been lucky, yet again. He wondered when the pot of luck would run out.

"You will wait out here," said Azara.

"Why?"

"Shut up and wait," she said. "We have already lost so much time."

The whole thing was pointless. The boy looked paler than ever, and Laris was all but sure his body'd be cold by now. There was no way his heart was still pumping blood, but still Azara insisted she knew what she was doing.

"If they come, kill them," said Azara. "Don't think twice about it." And she disappeared into the woods, the boy over her shoulder. It gave him time to think, to reflect. He'd been around for long enough to know not to trust so easily. Not even those who might appear to help. What was a Uressi doing this far south? Lurking in the shadows and stalking a boy, a boy who he'd seen in that palace all those weeks ago? Had she been stalking him too? He'd seen her twice now.

The moon was high in the sky by the time Azara Urisci emerged from the woods, the boy cradled in her arms. He was still pale, but he looked peaceful now, as if he were sleeping.

"It is done," she said as she rested him upon the leaves scattered below. Her hands were bloody, she wiped them against the leaves and the soil and then patted them against her own purple cloak. "It was near impossible."

Laris eyed the boy carefully. He was breathing, so she was not lying at least. It was curious, how had she done it?

The boy's eyes opened wide and he gasped loudly before sputtering and coughing.

"Sit up, boy," said Azara, giving him a hand.

"W-w…."

"Hmm?"

"Water," he said.

Azara laughed out loud. "Water won't help you now, my boy."

"Why not?" said Laris.

Azara said nothing at first. She simply got up and stretched her arms, swinging them from side to side. "We need to go."

"Go? Go where?" said Laris.

"North," said Azara. "As soon as is possible. After we fake the boy's death, of course."

"What?" said the lad but Azara hushed him.

"It will all make sense to you soon," she said.

North? "Will it be wise? Travelling to Ayleris?"

"I'm afraid we are travelling a little further than that."

"I'm not going to Uresso or Asmon or whatever barbaric wasteland you come from," said Laris, slapping his thighs. They'd never make it back into this country.

"Barbaric?" Azara laughed, but it was more of a cackle. "Did you and I see the same Sturrock today? The same Arvendon?" She sighed loudly. "Don't worry, we are not going to any barbaric wastelands. Besides, nobody is forcing you to go. The boy and I can travel alone, I am sure."

"We haven't any food," said Laris. "The boy's bread, he dropped it in those markets."

"I will find you food," said Azara. "Stay right here. And if any of them come, you will kill them." She wagged her finger at Laris.

"Yes, yes, I will kill them."

The boy looked utterly terrified. He sat by the small fire, shivering. His teeth chattered too, but it wasn't all that cold. Nowhere near as it could have been in Sturrock's woods, this was mild.

"What's your name?" said Laris.

"Jaspyn." The boy clutched his thigh.

"Does it still hurt?"

"Less," said Jaspyn.

There was still time. Laris could still run, leave the boy to the mad woman. It was none of his business, after all. It wasn't *him* the bluecoats were after. But then…why were they after the lad? Because he'd once had friends in high places? The boy was practically a beggar now, stealing bread from markets.

"What of your parents?" said Laris. "Your family? They still around?" He dreaded the answer.

"Yes," said Jaspyn. "But I haven't been able to see them, not since the night of the siege."

"That is a long time," said Laris. "Why haven't you gone home? Where have you been?"

Jaspyn sighed. "I've been on the streets since," he said. "Can't go home."

"Why not?"

"Because they haven't left me alone, the bluecoats. I don't know what they want from me, they've tried to kill me twice already and they never want to talk. They went to my house, the morning after it all happened…the bluecoats kept asking my parents about me, where I was and when they told them they didn't know, they threatened them. To hurt them, or maybe worse."

"And how do you know?" said Laris. "If you were not there."

"I was watching, listening, the first few days at least. They never knew I was there…I didn't want to put them in any danger."

"And you still don't," said Laris. "Do you know her? That woman?"

Jaspyn shook his head.

How peculiar. "And do you trust her?"

"Well, she saved my life."

"And do you trust her?"

"I don't know."

"That's a better answer," said Laris. "Nor do I."

"Do you know her?" said Jaspyn.

"Hmm." Laris was faced with a choice. "I saw her once in the woods, when she'd first arrived in the city."

"What was she here for?" said Jaspyn.

"You," said Laris. "She had a photograph of you in her pocket."

"Do you think…do you think she's been following me?" said Jaspyn.

Laris nodded. "Maybe your...*pals* from the palace have sent her, to find you."

Jaspyn shook his head. "I've never seen her before, nor have I heard of her. And if that were the case, she'd be taking me to Ayleris, no further."

"I say," Laris turned his head to make sure there wasn't a soul in sight before lowering his voice to a mere whisper. "I say we run. Not now, but after we have faked your death. I imagine she can help us with that."

"Run?" said Jaspyn, gulping. "Run where?"

"I don't know," said Laris. "Astonkirk? Jertonshield? I've lost count of which city flies Ashcrest's banner."

"I know one that certainly does not. Ayleris."

The Nynnevor Keep
Aren

"**D**elirium and general insanity, if I had to guess," said Pennyn, but Aren wasn't entirely convinced. There was something about the outburst that had made him shudder. Rhedas was mad, this much was certain, but it wasn't completely clear how much of what he was saying was a result of his lunacy. "All those peculiar fasts and rituals they have, it's bound to have an effect," said Pennyn.

"But what if there is some truth in what he had to say?" said Olivia suddenly, as if having read Aren's mind. "Sorry, I just don't think it is particularly useful for us to dismiss him like that. They came from afar; they must have come for good reason."

Pennyn glared at her before turning to Aren.

"There isn't any use following the word of a madman, or a fanatic, we have wars to fight," said Pennyn. "We don't have the time to worry about the North Parydon. Nor this healer from Veytora."

"I'm not completely inept," said Aren. "I won't blindly follow the word of anyone, be that a priest, *or* a chancellor. I know we have great threats in the south and the west, but that does not mean we have only one enemy."

"You're right," said Cyneric. "The most naïve assumption we can make is that this is a fight of good against evil."

"Precisely," said Aren. "It is far more complicated, we need to take action now. I'm going to announce a formal declaration of war."

"I'm going to assume you have made a decision on your Arms Counsel then?" said Pennyn. "Can't declare anything without an Arms Counsel."

In truth he had made his decision some time ago. "My uncle," said Aren. "Mentos."

Pennyn looked at him the same way he'd looked at Rhedas earlier. "Mentos Jeffyrs? I know we don't always see eye-to-eye, but are you sure that is the right decision? Do you think your uncle is capable of leading this kingdom into a war unlike any it has seen before?"

"My decisions are final."

"Aren, while I do respect your decision, I will point out that your uncle's reputation precedes him," said Cyneric. "Any vessel he's been on has ended up at the bottom of the sea. Yes, he's got years of battle experience in Asenia, there isn't any denying that, but, well… I don't usually pay much heed to rumours but…"

"He isn't very well liked, yes I know," said Aren. He also knew that his uncle wasn't the best strategist. Not the brightest either, even Rayne had said so. "But the truth is, I've got few people I can trust. Mentos is the only person I can trust outside of this room who has any proper experience in battle. He'll have Cyneric and Lord Ysser to advise him, but they have their own parts to play of course. We have all got our own duties. This way I don't have to worry about another Gavyn Escos."

"And what about Lady Rayne?" Cyneric replied.

"She has no experience in battle," said Aren. "Besides, she has the Department to look after."

His advisors nodded at him, though he couldn't tell if it were out of compulsion or genuine agreement.

"I'll send word out to Mentos, then. I can have him in Ayleris within the week."

"Sooner would be better."

"Actually," said a voice as the door creaked opened. "That won't be a problem. Mentos is already on his way." It was Lady Rayne. She held a grave but sorrowful expression as she entered the room and Aren didn't know why. Surely this was good news? He braced himself for the worst.

"What's the matter?" said Aren.

"Nothing, Aren," she smiled kindly. "I can send out word to him as soon as you want me to," she said. "And when you get the chance, I'd like to speak with you privately."

"Of course," he said. "But first, I'd like to tell you all of another decision I've taken. One that concerns the Crown Envoy."

"Crown Envoy?" said Olivia. "Is that not your Uncle Skander?"

"He cannot do it from Asenia, can he?" said Aren. "And it is an important seat, especially now. With him gone, we'll need another face to represent the Crown. A face with an important name, a respectable family."

"And who did you have in mind?" said Pennyn.

"Lara Hercan," said Aren, and once more his advisors looked at him as if he was a mindless child.

"Out of all the people you could have chosen to represent the monarchy," said Cyneric, chuckling softly. "You choose a *Hercan* heir. A girl whose ancestors built the Old Federation. There's irony in it isn't there."

It was precisely this irony which made it perfect. But Pennyn didn't seem to appreciate that irony. His voice was dark and serious.

"Oscon Hercan started the very institution that slowly erased Verenic culture, one step at a time, everywhere it went," said Pennyn. "We celebrate him now, of course, because he was the lesser evil of the time. We *had to* work with him and the old bluecoats to abolish the Sandaerian Dues. But that doesn't change what his family did, does it? There are still many in Verenia who wouldn't appreciate the Stars of the Free shining down upon them from up here."

Aren shook his head. "A Hercan waving the banner of the Crown?" said Aren. "That is powerful. That is how we will win more of the southerners, especially the common ones."

"And lose some more of the northerners?" said Pennyn.

"We shall see, won't we?" Aren replied.

"A risk," said Lady Rayne, toying with her fingers. "But certainly not an unreasonable one. Why not your cousin Jeryn, though? He seems like a sensible lad."

"He's a royal, it wouldn't send the same message," said Aren. "We don't want the Envoy looking like a puppet." He knew though, that that was exactly what the Envoy was.

"And is that it for your council, then?" said Olivia feebly. She'd been quite quiet throughout.

"Yes, I don't see the urgency to appoint a Justice Counsel or a Health Counsel for the moment. We are in a war, so... as soon as we can get Mentos here and –"

"And that is all?" she said. She looked frustrated, for some reason. Aren looked back at her with a blank and confused look.

"Have you all forgotten? What was said in this very room not too long ago?" she said.

"The Asellar girl?" said Aren.

"No, Aren. Not the bloody Asellar girl. I'm talking about what that man told us about the graver threat we are all facing. The dwellers," said Olivia. "Don't you want to reconsider having Lord Nazeris on your Council now? You've invited these people into your home, just as your mother did in Sturrock."

It was very unlike her, this outburst. Pennyn scowled at her, ready to open his mouth but Rayne stopped him at once.

"My dear girl," she said. "While I, more than anyone, sympathise with your worries," she looked at Aren for a brief moment. "And I, again more than anyone, understand that there are bigger powers at play here than playing battle with Soren Ashcrest," she added. "Rumours and *hearsay* scarcely ever help improve difficult situations. The rumours surrounding House Nazeris are of no good to anybody. There is no use in believing them. That is what you are speaking of, I assume?"

Olivia nodded.

"You've got Zaldroni blood in you too. Are we to lock you away until you prove you will never turn? No. Because the rumours about the Zaldroni descending from dwellers were all fabricated. A lie, a cruel lie. It was a troubling time, so a convenient falsehood helped to justify the Exile," she said. She shook her head wildly and tutted. "House Nazeris itself descends from the line of House Asellar. The Old Deryzi. Why do you think their crest bears the lynx? Same as the Asellars. Would you truly believe them to be of ill intent?"

"A perversion," said Olivia. "The white lynx represents purity. Theirs is bordered by a red stripe. What do you suppose that means?"

"Very little," said Rayne. "What do you even know about the ancient dwellers that supposedly walked this land?"

"Well, I know about Jerton's sacrifice, of course. We're all taught about it. Tilas Jerton's victory against them, against the dwellers. It's what led to the Exile."

"A game of politics and fear is what led to the Exile," said Rayne, shaking her head once more. "The Federation instilled that fear in the hearts of millions of people, the fear that they used to further their influence. Gain more power, gain in riches."

"So, are you suggesting there were never any dwellers here at all?" said Olivia.

"Maybe there were, maybe not. It doesn't matter," she shook her head. "The point is…that fear was used to cast aside people based on trivial matters like their blood and their name. They were ripped from their homes, attacked in the streets, given orders to cross the Strait into Zaldron, or to die. They were slaughtered at the hands of the bluecoats. We mustn't let that same fear be used by anybody ever again – judging the Nazeris family because of their blood and their name would be foolish and dangerous. I know Arcadius and I can tell you that there is *no way* he is a bad person."

Olivia stayed silent for a moment, moving her eyes around the ceiling as if thinking about something, then she spoke up.

"Aren. I've just…just remembered something."

"What?" said Aren.

"Do you remember the time when we were sat in your study," she said. "And I had that book…the book I got from Legacy Hall?"

He couldn't remember it at all. The weeks before the siege had become a blur.

"*The Sandaerian Promise*, it was called."

"Yes, barely," he said. Why was she talking about some book from weeks gone bye?

"I think that it may have had some clues about these dwellers and how they are thought to have been defeated. Something about a key, I forget…"

"Where is it now? The book?" said Cyneric.

"Legacy Hall," she frowned. "But Aren, I remember it referring to something, some alleged key… But it wasn't actually a key."

"What are you talking about?" said Pennyn.

"A way to put an end to them," said Olivia seriously. "Once and for all. I didn't read the whole chapter because I was so determined to find out more about…I wish I had kept it with me."

"You're sure of it?" said Cyneric. "That it was talking about these creatures? And that there is indeed a way?"

"Yes, I told you," said Olivia. The madness in her voice hadn't dwindled in the slightest. "A *key*. I knew I'd heard it somewhere, that Rhedas man, he said something about a key. The book said the same thing, that there is a key that can…that can stop them." She sighed loudly. "I wish I'd held on to it, I didn't think I'd need it.

There's no way we can get it from the palace is there? Sturrock is unsafe."

Pennyn, Cyneric and Rayne all shared a look.

"You are sure this book will be of use?" said Rayne. "This is important, girl."

"Yes, yes I'm sure of it!"

"The Nynnevor Keep, Aren," said the chancellor finally.

"Pardon me?" said Aren.

"It's a collection, a private one, of old books, scriptures, some artefacts, from the days of the Dues. It was one of the few things that survived the devastation up there, which is why it's a secret kept amongst only a few," said Rayne.

But before she could say any more, there was a knock at the door and a familiar face walked in, a guard that he recognised. He nodded at Lady Rayne. With a worried look on her face, she got up and cleared her throat. She walked over to the guard and tapped him on the shoulder twice as if to thank him. "Just a few moments, I do apologise," she said, finally turning to face Aren before shutting the door behind her.

"What was that all about?" asked Aren. "Never mind. Where is this… *Keep*? Can we find out if this book is there?" he said.

Pennyn shook his head. "Unfortunately, that isn't how it works. Somebody would have to go there. If it's called '*The Sandaerian Promise*' though, I'm all but certain you will find it there," he said.

"Oh, why?" said Aren.

"Because the Keep, it is beneath the North Parydon itself," said Pennyn. "Behind the Falls."

"Oh," said Aren. "Well, that is a shame. There's little we can do to retrieve it from there. Especially after the audience we just had with the Sandaerians."

"That is truly awful, I really think that it might help us, the book," said Olivia. "Or it might give us more information, tell us if there is any truth to what these priests are saying."

"Well," said Pennyn. "There are secret ways in, ways very few are familiar with," he said. "Through the tunnels."

"The tunnels beneath Ayleris?" said Aren.

"They're everywhere," said Pennyn. "All over Verenia. Of course, it'd be a long journey, an incredibly difficult one, but not impossible by any means."

"Through the tunnels all the way to the Falls?" said Olivia. "That's miles and miles away!"

"No, of course not. You would tunnel out of Ayleris, that's what the tunnels are for, much like the ones we used in Sturrock. Where do you think the old bluecoats got their ideas from? They were there so that the Deryzi could slip out of the castle into the safety of the darkness of night, if the need arose," said Pennyn. "That bit even a fool could do, even me. Then it's not too far by road to the Falls, and nobody would notice anybody had passed from the city gates. The tunnels *into Nynnevor* though, they're a lot harder to get through. Only a few are capable of getting in and out without being caught."

"That sounds very dangerous. Aren's the king, why can't he just order them to give us the book? After all, it is just a book," said Olivia. "Especially since we want it to fight *their* war. The one they brought to us."

"The Sandaerians are a very proud people," said Pennyn. "And not always to be trusted. *Ordering* them to do anything would be foolish."

"I could go," said Cyneric suddenly. "I know the tunnels. I've been into Nynnevor before. No one would notice I'm gone, it'd be a day at most."

"Are you sure?" said Aren. "I couldn't possibly ask you to put yourself in danger."

"No danger," said Cyneric. "I know the tunnels well. I'll take a motorcar there from outside the city walls, it'll be quick…"

"Maybe we should ask somebody else…"

"You cannot trust anybody else. Nor can you expect Pennyn to go, even if he were able to get through the tunnels into Nynnevor because too many would notice he were gone."

Aren felt he had no choice but to agree to it. "Then I wish you the very best of luck."

"I shall leave before dusk then," said Cyneric.

The door swung open once more and Lady Rayne entered the room, her head bowed. "Aren, may I have that word with you now?" she said, rather restless. "I'm not so sure it can wait, if you're done here."

"Yes, my lady. Could we get some privacy please?" said Aren to the others.

"Actually, perhaps Olivia'd ought to stay," said Rayne.

"Oh."

As the doors shut behind his advisors, Aren couldn't help but hold his breath for the worst – that's what being king had taught him, if anything. Had the bluecoats taken another city? Had she found another traitor amidst the castle's walls?

"I…" she croaked, her eyes misty and sad. This must have been one of the only times Aren had ever seen Rayne struggle with words. "I don't know how to say this."

"Just say it," said Aren, as he watched Olivia's heart sink with his own.

"Jaspyn Fenwern," said Rayne. "He's…"

"No," said Olivia, shaking her head. "No!"

"He's dead." She was quick about it. She looked Aren in the eyes as her words pierced through his heart. He took Olivia's hand into his own and held back his own tears. He stared at Rayne emptily and desperately fought the urge to break down.

"I received word this morning…that our forces were questioning a man who claimed he recognised the picture we'd sent down," said Rayne. "He said he witnessed something…several days after the Siege. Something awful."

"What…what did he see exactly?" said Aren, barely managing to get the words out.

"After the Siege, it was really bad down there. Arvendon, Hartyl Street, they had it the worst. Not just the bluecoats, even those pledged to the Crown, looters, it was a twisted mess. This witness, Tyrus, he was in an alleyway in Arvendon. He saw Jaspyn in the thick of it, he's sure, unmistakeable blazing hair and all. He was surrounded by looters, near the bridge," she said.

"Looters?"

She nodded. "Led by some dark-skinned woman. They weren't bluecoats. He reckons they knew him, the way he was ambushed." She paused for a moment, and there was a chilling, eerie silence.

"And they killed him?" said Aren.

"Well, no. He wasn't alone. There was a man apparently, I've already asked for a detailed description. Pale of face. Dishevelled. Scruffy, brown hair. He attacked Jaspyn and wouldn't let anyone near him, mad in his rage. As soon as the looters came close, he'd fight them off."

"Wait, he was protecting him?"

Rayne shook her head sadly. "It's unclear what his motives were, perhaps a lunatic. He…"

"How did Jaspyn die?" said Olivia, having stopped sobbing. Aren looked over at her. She was red, her eyes weren't filled with sorrow, they were filled with fury, her fists clenched tight. He looked at the red blotches where her nails were pressed into her pale skin. It looked as if it would've hurt her very much, but you couldn't tell, looking at her face. She was angry, not in pain.

"The man, the mad one, he did it," said Rayne. "We still aren't sure why he was fighting off the others, probably insanity, and from what the witness said it didn't seem like Jaspyn knew him either." There was another cold silence, as Rayne lowered her gaze. "Olivia, you're bleeding!"

Aren looked over at the dark blood dripping from her palms from where her nails had dug deep into her flesh.

"He can't be gone," she sobbed. "This isn't how his story ends. We don't even know if this man is telling the truth."

Rayne took in a deep breath. "I'm afraid it's true. We found the body exactly where the witness said it'd be." She took another pause before continuing. "Charred beyond recognition, but his parents are sure it is him."

Olivia shuddered and turned away, her bloody hands covering her face.

"His parents have been told? It must be so, so awful for them," said Aren. He tried not to think about it, but his mind kept picturing Jaspyn's frail, broken parents, already distraught over everything else that had happened to their family.

"Did you… Did you say *charred*?" said Olivia.

"The rumours of the dweller sightings in the south," she said, sighing. "The city is paranoid, the Sandaerians have made sure of it. It's not a secret anymore, this dread of the nightdwellers. The zealots have been making the most of the situation, striking their fear into whoever might buy it. It's caused people to start burning bodies in the streets out of fear that they may rise as the undead. We think that's what happened to Jaspyn's body."

Aren drew a deep breath, his lungs numb and his skin cold.

"I know what it is like to lose a brother," said Lady Rayne, stepping up towards them and placing a gentle arm on Aren's shoulder. "I cannot express in words how sorry I am, both of you. I wish I could tell you that this wasn't true, I wish I could tell you that there may still be hope that the witness was lying, or that we hadn't found the remains… I can't fathom how incredibly awful this must be and I want you to know that I'm here for you, for both of you."

"Coward," said Aren, and then immediately wished he hadn't. Rayne looked at him, sad and confused. "The witness," he added. "To watch such a thing happen, to watch it unfold from a distance, from the safety of an alleyway, hidden away, and not do anything. Not intervene. Cowardly."

Rayne and Olivia stayed silent. He wished they'd agree with him, he wished they'd tell him he was right, that the witness was to blame as well. Just as complicit. But they just stared at him. Eventually, Olivia broke her silence.

"After so long?" she said. "His remains were in the streets, in the streets of Arvendon. Beneath the bridge where the market stalls sell pears and baskets. He lay there for weeks, alone and dead."

A tear rolled down Rayne's cheek. "They haven't cleared up half of the bodies down there… there are too many to know where to begin. The streets are washed with blood. I can't imagine…I don't want to imagine. I've seen so many horrible things in my life but what I heard today made my heart shatter into a million pieces," she said. "They found him right there beneath some rubble, stretched over a broken stall cart, his arms twisted, the charred remains of…" She stopped again and sobbed. "Of…a…"

"Of what?" said Aren.

"In his arms," she sobbed. "There was a small animal, charred, a cat maybe. There are a lot of strays down there."

One Winner Alone
Eyan

"No, sir, y-you want to move this piece," said Renut, pointing to the wooden swordsman. "And then, I can…"

"No," said Eyan, moving it back. The steward wouldn't best him, not today. "I want to move *this* one," he said. The look of shock on the little man's face was enough of a win. The tent was dim, but his squirming face was in clear sight.

"Ah, I see," said the little man. "Yes, I d-do suppose that that would be a better move." He stared in silence at the Tiroz board for a good while, focussing, and then his face lit up. He moved his piece up half a triangle and looked up at Eyan, smiling, almost like a child. It was an innocent smile, but a proud one, nonetheless. Eyan looked down at the board. The little idiot had trapped himself. He could easily be beaten in a single move.

"Ah, fuck, you've gone and done it," he said to the little man. "I yield." He shrugged his shoulders. Renut all but jumped with joy before remembering who he was stood before.

"Th-thank you for playing," he said. "You're very good, sir."

That, he was. Even better than the little man knew.

"It's a good game," said Eyan. "Good for the mind, isn't it?"

Renut gulped. He looked terrified, perhaps a little confused.

"I asked you a question," said Eyan.

"Y-yes," said the little man. "It's a good game, a b-brilliant one!" He took a step back as if Eyan were about to strike him across the face.

"Renut, are you…are you scared of me?"

The little man shook his head frantically. "No, no. I am not. I fear only the One."

"Good," said Eyan. "Now, do you know why it is a brilliant game?"

Renut shook his head again, more gently this time.

"Because it reflects the battlefield, a real battlefield," said Eyan. "Sharpens the mind, shows you what to look for."

Renut didn't look convinced. "I'm sure it does," he said. "Not that you or the First Warden would need your m-minds sharpened at all. You will v-vanquish over the tyrants."

Eyan smiled. "That, we will," he said. "Every single time."

Renut looked up at him inquisitively, scratching his balding head with his left hand.

"Yes? What is it?"

"Just… I h-had a question."

"Well, go on," said Eyan.

"The tyrant king, he sits at Malysor," said Renut. "In Ayleris."

"Hmm."

"So why haven't you – I-I mean we – why haven't we attacked yet?" said Renut. "We have m-more than enough men. More than enough. Ayleris isn't far from h-here." The stuttering was getting worse and worse and it irritated Eyan.

"We've only just taken Fencliffe," said Eyan. "It's barely been a week. We sit now outside the walls of Jertonshield, the men inside, they kneel to the king no more. They serve only the First Warden."

"Y-yes, exactly," said Renut. "So why not Ayleris? Bring an end to it all?"

"Because after taking Fencliffe, Jertonshield, and all of the lands between Sturrock and Éterin, the men are tired. More tired than ever," said Eyan. "They need time, to rest, to recover properly or else they won't stand a chance in Ayleris."

"B-but, what about…" he stopped dead in his tracks, his eyes filled with horror. "Sorry, sorry."

"Speak, Renut."

"No, it's n-not my place."

"SPEAK!"

"O-okay, okay, I will," he said. "I just think, w-won't the king have time too? To rest, r-recover, the rest of it. Won't h-he have time to build his army? To prepare?"

Eyan smiled. "We'll cripple them before they have a chance to do any of that," he said proudly.

Renut looked at him, puzzled as ever. "C-cripple them? How so?"

"Oh," said Eyan. "The First Warden does plan on taking a city, two, in fact. Just not Ayleris. We'll let them keep their beloved Verenia for the time being."

He could almost see the cogs and wheels in Renut's little head turning. "Two cities…" he said. "You d-don't mean…*how*?"

"Right across the Strait," said Eyan. "That's how."

"The Strait?" said Renut. "B-but… Oh!" he lit up again.

Eyan smiled. "Yes, oh. We'll close the Neck, tighten our grip around it."

"Very c-clever," said the little man. "W-we'll let them keep Verenia…so, the two countries c-can live side by side…he'll allow that? The First Warden?"

"Oh, no, absolutely not. That was never in the cards," said Eyan. "I said we'll let them keep it *for the time being*. There is no end to this war where two countries emerge. There can only be one winner, one winner alone. It is much like this game," he said pointing at the Tiroz board between them. "There is no end to this war where both a First Warden and a sovereign king emerge."

Renut gulped. "Of course," he said. "A-and it won't be a s-sovereign king that emerges, it c-can't be."

Eyan smiled. "No, it can't." He got up from the old stool, making Renut flinch. "Right, I'm going to get some fresh air." He needed it. Being trapped in a hot tent with Renut was not how he'd wanted to spend his night.

He pulled back the flap and walked into the starless night. He took in a deep breath. The air was even less fresh out here. Thick, with smoke, from the fires they were burning in the camp. Suddenly, he felt sick. The tent seemed more welcoming than ever now. He tried to clear his head of it, of that night, but it was of no use. The smell…it was almost the same. He was in the palace again, then in the streets of Sturrock. Beneath the Arvendon Bridge, then at Wyntock End. His palms were sweaty, his forehead too. He breathed deeply, clenching his fists, looking into the fire, the wretched world spinning all around him. He closed his eyes, squeezing them tightly shut. He felt sicker still.

"Are you alright there, son?" It was his father's voice.

"Yes, I'm – I'm fine." Suddenly he was the one stuttering. He turned around, the First Warden wasn't alone. The cloaked woman was beside him, he wondered which one it was this time.

"Are you ready?" said his father. "To march eastward."

"Yes," said Eyan, though the only place he wanted to march was home. Sacrifices had to be made in war, though.

"I shall march with you to the river," came the woman's voice, taking her hood off. "Then I will head north." It was Linara Spenler.

"Great," said Eyan, still a bit dazed. He looked back into the fire. "Brilliant."

"Son," said Soren, placing his hand on Eyan's shoulder. It was a strange and foreign feeling. "Are you sure you're up for this? After what happened at the Valecrest, after what happened in Sturrock…you have more than proven your worth to me, to the Federation."

"Yes, I'm up for it," said Eyan. "Why wouldn't I be?"

"You're different now," said his father, snatching his hand away. "Distant. Cold." His voice grew darker. "I just want to make sure that you aren't, you know, having regrets."

He turned around to face the First Warden. "I have no regrets."

"Oh?" said Soren. "Because I did, when I first marched into battle. When I first killed a man," he said. "Let alone when I killed a man who had surrendered. The Insurgency was the first time I'd been faced with something like that, I know that it isn't easy."

Indeed, it hadn't been. He felt sick to his stomach, unable to get any proper sleep most nights. The faces all flashed before his eyes, he saw them everywhere he went. Even in sleep, he was never alone.

"But just because it isn't easy, doesn't mean it isn't necessary," said Soren sternly. "It is a necessary evil. You know why we fight this war, son."

Eyan nodded.

"She never did like me, Elvira. I wasn't listened to," said Soren. "Not when I warned them of the nightdwellers, not when I warned them of the Sandaerians, and not when…" His voice wavered for a moment, and he was vulnerable again, raw and helpless before Eyan's eyes. "Not when I warned them of the Asenian rebels. Told them that our lives were in danger, all of us. And what happened?"

Eyan fought back his own tears. "She died."

"She was *killed*," said Soren. "By the very mutineers I warned them against, all of them. That is the sacrifice I made for that Crown. That is what those people did to your mother, Eyan. Don't ever forget it. They're tyrants, the lot of them. They don't care for what you have to say, they never have. They killed her."

Linara scoffed. Soren turned to face her, scowling.

"Have you got something to say?" he growled.

"Nothing at all," she said.

"Good, because you should be careful, very careful with your words. That tongue of yours is loose, isn't it?"

She smiled at him emptily.

"Sir!" came a man's voice.

"What is it?" said Soren impatiently.

"One of the men, he's been bit. He's not doing so well," said the soldier.

The First Warden smiled cruelly. "I'm glad," he said. "I'd better go and take a look." He nodded at Eyan and slipped away.

Linara turned to face Eyan instead, the unpleasant thin smile still etched on her face. "The girls, I bet you're worried about them, aren't you?" she said.

"Why would I be?"

"Oh, don't pretend you haven't heard," said Linara. "The choices that lie ahead…the test."

He knew all too well, but he had plenty to worry about. She was being vile, she *knew* he had plenty to worry about. "Let us hope that their fathers choose well then," he said.

"I don't trust you, you know."

"It is a very good thing that you don't have to," said Eyan. "My father trusts me and that is all that matters."

"Well, he shouldn't."

"And why is that?" He wished he could shove her into the flames himself. Out of all of his father's acquaintances, this was quite possibly the one he hated the most. Probably even more than his father's masters.

"Because you are weak, you always have been," she said, bitterly. "And you grow weaker with every day that passes."

"I'm not weak!"

"Yes, you are. I know what really happened at the palace that day, we all do. Your father is blind and one day that blindness might just get him killed."

"I don't know what the fuck you think you know, but for –"

"They *all* saw it. All of them. Edi told me himself that you practically watched them leave through the tunnels, the king, the

Berywen girl, the royal family. You just stood by and watched. You could have followed them, you *should* have followed them, and you didn't."

"That isn't true!" His heart pounded inside his chest. His mouth and throat were dry.

"They know you only killed that chef to prove your loyalty, your worth. You didn't mean it. It wasn't for honour, nor for your country. They *know*, Eyan, and soon the First Warden will too. He'll see your weakness. Let us hope it is not too late by then."

Suddenly he wished he'd never left that sweaty tent.

The Mysterious Stranger
Rhedas

The books in his arms weighed almost as much as Rhedas Sandaerzi himself. He let out a tired groan and turned to Ferus, who didn't seem to be struggling at all. Perhaps the fast was doing him some good, perhaps it had given him strength somehow. Not something Rhedas cared for in the slightest. To give up his own *voice*? It was one of the few joys he had left in this life. It did also get him in a lot of trouble, like at the Malysor Castle that other day, for instance, but the beatings from Kyril had been worth it. He'd said what he'd said, and he'd needed his voice for that. His voice and his dreams.

Ferus cleared his throat loudly. Rhedas turned over to him. The minister's eyes slid over to the left.

"No," said Rhedas, pointing to the right. "It is this way. The other path leads right back to the Hall of Answers." He knew the way well by now. He'd been sure to learn it, or else Tamuz would think he was completely useless. "No, I said follow me!"

Rhedas hated working in the Hall of Answers. Absolutely despised it. He'd rather be working in the wells, or tending to the gardens, anything but this. Perhaps one day, he'd even get to hold sermons. But for now, he was condemned to this tedious task. The thought of it had him irate. Going through hundreds, maybe thousands of books, one at a time. Facing the wrath of Tamuz if they fell asleep whilst doing it. Checking each page, each scroll, each line, and then doing it all over the next day. It was foolish. Nobody in the rest of the kingdom would ever see these books, nor care for what lay within them. What was the point of it all? Who were they to amend scriptures written a thousand years ago, written in a different time? Who were *they* to decide what was truth, and what was not? Most of all, he hated working with Ferus. The man never uttered a word, leaving Rhedas a lot of time alone with his thoughts. Ferus looked at him as if he'd read his mind, his eyes bulging.

"What is it?" said Rhedas. Of course, the minister said nothing. Just smiled sheepishly, waddling his head around at the oil paintings around them. Rhedas should have known better. "Do *you* like it? Working in the Hall of Answers?"

Ferus nodded.

"Hmm? Why?" said Rhedas.

The fat minister scowled in silence.

"I just...I just thought maybe you wouldn't either," said Rhedas. "It seems awfully dull. Besides..."

Ferus cleared his throat and looked at him expectantly, as if asking him *what?*

"Well... who are *we* to decide what is truth and what is not? Who gave us that power?"

Ferus shrugged his shoulders daftly. Rhedas stopped and looked up at the oil painting above him. The noble creature stared down at him from it, as if watching over. Its silky white wings spread wide over the Falls...fierce lightning scarring the starry skies above.

"A year or so ago, we'd be marking any mention of skyverns as lies and myths, but now we know better, don't we? The real truth cannot be known, not by any man, except perhaps in death," said Rhedas. The weight of the books in his arms had doubled by now, he feared he might drop them. He just hoped Ferus wouldn't go and tell Tamuz. "It is pointless, all this. We could be using our time doing something more important...they're sacred and noble creatures, you know, skyverns. Clever too. They need to be protected, from what is happening in the south and the west, from what is happening where the three rivers meet."

Ferus gave him a puzzled look, then glanced up at the oil painting of the majestic animal, then down again, more confused than ever. Ah, of course, *he* didn't know. *He* didn't have the dreams.

"It's alright," said Rhedas. "There will come a time when she will have to choose.... let us hope that Her Eminence chooses wisely."

Ferus gulped.

"They should let me talk to her, guide her. She shouldn't have to face it alone," said Rhedas, lost in a cloud of his own thoughts. He wasn't mad, nor was he delusional. His dreams hadn't let him down yet. Kyril and Tamuz should see that, but they were just as lost as the rest. They wouldn't let him anywhere near her. He'd begged and begged to go to Veytora, but it had been useless. After Ayleris…they'd never agree.

Ferus cleared his throat again.

"Oh, splendid," said Rhedas. "We're here." He opened the heavy wooden doors to the Nynnevor Keep with his back, allowing Ferus to pass before letting them slam shut loudly behind them. The echoes followed for a good moment after. The hall was vast, the biggest he'd ever been in, in a dream or otherwise. Its bounds were endless, he could scarcely see the wall at the other end. Hundreds upon hundreds of shelves lined thin passages before his eyes, balconies on either side with even more shelves. Each shelf must have had a few hundred books on it. Absolutely vast. Between ladders and trolleys, the place was a labyrinth that he'd hate to be stuck in. And this was just the one hall, there were four others. An endless maze. It was a good thing he knew it well, though he couldn't say the same of Ferus. The fat minister's mouth was left open.

"Come on now, Ferus, this isn't your first time." But deep down he knew that he too was left speechless each time he came back here. "Follow me, here."

The alley of scrolls didn't have an end in sight. He pitied the fat minister, but each man fought his own fight.

"Be careful with the ladders," said Rhedas. "They slip."

Ferus looked to him expectantly once more.

"Oh, me? No, no, you do it alone, that is how you will learn." Rhedas knew it would take him a good few minutes to get to where he needed to be, and time was most certainly of the essence. "Off you go," he said, pointing down to the end of the long passage.

He had to set his books down as soon as soon as the fat minister was out of sight. His arms ached. He stretched them out, reaching upwards and backwards wildly before he picked the books up again, groaning all the while. Tamuz had better be happy with him.

It was just beneath the balcony that he spotted the thief. Dressed entirely in black, lurking in the shadows like a cat. The stranger all but tiptoed around, dagger in hand. Pale white skin, greasy black hair. Familiar, too familiar. Rhedas all but dropped the books. He slipped behind a shelf, putting the books down gently – he couldn't make a noise. He pushed aside the books neatly stored on the shelf in front of him to catch another glimpse of the intruder. His heart was in his mouth. A dagger, in the North Parydon. Weapons were forbidden, everybody knew that. This was a holy place, a sacred one. A *safe* one. He worked up the courage to peer around the bookshelf and deliberated following the thief. It was an effort convincing himself to do it, but he was a mere servant of the Parydon, this was his home, and this was his duty.

The mysterious stranger lurked some more, knocking over a book from beside him and it made Rhedas jump. To his surprise, the man bent down and picked it up. *A respectful thief.* Or perhaps just a cautious one. Rhedas followed closely behind him, quiet and careful. There was a thud. The stranger turned around and Rhedas ducked beneath a shelf, praying with all his might that he hadn't been seen. The thud had come from a distance, from the other corner of the vast hall. He thought it might have been Ferus, perhaps dropping a book or two. He perched his chin up onto the shelf once more and searched for the stranger. The man was still looking this way. The black hair, the emerald eyes. This wasn't a stranger at all. It was the one from the Malysor, the one who'd stood beside the king. What was his name? Something southern. *Cyneric.*

His first thought was to rush upstairs as quickly as he could and tell Kyril and Tamuz everything. He needed to prove himself, prove that he belonged here, prove that he was good at this. He couldn't leave the Parydon, he had nobody to turn to. The king couldn't send spies here, with weapons too. He shook his head. There was something about him, about this man, which he was drawn to. He couldn't place it. Had he seen Cyneric in a dream? He certainly didn't think so. He'd seen another, one who looked similar, but younger. A lot younger. Barely more than a boy. Same black hair, same emerald eyes. He'd seen the boy where the three rivers meet. And in puddles and puddles of blood too. He'd seen the boy atop a tower, a tall tower, by the Aspen trees. In peril. But peril that he'd brought onto himself. No, this wasn't that boy. This was a man. He closed his eyes tightly, shaking his head, panting. He cast his mind back to it. This man was there too, in the thick of it. He *needed* to be there.

He needed to be here too. He had to, or else how would Her Eminence bring the dawn?

He decided to keep quiet and watched as Cyneric disappeared into the distance.

An Old Rumour
Cyneric

The blistering heat was like fire, raining down on the road. Cyneric walked with purpose: cautiously and quickly. He wiped his sweat, searching frantically around the short walls beside the riverbank. He was sure it was here somewhere, the tunnel. If only he could have used the other, he was so much more familiar with it. Unfortunately, the funeral procession on the courtyard outside it meant that he'd have to wait for who knows how long. But he needed to get back to the Malysor, so, it had to be this one. He had only ever used it once, but his sharp memory had scarcely let him down, so he wasn't too worried. It was a very small tunnel, just big enough for him to crawl through, but it fed into a bigger one further in so at least he could look forward to standing and walking instead of being on his hands and knees all the way through. If only he could find it, time was of the essence and he grew tired.

He scanned the wall carefully – he didn't have time to scale it from end to end and the rucksack on his back grew heavier and heavier with every moment that passed whilst he stood here under the sweltering sun, so he tried to be quick about it. It wasn't easy. But Cyneric knew that Aren would be waiting for him, probably quite anxious too. He hadn't had the means to send word to the king about the goldmine he'd brought back. He'd been lucky, too. So close to being caught, *too* close. He was glad they'd been noisy coming into that damned hall, the pair of them, or else he'd have been found out for sure. But he hadn't, so he stood on the riverbank, tired and sweaty and in pain.

Where was the damned tunnel? He rarely panicked, he was usually good at keeping himself together, but it was *so hot*. And he had such little time. And this part of the riverbank had changed so much since he'd last been here with the queen. Many of the trees had been chopped down, much of the gravel was gone, leaving behind thin sand. Most of the bottom half of the wall was now covered in moss, thinly hidden by small wild shrubs that grew from the sand. He couldn't find the wattles that had once covered the tunnel, they had probably been torn away too. All he could see were the shrubs that lined the wall, masses of them. It was a marvel they'd grown in this heat. He walked up to them, pulling at them to see if the tunnel was behind them. There were nettles and thorns. He bit his bottom lip and fought the agony. Damn. All for nothing. He cursed out loud. Just as he was about to move past though, some of the bricks at the bottom of the wall behind the shrubbery stood out to him. They looked different, less faded. Less aged. He rapped his knuckles against them. There was the slightest hollow echo. He took off his bag from his back, spun it from over his shoulder and swung it directly into the bricks. They budged ever so slightly, the loose mortar cracking in between them. He did it again. The bricks wobbled. This wasn't going to be easy, was it? He took a few steps back, ran forwards and kicked the wall at full speed. The bricks fell inwards, creating a small opening. He took in a sharp breath through his teeth, fighting against the stabbing pain in his throbbing foot. He swung at the bricks again, taking out a few more, making just enough space for him to crawl through. He pushed his rucksack through in front of him. He wondered why the tunnel had been covered, but he did not care enough to stay around any longer. It was probably just to conceal it after the bushes had all been torn down. Oh well, it wasn't important right now. As soon as he was at the castle, he'd make arrangements to conceal it properly.

Cyneric crawled forwards, just about fitting inside. Relying solely on his memory and what he could feel with his hands, one by one he moved his hands and feet forward, clambering over debris left behind from years ago. He wished he could have just taken one of the normal entrances into the castle, but he'd be noticed for sure, and they couldn't afford the attention. His back ached from all the crawling…the Nynnevor tunnels had been just as bad. Luckily it had been a fairly easy endeavour, if not for the slight gamble. The book was easy to find, and he'd been in and out within the hour, perhaps even less.

Thankfully, the tunnel in front of him widened fairly quickly. He waited until the crawlspace allowed him just enough room to wriggle his hand into his pocket and pull out a small torch. He shone it in front of him and continued forward, hastening his pace now that he knew for certain that anyone near the riverbank wouldn't hear him, though there was very little chance anyone would wander that part of the shore anyway, if he were being honest. He kept to his hands and knees until there was enough room for him to kneel, then eventually stand, hunched over. He followed the etchings along the wall of the tunnel, tracing his fingers against the markings to make the precise, calculated turns that would take him to the castle.

The route led him into a cavern, one of many in the large network of tunnels beneath Ayleris. There were several openings. He was pretty certain it was the third on his left he'd take, or was it the fourth? He strode forwards towards the third, putting the rucksack back on his back and straightening it. He couldn't wait to stretch properly at home. He supposed that that was what the old castle was now…home. Carefully and quickly, he marched on through the rubble on the ground, shining his torch on the ground ahead of him. He used his other hand to trace the wall beside him, careful not to stray away. He paused. Another intersection. The crunch of the rubble beneath hadn't stopped, though. In fact, it was louder than ever. He looked ahead, shining his torch straight on. There was nothing there. He flinched at the footsteps and turned around in a hurry. There was a gentle clinking and clatter, it echoed in the tunnel and grew louder…louder. But before he had had any time to give it thought, he felt an immense thump on the back of his neck.

The sting was excruciating. He lost his balance, stumbling against the wall. A fire raged in the base of his skull, where it met his neck. His heart pounded in his head and the tunnels were a dark blur. He turned around as quickly as he could, letting go of the torch and pulling out his pistol from inside his jacket instead.

His vision was still hazy from the blow, but he aimed at the assailant. The four silhouettes danced in front of him as his eyes adjusted. No, there were two. He aimed for the taller one's head, but the shorter one was quick to swing around and kick the gun out of his hand. They both stood in front of him, the taller one armed with a rifle pointed at him whilst the shorter held a sword. His sight was almost back to normal now, but it was too late. He stared back at the masked figures in front of him. He tried to reach inside his pocket for his dagger, but a hand came up and stopped him.

"No."

It was the taller one who had spoken. It was a deep, serious voice. The man wore a plain black mask which covered his entire face from ear to ear, except the eyes. In the dim light of Cyneric's torch, which still shone up from the rubble below, he could see that he was dressed entirely in black, wearing what must have been a thick, black cloak. Even his hands were covered by black leather gloves. Through the holes in his mask where his eyes were, Cyneric could see that he had very pale skin, which glistened under the dim light of the torch. It was too dark for Cyneric to make out the colour of his eyes. The other figure was of a smaller stature, wearing a somewhat larger and looser cloak. His face was masked too, a loose hood over his head, silver chains and beads dangling down from it, in front of his face. His hands were also covered by the same black gloves. Cyneric couldn't make out anything about his face, it was well hidden by the beads in the low light, but he did wear a chain around his neck, a single fang hanging out in front of his chest.

"The bag," said the taller man. "Give it 'ere."

It was a very southern accent, he'd heard it for years.

"The bag!" he shouted again.

"Who are you? Who do you work for?" said Cyneric.

"Do you value your life?" said the man. "Hand the bag over and we might let you leave with your 'ead." Cyneric was all but certain they wouldn't.

"Why do you want the bag?" said Cyneric. How could they have possibly known what was inside? These weren't petty robbers, petty robbers wouldn't have made it into the tunnels.

"You ask too many questions," said the man. He edged closer towards Cyneric, until he was within an arm's length. He pressed his rifle against Cyneric's chest.

"It's dusty in 'ere ain't it?" said the man, sniffing. "The dust tickles my nose. I could sneeze right now, accidentally pull this trigger. And then I'd take the bag anyway."

Cyneric examined the man carefully. He definitely wasn't a noble, he sounded like he might be from Arvendon or maybe Wyntock End.

"Or you could leave this hole with your life," said the man. "All you gotta do is hand that over," he pointed at the bag again.

Cyneric nodded. He began to take off the bag from his back and lowered it slowly to the floor.

"Kick it to my mate over there," the man said, pointing to the veiled figure a few paces back.

Cyneric obliged, and the man lowered his rifle.

"Thank you, you've been a real help, Cyn," said the man.

Cyneric was utterly disgusted. Disappointed in himself. He was waiting for the right moment, a hasty move, anything to give him the chance to strike back. His assailants were far from hasty though. The man backed away swiftly, bag in hand, not turning his back on Cyneric. Just as he reached his accomplice, Cyneric thought they may turn around, maybe offer him an opportunity to attack, but he was wrong. The man suddenly stopped in his tracks.

"Daxian," he said. "I serve Daxian."

Before Cyneric could get a word out, he was facing down the barrel of a rifle once more and this time the man pulled the trigger. Cyneric yelled out in sheer agony, clutching at his side. Luckily for him, in haste, the man had just grazed his torso. Cyneric dove down, punching the man in his knees, causing him to tumble over. The man let out a shriek. Cyneric wasted no time, striking him quickly in the arm, knocking the rifle away from him. The second hooded figure plunged towards Cyneric, sword in arm aimed directly at his chest. Cyneric pulled out his own dagger and grabbed the fallen masked man by the shoulder, pulling him up. He pressed his cold blade against the man's neck, facing the hooded accomplice. The accomplice stood still in front of him.

"I'm going to pick up this bag, and walk to the castle now," said Cyneric, pressing the blade further into the man's neck. "And you're going to walk in the other direction."

The figure remained motionless, staring in silence. Cyneric took his first step backwards slowly and cautiously, waiting for his assailant to step back too. How would he get to the castle without being followed? He supposed he could take the tunnel leading east, he would have to crouch, but he could probably make it.

"Don't worry about your friend, I will be taking him with me to the castle," said Cyneric. He held an arm around the man's shoulder, covering his mouth with his hand. He ignored the man's muffled screams, there was no way this man was going to play the hero or distract him in any way.

"No harm will come to him from me as long as you step away and head back out the tunnels from wherever you came," said Cyneric. "If you take one step closer to me, though, I will end this man's life. There is no need for blood to be spilt today."

The figure stood lifeless, completely silent.

"Does it talk?" said Cyneric, growing impatient. He quickly calmed himself down before things got out of hand. "It's alright, I'm going to back away now, and walk towards the castle. You *will* turn around. The king is forgiving, your friend will be alright."

Without giving Cyneric a chance to think, the figure leapt forward and launched the sword directly at him, but he barely felt it. His hostage let out an excruciating howl though, as Cyneric moved his hand from the dying man's mouth and saw the sword buried deep in his chest. The figure pushed it further, twisting it as the poor sod let out an agonising scream until Cyneric felt its touch on his own stomach, a cold blade warmed by the dead man's blood. He quickly jumped back, pushing the dead man away from him and onto the figure with the silver veil. He looked down at his tunic, red with the blood of his enemy and his own. He clambered to his feet, still gripping onto his dagger, as the murderer before him pulled out the dirty sword, kicking the dead man off of it.

"Have you no honour?" he said to the cloaked figure. "You would kill your own just to get to me? And for what? For gold?" he gestured to the bag at his feet.

The lie worked. It distracted the hooded figure just long enough for Cyneric to stamp on his torch which was still shining on the floor and make for the bag on the ground. The dim light went out completely, leaving the tunnels almost pitch black. He grabbed the bag, not thinking twice about it and he dove down onto the ground. He crawled into the tunnel heading east closest to him, crouched, feeling the walls of the tunnel with his hand. He was so thankful that he knew these parts of the tunnels well. He didn't look back. He could hear blind shots behind him as the assailant picked up the gun, but he didn't slow down to think about it. He made straight on. It had been a gamble, and he wasn't in the clear yet, but it looked like he might just make it out alive. He knew the tunnels blind better than his attacker, who he could still hear struggling in the rubble of the cavern. He left the echoes behind and thanked his lucky stars.

His wound slowed him down immensely. He kept a hand tightly on it as he hobbled through as fast as he possibly could. A wave of relief hit him when he finally did reach the fortress' dungeons. He clambered up the stairs, cursing under his breath as the blood dripped from his side, leaving a dark red trail. He traipsed through the narrow halls directly towards the king's private chambers, rucksack in one hand, the other clutching his wound tightly. There was only one guard stationed outside his living quarters, and luckily for Cyneric, she recognised him immediately.

"Are you alright, sir?" she said, eyeing Cyneric's bloodied tunic, and the cuts and grazes on his cheek.

"Nothing to worry about," said Cyneric. It shamed him that he couldn't even remember the guard's name. After the siege they'd lost many of the old guards, the ones that Cyneric knew well. "Get the king, immediately."

"Sir, His Majesty is in the Throne Hall."

Cyneric paused for a moment, dropping the bag onto the floor.

"Could you summon him here, please?"

And with that, he slumped onto the floor, leaning against the wall. The guard nodded and ran down the corridor. She returned soon after, not only with the king, but also with Pennyn Runeval, Olivia Berywen, Ysser Banlin and Lara Hercan.

"Cyneric! What happened?" said Aren.

"A story for later, first of all… I managed to find what you were looking for," he said. He pointed at the rucksack next to him. Olivia winced at the blood, but the rest just looked at him in pity. He hated it. "Just ran into some trouble along the way," he mumbled. He held out his hand for the king to help him up. Groaning, he pushed himself up, using the wall to support him. It definitely wasn't the best of his moments, and he wasn't happy that so many were there to see him like this.

"You can stay there until the doctor arrives," said Aren, looking down at him. "Lean on the wall."

"Should I get somebody to help?" said Lara.

"No, no, don't worry. It's best if I stay up. Here, Olivia, I think this is for you. Make of it what you will."

Olivia looked startled at the state of Cyneric, but she held out her hand and took the bag from him. "Thank you. I don't remember the page–"

"Go on then, be on your way," said Cyneric. "Why don't you take it to your study."

Olivia gave him a confused glance, but Cyneric didn't want to make a scene out of it. He was distrusting even of those that stood before him right now. Except the king, he truly didn't know who was loyal. Somebody had been talking to the wrong sorts of people.

"It's alright Olivia, just go to my quarters," said Aren, handing her an old key. "Cyneric, help will be arriving very soon, tell us what happened."

Cyneric stared blankly.

"You can trust them," said Aren, but Cyneric wasn't so sure that he could.

"I was attacked in the tunnels," he said. "Two assailants. I believe that they'd purposely blocked off one of the entrances, so they could be sure I'd take the other, where they'd be waiting. They must have known the tunnels fairly well, or known someone who did," said Cyneric. He took a moment to catch his breath. "I was able to get away, but one of them was killed in the process. His body will still be down there, unless his accomplice got rid of it somehow. The other one didn't know the tunnels as well…and he stayed silent the whole time. Argh!" Cyneric winced again, squeezing his side.

"What did they look like?" said Aren.

"I didn't see either of their faces, not properly. One was pale and tall, the one that's dead," he said. "The other was shorter but was wearing some sort of hood so I could see nothing. Silver beads and chains covering his face, sort of like a veil."

"What did they want?" said Aren.

"The book. Or the bag, at least."

"What book?" said Lara. Aren turned around to answer but Cyneric was quick to stop him.

"Some book," said Cyneric sternly. "It isn't important."

"How could they possibly know? Were they…were they bluecoats?" said Pennyn.

"I don't know, not by the looks of it," said Cyneric. "But I wouldn't rule it out. Though he did tell me who they work for, the tall one, right before he shot me."

"Who?"

"Daxian," said Cyneric. "Whatever the hell that means. I don't know who or what Daxian is and whether or not he's a bluecoat, but he has some powerful allies and he's a step ahead of us."

He watched as the look on Pennyn's face changed. Suddenly the pity was gone. He was worried, truly worried and not just for the sake of appearances.

"Daxian," said the chancellor. "Are you sure?"

"What is that?" said Aren.

"Have you never heard the word before?" said Pennyn. "It was thrown around a lot during the Insurgency, but I suppose you're a little young for that."

"Oh?"

"It's an old legend, from the time of the old bluecoats."

Cyneric was very careful about what he said next. He groaned as the stinging all over his body worsened as he shuffled. "I'm not one to indulge conspiracies but I think that there may be a possibility, a small but significant possibility, that this attack was related to what our Sandaerian ministers had brought to our attention the other day."

"The…the dwellers?" said Lara Hercan.

Cyneric looked at her, his head tilted, and his eyebrows furrowed, and then over to the king.

"It's alright, Cyneric," said Aren. "I trust Lara, I've told her everything. It's important she knows."

Lara nodded and then shuffled uneasily.

He wasn't too sure how wise it had been on the king's part, but he put his doubts aside, there would be plenty time for those later. But the palace guard was still stood behind Ysser. They couldn't yet speak freely. "Off you go," said Cyneric, looking at the guard. "You are no longer required here." He waited until the woman was gone.

"I thought I had gotten away with it," said Cyneric. "I thought nobody had seen me in Nynnevor, nobody suspected me. But what if I'd been spotted?"

"I doubt it," said Pennyn. "It doesn't add up."

"So, how did the bluecoats find out exactly when and where you'd be?" said Aren.

"Well, that is the thing. There isn't any way they would know, unless I was seen up in Nynnevor. What if the Sandaerians tipped off the bluecoats about it?"

"Are you saying…"

"Then the fight is simpler than we make it to be," said Pennyn. "The bluecoats are working with the Sandaerians. The dwellers are in on it too – our enemy is clear."

"Hold on," said Aren. "Very few know about the tunnels, or indeed how to find their way inside them, that too in almost complete darkness. How would any of them know where to look?"

"Well, dwellers see much better than we do in the dark," said Lara. "They are creatures of the night." How did *she* know so much about them? Cyneric had always thought she was a sceptic, like the rest of them.

"Hmm."

"Why would they break faith with us?" said Lara. "The Sandaerians."

"The Sandaerians are loyal to their Deryz, nobody else, and with hundreds of them believing in this charlatan's tricks…"
"Oh, Develyn Asellar?" said Lara. Again, he was astounded by the extent of her knowledge in matters which didn't concern the girl.

"It isn't hard to believe that she'd be working with them, perhaps for her own gain," said Cyneric.

"Whoever they are working for, what did they want with those books?" said Aren. "Do they know something we don't? Something about the dwellers?"

"Perhaps they do," said Cyneric. "Which worries me more."

Olivia burst through the door, the dusty old book open in her hand. The page was creased and yellow, Cyneric couldn't make out what was scrawled across it.

"This!" said Olivia. "I remember seeing this, I knew I was forgetting something." She was pointing to a drawing in *The Sandaerian Promise*. "The *Key*."

"What is this?" said Cyneric. It wasn't anything he recognised, but a quick glance over at Aren's wide eyes and it was clear the king knew something.

"It's the key," she said. "It's not actually a key, of course, but it's called the Key of Blood by some because–"

"Argh!" Cyneric yelled out. He knew now why the king's eyes were wide.

"Are you alright?" said Olivia.

"Yes, yes, I just…aaarrgghh! Shit. My wound, it stings."

"Ysser," said Aren. "Would you see to where the doctor is?"

"Of course," he replied.

"In fact," Cyneric added. "Lara, could you accompany him? Many here speak Verenic, and, well, Ysser speaks none."

"Me?" said Lara. "Oh, erm, I don't speak much of it either, if I'm honest."

"But you speak more than him," said Cyneric, faking a laugh. "Please find me help." He winced loudly, pressing on his wound.

"Why did you get rid of them?" said Olivia.

"No time to explain now," said Cyneric. "But please, do tell us about that…that *thing*." He pointed to the drawing, its jagged, irregular edges. Its dark red gleam.

"Indeed," said Pennyn Runeval.

"Aleryc's Pendant," said Olivia. "But some call it the Key of Blood. I believe that it's the key we seek."

"What key?" said Cyneric.

"Remember Rhedas, the minister. He kept talking about *the Key*. He said we need it, I'm starting to think maybe he wasn't completely mad after all."

"Ah," said Cyneric, because he knew better than to question madmen by now. He looked over at Aren though, whose eyes were fixed on the page. He knew why, of course. But what could be done of it now?

"Look at this," said Olivia. "It's in Verenic… *Key of Blood, Stone of Sacrifice, Shield of Mankind*. It possesses the power to stop them," said Olivia. "The dwellers."

"How?" said Pennyn, crossing his arms and looking at her over the rim of his glasses.

"It doesn't say how, exactly."

"What does that say?" said Cyneric, pointing to a passage next to it.

Olivia shrugged her shoulders. "I'm afraid that is the extent of my Old Verenic," she said.

"But not mine," said Aren suddenly, clearing his throat. "Let's see. *Heaviest is the darkness of the perilous night, unto the death of innocence…*"

"The death of innocence?" came Olivia's voice.

Aren nodded. *"When the land stains red with the blood of the free, the blood of the shadows...the blood of the winds and the blood of the flames."*

"What on earth does that mean?" said Pennyn. "Sandaerian nonsense, at its best."

"The end will be nigh. Dawn shall set from destiny's stone itself. Only under the darkest, starless cover of despair."

It made Cyneric shudder. "Well done," he said, sarcastically. "It sounds sort of like...the madman's words, doesn't it?"

"Yes," said Olivia. "Exactly. I think he was describing this," she said pointing to the old, jagged relic again. "It can control them, or at least prevent them from killing somehow. If we were to get to it, we could stop the killing, and the famine too."

"Oh, we could do more than that," said Pennyn, a smile on his face. But Cyneric wasn't smiling, and neither was Aren. It had looked different when he'd last seen it, when he'd held it in his own hand. It was in its golden case then, the royal crest of House Aryssen engraved on it.

"I know where it is," said the king finally. Of course, Cyneric knew too. "The Pendant. Aleryc's Pendant. But I wish it wasn't there."

"Where?" said Olivia.

"In the Panderer's realm."

An eerie silence followed.

"Why?" said Pennyn.

"My mother gave it to me, along with my father's watch. She wanted me to wear it during the Recedon. I did a lot of my practice with it on me, actually. But in the hurry to get home, I forgot quite a few of my things... I... I left it there. Right beside my sparring gloves."

A wave of guilt pierced through Cyneric, shaking him worse than the wounds ever could. He had been so incredibly stupid, so careless. He was unworthy of his role, beside the king, beside the Council.

"But the Panderer's bloodgate... It's beneath the Valecrest," said Olivia. "In Sturrock."

"There's no way of getting down there," said Pennyn, shaking his head.

"And there aren't any other bloodgates?" asked Olivia.

Aren shook his head. "We know very little about them. There was one in Nynnevor once, but it no longer exists. It was destroyed during the Hercanian Uprisings, according to my mother anyway."

Pennyn narrowed his eyebrows. "Your Majesty, I'm not sure that's entirely the case, strictly speaking. What about the one here?"

"What?" said Aren.

"I'm sure that one of the old bloodgates was rumoured to be here in Ayleris, I'd bet it's somewhere here in the castle," said Pennyn. "Or in the Halls. Perhaps the University?"

"I've never heard this rumour," said Aren. But this rumour, Cyneric *had* heard. It was a pity his sharp memory was failing him, though. His mind went almost completely blank.

"With all due respect, Your Majesty, you've spent very little time here, in this world, and even less in Verenia," said Pennyn. Cyneric cast his mind back to his own time in the far north, with the queen.

"I think he might be right," he finally said. "I vaguely remember the queen telling me about her childhood summers up in the Riviera with Prince Skander." It was all coming back, bit by bit. "They'd spent a lot of their time in Verenia here at the Malysor and they'd spend the evenings looking for the lost bloodgates. Your grandmother had told them about them. They'd never had any luck though, of course."

"Do you think my uncle would remember more about it?" said Aren.

"No, I doubt it. He was very little," said Cyneric. "Besides, they it was just a child's game for them."

Aren had a sad look about him all of a sudden. "*Pendant*," he said. "That must have been what she'd said to Ysser."

"Who?" said Pennyn.

"My mother, when she was dying."

"Yes, I remember," said Cyneric.

"Maybe she knew that it was the way to stop it all," said Olivia.

"Then why…why would she have given it to me?" said Aren.

"Perhaps that is the precise reason she gave it to you," said Cyneric. "Because she knew it was the key."

"If I knew your mother at all, she was always two steps ahead of the game," said Pennyn. "Perhaps she gave it to you to protect it. So that you'd be able to use it once it was time."

"But why me?" Aren croaked. "I don't know anything about it. Nor did she ever mention it to me again. I don't know why she'd give it to me."

"Aren, you are blood of the Crown," said Pennyn Runeval. "Aren *Aleryc* Janus of the House Aryssen. It is in your name. The blood of the Deryzi of Old flows through your veins, and your heart beats to the March of the Skyvern. If not you, who else?"

Cyneric hoped that that would be enough. He hoped that Aren would be enough. But he never presumed to rely on fate alone.

"But how?" said Aren. "I don't have the damned thing, nor do I have any way of getting to it."

"I spent a lot of time in the dungeons far beneath this castle," said Olivia. "I'll help you. We can find it, the bloodgate, I know we can."

"Then let us get to work," said Cyneric. "But first, I need you all to pay close attention. I have an idea, but it will only work if you all listen to me carefully."

"An idea? What for?" said Pennyn.

"To weed out the snakes in our castle."

Key of Blood
Aren

It was dark in the tunnels. The walls smelled of the soot and dust that had gathered over the years. Despite the darkness, it was considerably hot, even amidst the deepest shadows of the dungeons beneath the castle. Aren made his way through the narrow passages carefully, with Olivia beside him, searching the walls on either side as he wiped the sweat from his brow. This must have been how Cyneric would have felt, sweating and panting in the tunnels beneath the city. At least Aren had company though, he'd probably go mad if Olivia wasn't with him. She stopped at every door they passed along the passage, examining it carefully.

"Are you sure it's here?" he said.

"No," said Olivia. "But we may as well have a gander, a little walk won't hurt us. I thought it'd be nice for us to hide away from the troubles above ground."

"Tell me, where are we going to find it?"

Olivia glared at him.

"I know, I know. You've explained it to me before, I'm just not completely convinced that it will work," said Aren.

"Nor am I," said Olivia. "We lose very little if it doesn't, we gain incredibly if it does. Take it up with Cyneric."

Her eyes wandered over to the side. "The door, Aren," she pointed at a grey, worn-down door on his side of the tunnel. He pushed it inward, to no avail.

"Locked again," he said.

"It's a marvel how many of the doors in the king's castle are locked to the king himself," said Olivia.

"This isn't the capital, hasn't been for hundreds of years. Most of these doors have been locked for generations."

Aren glanced over to another more battered door further down the tunnel. It was different, had markings on it. He walked over to examine it more closely.

"Verenic?" said Olivia.

"Old Verenic," said Aren. "It'd be difficult for me to read though, even if it wasn't so faded and patchy."

"I wonder what the Deryzi used it for," she said, pushing at it.

"It isn't worth it, another locked one," said Aren.

She sighed. "Let's just go back, it was a silly idea."

"To be honest now that we've been down here for a while, I'm rather enjoying it," Aren said to her. "Even if half the doors are locked."

Olivia's somewhat sullen eyes sparkled, lighting up her face. But she turned her eyes away from his, smiling into the darkness.

"Being so far beneath the castle, it gives me a sense of peace," said Aren. "As if the wars can rage on above and we'll be just fine. It's a false sense of peace, I know, but that makes it no less welcoming."

Aren could just about see the corner of Olivia's smile fade away in the shadows.

"What's the matter?" he asked.

"Nothing."

There was a sudden thud.

"What do you suppose that was?" asked Olivia.

Aren shrugged his shoulders. "Maybe it's the sky finally falling down upon us. I'd welcome it with open arms."

Olivia looked worried, though.

"Don't worry, it was probably just some old rocks falling. If there's any trouble, Cyneric knows exactly where we are," said Aren. "Do you want to go back up?"

She looked uneasy. "Let's stay a while longer."

Aren smiled at her. "Which way?"

"My guess is no better than yours," she said.

He pondered for a moment. "Let's go this way," he said, pointing to his right, but Olivia didn't budge. She looked pale, leaning against the sooty wall.

"I'm tired."

"Let's sit, then," he said.

"Down here?" said Olivia.

"Well, we can head back up if you'd prefer."

"No, let's sit here."

Aren wiped the sweat from his forehead again as they sat down on the dirty ground.

"Why did you ask me down here today?" Olivia asked.

"You know why, to find the –"

"No, I mean, why *me*? It didn't have to be. Cyneric could have easily helped you. He knows the dungeons just as well as I do."

"For the sake of my own sanity," he said, chuckling.

She smiled, sliding her hand to her side, beside Aren's. It was cold, even in this heat. "He can be very finicky, can't he?"

"It's that exact quality of his which I admire the most, though, and the one which has probably saved my life the most over the years."

"Well, we certainly can't have you leaving us, now, can we?"

"The life of a king is no more valuable than that of his soldiers," Aren replied.

"I disagree. A king's death has far greater effects than the death of a common soldier, who rots away behind enemy lines. We don't even know their names."

"Just because we don't know all of their names doesn't make them any less important than me."

"You're foolish to think so," she said. "They are no less important than you, of course, but unfortunately it is just the way our world works…you have a much bigger influence in life, therefore you would move mountains even in death."

"Is that so?" said Aren. "I suppose we shall have to disagree."

"It's a silly comparison," said Olivia. "The castle doesn't stir at the death of a common boy or a common girl. How many hundreds lost their lives during the siege?"

"I know," said Aren. "And we celebrated their lives, we mourned them all."

"You don't get it at all, do you?" she snatched her hand away from his, the smile wiped from her face. "When a noble dies, we don't spare any expense in mourning them. We'd go to war for them. Daria died and nobody at the Valecrest showed more than a morsel of sorrow for it."

"Olivia, you know I–"

"Jaspyn died too. I lost him forever. And what happened? Did we march south? Did we hang those that hurt him? So don't pretend all lives are worth the same when we've built a world that sets some apart from others."

And just like that, his heart burst into a million pieces.

"I lost him too, Olivia."

"I know."

The pair were silent for a moment. Aren stared into the darkness at the brick wall opposite them. He dared not look at her, but he could sense from the shakiness of her breath in the silence that she'd begun to cry. He wanted to comfort her, he wanted to be there for her, but he couldn't, so he sat quiet and still.

"Aren," she sniffled.

"I know," he said. "It hurts me every day. I haven't forgotten."

"No, look," she pointed into the darkness, wiping away a tear.

"What?"

"The door, that one look!"

She pointed at the dented door opposite them, a little further down the tunnel.

"What about it?" said Aren.

"It's more broken down than the rest, look at the bottom of it."

The wood at the bottom was fraying. It had a faded green touch to it, distinctly duller than the rest of the door.

"Flooding, do you think?" asked Aren.

"Possibly," said Olivia. "Don't you think it'd be easier to break it down?" She got up and began walking slowly towards the door before he'd had a chance to answer.

"You want to break it down?" said Aren.

She chuckled quietly. "We may as well." She looked over at him. "Do you want to do it?" she asked. He had no such interests.

"Wait," he said, placing his hand on the knob and twisting sharply. To his surprise, the door creaked opened, revealing a tiny, dingy room with a few small trunks inside.

"Just our luck, isn't it?" Olivia said. "When we're ready to break down a door, of course it opens."

He laughed softly. "This looks as if it could be the one, though, doesn't it?"

"It's perfect," she said. "Look…they're unlocked." Aren glanced over them, each had the ancient crest of House Malysor on them. It might just work, if they were careful.

Aren knelt down and rustled through the many old artefacts, pieces of jewellery and debris that filled the open trunk. Probably ancient relics, from the days that kings and queens had barrels of heirlooms and riches presented to them in court. Nothing of use, nothing with the garnets, nor with any crest.

"I'll check this one," said Olivia, kneeling down to one of the closed trunks. She pulled the lid open, and a gust of old dust flew up into the air. They sifted through the trunks in silence.

"Aren!" She yelled, calling him over. "And there it is," she said. "Just right." She was holding an old, ornate bronze key. Aren held out his hand and she placed it in his palm. It had the crest of House Malysor on it, it had the red garnets, the same ones which decorated his dagger. It was perfect in every way. He wrapped his fingers around the old thing and slid it carefully into his pocket. "We'd better head up then," he said.

The journey up felt quicker. Perhaps it was the cold air between the two of them, or the rush end excitement to get back into the castle. Suddenly, cracks of sunshine peeked through from above them as they reached the familiar halls outside the Council's Chamber. It was as if the troubles of the war had been put on hold whilst he had been down there and as soon as he was back above ground, it all came back. It was like a thick sadness, as if he could just sense that something awful was about happen.

"We should find Cyneric," said Olivia. "He'll know what to do."

"He's at the Ayleris Command," said Aren. "This can wait."

"I don't think it can," said Olivia, grabbing him. "Come, now! Let us–"

"Your Majesty!" It was Ysser Banlin, yelling frantically from across the hall. "Your Majesty, my lady…"

"What's the matter?" Aren asked.

"It's news from the east, sir. Medlanta. The peninsula has fallen."

"Medlanta? What?"

"Ships came into the harbour, bluecoats. They pillaged straight through the City Guard."

"But Lyndan, it's safe," said Aren. "We've got hundreds there."

"They had thousands," said Ysser. "Lyndan is…well, it's lost."

"Aren…" said Olivia. "Aren, Rayne – she said…she said–"

"It's…*lost?*" Aren was fuming. He foresaw this. How could he have been so stupid as to listen to these fools? It was over for them now. They'd had a chance to protect the harbour and they'd lost it.

"How many fell?"

Ysser shuffled on his feet, looking down in shame.

"How many, my lord?" said Aren. "I will not ask a third time."

"We haven't got all the numbers yet, but it's looking like it's in the hundreds," said Ysser. "At least half."

Hundreds. Maybe if he had trusted himself, used his own intuition, fewer of his men would have died in the east. Maybe he wouldn't have lost Lyndan to Soren Ashcrest. This was all happening while he was king, it was something to be ashamed of. Of course, without Lady Rayne there, it would have been much easier for the bluecoats to stage a coup. He should have known. He *did* know. Never mind, the past could not be changed. His enemies had made their choices. An act of treason. An act of war. He knew what needed to be done now.

"Prepare for war, my lord," said Aren.

"Your Majesty…the Crown Chancellor would strongly advise against it, he wouldn't –"

"Be quiet," said Aren. "And prepare the royal forces for battle. We *will* fight at the Medlantan frontier, and we will win back what has been taken from us."

The Blue and Gold

Eyan

yan picked up the goblet and drank it all in one go. He looked around him at the pompous, proud faces. Drinking wine, eating like fat pigs. None of them had been there. Not one. Not his father, not the rest. They hadn't seen the things he'd seen. They hadn't heard the voices, screaming out in despair, in anguish.

"Master Eyan?" said the little man.

"What is it?"

"Y-you're…you're going to get sick," said Renut. "Not all at once."

"Then so be it," said Eyan, getting up from his chair.

"Eyan," said his father from the other end of the table. "Off so quick?"

"I must rest," he said. "My apologies. It has been a tough few days."

His father's generals all fell to a silence so thick it was suffocating.

"Tough, is it?" said Fraston Spenler. "Tough? Tough is marching into the enemy's territory, right into the heart of it. That's what my sister has done, that's tough."

"I meant no disrespect, it's just—"

"Into the very *heart* of Verenia," said Fraston, raising his glass to a chorus of cheers from the other generals, their mouths still full. "The Falls themselves."

Eyan was sick of it. He knew that Linara's travels north were about as tough as a cloak made of velvet. She wasn't alone, everyone knew that. It was barely enemy territory.

"Aye!" shouted another man. "Tough is marching into battle across the Neck, that's what our brothers and sisters are doing right now! Tough as shit."

Whilst you munch on last night's leftovers. A thousand miles away, where the dead cannot haunt you. But Eyan kept his thoughts inside his head.

"They hold the Neck, so that those behind it can be free! So that Lyndan shall belong to the tyrant no longer, so that it can return to the Free as it always should have!" The man was yelling maniacally, waving his fork around, a bit of mutton still on it. He stared down Eyan. "That's tough," said the general, finally stuffing the piece of mutton into his mouth and chewing hard.

"I know," said Eyan, staring right back at him. "I know because I was there."

The man slammed his fork down and got up, fuming. "What do you mean to say?"

"Stop it, the both of you," said Soren. "Eyan, you will apologise. Where are your manners?"

Probably still in the field of battle, or rather the field of slaughter, he supposed. "I'm sorry, sir."

"Wonderful," said the First Warden. "Now off you go," he shooed him with his hands as if he were a pest of sorts.

Renut got up from his seat too and followed him out of the tent.

"Who asked you to be my shadow?" said Eyan, annoyed.

"S-sorry," said the little man. "What d-did you see out there? At the Neck."

Eyan shook his head. "It wasn't as bad as Sturrock," he said. "Nowhere near. But not quite as easy as Jertonshield either. Blood was shed."

"B-but we won," said Renut. "Now, they f-fly the *Blue and Gold.*"

"It is too early to celebrate. Far too early," he said, shaking his head again. "We wouldn't have won if it wasn't for our guests…the ones from across the Strait. We've got to actually *hold* the Neck, not just seize it…*that* is the hard bit. The Crown forces march on, Rayne Dresden's forces march on. That's what today is all about, yet they sit in there as if we've won this war."

Renut took a deep breath. "But w-we have taken the city," he said. "We must take s-some time to rejoice. W-when do we march onto the next?"

"Tonight," said Eyan. "Not *we*, just me."

Renut looked back in horror. "Y-your pardon, sir?"

"He hasn't told the rest," said Eyan. "Father. He suspects there's a mole amongst his generals. But I march tonight, and Linara's men will meet me there." He took a moment to look around him, his ears pricking up at the familiar crunch of the gravel. Nobody was there, of course. "It is more important, this next one. If we were to succeed…" he gulped. "There would be no stopping us at all. We'd rule the skies and the seas."

"Just h-her men?" said Renut. "Linara Spenler's? That is only…" He looked up at the blue skies, concentrating hard and then his face lit up again. "Ah, only fifty odd."

"Our friends from the south will be joining us," said Eyan. "Our friends from Éterin…Harvus Berywen has promised."

Renut let out a gasp. "That is a g-good thing, no? M-means that he can be trusted? That the First Warden m-might show some mercy?"

He didn't know about mercy, but his father was by no means trusting of the Berywen family, none of them. "I tire of this cat-and-mouse game," said Eyan. "Moving from city to city…it's tiring now. I want it to be over now."

"You want t-to kill Aren Aryssen?"

Eyan looked down. "If that is what it takes."

"That *is* what it t-takes," said Renut. "There c-can only be one winner."

Eyan sighed. "I suppose so."

"Did you s-see anyone?" said Renut. "That you r-recognised? In Medlanta?"

"No," said Eyan. "The Crown forces hadn't arrived yet. I got out before they had."

"And o-our…*friends*?" said Renut, his beady eyes wide. Eyan looked back at him thinly, the side of his face curled into a half-scowl.

"Our *friends*," Renut continued. "The ones which rise from within the shadows."

Eyan nodded sullenly. "Yes, yes they had arrived," he said. "Like I said, it wasn't quite as bad as Sturrock, could've been a whole lot worse," he muttered, his head bowed. But he knew that the things he'd seen would stay with him. He knew restless nights lay ahead.

"Is it a w-wise idea?" said Renut. "Trusting them? After what they've d-done?"

Eyan didn't know how to answer him. He looked around at the sandy wastelands surrounding the camp. He'd have much rather stayed in Medlanta. At least he wouldn't have had to face what was still to come. He looked up at the city walls, so far in the distance, its two watchtowers looming over it. They looked tiny from here. "Let us simply hope that there is less bloodshed in New Castisa."

The Blade

Aren

Aren pushed around the piece of chicken on his plate. It had been a while since he'd eaten. He had no interest in it. It had already been a few days since Lyndan fell to the bluecoats and he'd eaten less and less each day that passed. How could he? When his subjects were being starved out on the Medlantan frontier?

He didn't feel hungry. More than anything, he felt alone. Uncle Mentos and Ysser had led the armies east, with Cyneric and Lady Rayne just behind them. Éline and Lara had spent most of their time with Lord Nazeris. Pennyn was cold and distant. Not by coincidence either. But Aren cared little, his decision had been final. Olivia, meanwhile, was more withdrawn than ever. She'd spent little time with Aren since that day in the tunnels.

"I'm afraid it isn't good, Your Majesty. The news."

Aren looked up at his chancellor, who had a more horrid expression on his face than usual.

"What?" said Aren. By now, he knew that no type of news was good news. His advisors seldom came to him bearing news of their good fortune. It was wiser to be prepared for the worst, always.

"Medlanta. We've just heard back. It was a huge loss for the Crown, sir." Pennyn bowed his head. The shame was a facade, the chancellor sounded smug, Aren could hear it in his voice.

"Where did you get this news from? Lady Rayne?"

Pennyn shook his head. "Lord Ysser himself. They're on their way back, the ones who've survived, Lord Ysser is quite badly hurt. Lady Rayne has been evacuated…out of the camps into a village nearby. Ysser has an aunt who lives there apparently, just outside of Astonkirk."

"Evacuated?" The word felt awfully real.

The chancellor nodded. "It was *far* too dangerous for the Countess of Lyndan to be caught in the middle of a battle as the enemy drew closer." Again, his voice was smug, but Aren pretended not to notice.

"And Cyneric?"

Pennyn looked almost disappointed with the tone with which he'd been met. "Cyneric is fine. He is on his way back as well, he should be here within the hour, and the rest before nightfall," he said.

"But what has he to say about Lyndan?" said Aren. "How could we possibly have lost? We outnumber the bluecoats, the reports we received from Rayne's spies made our victory all but certain! We just had to close the Neck, secure the borders. Cyneric told me that himself."

"With all due respect, Your Majesty, Cyneric Porter is not the Chief of Ayleris Command, nor is he the Arms Counsel. He has–"

"Answer my question, chancellor."

"Cyneric can speak to you himself when he arrives," said Pennyn, stepping back and folding his arms, his face stern and serious. "I have not heard his thoughts on the matter, nor am I interested in them," he muttered.

"And what are *your* thoughts on the matter?" asked Aren.

Pennyn sighed. "From what I've heard, their men far outnumbered ours at the vanguard. What's more, they held their ground, and they held it well. They strengthened the Neck better than we could have ever fathomed, there was no way through. They didn't extend their forces westward or try to push back the Verenic forces, they just…they just stayed there. Held their ground."

"The Landridgian forces."

"Pardon?"

"Not the Verenic forces, the *Landridgian* forces. I am the King of Landridge all in one piece, not just of Verenia. The Crown forces are Landridgian."

"You're right, of course, Your Majesty," said Pennyn and the sternness was gone.

"How did they get so many ships in? It doesn't make any sense," said Aren. "We control the seas in the south, and we've all but cut them off. One or two boats sneaking past is one thing, not a whole bloody armada. There was no way for them to get so many bluecoats in, not with us watching. Not from the south." Aren got up from his seat and began pacing around the room. *Not from the south.* A thought crossed his mind, a terrible one, which made his heart sink. "Is it possible, that it was with the help of the Sandaerians?" he said.

"I wish I could say it wasn't," said Pennyn. "I'd really hoped we were wrong about them, I'd really hoped that they could be trusted."

"It makes sense, though, doesn't it?" said Aren. "They're right across the Strait, they have good access to the peninsula…and the means to get past Crown forces on the water without raising too many eyebrows."

"I can't say it would surprise me," said Pennyn. "Nynnevor is all but the throw of a stone away."

"Surely Lord Hercan would have noticed something?"

Pennyn shrugged his shoulders. "Perhaps we are thinking about it too much."

"Arrange for Lady Rayne to come and speak with me as soon as she is back."

"Of course," said Pennyn.

The thunderous footsteps of heavy boots emerged from down the corridor. Aren peered ahead to catch a glance of who it was. Suddenly, he felt a tad more comfortable. It was Cyneric, some soldiers behind him. He gestured at them to leave and darted straight for Aren.

"Cyneric, I'm so glad you're fine. What's happening –"

"We have very little time," Cyneric interrupted Aren. "It's worse than you've heard. Both of you."

"We know about the harbour," said Pennyn.

"Forget about the fucking harbour," said Cyneric. "New Castisa. It's fallen. To the bluecoats."

"It's…fallen?" said Aren emptily.

"They've been playing us. They made us push our forces east, to a battle that we would never win."

"We left a good few hundred men in New Castisa," said Pennyn.

"Not enough. Like I said, they've been playing us," said Cyneric. "That's why they took Medlanta first. Whilst we were fighting whoever these soldiers were on the peninsula, Ashcrest sent his own troops east from Jertonshield. His lad led them himself, from what I hear."

"So, we've lost the harbour and we've now lost the dynes too, all in one day?" said Aren. "How did we lose Lyndan? You told me it would work, you told me we had the numbers."

"There were too many men. Far too many, Aren. The battle was all but lost by the time I'd even reached the border. There were more men than there should have been, and all at that bloody Neck. They were stronger than us, faster too."

"You don't think…"

Cyneric nodded.

"What do we do now?" said Aren.

"I don't know," Pennyn replied, whilst Cyneric remained silent.

"They have New Castisa. What's to stop them from rowing up the river now and staging a siege? Or from bombing us to a crisp? They have the aces now, they have the skies."

"We have to win back New Castisa. At any cost," said Cyneric.

"How can we stand a fair chance? They are stronger. They have dwellers. Cyneric. They control the harbour, the aerodynes, the river."

"We orchestrate our movements very carefully. One step at a time," said Pennyn. The easiest way to destroy them now would be from the inside."

From the inside. How?

The doors slammed open. There were no knocks.

"Aren!" she yelled, with no regard for those around her. A guard clambered in behind her, but he was too late. The three men looked at Olivia Berywen in confusion as she swatted them away from her.

"I'd like to speak with you in private," she said to Aren. "Now."

"Olivia, this definitely isn't the time."

"It's urgent, Aren." She looked delirious, her eyes were fixed on him. It must have been serious. He nodded at his advisors and the room quickly became empty. They stood opposite each other in silence for a short moment before he cleared his throat to speak.

"Now is not the time, Olivia," he said. "This isn't what we discussed, we have to wait for the rest. It might not even work now, it's all going to shit."

"I'm not talking about Cyneric's plan," said Olivia, grinning madly. "I've found something." Aren knew better than to get his hopes up though, as he reminded himself to expect the worst.

"I think I might know how to retrieve the pendant, Aren. We can stop them." Her grin widened, and she rubbed her hands together in excitement as if she were a small child.

Aren looked blankly at her. "How?"

"The lost bloodgate," she said. "I think it's in this castle. I think I've found it."

Aren waited for the worst. He anticipated more terrible news, but the smile on Olivia's face only grew brighter.

"Tell me everything," he said. "From the beginning. Where do you think it is? And how did you find it?"

"We don't have time for all that," said Olivia, grabbing him by the arm. "It involves a lot of boring translation and reading, but I'm almost certain it'll work. I'm just not sure how to open it, we need you and your Aryssen blood for that."

"Where is it?" If she wasn't mistaken, if she actually had found another bloodgate into the Panderer's realm, maybe they actually stood a fair chance after all.

"Do you remember when we were down in the tunnels?"

He nodded. Of course he remembered.

"The door with the Old Verenic scriptures on it," she said.

"Scriptures?"

"Yes, I did some reading, and I think I understand, well *we* did some reading –"

"Who is we?" said Aren.

"Well, Lara helped me."

Aren glared at her. "Are you sure that was wise?"

"Our plans are not to happen for some time anyway," said Olivia. "I *had* to trust her – I needed her help."

"Right, well, let's see this bloodgate, then." He wouldn't believe it until he saw it with his own eyes.

"Now?"

"Yes, I've got my dagger with me."

It was just as it was the other day. Except the tunnels seemed even darker, even narrower.

"You brought Lara down here?" said Aren.

"Heavens, no. I couldn't if I tried, she wouldn't have it," she said. "I drew it out for her, the writing. She couldn't completely understand it, she's still learning, of course, but she helped a great deal. I used the books to piece it all together, but I couldn't have done it without her."

"How are you so sure that it is the bloodgate?"

"There's a drawing of the door, that same door, in *The Sandaerian Promise*. Except, with more of the writing on it. Look here, half of it is faded," she said, pulling out a folded piece of paper with ancient writing scrawled across it.

"How nice," muttered Aren. "That bloody *Sandaerian Promise*."

"*Stone of passage brings the winds. Realm of Sin, of Corruption and Guilt. Of Blood of the Crown…*"

"The *Crown*? It mentions that?" he asked her.

"Well… not exactly. It doesn't translate well. *Dendrus* is… the shoulders that the faith rests upon, the shoulders of the Deryz. That is what Lara told me."

"I see," said Aren. "What else does it say?"

"I couldn't piece it all together perfectly," she muttered. "The winds? It went on to mention something about mountains, something else about some stars…*stars falling from the night, into the embers of the old*… Blood of the free, blood of the shadows …Neither of us could understand most of the nonsense, but the pieces about the *stone of passage* and the *realm of sin* seemed as if they were promising."

"Realm of sin?" Aren laughed quietly. It was an interesting way to describe the world in which he'd spent his childhood.

"Look," said Olivia, pointing to the empty dark wall. He gave her a confused look. "See how the tunnel turns left from here?" she said. "And then, look, just across over there. See how it curves back round?" He wasn't sure what to make of it. "Now, come now Aren. Just straight on from over here," she pointed.

There it was. Battered, as ever. Olivia looked at him as if she was expecting more of a reaction, but he wouldn't celebrate just yet. He was half convinced she'd gone mad, this tattered, bruised old piece of wood couldn't be it, surely?

"There isn't anything behind it," she said, pointing at the bend in the tunnel. "It's just the wall, and then the tunnel comes round behind here, you just saw it. It's a false door."

And that's when it hit him. Suddenly, the prospect of this actually working wasn't such a distant dream.

"Well, shall we get on with it then?" she said.

He was suddenly nervous. His knees were shaky, and he felt an impending sense of doom, though he couldn't quite rationalise why. If the worst came to be, if Olivia was mistaken, then this door wouldn't lead him anywhere. He would lose nothing. The kingdom would lose nothing. Then why was his heart racing?

"Of course," he replied. He pulled out the dagger and held it as if it were made of glass, carefully in between his fingertips.

"Aren, what is that?" Olivia exclaimed, her voice suddenly riddled with a sense of fear. Of course, Aren realised that she'd never seen it before. She'd never before been to the Panderer's realm, so she had no idea what this dagger was capable of.

"It's for the bloodgate," he said calmly.

"Do you think it's the door, then?" she asked.

He shrugged his shoulders.

"What's the dagger got to do with opening the bloodgate?" said Olivia.

"It isn't easy to explain," said Aren. "Now, this is quite an unusual experience, so I want to describe it to you beforehand. It isn't going to hurt. Just remember that."

She nodded quickly. "What do you need me to do?"

"I'm going to say some things in my tongue…and then when I look at you, I need you to close your eyes. Eventually, if it works, and you'll know when it works, we'll turn around and lean our backs against the door. You're going to hold the edge of the blade and I'll hold the other end. That's incredibly important – don't forget it. I can't do this without you."

"I won't."

"One more thing. You might see something unfamiliar. Strange. Maybe even unpleasant. Something you think isn't really there – or shouldn't be. Pay it no attention. It's incredibly important you stay completely focussed."

"Focussed on what?"

"The blade, of course," he said. "I'm going to begin now."

She looked terrified, but he had no time to waste. Aren started the ancient ritual. He held the dagger up to his forehead, and gently brought the surface of the blade to his skin.

Olivia let out a loud gasp.

"Olivia…" He brought his arm back down. "Olivia, you can't do that. I'm not going to hurt anybody."

"I know, I'm sorry, it's just–"

"I'm going to start again. I need you to be silent and remember what I said."

"I do."

He lifted the blade up to the skin of his forehead once more, and without delay slowly slid it across, muttering the familiar incantation. Moments later, he turned to face his friend, keeping his head down the whole while, and lifted the blade to her forehead. He was careful and particular about the prayers he was muttering. He didn't look her in the eyes, it might have distracted her. She had to focus on the blade and nothing else.

As soon as he was done, he looked up directly at her and gave her a gentle nod. She closed her eyes. He turned to face the door and did the same. His dagger's hilt firmly in his hand, he prepared. He took no more than a moment. He held his blade at his hip with his eyes closed, took in a deep breath, and sharply plunged it forward into the old door in front of him.

The Door
Olivia

Olivia worked up the courage to say something and opened her mouth but could only let out a croak.

"Hmm?"

"Aren, is it working?"

"Why don't you open your eyes now," said the king.

"I'm too scared."

"Don't be."

But her hand was trembling. The anticipation is what scared her the most. What waited for her when she opened her eyes? What was she so afraid of?

Hesitantly, she opened them, just a crack. The dim light snuck in almost immediately, a flash of silver and red and brown and she closed them again, gasping. Were her eyes playing tricks? But then again, who was *she* to define the limits of possibility? She should know better by now. Making sense of it, magic and power, was a fool's game.

Her eyes hadn't played tricks, she soon realised as she opened them once more, wholly this time. The blade was stained. A dark streak of blood flowing down it, from where it had pierced the door. Or at least, it looked like blood. It couldn't be, surely? She hadn't felt the blade pierce her own skin, nor was there any blood on Aren's forehead. Where could it have come from? Wood does not bleed, nor does brick. But then again, here she was, stood before an old, battered door, expecting a bloodgate to open up before her. A bloodgate that would take her to another world…far, far away from this one. Magic was real, despite everything she'd been told as a child.

"Better not to ask," he said, noticing her. "Now when I say go, I'm going to hold this dagger up from the hilt, and you'll hold it from the blade, and–"

"The blade?" she whimpered. "The blood-stained-"

"Shhh…we need to be quiet. Don't worry about the blood, it'll be gone. As I said, you're going to hold the blade and we'll turn around slowly so that our backs are against the door."

"What then?"

"We lean back against it."

"Against what?" asked Olivia.

"The door," said Aren, as if it were painfully obvious. "Pay close attention."

Her stomach churned and she felt a sharp pain in her chest. Her hands were still trembling, she had no control over them now. Reluctantly though, she nodded, and Aren began the ancient ritual. She gasped as the blade touched her skin. His movements were rehearsed to perfection. She shuddered though, clenching her fists. It didn't matter to her that he'd probably done this a thousand times, or that he'd never do anything to hurt her. She felt cold, her breath icy all of a sudden. It was like nothing she'd felt ever before. Her hands were pale, tainted only by the deep red touch of blood smeared across her palms.

As she took a hasty breath, turning to face away from the door, her mind wandered. It was sorcery, of a kind. It wasn't right… was it? It couldn't be. There had to be a cost…there always was with blood magic. She cast her thoughts aside and leaned back, ever so slowly. Making sense of it was a fool's game.

There was a deafening cracking sound. She carried on, easing backwards bit by bit, not even noticing the world slip away from around her. She waited for the cold, hard door to press against the small of her back but felt no more than a light brush. There was no cold, hard door behind her. There was nothing. Empty space. Her eyes twitched and she looked around her frantically at a greyish haze of nothingness. She didn't quite know what it all was. It wasn't until a few short moments later when cracks of colour seeped in and an abysmally lit, dull room started to materialise around her. It was the smell of stale cat piss she noticed first, a vile one, worse than the tunnels she'd been in not long ago. Instantly something about it all felt unnatural, as if it wasn't real at all. She rubbed her eyes and blinked as the haze started to clear. The room could have been a cellar, or a really unkempt pantry of some sort. Dusty and full of shadows, piles and piles of rubbish in the corner.

"Shall we?" said Aren, turning towards her. She nodded quickly and quietly, eager and scared to follow her friend into his world.

He stumbled over some small boxes on the floor and walked towards the door, smiling as he opened it. She scampered like a blind mouse behind him as he walked out into the small open space, a crack of grey light shining down from the stairs, if you could even call it light. She followed him up and through another set of doors, into what appeared to be an old library. She wanted a closer look at some of the books that had been left behind and neglected for what looked like centuries. She wondered what the Panderer read and wrote about. All the stories of the horror of these people – where had they come from? There was so much to think about, but she stopped her curiosity from getting the better of her. Aren sped on, not turning around even once and so she followed.

When they finally made it out of the door, the air was cold, much colder than she was used to – sort of like a sharp Pyburrock chill. There was no sun, just a dull grey that lingered above them. There were trees lining the narrow road just outside. Further up the hill was a rusty black gate, some open grassland behind it. In the distance, motorcars, of all colours. Very different to the ones she knew. A single grey path parted the fields, some bare trees dotted around it. But where was he taking her? The path didn't seem to lead anywhere at all.

Why was he smiling? She couldn't figure it out. He looked almost yearningly at the dull suburbia around him. It wasn't something that her eyes could get used to though…it was a strange and cold land. A part of her still wasn't convinced that she wasn't in a lingering nightmare.

There was a loud rumble and the trees around them stirred as a thin, white demon soared above them. She let out a loud gasp and clutched tightly to Aren's arms, but he just chuckled softly.

"What was *that*?" she said. "Why did it look like that?"

"A *jet plane*," said Aren admiringly, still looking up. "An aerodyne. Did you see how fast it was? Did you feel its ferocious roar in your heart?"

Whatever she'd felt in her heart, she wasn't sure she liked it at all. "Aren, where are we going?"

"To the school," he said, still not looking at her.

"Will there be a lot of people there?"

"No, there isn't any school today," he chuckled, looking at the state of her. "Or else I wouldn't bring you with me, would I?"

She didn't know if she should have laughed at that.

"I just mean, you aren't exactly dressed like you belong here."

"Nor are you," she said.

"Yes, but people know me here. And I've grown used to coming up with excuses in case somebody asks questions."

She nodded and decided to spare him any more questions.

The path was empty, but they kept an eye out for any stray wanderers. Aren reassured her that this part of town was fairly quiet most of the time and that this was the quickest way to get to the school, but something about it all scared her nonetheless.

"Wait," whispered Aren, slightly unnerved. "Thought I heard a voice, a child maybe," he muttered.

"There," she said, pointing to the trees further up the path.

"Ah yes," he said. "She looks familiar … but then it is a small town."

The little girl did look familiar, even to Olivia, who'd never before been to this barren town.

"We'll wait for her to leave, just in case," said Aren.

"She looked a bit like Daria," whispered Olivia. "Maybe that's why she looked familiar."

"I think we can go on," said Aren. "She's gone."

The remainder of their journey was even quieter than before. When they finally arrived at the wall outside the grand entrance to the old school building, the sun was lower in the sky, or so Olivia guessed. She couldn't see it through the thick grey clouds above. The evening chill sent a shiver down her spine and brought with it a gentle dimness, foreboding sunset. The darkness came almost all at once. Days seemed shorter here, even shorter than Sturrock during the winters.

"Okay, we'll go in through the doors at the side of the building – stay with me and stay quiet, it'll be safer that way," said Aren. "Olivia, if we do encounter anyone, maybe it's for the best if you remain quiet," he said. "You do not speak the tongue. I can tell them a lie and we can get out of there as soon as we can, but I think it will be easier if we don't raise too many questions."

"Not to worry, Your Majesty," she replied. She didn't care for the tone he'd taken.

They set off over the wall to the side of the building. She blindly followed Aren through the muddy field. He looked like he knew a way in, but to her the sullen grey walls and grimy glass windows all looked the same.

"And just how often did you used to sneak out of here when you should have been studying?" Olivia asked him, as they reached a low archway behind a large rose bush.

He laughed. "Not very often at all."

"Then how do…"

"Cyneric." Aren turned toward her. "You know how he is…always have a way in, always have a way out. Right, come on."

They clambered through the small tunnel straight into the side of the building. It wasn't a difficult feat; in fact, this building wasn't very well protected at all. The schools in her world, in *their* world, were better suited, more practical.

They reached a short wall, a brick or two loose at its base and he effortlessly clawed his way over it, signalling at her to follow. She was reluctant but gathered herself and climbed over, finding herself on a raised wooden platform now, bordering a large window. Aren pulled out his dagger and began picking at the rusty handle.

Olivia frantically looked around, but Aren had been right – there was simply no one around at all. An odd, lifeless world. It felt like a sullen hell. The window creaked open, just wide enough for each of them to fit through and the inside of the horrible place might have looked even sadder than the outside.

"It smells rather interesting, I must say," said Olivia, noticing another foul, rotten sort of smell. "Not sure how you spent years in here."

"With difficulty," said Aren. "Unsure if the smells were a major part of my worries during my time here, though."

She nodded, shuffling on her feet. The bottoms of her shoes were sticky, and she'd brought in mud with her, leaving a trail from the window but somehow, she didn't think anybody in this place would ever notice. The walls were cracked, the paint chipped, and she could hear a constant drip of water down the old corridor.

"Right, as far as I know, the pendant should be in the utility room," he muttered to himself, walking briskly past some doors with strange writing on them. "I do hope we find it there, I'd dread to think that we'd made this journey without reason," said Aren.

"It has to be there." She didn't know if he was reassuring her or himself.

She hoped they'd find the damned thing. If they didn't, she didn't know if they'd win this war. She didn't know exactly what role it played but she knew enough to be able to bet her life on the fact that it could not, under any circumstances, be lost. She could only imagine the devastation. They had to stop the dwellers.

"This is where I hid a lot of my things while I was at school, bits and pieces for my training, letters from my mother," said Aren, as they approached the door. "Not even the *caretakers* ventured up here too often, and even if they did – there were always plenty of good hiding places."

She didn't care to ask what a *caretaker* was at school, nor why Aren knew of so many hiding places. "Is it locked?" she said.

"That's the best part, it never needs to be," said Aren, pushing the door wide open. "Nobody cares about it."

Nobody seemed to care about anything in this odd place.

He darted straight towards a shelf with many dusty old pots and containers on it. She couldn't see what he was doing but she waited behind him as he cluttered around with the old things, muttering to himself.

"And there it is," he said loudly. It had seemed far too easy. He held up the sparkling dark vermillion stone up by its chain, hanging it in front of her eyes. It peeked out of its golden case, emblazoned with the royal crest of House Aryssen.

"Aleryc's Pendant," she said. "I almost can't believe that we've found it. Maybe something terrible will happen now so we can't take it back with us."

"Best not tempt fate, Olivia."

"I suppose not," she said. "Although would it be so bad, being stuck here forever?"

He looked back at her if she'd gone mad. "This world has its own kinds of sordid doings," he replied. "The peace would be temporary."

He once again looked over the shelves and pulled out a pair of sparring gloves – she recognised them immediately, almost identical to what her brother Chrysan used when training back in Éterin.

"Truly, Aren, you never cease to shock me. Sparring gloves? Don't tell me Cyneric can't fetch you another pair in Ayleris."

"Somewhat more value attached to these ones," he said. "I've always trained with them."

He stuffed the pendant and gloves deep into his pocket and ushered her out of the room, shutting the door tightly behind himself.

"Wait – what are you doing?" she said to him. "It's a pendant – why don't you wear it?"

Aren laughed. But then, he gave her a look of intrigue. "Do you reckon that's how it works?"

"I don't dabble much in blood magic, Aren, so, your guess is as good as mine, but it *is* a pendant, one passed down in *your* family. Maybe you should put it on."

He gave her a look comparable to a shrug of the shoulders and then a simple nod. He took the pendant out of his pocket by its chain and wore it around his neck. The moment it kissed his skin she expected an eruption of some sort. A surge in energy, perhaps. An overwhelming burst of power. Of magic. But nothing. All that had changed was a look of impatience on Aren's face. She scowled.

"I guess it isn't that easy," she said. "At least it's safer there than in your pocket."

"Right, let's set off," he said, ignoring her again.

They left the building the same way they'd come in. As true night set in, Olivia wondered what would be happening back at home at that exact moment. Would the castle be getting ready for dinner? Would the lords and ladies be wondering where their king is? They'd been gone for some time now.

A dog suddenly barked somewhere behind her. Then, a shrill squeal of a child. She turned around, startled. To her astonishment, the little girl from earlier that evening glared up at her. It was a bit like looking down at Daria, and it gave her chills. Beside the child stood an older girl, probably closer to Olivia's own age. She had bright auburn hair much like the younger girl. Sisters, perhaps, she thought to herself.

"Aren?"

It was the older girl that had spoken. It spooked Olivia. She silently glanced over at him, and he looked as if he'd seen a ghost.

The girl spoke with an icy voice, looking at Aren, and then at Olivia, and then back at Aren. Olivia couldn't understand the tongue, but she could feel the judgement in the Panderer's gaze…

looking at every part of her, from her eyes to her blouse, to her hands... her *hands*. Olivia looked down, lifting her palms up, but the blood was completely gone, just her pale, slightly muddy skin left behind.

The Panderer hadn't stopped talking. She was furious, by the sounds of it. And Aren fearful, maybe apologetic...she wondered what the two spoke about. Aren had looked over at Olivia twice now, pointing and gesturing wildly. The Panderer smiled, but she didn't look happy. Not one bit. Aren, meanwhile, was pale, smiling awkwardly at her.

"Olivia," said the Panderer. Her accent was foreign and strange. Olivia couldn't understand the tongue at all, but the Panderer spoke slowly and surely, as if speaking to a child. A deaf child.

"Shannon," said Aren, nodding over at the Panderer with his eyes.

Olivia went red, smiling and nodding in response. Suddenly the little Panderer jumped up and waved frantically. It left a weird feeling in Olivia's stomach. Then, the older girl, Shannon, smiled and waved before brushing past her and heading off in the opposite direction.

"What did she want?" said Olivia. "Who is she?"

"Oh, an old friend," said Aren. "She didn't want anything. Just wanted to know why I'd left so quickly, why I'm back... How long I'm staying here for."

"Oh?"

"Yes," said Aren. "Now come on, let's leave before somebody else finds us."

As Good a Time as Any
Aren

ren toyed with the jagged relic, rubbing it between his thumb and finger. He was slumped in a chair in the corner of his study, deep in thought.

"You've been at it for days, you've tried everything," said Cyneric. "Give it a rest. They're going to be ready soon, we don't want to keep them waiting or they'll suspect something is wrong."

"He's right, Aren," Olivia added. "Maybe we were wrong, maybe this isn't the way."

"They can wait," replied Aren. It *had* to be the way. It had to be his destiny. "I thought maybe if I brought it back here, maybe it would become clearer. You're sure there's nothing in the book?" he said, turning to Olivia. "So much for the *Promise.*"

"No, I'm sorry. I've looked again. There's absolutely nothing anywhere."

"Aren, I don't think it would be wise for you to be carrying it around all the time," said Cyneric, folding his arms. "Just lying around in your pocket, especially in times like this…I just think it is far more dangerous."

Aren thought about it. "For me or the pendant?" he laughed. Cyneric shrugged.

"Both, actually."

Perhaps he was right. If it were to fall into the wrong hands, he didn't know what might happen. Just because he didn't know how it worked didn't mean that nobody did.

"What would be the alternative? Keeping it locked away isn't exactly any safer, is it?" said Aren. "Vaults are meant to be broken into."

"Well, no-one said anything about locking it away. Give it to me, I'll hold onto it myself," said Cyneric, holding out his palm.

Aren eyed him. He'd known Cyneric for almost all his life now. They had been through plenty together, and the Panderer's loyalty had never faltered. He'd never given Aren any reason to doubt him…yet…why did he want it? He brushed aside his silly thoughts, Cyneric was his oldest friend. If he could not trust his oldest friend, he could not trust anybody. But still, he didn't think it wise to give it to him.

"But I don't really know that it's any safer with you," said Aren. "You're by my side all the time. The only times you aren't by my side are when you're…well, out fighting."

"And?"

"I know you'd guard it with your life, but I don't know if we can afford that. We need you doing what you do best." He shook his head.

"I can do what I do best while still protecting the pendant," said Cyneric.

"Really? So, you'd march into battle with *that* thing on you?" said Aren. "Somehow I don't think that would be the cleverest idea."

Cyneric laughed. "No, I don't suppose it would." He leaned against the shelves beside him, toying with a wooden splinter, and the smile faded from his face. "It's bigger than you, this pendant."

"I know."

"No, but I want to be clear. If we went to war…"

"He knows," said Olivia. "We all know"

"If we went to war," said Cyneric, completely ignoring her. "And you were to fall, that *thing* need not fall into the wrong hands."

"What about me?" Olivia said suddenly. "I can keep it safe for you."

It wasn't completely outrageous. She was practically under lock and key at the castle. And he *could* trust her, couldn't he? After all, she couldn't be judged for the actions of her kin. Olivia had had plenty of opportunities to betray him if she had wanted and she had proven herself time and time again. He wondered though, if it was fair to burden her with something like this, something which could put her life in danger?

"It's not safe."

"Nobody will know it's with me," she said. "We're sworn to secrecy, the three of us, and nobody else knows about the pendant. Who would be able to guess that I have it?"

It wasn't without its problems, but Aren supposed that she might just be right. Olivia scarcely spoke with those outside the castle…it'd be safe with her. And as for her own safety…she was a Berywen, there was no way the bluecoats would risk losing such a powerful ally – Lord Berywen wouldn't have it. Perhaps the situation could be used to their advantage. Perhaps.

"Very well," he said. "Tell no one. Absolutely no one. This cannot leave this room."

"Of course," she said. Cyneric nodded too.

Olivia held out her hand in front of Aren.

"What are those?" Aren asked, passing his fingers over the red crescents dotted across her palm.

She shrugged her shoulders. "I've got sharp nails."

"And do you make it a habit to use them?" he laughed.

"Just give it here, Aren."

Reluctantly, Aren handed the ancient relic over and sighed, careful not to let her see.

"Right, you've kept them waiting long enough," said Cyneric, slapping his hands on his thighs and getting up from the wooden chair. "Any longer and they might really start thinking that something is wrong."

"Do you think it's time?" said Aren.

"As good a time as any," he said.

"Do you want me there?" said Olivia.

"It works out better if you are," said Cyneric. "More convincing."

"Pennyn, Ysser… Rayne and Mentos," said Aren. "Is that all?"

Cyneric nodded. "And Lara."

"Perfect. Let's get on with it then," he said, getting up out of his own seat.

"Hold on," said Cyneric, putting his hand up as they approached the room. "Olivia, you go in first and then wait. We will join you in a few moments. It'll be suspicious if the three of us were to walk in together, all at once."

Aren waited until the door had shut behind her. "Do you think I made the right choice, giving it to her?" he said to Cyneric.

"I don't see what other options you had, given the circumstances."

"That isn't a yes," said Aren.

"It isn't a no either," replied his mentor. "Right, let's go."

They walked into the hall, just one long table laid out in the centre. Pennyn Runeval was sat at the opposite end of the table, his lips pressed tightly together, and his arms laid out on the table, fingers drumming a jaunty rhythm. Along the table, the others eagerly rose up all at once as he entered.

"Please sit," said Aren. "I know you all have important roles in court, duties without which this war effort would be futile. So, I'll keep this short. As short as is possible."

Pennyn Runeval grunted and crossed his arms.

"Now, what I'm saying may come as a surprise to some of you. I understand this, I know it may be a lot to take in, but these are uncertain and unruly times in which we live." He chewed on the words; they weren't his after all. He'd have chosen different ones, but if it needed to be done, it needed to be done, so he took a shallow breath and continued. "You've all heard the stories about the bloodgates, the mystical passages into other realms…the ones capable of taking you from one place to another," he said. A mixture of faces looked back at him. Curious. Confused. Frightened, perhaps? It was Pennyn's that stuck out…the chancellor was as cynical as ever. "It's real…the magic – it's all real." He paused and let them take it in. "The bloodgates, they're enchanted by an ancient spell… one capable of much greater than the stories would have us believe. It is possible to move from one to another, with blood magic."

"Blood magic?!" said Ysser.

"Yes, blood magic," said Aren, turning to face him. "And there are a few in our kingdom, the bloodgates. Ancient things, from the time before the Deryzi."

Lara Hercan looked puzzled. "From hundreds and hundreds of years ago?"

Lord Ysser scoffed. "*Bloodgates?*" He rolled his eyes and chuckled.

Aren looked each of them in the eyes as he talked, moving from one face to the next. His eyes were met by a steely, cold gaze as he glanced over at Pennyn. Mentos, on the other hand, looked fearful, wringing his hands together.

"Did the Sandaerzi feed you this, Your Majesty?" said Ysser.

"You will respect your king," said Lady Rayne sternly, slamming her fist on the table and scowling at him before turning to face Aren. "But I'm afraid I must ask you too, where have you got this information from?" A part of the ploy.

"I understand your disbelief – all of you. This is information very few are privy to. I have chosen to trust you all with it because I believe it is in the best interests of the kingdom." He took a step forward and leaned against the table, turning to Ysser. "This is reliable information, and all I can say, my lord, is that it is not from the North Parydon. This is something I have witnessed with my own eyes."

"With your own eyes?" said Mentos.

"Yes, uncle. And that's as far as I'll dwell on the matter."

"But how-"

Cyneric put up his hand. "That is as far as the king would dwell on it."

"Thank you," said Aren. "The more pressing issue at hand, I believe that we can use this…this *magic* to our advantage."

"How so?" said Rayne. Again, a part of the ploy.

"Well, as I mentioned already, there are more than one of these bloodgates within our kingdom. We have recently learnt of one within Ayleris, not too far from the castle actually."

"Oh? Here in Ayleris?" said Olivia, speaking for the first time. "And where are the others?"

"It's just one of them in particular that we should concern ourselves with. The one within the Valecrest. I believe we can take the war south. Attack the traitors from the inside."

This time, each face wore the same expression. Fear and concern all round.

"I have in my pocket a key," said Aren, pulling it out. He held up the old bronze thing to the rest of the room. "The Key of Blood. It has the power to open the bloodgate and take with it up to five or six men, maybe more. They'll never see us coming."

Pennyn's head shook and then sank into his hands. He'd rehearsed well for it, it seemed.

"Is there a problem, Crown Chancellor?"

"And so, we would use blood magic to get an army inside the palace?" he said mockingly. The performance was almost too convincing.

"Not an army. All we need is five good men. Trained men."

"And just what will we do with five men, exactly?" said Pennyn.

"The Crown forces will be waiting on the outside," said Aren. "A perfect siege. And that is where you both come in," he said, looking at Rayne Dresden and Mentos Jeffyrs.

"This is a foolish and hasty plan," said Pennyn. "We'll lose far more than we gain."

"Where exactly is the bloodgate, Aren?" said Mentos, ignoring the Crown Chancellor. "Where in Ayleris?"

Aren smiled. "Just up the river. At the Halls of Femoren Deryz."

"I think it is possible," said Mentos. He turned towards Rayne. "What say you? I think if we coordinated it well, we could take back Sturrock from those that have usurped us. How soon can you get word from your people?"

The High Lady rolled her eyes at him. "I don't think it's impossible, but I must say I'm surprised that this is the plan we are going with," she said to Aren. "Well, I can get word from my people within the day at best."

"Then, it is settled," said Aren. He turned around to Cyneric, placing the old key in his mentor's palm. "Could you put it back where it belongs."

Cyneric nodded and took a step back, placing it in his pocket.

"I'm sorry," said Ysser. "I'm not entirely sure I believe in all this…this nonsense."

"You can be one of the first men to go in then, Lord Ysser," said Aren, deliberately condescending in his tone. "As part of our five-man army. Perhaps seeing it yourself will help you believe."

The man scowled at him briefly, then nodded. "Very well then, Your Majesty."

"Olivia and Lara, I'll need your help too, with learning more about the actual bloodgates themselves," said Aren.

"I don't see how we can help," said Lara.

"You've proven to be quite well-read on Verenic history, Lara," he said. "The tongue too. And Olivia…she reads a lot of books," he said. "She is good at puzzles too."

His Council shared a look of uncertainty and disbelief and he found himself praying that the ruse would work.

"We will speak again very soon. That is all for now," he said to them all, signalling for them to leave. He waited until he was alone with Cyneric and Olivia.

"Do you think they bought it?" she said.

"I think it was very well sold," said Cyneric. "Rayne and Pennyn did well, that ought to cause a stir. Now we wait. Traitors thrive on information so it shouldn't be too long before they act. We've only got three people to look at closely."

"And it has to be one of them," said Olivia. "Or somebody they speak to. It cannot be anybody else."

"Why Lara?" said Aren, drumming his fingers on his thigh.

"Because I told her about Nynnevor," said Olivia.

"And why did you do that?" said Cyneric.

"Because we can trust her, and this is the only way to prove for certain that we can."

"Ah," said Cyneric. "Brilliant. Now listen, both of you. I'm going to keep this key with me," he continued. "Olivia, you and I should not be in the same place for too long. They know I have it, so I don't want to endanger you, nor the..." he looked over his shoulder as if to check for ears on the walls. "Nor the pendant."

"I completely agree," said Aren.

"It would probably not be wise for the three of us to spend time together, *especially* not the two of you," said Cyneric pointing at the pair of them. "That way we can keep a close eye on each of them too, we'll need to split ourselves up to do that."

Olivia frowned at Aren.

"It's temporary," he said to her.

"I know," she said. "It always is, at first."

"You will probably have the most difficult duties of us all," said Cyneric, placing his hand on Aren's shoulder. "Everyone wants a piece of the king so just make sure that there is enough of you to go around."

"We can only hope," said Aren.

"I suppose it would make sense for *you* to stick to Lara," Cyneric said to Olivia. "You'd probably be safest with her anyway, she spends most of her time right here at court these days from what I hear." He began muttering under his breath. "Anyway, Pennyn, Rayne and I will cover the leftovers," said Cyneric, likening the Crown Council to unwanted meat. "We won't leave a single stone unturned. As much as an Aspen tree stirs in the desert and we'll hear about it."

"Actually, there are no Aspen trees in the desert," muttered Olivia. She was met with silence.

"It needs to be perfect," said Aren. He'd grown more and more distrusting of the man who once was so close to his mother. He was dubious, secretly, that Cyneric had included Pennyn in his plan, but he cast his worries aside – there was work to be done.

It wasn't until a couple of days later that his fears really began to plague his mind. None of them had given anything away, from what he'd heard. He sat deep in thought, scrawling across a piece of paper on his desk but a soft knock on his door caught him off-guard. He could tell by now that this was Olivia.

"Come in," he said.

"Aren," said Olivia. "Don't you have to attend court this afternoon?"

"Yes, you're right," said Aren, suddenly reminded of his royal duties. In such times it felt strange that this sort of thing was still expected of him and if he were honest with himself, holding court was often one of his least favourite obligations. Nevertheless, he was not one to forget the burdens thrust upon him by the Crown, no matter how trivial they may have seemed. "I'll go now. Care to join me?"

"I'd probably do better not to," said Olivia. "Cyneric's already had a go at me for distracting you. He just sent me over to fetch you, I'm on my way out."

"Oh, really? Where are you going?"

"Ayleris Command. Lara's decided to take her duties as Crown Envoy quite seriously, it seems," she chuckled. "She said she's going to pay a visit to all the men and women working to defend us, that it might be good for morale."

"Ah, I see. That does seem clever," said Aren. "Well, I'll see you later on then."

That afternoon, the Throne Hall was abuzz. From the moment he walked in it seemed people from all over Ayleris had shown up to the castle, all with complicated, petty problems of their own. Some were apologetic, others were arrogant, sneering at him as he sat on his throne. He felt quite alone in their midst. For one of the first times in his reign, none of the people closest to him stood beside him. None, except Pennyn Runeval.

He'd been sat there for a good while, enduring the mundanity of farmers looking to turn a profit off of each other, when the chancellor ushered them out to make space for the next arrival. A royal guard first entered and boisterously began to present himself to the king. He stood in the archway of the room, hands on his hip, not getting any closer.

"Your Majesty, Tarwen Fetterly. May I just say sir, it is a true, true honour to be of assistance to you. I hope I am not wasting your time, I know that you are an incredibly busy man. Sir, I myself wish I hadn't spent the day with these buffoons but alas – they insisted. I hope–"

"On with it, please," said Aren, smiling softly. A quick glance to his side and Pennyn was glaring at the balding man as if he were dirt on the floor.

"Right, of course sir, well these men – they claim you know them but they're grubby folk if you ask me, that's why I was avoiding taking up your time by bringing 'em in. I found 'em just outside of the Command, I was just patrolling the grounds of Femoren Deryz when I happened upon this man, he was having a piss in the –"

"Good heavens, man!" said a dark, gruff voice behind him. "Even my own mother'd never given me such a grand introduction. Grubby? You, perhaps."

It was a familiar voice. The tall figure walked into the arch, behind Tarwen, out of view.

"Shut up, you! Nobody invited you to speak," said Tarwen.

"I presume there's a reason you've brought him here to us," said Pennyn. "If it wasn't to speak, what was it? Who is this man?"

"Right, of course," Tarwen cleared his throat. "May I present to you, Laris Honfrey,"

"Hontren," said the man behind him, walking into the light. "Laris Hontren. But of course, I don't need to introduce myself to youse."

Immediately, Aren recognised him. He was in chains and cuffs, but the scruffy hair and the scars he bore were unmistakeable.

"Aren..." Pennyn whispered.

Almost immediately, Aren realised that the astonished look on the chancellor's face wasn't just from seeing one familiar face.

Another, smaller, shadowy figure stood next to Laris, also bound by shackles. As he walked further into the light, Aren realised it was a figure Aren recognised all too well. He looked incredibly different, unrecognisable, even. His skin, paler than ever. He looked thin, almost sickly, and his hair was long, slick and black, though its reddish-brown roots had started to show. He'd never seen him like this before, without his distinct fiery hair. Jaspyn Fenwern was alive. Before Aren could open his mouth to speak, Laris stopped him.

"Now if you'd let the court know just how well we know each other, Your Majesty, perhaps we'd be able to discuss some other *very* important things," he said, winking. "I've got me nephew here too, he wanted to see the New Capital and all, why don't you say 'ello, Ferret?"

Jaspyn Fenwern nodded, with wild eyes. "Good afternoon, Your Majesty," he said weakly, and Aren gripped the wood of his chair tightly, holding back his tears.

"Laris, we'll have plenty of time to talk," said Pennyn.

"What took you so long to bring these men to me," said Aren to Tarwen. "They are friends of the Crown."

"Wha–"

"When did you find them, Mr. Fetterly?"

"Yesterday morning."

Aren was mortified. "And I'm only just seeing them now. Why? Where did you have them stay?"

The man dropped his gaze, remorseful. "At the holding cells beneath the Halls."

"You kept them *imprisoned*?" said Aren, raising his voice. "Were you hoping for a medallion, a reward of some kind? Or was it some sort of…*glory*?"

Laris Hontren smirked at his captor.

Tarwen Fetterly's eyes narrowed. "He was pissing in the fountain," he said, pointing at Laris. "We put those kinds of men behind bars around 'ere. B'sides, if we brought every man that claimed he knew you to the castle there'd be hundreds of peasants in 'ere and no room for the fancy folk. You do realise you're the king, Your Majesty? Thousands of men who want to do you harm lurk the narrow streets of this city, do you expect us to bring them all to your door?" He'd started shouting and his voice echoed around them.

"I understand," said the king calmly. He was wary of the countless eyes upon him, many of them common folk, whose gazes were swinging between him, and the rugged looking group stood opposite. "I'm glad you brought these men to me, even if it was late. How can the Crown reward you?"

Tarwen calmed down as well. "I wasn't looking for no reward," he said, but his eyes said differently. "But I suppose gold can never hurt, especially us folk out there, fighting the good fight."

Fighting the good fight? There were men actually putting their lives at stake for him, for the monarchy, going into foreign fields to fight losing battles and uphold his peace, and then there were people like this man. The pursuit of gold. Glory. Nonetheless, Aren couldn't express his abhorrence openly here, there were far too many prying eyes.

"Very well, Mr. Ruvenal, see to it that Mr. Fetterly is fairly compensated."

He cast his eyes back to the sickly boy before him. Jaspyn was dead, Rayne's men saw him. Had she been lying to him? No, she wouldn't lie, what reason would she have? Then how had he survived? What was he doing with Laris Hontren? He'd had enough. He needed answers now. He looked to Pennyn, who nodded back to him as if he'd read his mind.

"That will be all for today, thank you all for your patience," said Pennyn, then turned to face Jaspyn and Laris. "You both, please take a seat."

"Wait –" said Jaspyn suddenly.

"Yes?" said the Crown Chancellor.

Jaspyn turned to look at Tarwen. "Hartyl. My cat, sir. When can I get him back?"

"Was the cat threatening the castle's security too, Mr Fetterly?" said Pennyn coldly.

Tarwen scoffed. "I'll make arrangements to have him sent here too," he said, before leaving the room promptly, giving Jaspyn no opportunity to thank him.

"That will be all," said Aren. And Pennyn raised his hand and signalled at the guards, who ushered them all out like sheep.

"Not you two," said Pennyn as the black-haired boy and his rough-looking accomplice began to shuffle towards the door. "The king would like a word."

"Aren?" Jaspyn finally said, once the room was empty. "Where's Olivia?" He spoke so calmly, so nonchalantly that you'd never believe he'd risen from death's door.

Aren could finally hold it in no longer and he spoke all at once. "Jaspyn, what happened to you? Why are you with *him*?" he asked, pointing at Laris. "How did you…how are you here?" Aren was barely coherent but he didn't slow down.

"Erm, because '*he*' saved the idiot's life," said Laris, referring to himself. "The idiot and his idiot cat."

"What is he talking about, Jaspyn?" Aren's voice was trembling now.

A look of terror struck Jaspyn's face. "The siege, Aren." His voice was still calm. "They came for me, they tried to kill me. The rebels. Where is Olivia?"

"She's at the Command, with Lara." Aren's face felt hot and he felt dizzy. Just hearing about everything that had happened made him feel sick to his stomach. These people were monsters, and they would pay for it all. Everything they'd put his loved ones through.

"They attacked me in the streets while it was all happening… I escaped, but my house… They ripped everything to shreds. I went back there a week later after the dust had settled and everything was torn apart. I didn't want to put my parents in any danger, they were still alive, last I saw…"

"I don't know what to say," said Aren. "I'm just really glad you're alive, we all thought you…"

"That's because Laris found me, while I was on the streets. I thought he was one of the bluecoats at first, actually, but he rescued me. I owe him my life."

"Would you look at that – the boy's in love," said Laris. "My question is why were *your* enemies so damn persistent on killing this lad," he waved a dirty finger, no nail, at Aren.

"Because they're my enemies," said Aren. "They'd stop at nothing to hurt me, even if it meant capturing or killing innocents close to me."

Laris looked unconvinced. "The way they had us on the run, you'd think there might've been more to it than that."

"Thankfully, Laris helped me fake my death," said Jaspyn. "It was really difficult to make it believable, we laid everything out beforehand."

"The cat was a nice touch though, weren't she?" said Laris, smiling unnervingly.

"I don't know about that," said Jaspyn.

"Oh, relax. The thing was dead anyway."

"I just hope it gave my family closure, I suppose. I know that they were worried sick, and I feel really guilty leaving them there but I…I just didn't want them to get hurt."

"Wait, your family believes you're dead?" said Aren.

"The whole world believes I'm dead. I'd like to keep it that way, too."

"You're safe here," said Aren. "You can get rid of that ridiculous hair."

"I'm sure I am. But the things I've seen, though…It leaves behind scars. I can't get them out of my head."

"I've been hearing of what it's like down there, I can only imagine…" said Aren.

"Don't imagine," said Laris. "Just listen."

"Take it from me, Aren. The bluecoats…they're…they're out for blood. Families are being separated, homes destroyed… All for what?"

"Where do you think we found the corpses to fake the lad's death?" said Laris. "Innocents are dying for your bloody crown."

It was a grim thought. Aren had spent so much time focussing on how to beat Soren Ashcrest that he'd almost lost sight of what was actually going on down there. It was happening to his people. To families.

"We will win this war," said Aren.

"At what cost?" said his friend. Aren had no answer for him.

The doors opened again loudly, and Lady Rayne Dresden walked in, a frightened look on her face.

"Your Majesty," she said sternly. "Our emissaries have sent word. A small army has been spotted up the river."

Aren's mind began to race. "How big is a small army?"

She shrugged her shoulders. "A handful of boats? They must have left New Castisa just today."

This was his chance. It would have to be now, no matter what. "We're going to take the war to them."

Nothing But Black
Olivia

It had felt like hours. Olivia wondered how long it would drag, this dull affair. Her eyes were shutting as Lara spoke to yet another officer, commending him for his admirable efforts to defend the New Capital. It wasn't that Olivia was impervious to the Verenic struggle, nor inconsiderate, but it was almost as if this was a rehearsed performance for Lara. It came naturally to her, all this. For Olivia, it wasn't quite the same.

She'd been watching her friend closely. It gave her something to put her focus on while the dry conversations around her droned on. She was hungry, she hadn't eaten for hours, but Lara just kept going on and on.

"Lady Olivia, Weryc here fought valiantly at the Medlantan frontier," said Lara Hercan.

"Is that right?"

"Yes, ma'am."

"Yes, *my lady!*" shouted a higher-ranking guard behind him.

Lara smiled at them both. "You needn't worry about formalities," she said.

"I'm very honoured to make your acquaintance," said Olivia. "Thank you for your service to our great kingdom."

"That means a lot to me, my lady," the man said. "I pray for your family's safety. It's a terrible thing, what's happening in this country."

"I'm grateful." She hoped prayers might be enough but was beginning to doubt it.

"Right, Lady Olivia and I should probably excuse ourselves now," said Lara, bidding them farewell before leaving the hall.

"How perfect of you," said Olivia, making sure they were well out of earshot. "You've really settled in well, haven't you? Crown Envoy, and all."

Lara smiled. "Thank you, that means a lot coming from you."

"Whatever do you mean, coming from me?"

Lara took a deep breath. "You, the Crown's right hand."

Olivia laughed. "I'm not anybody's right hand."

"But you are, you don't see it yet, but you will," said Lara. "He involves you in everything. Sometimes, it makes me think…"

"Think? Think what?"

"Just that *I* could do more, maybe even *be* more," said Lara. Olivia felt to laugh out loud once again. What more would the girl want to be? Perhaps Crown Chancellor.

"You and I, we're similar in a way," Lara went on. "We've got important family names, both of us. Even though your family fights for the wrong side, their name is powerful. You don't let that define you, though. You are stronger than just your name. It's something I wish I was."

"I'm not sure I understand, if I'm being honest."

"You know…you're an asset to Aren. You've proven yourself time and time again, regardless of the family you belong to. Me, however, my family is one of the strongest supporters of the monarchy these days, yet too often I find myself struggling to find my worth here, my purpose."

"But you do have a purpose, Lara," said Olivia, and she meant it. They owed a lot to Lara, a lot more, perhaps, than her friend realised.

"Yes, I know. That's why things like this, the little things, are important to me. I want to invest as much of my time into them as I can because I feel as if in my own little way, I'm playing my part in the war effort." It was a nice idea, Olivia wished she could share that optimism, but she knew far too much for that.

"I think it's brilliant what you did here today," said Olivia.

Lara laughed. "Thank you, but I can't claim praise for it entirely, I'd have never thought of it myself if it weren't for my father," she said.

"Oh, did he give you the idea?"

"Yes, he thought it'd be good for morale, he insisted actually. Wouldn't even let me hold off until tomorrow morning, what with more of the wounded returning today, from Astonkirk. That's why the plan was so sudden."

"He sounds wise," said Olivia. "Do you see him a lot?"

"Less and less every day, even before I came down here. We used to see each other a lot more down in the capital, but it's just not been the same since."

"I suppose that…can be understood," she said. "I scarcely saw my father anyway while he was the Means Counsel, he was always travelling the country, going from city to city," she shrugged her shoulders. "So, it didn't come as too much of a blow when it hit me that I couldn't see him at all anymore."

Lara looked at her sadly. "Don't worry, you'll see him again. I know you will." Olivia didn't know, though. She didn't know if her father was going to make it out of this war alive. Her brother either. She kept her mouth shut though as they arrived at the doors of the Guards' Mess, where she hoped they'd finally get some food. There was mould growing out of a pan left on the tabletop, and the whole place smelled of rotten eggs.

"Oh, actually, I know a very nice inn not too far from here, do you want to go there instead?" said Lara, probably noticing Olivia looking somewhat repulsed at the state of the room. "It isn't too far, I promise, it's just up the road."

"Yes, sure," said Olivia. She'd already waited so long, what was a few more minutes? Besides, this would give her more time to talk to Lara, with nobody else around to listen.

"Do you know a lot of Sandaerians?"

"Is this about that thing about the key?" said Lara.

"No, no. I'm just wondering. Having grown up between Éterin and Sturrock myself I can't say I've known any."

"What do you mean? There's plenty of Sandaerians down in the south."

Olivia raised her brows. "Oh? I thought they were mostly up here."

Lara shrugged. "They live all over. There are very few of them now, though. Whether that be in the north or the south," she said. "Outside of Nynnevor anyway, of course… Oh, and Veytora."

"Really? Veytora?"

Lara's smile wore thin. "The healer, I'm sure you've heard about her…she's drawn quite a crowd in the Nevebaris."

"The Asellar girl?"

"Yes," said Lara in hushed tones. "This stays between us, but I've heard whispers. The Sandaerians don't much talk about her outside of their circles."

"Where are these whispers from, then?"

"I shouldn't talk about it," said Lara. "Just here and there. Mostly from the University. Some of them even have fathers in the North Parydon, you see… I reckon they're conspiring in the whole thing."

"Have you told Aren that?" said Olivia. "Do you think she's a real threat? I've heard some things here and there too," she added.

"She's prophesied, Olivia, or so they believe anyway. They think she's the Last Deryz returned – *their* Last Deryz. If you ask me, I think she has the potential to cause quite a stir."

Enemies everywhere. It was frightening when she thought about it.

"OLIVIA!"

It was at that moment that Olivia felt a pain she'd never felt before. An excruciating, stinging blow to the back of her neck. Lara's bellows faded away as she fell to her knees, the world clouding and fading around her. She blinked until she could see again, and the screams returned once more. Next to her, Lara cried out at the top of her lungs in agony, blood dripping from the side of her face.

Olivia bawled in anguish, looking up at her attacker. The pain was overwhelming, she could scarcely piece together what he looked like. Young, swarthy, thick curly hair, almost like Aren.

"Olivia, over there!" Lara shouted.

He wasn't alone, there were three of them. Two men and a woman. She frantically looked around her for something, anything, that could be used as a weapon.

"Lara! Pick that up," she shouted, pointing at a fallen branch.

She looked back at their assailants, anxious as they edged closer towards them, encircling them.

"Fucking Weslin scum," one of them said. "This ought to speak to the traitor king, the bastard!"

"You lay a hand on either of us, sir, and you declare war on your own," said Lara. "We're already in the midst of a war, we are on *your* side! You really want the king worrying about a rebellion from within? From his own blood?"

"The king needs to learn a lesson or two about southern treachery," the woman among them said, walking closer and closer, a baton in her hand.

Olivia wanted to cry. She wanted to close her eyes and make her peace. These weren't the kind of people to negotiate. More than anything, she felt lightheaded from the pain.

"Take us, then," said Lara. "We'll mean much more to the king alive than dead."

The woman just chuckled. Olivia's heart was racing and pounding in her chest. She was close to giving up, so close. She felt tired and just wanted the pain to go away.

There was a sudden blur behind the woman. Olivia blinked to adjust her eyes. The next thing she saw was an arrow pierce outward of the woman's neck, skewering her throat. The woman gasped and gagged as the dark red blood spurted from her mouth and flowed down her neck. Her eyes spread far and wide as she tried to look down at her body. Another arrow pierced her chest. Her skull hit the ground right in front of Olivia, her dead eyes still open.

"Vera!" yelled the accomplice, rushing to the dead woman's side. "No! How could you?!" he looked up to see where the arrow had come from. Olivia glanced up behind the dead woman. It was Ysser Banlin, bow in hand.

"Ysser, over there!" shouted Olivia, as the other man threw himself towards the soldier. Ysser ducked as the assailant swung a baton at his head, punching the man's kneecap. The man yelled sharply in pain as he stumbled but his accomplice had already pulled out a dagger and was hurtling into Ysser's side. Ysser rolled over, dodging the knife, just as three more men, all dressed in royal uniforms emerged from the Halls. Olivia could see a fourth closely behind them, pistol in hand. The guards leapt into action – one disarming an assailant as another launched his sword hastily, slicing the other curly haired man's arm.

They encircled the two men, taking swings at them but with no luck. As steel hit steel, the armed guard waited for a clean shot. His hand was shaking, Olivia could see it quiver even from where she was. One stray shot and it could be disastrous. She looked over at Lara who was still bleeding really quite badly. She needed help. One clean shot, that's all they needed.

A deafening crack and it was as if her prayers had been answered. It echoed ferociously, making Lara clutch her ears in agony. The man was thrown backwards onto the floor, his ragged tunic dark red with his blood. His companion looked over at him, his eyes screaming vengeance, pain, remorse. It had been just enough to give Ysser the chance to pick up a fallen sword and plunge it upward, impaling the last man's chest. It was a clean, fatal blow.

Lord Ysser ran towards them, dropping his sword as the bells from the Halls of Femoren Deryz began ringing thunderously. It was painful to the ear, after the pounding headache she now had. He held her bleeding arm up first.

"My lady! Are you alright? Where did they come from, did you see? We need to get you seen to by a doctor, guards – call for help. The bells are ringing, the king should be on his way soon."

There was no response from the guards, now behind her. Olivia turned around and gasped.

"What is it? Guards, I said–"

Ysser saw it too. Olivia saw it in his eyes.

"What the fuck do you think you're doing? Let her go, you unhand her right this instant!" shouted Ysser. But the guard kept his pistol firmly pressed to Lara Hercan's head. There was a cold, dead silence as the others walked over to Ysser and Olivia, each holding a piece of white cloth. The smell was foul, even from a distance.

"Not a word from any of you," said the guard holding the gun. He had a deep voice and spoke in a southern accent, one similar to her own. Olivia didn't recognise him as one of the hundreds of men she'd met earlier today. His face was pale as snow and his eyes bloodshot, as if he hadn't slept in years. It was the first time she noticed just how scary he looked. Why were they doing this? Why had they bothered saving her life if they had just wanted to kill her? And then the damp cloth covered her nose and mouth and the world slowly faded to a blur around her, until there was nothing but black.

For the Crown

Jaspyn

"But it will take some time, Your Majesty," said Mentos Jeffyrs. Jaspyn found his voice the most annoying out of all of them.

"We don't have the luxury of time," said Aren. "They've given us until sundown tomorrow, at the most."

Jaspyn had been watching the pair argue in the Throne Hall for a while now. Cyneric was sat beside him, listening eagerly, with Laris sat slumped on the other side, tired and uninterested. Aside from the echoes of their solemn voices, the castle was eerie. Jaspyn had never seen it before, any of it. The mighty Malysor Castle. The historic city of Ayleris. He'd always dreamed of strolling through the streets and the markets, but the little time he'd spent in Ayleris had proven to be brutal. He was bruised and burnt and now wanted for nothing but some peace and quiet. The city had been cruel. He hadn't been here a day and his world was crumbling around him all over again.

"And do you truly believe a couple of hours is sufficient? To plan a battle?" said Mentos.

"It's all we have," said Aren. "I won't repeat myself, rally your men, uncle."

"Why don't we just give them what they want?"

"Treachery is in their blood," said Aren, pacing around the hall. "Giving them what they want will take away any chance that Olivia and Lara have of getting out without getting hurt."

Jaspyn had never seen him like this. Mad, frantic, but as bold as a king. Truth be told, growing up it had always been a little hard for him to imagine Aren as a king. He didn't seem kingly, not in the slightest. Now though, it was different. Thrust into the thick of it all, he'd managed to keep the peace in Verenia, for the most part anyway.

"They will get out of this alive," said Cyneric. "All three of them." Jaspyn hoped so. It made him feel guilty, but he wished it had been anyone else. Not Olivia and Lara.

"Very well, Your Majesty," the noble finally conceded. "I will make arrangements at once."

"Hold on, Aren," the chancellor walked in without as much as a knock. "I've just been to the Guards' Fast. The Berywen boy is here."

"Chrysan?" said Aren.

Pennyn nodded. "He's had a change of heart, he says. Realised he's fighting for the wrong side, and all."

Aren frowned. "Why *now*? What's changed?" he said. "What happens when he hears that his sister's been taken, snatched from in front of our eyes? After we told him that she'd be safe here?"

"He already *knows*," said Pennyn impatiently. "That's why he wants to fight for us, for Olivia."

The king raised his eyebrows as if in disbelief.

"The bells started ringing little more than an hour ago," said Aren. "He couldn't have found out about Olivia before then. You'd have me believe he made the journey from whatever Éterin backwaters he was stationed at in such short a time?"

"He didn't. Remember the men we spotted up the river?" said Pennyn.

"The small army," said Aren.

"Yes, them. They weren't bluecoats at all. Not anymore, anyway, if he is to be believed," said Pennyn rather coyly. "The boy managed to sneak out of New Castisa with some of their men, those loyal to his family. He wants to talk, to discuss terms of peace with the Berywens."

"Why?" said Cyneric.

"Éterin is surrounded and Lord Berywen fears an ambush," Pennyn replied.

"Hmm."

Jaspyn had never known Chrysan Berywen to concern himself with terms of peace. The man was temperamental on his best days.

"I know you're wary of trusting him, Your Majesty. But the truth is we need every advantage, every edge over the bluecoats that we can possibly get," said Pennyn. "The lad isn't stupid, his sister was captured by his own people, and he knows that we'd have made every possible effort to keep her safe. We've faced them in a field of battle once already, and it was a massive loss on our part. Chrysan can help us. He knows them from the inside, every strategy, every move."

"And what if he's been sent here as a spy?" said Cyneric.

"Then I suppose he'll die here as a spy," said Pennyn. "A foolish one."

"You think he's telling the truth?" said Cyneric.

"We've searched him, top to bottom, the boy has nothing that he might be using to feed his masters down in Sturrock, we'll watch him closely. But he has been pretty transparent, he wants nothing from us save the opportunity to serve in the battle to come, for his sister he says."

"And how does Lord Berywen feel about it?" said Aren.

"It came from Lord Berywen himself," said Pennyn. "He made his mind up some time ago. He wanted to help us, but they have Éterin surrounded. He sent emissaries, they were taken. He tried to send troops up to Ayleris, to serve in the Crown's name because…"

"Because what?" said Aren. "What could have possibly changed his mind?"

"Because he had reason to believe that his daughter was in danger," said Pennyn. "The boy doesn't know the ins and outs of it but there has been bad blood between his father and Soren. Issues of trust."

"So he sent word to his son," said Aren. "In New Castisa."

Pennyn nodded. "I don't see why he would be lying, if I'm being frank. Ashcrest betrayed them, the Berywens." He took a moment, appearing to mull it over. "He says that we need to fight in New Castisa, to take it back. He says that that is the only way his sister might live."

"And what assurance do we have that Ashcrest won't march his men into Ayleris?" said Cyneric. "Or that they won't fly the aces over us, desecrate our armies before we even make it to the city walls."

"They set fire to all the aces, each and every one," said Pennyn. "Chrysan and his men, before they sailed for Ayleris. There is no longer any Aerial Command."

Aren looked around the room, setting his eyes on Jaspyn as if to gauge his thoughts on the matter. Jaspyn wished he knew, but the truth of the matter was that this could very easily be a trap, or this might be their way of winning an impossible war…there was no way of knowing for certain. Luckily, Aren cleared his throat and rose up to speak.

"If he's prepared to give his life, let him serve in the vanguard."

A sinister silence followed. "Are you sure?" said Pennyn.

"No doubts about it, chancellor," said the king and Pennyn shrugged his shoulders. Jaspyn wasn't completely sure if he had his own doubts, but they didn't have much of a choice except to let him serve, did they?

"It's settled then," said Mentos. "I'll be on my way now, there's a war coming, after all."

Jaspyn worked up the courage to say something. He'd been listening silently, taking it all in, but he thought now was as good a time as any to say his piece. He waited until Mentos had left the room…the Arms Counsel still intimidated him, and he wasn't sure he'd like what needed to be said. Then again, he wasn't sure anyone would.

"Aren," he said softly. "Put me in the vanguard too."

His friend looked back at him as if he'd been cursed at. "Did you hit your head on the way in?"

Cyneric Porter and Laris Hontren burst into laughter.

"I'm deadly serious. I want to fight at the head," said Jaspyn, more loudly this time.

"I wasn't aware you were fighting at all," said Pennyn.

"He isn't," said Aren firmly. "Where did this come from all of a sudden? You've got almost no fighting experience, you've never set foot in a battlefield."

"And have you?" said Jaspyn. He immediately knew he'd crossed the line. He shouldn't have said that. Aren was the king after all, the commander of the forces.

"No, Jaspyn, I haven't. But I *have* spent years training for this sort of thing. Besides, what sort of king doesn't lead his men into battle?"

"*Lead* being used symbolically there, I hope," said Cyneric. "Because there's no way we're putting you at the head."

"I suppose not," said Aren. "Nor are we putting *him* at the head. Or anywhere on that field. And that is a command, if it must be so. You've only just crawled out of your grave, are you in such a hurry to fall back in?"

"Aren, trust me on this. I'll serve you much better at the front," said Jaspyn. Deep down though, he knew he'd be happy just being allowed to fight, no matter where he stood. He knew he could help. He knew what he'd been through, how he'd changed. He hadn't been back for long, but he already felt set aside, forgotten. He hoped he'd prove himself in battle, he knew he could. He'd be an asset…they needed to see it.

"My word is final, Jaspyn."

He looked at the king scornfully. For a moment, the two old friends just stared at each other in silence.

"However, if it is truly your wish, then you can fight alongside me. But you're not fighting in the vanguard."

Jaspyn smiled. "That will do."

"Now hold on a second," said Laris. It was the first time he'd opened his mouth on the matter, except to laugh or scoff from time to time. Jaspyn had thought he'd fallen asleep, bored of the whole thing. It wasn't *his* friends on the line, after all. "Hold on."

The king looked to him with narrowed eyes.

"Yes?"

"I reckon I could offer you a deal," said Laris.

"And what do you have that the Crown might need?" said Pennyn.

"My services," he said, smiling. "My life, if need be. You know what I ask in return, though."

Aren gave him a thin, knowing smile.

"What do you want?" said Jaspyn, glancing over at Laris.

"He wants to meet the Lady Wynter," said Aren. "Trouble is, the lady is gone. To Asenian shores, no less."

"Well what the fuck is she doing there?"

"Doesn't matter, she's out of reach," said Aren.

"Well then, in return for my services I want safe passage to Asenia too."

Aren stared at him for a moment, considering the proposal. "The Crown doesn't *need* your 'services', frankly speaking."

"Yes, but what do you have to lose? I'll probably die in that war anyway, so you'll never have to deliver on your end of the bargain. Heck, *you'll* probably die too." He looked coyly at the king and then over at Jaspyn, giving him a sly wink though Jaspyn didn't really understand why.

"And what do you have to gain from dying for the Crown?" said Pennyn.

Laris shrugged his shoulders. "If I die, I die a hero. A martyr, in Wynter's eyes. If I live, I live to see another frosty winter." He grinned, bearing his disgusting teeth. "Just make sure you tell 'er I was killed in action and all that," he winked at Aren.

"We don't tend to get frosty winters up here," said Pennyn, giving a rare smile. Laris just shrugged his shoulders. The man was delusional, Jaspyn thought, still, this was new. He'd gotten used to Laris' many quirks over the weeks they'd spent together, but this was a side he'd never seen.

"Very well," said Aren. "You may fight in the king's name at New Castisa."

Laris gave him a little grunt, presumably content with the outcome.

"Your Majesty," said Pennyn. "I believe it would be wise for you to speak to the Berywen boy yourself, maybe see if he'll say anything more to you."

The king nodded, looking nervously over at Jaspyn. "Could I please have the room?"

"Oh," said Jaspyn, caught off-guard. Perhaps he wanted to keep Jaspyn hidden. Not everybody knew yet that he was back, for good reason too. Or perhaps…it was an issue of trust. "Yes, I-I mean, of course," said Jaspyn, getting up to leave.

"That includes you, Laris," said Pennyn.

"Alright, alright," he said, getting up as well.

"You can wait for me in my study," said Aren. "Won't be long."

Jaspyn nodded at him before walking out of the largely empty hall. He only turned around for a brief glance. He could hear nothing of Aren's whispers with Cyneric Porter and Pennyn Runeval, just murmurs before the doors shut behind him and Laris.

"No, no, we don't need your help," said Laris to a guard who began accompanying them, waving his hands at the woman.

"You can't just shoo them away Laris, they're royal guards. Besides, we don't even know where we're going."

"Aye, it's a big castle, why don't we have us an adventure."

"Because it's not *our* castle."

Laris laughed raucously. "Nor is it the boy king's."

"You can't say things like that here," said Jaspyn in hushed tones, looking around to see if the guard had heard him. "You'll get in trouble."

Laris gave him a sidewards glance. "Why did you offer up your life to fight in his stupid war?"

"It's not a *stupid war*," said Jaspyn. "My friends are gone, I want to fight for them. Besides, why did you? They're not your friends, are they?"

"I gave my reasons in that bloody hall."

"You and I both know the odds they'll actually let you see her," said Jaspyn. "She's a noblewoman, a married one too. How do you even know her?"

The corners of Laris' mouth curled up slightly, but he gave nothing away. "Why don't we talk about the real elephant in the room," he said, lowering his voice. "When are you going to tell him, lad?"

"When the time is right," said Jaspyn. Deep down though, a part of him wished it would never come. "When are *you* going to tell him? That you weren't the one that saved me? That it was that Uressi woman?"

He smiled. "Never."

Zytora

Olivia

The next time Olivia's eyes opened, she was in a small, dark room, maybe a cellar or a crypt. The ground beneath her feet was bare and dry. She frantically tried to jump off her feet, but it was of no use. She was pinned, her hands bound behind her, around a column of sorts. She was still groggy, and her head throbbed. She wriggled her hands behind her to see if there were any way she could break free, but it was impossible. Lara was tied up opposite her, her eyes still closed. She looked to her left, Lord Ysser's face was turned away, so she couldn't tell if he was conscious. The guard from before was stood in the distance, behind him, whispering to another man. Except, he wasn't wearing his uniform anymore. He wore a dark hooded cloak now, which cast a shadow over half of his face. She didn't need to see it, though. She'd remember that face forever.

The other man wore a beige cloak, like a Verenian Minister. She dared not make a sound, but she listened closely, trying her best to make out their whispers.

"Before sundown, else they won't be happy," the hooded figure said. "It's one thing having to worry about the bloody Asellar bitch, we don't need these delays."

"Are you sure it's possible?" said the other man.

"You watch."

There was a bitter contempt in his voice, like he had little to lose. She tried to piece it together. Who were they? What did they want from them? She squinted through the pain, trying to make out any weapons. A sword, and a rifle. Perhaps a dagger too. She fought the urge to sleep again, she had to stay alert. She wriggled her eyes around, clenched her fists. The skin on her palms had barely healed, so it stung but she squeezed anyway. That was when a stir in the corner of her eye caught her attention. Sudden and brief. It was Ysser's head that had twitched. He was alive, awake. She wanted to whisper to him, but it was too dangerous. She dared not move her head.

"You wait until all this blows over, if she doesn't get what she wants she'll make sure nobody does. Fucking spoilt brat," the man continued, speaking louder now.

"But we will win," said the other man. "The Order doesn't run us forever. When we get what we want, what power do they hold over *us*. They should be fearing us, all of them. No need to squander our time over the petty politics of–"

"When we win, they will all bow to Daxian, as will we." said a third voice. This one was deeper. It emerged from behind the two men. "Stay true to your pledges or face the wrath just as the rest."

"Nobody said anything about breaking trust with the Order," said the man in the beige cloak, his voice suddenly shaky.

"Your sort will be the first to go," said the deep voice. "If there is one thing Daxian does not stand for, it's disloyalty and dishonour. Our people swore an oath, and for it we were promised freedom. Freedom to live as we once lived. To live as we did before the Exile. In fact, to live as we did for hundreds of years without a care for Deryzi, Warden or Crown. But every oath has its price."

"Aye, we promised them a kingdom," said the hooded man. "And indeed, a kingdom they shall have, but we will play no part in the bloodshed that happens in its wake."

"We will just have to see then, won't we. I believe we'll have a role to play in Soren's plans. All of us. You just wait till sundown."

Soren? Olivia didn't like the sound of it, any of it. What was going to happen at sundown?

"Quiet! The bastard's come to," said the hooded figure. She squeezed her eyes tightly shut. She heard the men come closer and closer. Then a sharp, deafening cry of pain.

"ARRGGGHHHH! STOP! STOP IT! PLEASE!"

She winced, forcefully keeping her eyes shut as she dreaded to envision what was being done to Ysser. She twisted her wrists around behind her back, hoping she might be able to break free. It wasn't possible. The rope wasn't that tightly bound, but it was thick. So thick that it left no room for her to manoeuvre herself out of it.

"STOP IT! I'M AWAKE! I'M AWAKE!" he shouted, but his screaming didn't stop. "STOP! PLEASE!"

She reached around behind her, stretching her fingers as far as they could go. Searching for something, anything. That was when she remembered. She remembered what was in her back pocket, tucked safely away beneath her blouse. She could still feel its cold touch on her skin. Is that what they were after? Could it be possible that they somehow knew?

"Look 'ere, this one's pretending too," said a voice. Her heart stopped as his footsteps drew closer and closer…and then further away. "We don't like pretenders up here, open your eyes, girl." She squinted ever so slightly. It was enough to see that their backs were turned to her, it was Lara that they were speaking to. "Go on, open your eyes!" the man shouted.

"You will not lay a finger on her," said the other. "We're already looking at a lot of trouble with how far those idiots went, she will bear these scars for a long time."

Olivia heard a whimper from Lara. And then, she herself opened her eyes.

"Good, you're all here," said the deep voice.

"Do you want to get started or shall I?" said the hooded man. "Right, me, then."

His piercing gaze landed upon Olivia. "You see, dove, I've got a task to complete. None of you lot are leaving this shithole until I get what I want. Now, truth be told, I don't exactly know what that is. But one of you must."

"We don't know what you're looking for," said Lara. "We don't even know who you are."

The man in the beige cloak struck her across her face. Lara winced in pain, then drew a sharp, short breath through her teeth, suppressing a scream. He held a wooden-hilted dagger in front of her face menacingly.

"I said not a single finger," the third man said, toying with the rifle on his side. He walked over to the one in beige, his hand tucked into a deep pocket. "He'll have our heads." Then with a single, clean jolt forwards he drove his dagger through the man's chest, killing him. Lara let out a loud gasp and a tear rolled down her cheek. Olivia was numb though.

"As we were saying, it doesn't matter if you don't know what it is we're looking for, truth be told," said the hooded man again. "Your king does, and it'll be a simple trade – your lives for this hidden treasure."

"You're talking about the Key of Blood," said Olivia. All the pieces were falling into place and the picture was an ugly one. He walked up to her, a cruel expression on his face. His eyes were a deep blue and his skin waxy, lifeless.

"It speaks!" he exclaimed, laughing maniacally.

"Aren told us about the Key," she said. "Let the king come – you will get what you want. He will need assurance though, that our lives will be spared, as you say."

The man's face was stony, not a sign of remorse. Olivia was horrified by it. That is when the pieces came together, all at once. Of course. How could she not have seen it earlier? It wasn't a coincidence that Lara Hercan was so keen on paying a visit to the Halls of Femoren Deryz when just a few days past she'd found out, or thought that she'd found out, that the Halls housed a bloodgate. A work of magic. A weapon. A weapon that could be used using the Key of Blood. The lie had worked. But of course, Lara wasn't the one who'd insisted on going over there though, was she? Her father. Lord Hercan had insisted she go today. He'd been persistent. *The honourable Lord Perwell Hercan.* Could he do this to his own king? To his own daughter?

"Aren Aryssen will make no such demands," said the madman, pacing in front of her.

But how could he have known that they'd be attacked outside? Had it all been a part of the ruse? Her mind raced wildly. *Not a finger*, the third man had said. *He'll have our heads*, he'd said. It was becoming clear now. She felt stupid, hurt, betrayed. She hoped Lara hadn't been in on it. She couldn't have been, could she? Had it all just been a lie?

"Careful now, we don't want a mess on our hands do we, girl?" the man said to her.

"What do you want?" said Olivia, loudly.

He smiled at her cunningly. "You know what we want, you're a clever girl, aren't ya?"

She twisted and turned her hands, rubbing her wrists against the ropes behind her, hoping, against all odds, that they'd come free. Nothing. She clenched her fists tightly, frustrated, and she started to pray. All the prayers she knew, everything she'd been taught at the Aneglin as a little girl. She muttered under her breath whilst she clenched her fists tightly, her nails digging deep into her skin.

From behind the murderer, Lara widened her eyes, raising her brow at Olivia. She was trying to get Olivia's attention, whilst the men's backs were turned. She jerked her head sharply back, eyes still wide, wriggling her tied arms. What was she trying to say?

"Are you praying, girl?" said the man. "Probably for the best, wouldn't you say?" He turned back to face Lara, who stopped wriggling suddenly, looking forward again.

"Yes, sir. I think that would be for the best. In fact, I was just going to say a prayer of my own," said Lara.

"Oh, didn't take *you* for a religious girl," he said. "The kind of family you come from. Well, have at it. Go on, we're all curious."

The man sounded utterly mad. Olivia didn't know what to make of it.

"*Zytora*," said Lara. She glared straight through the man as if he were not there and into Olivia's eyes. "*Y valyzon terovezan…zytora ulvezon…Zytora…*"

She kept muttering the Verenic incantation as if she too were mad. It sounded familiar, but Olivia hadn't a clue what it meant. The men must have been southern too because they didn't show any sign of understanding.

"Full of surprises, aren't ya? Speaking the moon language like that."

"*Zytora…vyre avizan zytora…*"

Olivia had definitely heard the word before. *Zytora*. It was so common. Lara was trying to tell her something. She cast her mind back.

"Alright that's enough," said the man, his face serious all of a sudden. "Shut up now."

Zytora. She racked her brain. The books…the *Promise. Alto, dalto, heryzto…zytora*. Time. Lara needed time. Whatever for?

"Who do you work for?" said Olivia. She hoped to stall the men, but she didn't know what Lara had in mind. She hoped it was something clever.

"Do you think it's that easy?" he laughed. "We work for ourselves."

"You serve someone. Who?"

The man looked agitated now. "That's it. Not a peep out of you. Did daddy never teach you not to talk back to your elders?"

It was at that exact moment that Olivia saw Lara's hand come loose. It was quick. She'd tucked it behind herself straight away.

Olivia almost couldn't believe that it had happened. Perhaps just her mind playing tricks? No, she was sure of what she'd seen.

"You're cowards, the lot of you," said Ysser Banlin, before a quick glance over at Lara. Had he seen it too?

"What the fuck did you say to me?" the man punched Ysser in the chest.

"Argh!"

With the men distracted, Olivia had a chance to get Lara's attention. Lara smiled and mouthed the words *"use your belt."* It was of no use. Olivia felt her belt, it was nowhere near as sharp enough. The rope was far too thick. But if she could just reach the pendant...maybe, just maybe its jagged edges would be sharp enough to cut her loose. With two of them free and able to move, maybe they could try to take on the two men. It seemed like a stretch. The men were strong and fast, and it was obvious that they'd stop at nothing to get what they wanted. That was all the more reason to at least *try* to escape, though. She didn't know how, but that didn't matter for now. She tugged and tugged at the rope, reaching upward to seize the pendant. Every second was critical. A bead of sweat trickled down her forehead. She looked down at the dagger on the floor, next to the dead man. She didn't know if either her or Lara could get to it fast enough, if it came to it.

"We don't want to send you to your king in pieces, but we only really need one of you alive. And if that is what it takes to grab his attention, then indeed that is what shall be done."

Olivia ignored him. She kept at it, reaching further and further. The rope seemed to have come slightly loose, or maybe that was in her head. And then, it happened. It was in her hand. She clutched the cold thing tightly behind her back. She couldn't let it drop, that wasn't how it'd end.

"Right, who are we starting off with then?" said the madman. He was taunting her. Both of the men walked around, each taking turns to stare every one of them down. Scare them into turning on their king.

"No volunteers, eh?"

Olivia fiddled with the relic, trying to rub its sharp edges against the rope, praying it would wear down. Bit by bit. Time was scarce, though. She muttered her prayers in her head as she continued pushing the pendant up against the rope and sawing through it slowly, ever so slowly. It hurt her hands, but she didn't stop.

There was a gentle thud. Olivia's heart sank. It was Lara. She stood there, dead still, her hands out to the sides. A piece of her belt lay there on the floor beneath her. They were suddenly out of time. Lara darted towards Olivia, hiding behind her as the hooded man picked up his gun once more. The other man stopped his hand.

"No," he said. "Lara, don't. You don't want to."

Lara was frantically trying to untie Olivia's hands.

"You can bet your life that I do," she said. There was a loud bang and Olivia felt the bullet fly past her. But Lara kept fiddling with the rope.

"The next shot won't miss your pretty friend there," said the hooded man.

The rope had loosened enough for Olivia to try to cut through it. She ran to Ysser and began again, working the rope with her fingers.

Bang. Ysser howled and cried in sheer agony as blood seeped through his breeches.

"This man may never walk again, Lara. Take your life, and leave, before you take someone else's with your stupidity," the man said, shaking his head. "The next shot will be between his eyes."

She looked mortified. She turned to Olivia, as if to say sorry.

"Go, Lara. Go now," said Olivia. She had plans of her own. Lara let go of the rope and darted for the stairs opposite. As the men watched her leave, Olivia's hands came loose, and she seized the chance to launch herself forward to pick up the dagger the dead man had been holding. She hadn't been fast enough. The cloaked figure pointed his gun at her head, looking into her eyes, while the other pulled out his own dagger and held it to Ysser Banlin's throat.

"You shouldn't have done that," he said, pressing the knife deeper and deeper into Ysser's skin. Blood dripped down his neck and stained his tunic.

"Stop! Please. I'm sorry," Olivia yelled.

"Too late, bitch. It won't be an easy death either now," he said. He pressed the knife against Ysser's forehead, sinking deeper and deeper into his skin, slicing down the side of his brow. Olivia could do nothing except look at the man's scarred face in horror. In dread. She couldn't stop this. It would all be over soon, for all of them. She clenched her fists harder and harder, sobbing as the mad men mutilated Ysser Banlin. He yelled out in agony and she screamed and begged for them to stop, but nothing. She closed her eyes. The helplessness, the despair she felt was unlike anything she'd ever felt before. She clenched her fists even harder, letting the jagged pendant tear open the flesh of her palms, opening old wounds. She was numb to it. The pain didn't stop her. She pushed harder and harder, snivelling like a child as the blood trickled down her hands.

"I'll convince Aren myself, just let him go!" she screamed.

A drop of blood balanced on her thumb, hanging below. She desperately clung onto hope that they weren't too far from help and that Lara would be back with someone. It seemed less and less likely. She hadn't a clue where they were. She hadn't a clue if she'd see Aren ever again.

"Run, my lady! Just go! Please! Don't worry about me!" yelled Ysser, crying. "Just go!"

The drop of blood fell from her hand down to the earth below. She was overcome with emotion. And then, she felt the warmth. The pendant in her hand grew hotter and hotter, suddenly difficult for her to hold onto. She winced at her wounds and opened her palm, confused. It was glowing. Burning, almost. The red of the stone glimmered where her bloodied hands had stained the relic. The golden casing sparkled. She looked at it, stunned, as she heard a loud whimper of pain.

But it wasn't Ysser. She looked up to see the man holding the gun, scowling at her, utterly dazed. His eyes were redder than ever. Completely bloodshot. He looked almost ill. The man next to him let out an agonising scream as he dropped his dagger. They both withdrew from Ysser, walking closer to her instead.

"What have you done? You fucking bitch." She ran to Ysser's side, racing against them, but they were too fast. Thirsty for blood.

"Don't you dare hurt her!" Ysser yelled. "Kill me. Take me. Offer me to the king."

"We don't give a shit about you anymore. It's her we want."

She ran behind Ysser, using him as cover but they were already there. Olivia had just enough of a chance, the slimmest chance, to sneak the pendant from her bloodied hand into the pocket of Ysser's breeches. He looked at her, confused, but she just stared blankly back as if to tell him to keep quiet. She hoped it'd get to where it needed to be.

She saw the men's expressions descend into utter lunacy, falling to their primal urges. She was terrified, even more so than before.

One of them grabbed her by her hands and dragged her towards the stairs. She tried to break free, but they were too strong. Far too strong. She looked at the other one, yearning for some mercy but it was a lost cause. The blacks of his eyes widened, as she stared into the soul of the devil. He hissed and opened his mouth, baring his two fangs at her.

The Truth and the Justice
Eyan

Eyan crossed his arms. "Did you have to make such a mess of it?" he said. But Garlen wasn't having it.

"A *mess*?" he said, in his deep voice. "How were we to know what would happen?"

"But still," said Eyan, eyeing the dweller up and down. "Did you have to scare her so much? Was that necessary?"

"Maybe it wasn't," said Garlen. "That doesn't mean I didn't enjoy it." The cruel man bore a dreadful smile.

"And yet you left the guard?" said Eyan. "The very same who smuggled Aren Aryssen out of Sturrock. You just left him there, untouched?"

"We couldn't kill him now, could we? Believe me, if I could, I would have done it. Now, that's not to say he was untouched," muttered Garlen, still smiling. "Don't worry, we gave him quite a scare as well."

"And what of the other? Did you enjoy scaring her too? You think *he'd* like that?"

Garlen's grin vanished. "I am scared of nobody."

"Really?" said Eyan. "Not even Daxian?"

"Fuck off," said the dweller. "She has given me no reason to fear her. Don't you have something better to do, boy? The enemy draws closer. Your father won't be happy if it is a loss for you this time."

"Oh, I am well aware," said Eyan. "And we are more than ready, let them come."

Fraston Spenler emerged from behind the dweller, much to Eyan's dismay. "All ready, lads?"

"More than ready," said Eyan. "When will your sister arrive? With our guests?"

He frowned. "She will not be joining us, not for this one. But our...*guests*, well, they are already on the way."

"And why is that?" said Eyan. "Backing out at the last minute?"

"She has other business to tend to in the Falls," said Fraston, shaking his head as if the matter was not even worth his time. "Important business."

"What could be more important than–"

"Mind to yourself," said Fraston. "If something comes of it, we will tell the First Warden ourselves." Eyan changed his mind, perhaps he hated Fraston more than his foul sister after all.

"Very well," he said. "Now I must excuse myself, I want to see her before it all happens."

Garlen raised his brow. "You want...to *see* her? You aren't going soft on us, are you? It isn't true? What they say of the First Warden's son?"

"If it comes to it, I will cut her throat myself," said Eyan. "I'm not soft, just fair. That is all we are fighting for, after all, isn't it? That is what it means, the Federation."

Fraston laughed and then ruffled Eyan's hair as if he were a little child. "Of course, of course." He continued to laugh maniacally.

The sun was low in the sky outside, the night was almost upon them. He squinted to catch a glimpse of the enemy, by the woods, but he was blinded by the rising smoke surrounding his own camp, by the watchtowers. Oh well, he'd see his old friends soon enough. He walked through the camp, soldiers all around him. Rifles, bows, swords at the ready. Blood would be shed today. But it was necessary, to make the world a better place.

He peered inside the large, black tent at the centre of it all. The tent of his father's masters. Barrels and barrels of arrows, full to the brim. Piles of steel daggers in the corner, scattered and strewn. But no Olivia.

"What's it to you?" came her chilling voice. The silver veiled shrew.

"Your pardon?" said Eyan.

"What are you going in there for?"

"Olivia, where is she? I want to talk to her."

"I had her moved," said the masked one. "Linara told me what happened down at the Valecrest. We can't have a repeat of that today, not if it comes to battle."

"And where is Linara now?" said Eyan, making no effort to conceal his disdain. "I don't know what she told you, but I couldn't get to them at the palace, there was no way. That damn guard, Ysser, he knew the tunnels too well." He couldn't tell what was going on behind those damned silver beads.

"Let us talk strategy."

"We have talked and talked of it," said Eyan Ashcrest. "Since long before you arrived."

"Then let us talk of it some more."

Eyan scowled. "My father's own men, they will be at the back," said Eyan. "We'll be shielded by the front and sides that way, and we can have the gunmen up on the slope."

"Truly your father's son."

"Yeah, well…" he didn't know what to say to that. "I need to speak to her, Olivia, so tell me where she is. Perhaps I can get something out of her. End this before it begins, without losing any more of our people."

"It isn't happening. Don't ask again, or you might find yourself thrust into the thick of the enemy's armies when you least expect it." The voice grew dark and serious. Eyan didn't appreciate threats. He'd warned his father that these people couldn't be trusted, none of them. This one least of all.

"Fine," said Eyan. "I should go, prepare myself."

"Yes, you should."

Eyan scoffed. "And will you be joining me at the head?"

The beads rattled as a warm summer breeze swung them gently from side to side. Behind them, darkness. Just pale, blue eyes. Cruel eyes. The mask covered the rest.

"Yes, of course I will."

"Then all I ask is that you let me do the talking," said Eyan. "*All* of the talking."

"When have you known me to talk to my enemies?"

"Yes, but that puppet of yours too," said Eyan. "Garlen. I don't want him to say something stupid, ruin the whole thing."

"Don't worry. He will say no more and no less than what is required of him."

"Master!" came a ratty voice from behind Eyan. At long last.

"Where have you been?" said Eyan.

"I – I've b-been looking for…you," said Renut, passing his eyes over Eyan to the one who stood beside him.

"It's alright, I'll let you sort your quarrels." The tent swung open and suddenly Eyan was left alone with the little man. He let out a loud sigh, finally loosening up his shoulders. A moment longer looking at that disgusting veil would have been a moment too long.

"I…I c-can't find her anywhere," said Renut. "Lady Olivia." The little man was wearing armour, and a lot of it too. Hung from his shoulder, a longbow taller than his entire body. An empty quiver dangled from his tiny waist.

"Do you even know how to use that thing?" Eyan laughed. The little man placed his hands on his hips and looked up at Eyan with a furrowed brow.

"Why w-wouldn't I?" he said. "I grew up on the Pyburrock shores, y-you know." Eyan stepped up right close to his face and the man took two backwards steps, stumbling over a rock.

"I know you did," said Eyan. "But I've never seen you fight. As luck would have it, nobody has. Nobody alive anyway."

"Well, I c-can handle myself," he said, sweat trickling from his greasy, scruffy black hair down the side of his temple. "I c-can. You'll s-see today."

Eyan smiled. "Let us hope it doesn't come to it. It wouldn't be good for anybody."

Renut screwed up his face and crossed his dainty arms. "Why?" he said. "A n-necessary evil. Has to b-be that way."

"No," said Eyan. "It doesn't."

"I d-dare say the First Warden w-would not like that," said Renut. "What y-you've just said."

"Yeah, well, I don't have to agree with everything my father says, do I?" said Eyan. "Doesn't mean that I won't fight for him. I will fight with all the strength I have within me because…well the alternative is a mad tyrant who rules with fear and guilt."

"Well…w-who said that serving the f-false king is the only alternative?"

Eyan gave the little man a puzzled look.

Renut shrugged. "Of c-course. It isn't like w-we would ever betray the First Warden… he is…he is the…" The little man looked around him like a stray cat caught in the markets. "He is the truth, and h-he is the justice."

"Well…yes." Eyan felt a great burden upon his chest. His loosened shoulders tightened once more, and he drew in a deep breath. "He is the best ruler that this country could ever have. Stern, but not cruel. Fair, but not soft." It was a pity that his masters never let him be the kind of ruler that Eyan knew his father could be.

Sundown

Aren

Aren stood atop a wagon, gazing out into the battlefield before him. The enemy was close. He could see the traitor's armies on the horizon, barely visible, smoke rising from their midst. In the far distance, masked by a summer haze, he could make out the outline of the watchtowers of New Castisa.

"Four artilleries on the southern front, four on the west, facing us," said," said Mentos Jeffyrs, squinting through a pair of binoculars.

"We should march on," said Cyneric to Aren. "If you still want to do this before nightfall."

"Are you certain we cannot wait for the dawn?" said Mentos.

"The sun is with us now, uncle," said Aren. "Come dawn, it will rise from behind them, we won't see a thing."

"And during the night? We won't see a thing then either," said Mentos.

"We have waited long enough. They have one of our own, they've had the audacity to bargain her life as if it's a game to them," said Aren. "No…we will use the hours we have left before sundown to strike hard and strike fast, yes they have the advantage of higher terrain, but we have more men, and for now anyway, we have the light of day."

"Then we will flank them while they're thin in numbers," said Cyneric. "Any word from Rayne?"

"If they are thin in numbers then there's a reason for that," said Mentos. "Soren Ashcrest is no fool, and I'd count on him having a trick or two up his sleeve."

"No word from the Lady," said Aren, shaking his head. He clambered off of the wagon. "Why haven't they made a move yet?"

"They're waiting for you to make a move," said Mentos.

"Why? They have the ground."

"They also have Lady Olivia," said Mentos. "They're teasing us, they want to draw us in because they know we outnumber them."

"Only just," said Aren.

"We also have more artilleries," said Mentos. "With the Dresden forces, we'll be able to flank them comfortably and force them to retreat, even in the darkness of night, should it come. I just hope it doesn't, because I've seen things go wrong when the sun goes down."

Aren nodded and stretched his arms. He trotted over to the large tent perched beside them, in the thick of the camp.

"May I come in?" he said softly.

"Yes," came Lara Hercan's familiar voice.

She was sat beside Jaspyn, tending to Ysser's wounds as he winced in pain.

"We march today," said Aren. Jaspyn nodded at him quietly.

"I'm marching with you," said Lord Ysser, clutching at his side.

"My lord, I mean no disrespect, but you've seen better days," said Aren.

"And I'll see worse yet."

"No, sir, you won't. You'll die or worse… You'll slow us down. I need you for the wars to come, Lord Ysser." It was a cruel thing to say but it was necessary.

"I can still fight, I can still run, and you need every man you've got on the ground."

"No, my lord. And that is that."

"Jeryn wanted to fight too, my lord," said Lara, to Ysser Banlin. "I think at times like this it's just as courageous to choose not to fight. If Jeryn lost his life, House Hercan would be lost forever."

"No, Lara. You would carry the name of House Hercan," said Aren. "In my eyes anyway, if not in the eyes of the Aneglin."

Lara looked back at him, almost annoyed. "The father holds the right of choosing which name a child shall bear."

Aren shrugged at her. "Choose a father that will respect your wishes."

"If it were that simple," Lara muttered under her breath.

"Should it come to battle, an actual battle, I want you by my side," said Aren to Jaspyn. "Cyneric and Laris will be beside us."

"Are you sure it's wise for the king to march into the battlefield?" said Jaspyn.

"It may not even come to battle," said Aren. "They may choose to negotiate, they may stand down when they see our full show of force, but for all this to happen, I need to be there."

"Not on the front lines, surely," said Ysser.

Aren shook his head. "We'll be at a fair distance, Pennyn has agreed to represent me at the head."

"Then why go at all?" said Jaspyn.

"Because I need to be there no matter what the outcome. If it comes to a bloodbath, especially," said Aren. "I don't want to be the kind of king that orders his armies into war without ever stepping out into the field himself. Many of the men here with us today will not be going home, should it come to battle."

"Don't say that," said Lara. "That's grim."

"Well, it's the truth."

"Be careful," said Lara.

"Oh, thanks," said Jaspyn, smugly.

"No, I'm being serious. When I was in their midst…I saw things. Those men…" she lowered her voice to a whisper. "They weren't living men, Aren."

Nothing was going to scare Aren out of this war, not even baseless rumours about dwellers and mystics.

"I'm not sure what you saw but you were scared, terrified," said Aren. "You didn't know if you were going to make it home alive, that can take its toll on you."

"This is why I didn't mention anything before," said Lara spitefully. "I knew you'd think I was mad, but I know what I saw."

"You're not mad," said Lord Ysser, his face dark and serious. "I saw it too."

Aren narrowed his eyes. Coming from Ysser Banlin, the great sceptic at court, the story perhaps held more gravity. He didn't care, though. Dwellers or not, they would pay. They would all pay.

"We're just telling you what we saw," said Ysser. "And when Olivia gave it to me, the–"

"And you're sure of what you saw?" Aren interrupted the soldier deliberately. He didn't want to talk about the pendant, not here. It was in his own pocket now, where it probably should have always stayed. Maybe Olivia would be in a safer place now if it had, or maybe it'd have made no difference, there was no telling now.

Lord Ysser nodded. "My eyes have never failed me before, and you know better than most how I feel about stories of darkness and its monsters. Lies, most of them. This though, now I am not so sure."

If it were true, if Ashcrest and his traitor friends had somehow gained dominion over these creatures, the pendant would prove even more crucial than he'd thought. It was a pity he hadn't the faintest idea how to use it. He rubbed his hand over his pocket lightly and felt that it was still there. It'd been stained with the blood of his friend when Ysser had handed it to him. The blood of an innocent. He had little to lose now, leaving the pendant in the hands of another wasn't an option, never again. He dared not let it leave his sight, even if it meant marching into battle with it.

"Your Majesty, if I may," said Ysser, getting up suddenly with a tired groan. "If you could follow me outside." Ysser looked as if he had something important to say – something more. So, the king obliged.

"The pendant, sir," said Ysser. "I wanted to tell you before, back in Ayleris, but I haven't been able to steal a moment alone with you, and of course, the nature of this thing…it is quite sensitive."

"Yes, that it is."

"Well, when they took Olivia, the men – it was as if something had changed inside them. It wasn't their plan, they were just looking for the Key," said Ysser. "It was clear that they were hesitant, somehow."

"What do you mean something changed?"

"Olivia – she'd almost escaped, just as Lara had. They were taunting her. They were torturing her, making her watch as they…" He stopped. He looked around at the tents surrounding them, as if he'd seen or heard someone. "Anyway," he said continuing forwards. "Just before they took her, their faces…they started to almost waste away. Paler and paler, almost sickly, and their eyes…bloodshot as ever. Red as rubies, I tell you."

Aren's mind began to race. "And the pendant was in her hand?"

"Yes, but it is something I cannot explain – as if something had stopped them, dead in their tracks. Suddenly all they wanted was her, they didn't hurt me anymore after that, they didn't even look at me as I offered my own life for hers," said Ysser. "I didn't expect to make it out of there alive, I still don't know how I did. But they only cared about her, I still don't know why."

Aren's mind wandered some more. "They *didn't* hurt you anymore or they *couldn't*?" he asked.

"I don't see how the two are different," said Ysser.

"Well, it's as you said…something changed. This wasn't their plan. If all they had wanted was to capture her, why had they not done it earlier? In fact, why had they taken all of you anyway? If they had only wanted her?" said Aren. "Why hadn't they killed you all the first chance they'd had?"

Ysser looked at him curiously. "I don't know."

Aren's head was heavy. He frantically tried to remember the words he'd read. *Key of blood. Stone of sacrifice. Shield of mankind.* It was prophesied. He knew that Aleryc's Pendant was the Key of Blood, he knew it had a role to play in stopping the dwellers, he just didn't know how. Could she have figured out how to use it? How to stop the dwellers? *Stone of sacrifice.* Did it mean that the threat was over? It didn't matter. Not right now, anyway. Olivia was in trouble. The enemy was here.

"My lord," said Aren. "It is against my wishes, you marching into battle with us. But since I cannot stop you, not from seeking justice anyway, I have a small request."

"Anything," said Lord Ysser.

"Jaspyn. Keep him close, will you?" said Aren. "Another who is marching into battle against my wishes, but one who is less skilled in the nuances of the battlefield than yourself."

"Your Majesty, with respect, if you were to order him stand down, he'd be bound by the King's Law to stay back," said Ysser.

"There are some forces stronger than law, and I fear I would strike resentment in his heart were I to stop him."

"Hmm."

"He's been through so much…Olivia was already gone by the time he got here. I cannot stop him from fighting for her, but I can ask you to not let him out of your sight."

"I shudder to think what the lad will think of that," said Ysser.

"He cannot find out," said Aren. "Stay close to him and keep a keen eye, you're injured as it is, my lord, may come in handy to have a friend rather than foe close by should you fall on the battlefield. Let him believe he's fighting his battle, if that'll make him happy."

"Understood," said Ysser. He didn't look happy about it, but Aren was in no mood for a debate. He looked over at the horsemen riding out outside of camp and disappearing behind the Aspen trees next to them. He saw the artilleries being wheeled out of the tents in the next row, his uncle Mentos walking behind them, talking to another younger man, clad in the Crown's burgundy.

"Lord Ysser, it is time."

The Gift
Rhedas

Rhedas scurried down the stairs as fast as he possibly could without tumbling and cracking open his skull. He stopped to lean against the wall, panting and catching his breath. There was no time. He clambered down some more steps, holding onto the wall to support him.

"Good heavens," came Master Tamuz's voice. He'd crept up behind him. Rhedas flinched, bracing for a thump on the back of his neck but it never came. "Where are you off to in such a rush? Not running from the Parydon I hope."

"No, no," said Rhedas. "I would never dream of it."

Master Tamuz set down the books he was carrying and raised his brow. "Then where?"

"New Castisa has fallen. They are coming north, the bluecoats."

"And so you are marching to fight in their petty war?" Master Tamuz laughed.

"No, no," said Rhedas. "I have…I have something I must do."

"Tell me," said Tamuz. "We are here to support one another, after all."

"No, this is something in which you cannot support me," said Rhedas.

"Why can I not?"

"Because you will not believe me."

"And what makes you think that?"

Rhedas sighed. "I don't…I don't have time for all this!" He regretted it instantly and braced himself. But once again, there was no smack across the face. No shouting, no cursing. Just Tamuz's half-worried smile.

"So?" he said. "Why will I not believe you?"

"You never do," said Rhedas. "None of you. Not you, not Kyril."

Tamuz crossed his arms. "We believed Ferus, didn't we? When the lad told us he saw them, the creatures of the night."

"Then why?" Rhedas cried. "Why won't you believe me?! Why didn't you let me talk to her?!"

"Talk to whom?"

"Her Eminence," said Rhedas.

"For she was in Veytora," said Tamuz. "How can we send you there? Without very good reason."

"Please, just…just let me go!" Rhedas cried. Time was running out.

"Fine, my boy, go. But where will you go? How will you manage?"

Rhedas groaned. "I don't know."

"Let me help. Tell me what is happening, what has you so worried and perhaps, *perhaps* we can make arrangements to speak to Her Eminence."

"You…you will believe me now?"

Tamuz shrugged. "I do not know. But I do know that your…*dreams*, they might be more than a nuisance, a madness. They might just…they might just be a gift. That is why you were sent our way, perhaps."

"What makes you think so?"

"Well, you knew that King Aren would take the throne. You knew that he would sit at Ayleris once more, as his forefathers once did. Perhaps your dreams might tell us more."

Rhedas waved his hands around. "Thank you. That is *exactly* what I have been saying too." *Great peril*. He needed to reach her right this instant. The night was setting in and the Aspens stirred not too far from the enemy, the true enemy.

"Calm yourself," said Master Tamuz. "Now tell me everything."

"The dream I had, the one about Her Eminence…I…I think I may have misunderstood it."

"How so?"

"I think there was another in the dream. Another with black hair and emerald eyes. Another that shall face deceit. The Stars of Deceit. I…I tried to warn them all." He sobbed. "They all think me mad, every last one of them. It is the Key, that is the only way it might end." He looked around, his eyes moving wildly. "But now…now it is done. The blood has fallen, the land is sacred."

"Slow down," said Tamuz, placing a hand on his shoulder. "You are beginning to sound mad again. Slow down and tell me everything."

"There is no point in telling you," said Rhedas. "There is nothing you can do to help. I need...I need to talk to Her Eminence."

Tamuz opened his book and ripped out an old, yellowed page. He pulled a pen from inside his cloak and looked at Rhedas expectantly. "Well?"

"Hmm?"

"I shall write a letter on your behalf," said Tamuz.

"You shall write it?"

Tamuz frowned. "Well, you, for one, cannot write. So tell me, I will write it all down and we shall send it to her at once."

"Oh," said Rhedas. He wasn't sure they'd have time. "Okay. *Dear Queen Develyn Asellar,*" he began.

"Who has said that she is a queen?" Tamuz slammed his book shut, frowning. "She is the Last Deryz Returned. If you are one of us, you will stop with this nonsense of kings and queens and wardens."

"You said you will believe me, my dreams," said Rhedas. "This I have seen in them. This is how it must be."

Tamuz sighed. "Alright, my boy. Continue."

"*Dear Queen Develyn Asellar. The ones who wear the bluecoats, the ones who rise from the shadows, they are upon us. Upon the north. You need to help. You need to help for Azara Urisci has failed. He fights alongside his king, the boy with the fiery hair. He fights tonight and tonight many around him shall die.*"

Tamuz looked at him with his eyebrows furrowed. "What nonsense are you speaking, my boy? Do you wish to be smacked again?"

"Her Eminence will make sense of it. Please, please just write the letter."

"Fine," said Tamuz, scrawling down the nonsense.

"*Without you, the king shall fall. The north shall fall.*"

"Is it the truth?" said Tamuz.

"I cannot say," said Rhedas. "But soon we shall know."

"Do you wish to write anything more?" said Tamuz.

"Yes," said Rhedas, clearing his throat. But then there was a low rumble and the setting sun quickly faded and the skies above them darkened. Tamuz looked around, putting his pen back inside his cloak and there was suddenly a ferocious roar which made Rhedas jump.

"Look!" Master Tamuz shouted, pointing up at the dark clouds. "Look at it!"

There was a piercing screech and then a crack as a bolt of lightning struck down on the Great Tower.

"Master!" came Kyril's voice. He was panting, running up the stairs. "Master! It is her. She has come."

"Her…Her Eminence?" Rhedas croaked.

Kyril nodded.

"Why has she come?" Tamuz said calmly. Suddenly the skies opened, and the rains fell down, hard upon them. Tamuz gasped out loud, wiping his bald scalp.

"I don't know," said Kyril. "But the southern man, that lord, his armies are gone."

"Lord Hercan?" said Tamuz.

"Yes," said Kyril. "But this time he has gone with them. There was a woman with him, a southern woman, dark hair."

"Linara Spenler?" said Rhedas.

The pair looked at him, bewildered.

"Why, yes," said Kyril. "What do you know of her?"

"Nothing," said Rhedas. "But now we must find her, she is close, Her Eminence."

"Why?" said Kyril. The rain grew stronger, flying at them sideways now. Rhedas' hair flew in the wind as there was another thunderous clap from above.

"Do not worry about it," said Tamuz. "It is between Rhedas and I."

Rhedas turned to his master. "That letter you wrote, hold on to it tightly."

"Why?" said Tamuz, scowling.

"She isn't happy," said Rhedas. "We need to tell her everything, and fast. The sun is going to set soon and when that happens it'll be too late."

The Silver Veil
Aren

Aren looked back to face his armies, squinting through the blinding summer sun. He turned back forward, peering over his soldiers in the vanguard to survey the bluecoats opposite. The slope meant that he had a clearer view of the enemy, despite his stature. Unfortunately, it also gave Ashcrest's men a tactical advantage over him on the field. He'd hoped it wouldn't have come to this. He dared not show a sign of weakness to his armies, but he was terrified to his core.

"Aren, look," said Jaspyn. He was stood beside him, squeezed between Ysser Banlin and Laris Hontren. The castle guards surrounded them, with Mentos Jeffyrs on the left flank. Jaspyn had a look of sheer disgust on his face, deep hatred in his eyes. "I'm going to kill him, Aren. I'm going to do it."

Aren stretched his head to see what Jaspyn was looking at. Immediately, his own heart filled with contempt, and he held back the urge to charge straight through the soldiers in front of him, right at Eyan Ashcrest. He could see the bastard clear as day.

"Look at the smug look on the piece of shit's face," said Jaspyn again.

"If neither of you kill him, I will," said Cyneric.

The traitor was stood just beside a figure, a shorter figure, masked by what appeared to be a veil of sorts, with silver beads glimmering in the evening sun. He was talking to one of his other soldiers though, a tall man mounting a bow. Quite peculiar indeed. He cast his eyes over the rest and that is when Aren noticed, the majority of the enemy's frontlines bore similar, weaker weapons – no match for a bullet. Wooden bows, arrows, swords, daggers, spears and who knew what else. Ashcrest was no fool, why would he arm his vanguard with weapons he knew would be no match for the artillery they'd face in battle today. That's when he looked over

at Jaspyn and saw the wooden bow on his back and the quiver on
his side, full of arrows. Gripped tightly in his hand, a long, steel
sword. The rifle hung beside him, slung over his shoulder.

"Have you gone mad?" said Aren. "With those weapons."

"He insisted," said Lord Ysser from behind them.

"He's going to die out there," said Aren. Jaspyn shrugged and
smiled back at him.

"Well, it's too late for me to go back now," he said. "I'll be fine,
Aren."

"Aren, that one," hissed Cyneric. "The short one, next to the
Ashcrest boy. With the veil." He was pointing at the masked figure
stood behind Eyan.

"What about him?"

"That's the one from that day in the tunnels, when I was
attacked."

"You can have that one to yourself then," said Jaspyn.

Cyneric grinned. "I will. But I meant, he serves Daxian."

Aren rolled his eyes. "I've lost count of my enemies, Cyneric,
they're all sort of merging into one big monster in my head."

"Slay the monster," came a voice. It was Laris.

"Nobody invited your input, Hontren," said Cyneric.

Laris grunted but grinned all the same.

"But yes, Aren. He isn't wrong," Cyneric continued. "You have
loyalty, respect and by the looks of things from here, you have the
upper hand when it comes to weapons too. You're destined to slay
the monster."

"The promise of destiny can be blinding," said Aren.

"What a coward," said Ysser. Aren turned, astonished. The
soldier's face went red as he realised what he'd said. "Sorry – I was
talking about the First Warden–"

"Don't call him that," hissed Aren.

"Sorry, Soren Ashcrest. I j-just meant, what kind of man sends
his own son into battle in his stead?"

"Oh, Eyan is far from innocent in all this," said Aren. His head
filled with memories from the night of the siege. He'd never forget
how brutally and mercilessly Eyan had murdered innocents in the
palace – the icy look in his eyes whilst he'd done it. A man he'd
once called his friend.

"Attention!" shouted a voice. "Quiet! Attention!" A chorus of
soldiers repeated the command, on both sides until the field fell to

near silence. The sound of trees rustling in the woods behind them was all that remained.

Eyan Ashcrest walked up, out of the confines of his own army. He walked with a certain confidence, as if he were suited to be a battle commander – something Aren was envious of, and ashamed to admit so. It looked as if it came to him naturally, more than he could say of himself.

As planned, Pennyn walked up slowly towards him. It looked like Eyan was looking to talk at least, but Aren couldn't see Olivia anywhere. Perhaps they'd kept her amidst all the innocents within the city, as a hostage. New Castisa was under their control now and they'd be fools to bring her out here, into the open. But he was prepared to give up almost anything for his friend back. He didn't care what people might think.

"Just you then, chancellor?" said Eyan. He spoke loudly and clearly, as if with the intention of Aren hearing. Perhaps he'd seen him stood here, within the safety of his army. Aren had half a mind to march up to him, but he had to stick to the plan.

"Just you then, Mr. Ashcrest?" said Pennyn. "Where's your father? We'd have thought he'd have been here to lead his armies – after all, for many it'll be the last battle they fight for this so-called Federation."

Pennyn spoke loudly too. It was all part of the ploy, put together by Mentos. If he could highlight the reality of the situation to the bluecoats, perhaps less of them would be willing to die for the tyrant who kidnapped innocent girls and cared little for soldiers' lives. Perhaps their numbers might dwindle, but Aren didn't count on it.

"Such petty skirmishes aren't a wise way to spend his time, wouldn't you say?" said Eyan. "Besides, this will all be over fairly soon, then I can go back and help him bring this country out of its grave, the one *you people* dug."

"Let us not dwell for too long, time is scarce," said Pennyn. Aren knew that he was trying his best to steer the conversation in a different direction altogether. "There is no need for innocent blood to be shed tonight. I believe you have taken a hostage, an innocent."

"*Hostage?* Not the word I'd use personally. And innocent? That's a bold way of describing Olivia Berywen."

Eyan had gone quieter, a lot quieter. Aren struggled to hear what was being said.

"By taking Lady Olivia, you have broken peace, whatever little peace we had between us," said Pennyn. "We're giving you one final chance to hand her over, and we will retreat. Your men can go home, and we can all live to fight another day."

Aren was completely oblivious now, to Eyan's words.

"*What peace?*" said Jaspyn. "That's what he's saying."

"You can hear him?" said Aren. Jaspyn raised his hand to hush him. "*What… suburban fantasy have you been living, old man?*" he continued. "*Besides, Olivia Berywen…has committed…treason…against her own cause…she's our prisoner…*" He stopped and looked at Aren.

"No, don't stop," said the king. "I want to hear everything."

"*She will…face a fair trial… under the laws upheld by the First Warden…We aren't like you lot…she will be safe in our custody,*" he said. He took pauses as he listened in to the traitor's words. "*Until we can hand her over to House Berywen, safe and sound… on our terms and our terms alone…The Crown shall have nothing to do with it.*"

"What treason?!" bellowed a voice, loud enough that Aren didn't need Jaspyn to repeat it. It was Chrysan's. Aren's heart stopped altogether. He wished he wouldn't have intervened. He knew Chrysan's temper all too well, and unfortunately, so did Eyan.

"Ah, I thought I'd spotted you earlier," said Eyan, loudly again. "You dare question the treason of your family? Well, since you had the audacity, let it be known to all the men and women here today. This man is a traitor. His mother and father, traitors, the both of them. And his bitch sister, well she might be the deadliest snake in the pit. Her venom cost the lives of hundreds of innocent Landridgian soldiers fighting for the noble cause of this Federation."

"What the fuck did you just say?!" Chrysan yelled, pointing up his loaded rifle at the spiteful man. Aren held his breath as a dozen or so men by Eyan's side picked up arms against Olivia's brother, each ready to take their shot. The men in the enemy's vanguard raised their bows.

Pennyn raised his hands and gestured to Chrysan to stand down.

"Enough of this, Eyan," said the Crown Chancellor. "Tell us what you want, and we can end this."

"Do you think we can be so easily bought?" said Eyan, raising his voice again. "These men are loyal. It's in our blood. What sort of message do you think it would send if we handed you over a traitor? A turncoat? Do you think you can just wave around a piece of bait and we'll fold? We won't rest until the power is once again in the hands of the people, not in some golden crown laced with the blood of generations of anguish and suffering."

Aren had a wildly unsettled feeling in his core. He watched as some of the Verenic soldiers murmured amongst themselves in front of him. Then the masked figure whispered something to the man just behind Eyan.

"Aren, resist," said Cyneric from beside him in hushed tones. "I know this is painful, it is for me as well, but we mustn't say anything."

"I wasn't going to," said Aren, before shifting his focus back to the enemy.

"What crime has the girl committed, exactly?" said Pennyn finally, changing the subject.

"Feeding us false information in order to betray the Federalist cause that her family is sworn to protect and serve, for one. Using her father to feed your king intimate information. There's plenty to choose from."

It was all lies. By the malicious smile on Eyan's face, Aren knew his intentions were nefarious. He just needed it to look like Olivia was a traitor so he could keep her as prisoner, to buy time and give him leverage over Aren.

"We deny the charges, outright," said Pennyn.

"Well, the charges aren't yours to deny. This is a matter of the Federation, we will speak of the Berywens' treachery only with House Berywen themselves, and only with them shall we negotiate Olivia's release," said Eyan.

"You've got a Berywen son right here," said Chrysan, speaking up again. This time, there was a certain shakiness in his voice. "Tell me what you want from us if I'm to get my sister back. Where is she?" he shouted.

Eyan smiled thinly. "Not too far from here. Safe, don't worry." He paused for a moment. "Convince your *king*, if I can even call him that, to retreat. Convince your men to stand down. Then maybe, perchance, we might talk about your sister."

Chrysan froze, then turned around and searched the crowd until his eyes landed upon Aren's. There was a fear in his eyes behind the fury. A chorus of soldiers between them turned too, to face him. But their eyes had no fear nor fury, their eyes carried a glimmer of hatred, of determination.

"Ah at last, the king arrives," said Eyan. "So, what's it going to be, *highness*?" he said, mockingly. Aren looked him dead in the eyes and said nothing. He simply nodded at Pennyn.

"We will stand down, retreat, like we said," said Pennyn. "And we can talk about borders another day, when–"

"You will take your troops north into the depths of Verenia and you will stay there," said Eyan.

"Now you're pushing it," said Pennyn, calmly. "We will give you New Castisa, Eyan."

"You cannot give what isn't yours to give," said another voice, suddenly. It was the taller man, the one stood beside the masked figure. Eyan looked back at the pair of them, almost annoyed, then turned back around to face Pennyn.

"I am feeling rather generous today though, so I will give you our prisoner, as a gesture of good faith. If, and only if, you swear allegiance to the First Warden right here and now, Chrysan," said Eyan. "Lay down your weapons, convince your men to do the same, and walk over here and pledge allegiance once more to the Free."

"These men aren't mine to command," said Chrysan, again turning back to look at Aren. Aren was wary of trusting Eyan's word. He didn't know what to do, but the despair in Chrysan's eyes was enough to take the risk. The bluecoats were outnumbered anyway. He nodded at Chrysan.

"Stand down," he shouted. A chorus of soldiers repeated the order, until the entire vanguard had laid down their weapons. Aren noticed the masked figure whisper once again in the ear of the tall man behind Eyan.

"Very well. Bring her out," said Eyan to his men, who parted to reveal a hooded Olivia Berywen, still in the dress Aren had last seen her in, tattered, bruised and bloody, her face entirely covered.

"How do we know that that is her?" said Pennyn. "And not some villager you've dressed in her clothes?"

Eyan nodded at his men, who unmasked her. Her mouth was shut tightly with a rag of sorts, and her eyes red, tears still coming down her rosy cheeks. She looked straight through her brother, to Aren, to Jaspyn.

"Now, I'll let her walk over to you Chrysan, if you walk a couple of paces closer–"

"We want the false king to pledge allegiance to the First Warden," came a deep voice. It was the taller man again. "And we want him to promise to exile himself and his family to the Asenian wastelands from whence they hail."

Eyan looked back at the man as if he'd spoken out of turn. He then looked back at the masked figure, who hadn't yet uttered a single word.

"That isn't happening," said Pennyn. "You call yourselves the Free, as Oscon Hercan's men did. You claim to be virtuous…Staying true to your word is a vital part of that."

Eyan walked back to his accomplices and listened to the masked figure's dubious whispers.

"New Castisa isn't enough," said Eyan. "We want something else, from the king himself."

"Well, what is it?" said Pennyn.

Eyan looked Aren directly in the eyes. "We want the Key of Blood. I believe that the king will know exactly what I speak of. And no decoys this time, we will know, you can trust me on this."

"You shall have it," said Aren. Right now, he was willing to do whatever it would take to free Olivia. Even giving them the pendant. Every moment she spent behind enemy lines was a moment her life fell in greater danger. "But only *after* we get her back. In the meantime, my men are not armed, we are standing down, there is nothing we can do to cause you harm."

Eyan thought about it for a moment before nodding. "Olivia, I want you to walk in a straight line, slowly, to your brother. Once you've–"

"Actually," said the man from behind Eyan again. "We have more to say." Eyan looked furious now, but he nodded and let the man speak. "*You*," the man pointed to Chrysan. "Your blood has betrayed us once before. To prove your loyalty, take the life of one man, any man, who fights for this false king."

Aren's felt sick to his stomach. Before Pennyn had had a chance to open his mouth to say anything, Chrysan swung up his rifle to his hip and shot it twice through the chest of a Verenic soldier stood beside him in the vanguard. The soldier fell to his knees before hitting the ground hard, face down, dead. The Verenic forces around Chrysan picked up their own weapons and pointed them once again, but this time at the Berywen boy. It had all happened so fast. Eyan stared, in silence, whilst the taller one smiled, bearing his ugly teeth.

"Stand down," Aren said to his soldiers, breaking the deafening silence.

"But he killed an innocent!" a voice came from the vanguard. "A *soldier!*" The crowd jeered in agreement, waving their weapons in the air.

"You heard your king, stand down!" Pennyn bellowed and the soldiers obliged.

Eyan looked over at the masked figure, who nodded. He turned back and clapped his hands together slowly. "Well, you've definitely earned our trust, for the time being anyway."

"Blood has been shed, Ashcrest, we won't forget this," said Pennyn. "Now hand over your prisoner before any other innocent lives are lost."

Eyan nodded at Olivia, who set off from within the bluecoat armies, walking slowly and steadily, her eyes white with horror. On the other side, Pennyn stood with Chrysan, waiting for her. Suddenly, the taller man yelled out.

"Stop!"

They whispered amongst themselves once more. "We will hand her over to Lord Berywen and only Lord Berywen," the man said out loud. "In return, we demand the permanent exile of House Berywen from Éterin."

"I don't see that you understand how negotiations take place," said Pennyn. "Ashcrest, control your men. We're already giving you New Castisa, how can we–"

"Like I said before, New Castisa isn't yours to give," said the tall man.

"That's enough out of you, Garlen," said Eyan Ashcrest. "Look chancellor, we will give *you* Lyndan. The harbour and all."

"That isn't enough. Not for New Castisa and Éterin."

"How about you hand over the Key of Blood before we give you the prisoner," said the man named Garlen. "Then we can all–"

The masked figure beside him signalled with a raised hand once more, asking him to stop. There was a sudden silence in the field. For a moment, everything was still, very still. Aren looked at the figure, then at Olivia who was stopped dead in her tracks and over at Chrysan and Pennyn. It happened so quickly. All Aren could hear was the distant rattle of the silver beads swinging in front of the masked figure's face as he took a sharp step forward. In one swift motion, he launched the dagger, which hurtled straight towards the king. It wasn't aimed at him, though. It was almost as if time itself had stopped. The dagger's silver blade buried itself in the side of Olivia's neck, and blood spurted out as she let out a stifled cry of agony, choking. The bluecoats from the army's flanks fired their rifles almost at once, tearing through Olivia Berywen's chest as she fell to the ground, her eyes still open. There was an eerie silence after the last echoes of the riflemen's shots faded. Aren's heart burst into a thousand pieces as the last bit of innocence inside him died, with Olivia. Aren couldn't hear anything anymore. The screams all echoed, distant.

"I'm going to fucking kill you!" Jaspyn roared at Eyan. "You fucking watch me!"

Chrysan led out an agonising cry, cursing and swearing at everyone around him as he ran towards his fallen sister's lifeless body.

Eyan Ashcrest stood silently, in awe. His eyes were wide open and his face pale as snow. He turned around suddenly to look at those stood behind him, the ones who had launched the attack. The masked figure stood motionless, proudly.

"You–"

There was a sharp bang as Chrysan fired his rifle, grazing Eyan's leg. A storm of more gunshots followed as Aren's forces opened fire on the enemy's vanguard. Eyan dove back, shielding himself behind his soldiers. There was a deafening explosion as the enemy forces launched an artillery directly towards the king's men. The shell landed a distance behind Aren and took out a handful of his men with it. The ground was suddenly red and muddy with puddles of their blood.

"Advance!" yelled Aren. Once again, the command echoed through the field, repeated by his soldiers through the cries of anguish as they charged ahead. Aren searched the crowds for Mentos, who'd give him the signal to command the flanks of his army when it was time, as per the plan. He couldn't see through the swarm of men and the rising smoke from the artilleries. It couldn't wait. He was already losing too many. He wondered if Chrysan was still alive. He looked ahead, through the vanguard, at the men on the enemy frontlines. Something was off. He looked at his own men taking bullets to the chest, stumbling and falling to their deaths. Their shields were of little use. In fact, none of the shots were coming from the soldiers at the frontlines at all – they were all being shot by soldiers further back, on higher ground. He scrambled through the crowd to get a closer look, Cyneric by his side.

"Look – their men, they aren't –"

He looked to his left, but Jaspyn was gone. He couldn't see Ysser either. There was no time to worry about their whereabouts – he didn't care. Olivia won't have died in vain, she can't have.

"What about their bloody men?!" yelled Cyneric, taking cover.

"Look – look at the front. So few of them have shields, why are we losing so many more than they are?" shouted Aren, clambering over the bodies of his castle guards.

"Hold on," said Cyneric, holding up his shield in front of them. "Look, the ones at the front – the ones with bows, arrows, swords, they're –"

Cyneric didn't finish his sentence. An arrow landed in his right arm, burying itself in the outer layers of his flesh. He screamed as blood gushed out, the arrow still stuck in his arm.

"Look out!"

Another arrow landed just beside them. It had barely missed Cyneric's head. He breathed out heavily, lifting his shield up above himself. "Here, give it here," said Aren, lifting the shield above them. It gave Cyneric just enough time to take in a deep breath and pull out the arrow from his arm, wincing. As Cyneric took back the shield, Aren looked ahead to what he was pointing at. He was convinced his eyes were deceiving him, but it was clear as day.

"Are they…"

"Yes."

"Nobody can cheat death, Cyneric."

"No *man* can cheat death," said Cyneric. "The dwellers… we can't kill them. That's why the rest of them…they're hiding behind them." It was lost just as it had begun. How could they win?

"AREN!" a voice shouted in the distance. Mentos waved at him from the left flank.

"Aren, it's time. We're already lost so many, give the command," said Cyneric.

Aren nodded at him frantically in agreement. "Flanks!" he shouted.

No soldiers repeated his command. The castle guards were dead. Every single one. The sound of gunfire and screams were deafening.

"Louder, Aren!" Cyneric shouted. "FLANKS!" Cyneric barked at the top of his lungs and Mentos Jeffyrs charged forward, leading the left flank up the slope. The right flank followed suit and the shield of dwellers protecting the bluecoats thinned, dispersing to either edge.

"ARTILLERIES!" bellowed a soldier from behind him and they were launched, hurtling towards the enemy.

Aren couldn't see Eyan Ashcrest, nor the others he intended to kill, they'd disappeared into their armies. He had blood on his mind, not any justice. He longed to kill the masked one first, the one who'd thrown the knife. It wasn't a quick death he had planned either. He couldn't get Olivia's face out of his head. The way she looked to him, to her brother, the despair in her eyes.

There were two massive explosions as the shells took out some of Eyan's men. He watched as the dwellers in the vanguard rose up from the smoke of the artillery fire with little more than dirty scratches and bruises to bear.

"How…" Cyneric's voice came from behind him. He sounded tired. But not all hope was lost, the explosions had taken out a fair few stood behind the front lines too, the living men. The watchtowers of New Castisa weren't too far now, they'd forced the bluecoats to retreat. They'd pushed quite a bit up the slope now.

"Come, Cyneric."

Aren scrambled to his feet, panting, and set off again, Cyneric by his side. They raced through the piles of dead men straight into the thick of it.

"Aren! You're not martyring yourself here tonight. Stay back!"

"I'm going to kill them, Cyneric."

"Not if you get yourself killed first. One stray bullet would do it. Stay here with me, we've pushed them back quite a bit – let your armies do the rest."

"I can't just stand here and watch," said Aren.

"I'm not asking you to. Fight, but fight from here."

Aren stopped. "What's that?" he asked.

There was a loud stir coming from the north-east. A sort of low buzzing, droning sound. It got louder and louder until Aren could see silhouettes of horses and motorcars and carriages, massive carriage, emerge from behind the watchtowers. Was it the Dresden forces? Had word reached Lady Rayne in time? No…these were heavily armoured motorcars, just like the Crown forces' own. They drew closer and closer until Aren could see the standard that was emblazoned on them. It was as if his prayers had been answered. He sighed in relief, looking at Cyneric.

"The Hercanian Stars!" he said, pointing frantically at the noble crest. "Did we…did we send word to Lord Hercan?"

Cyneric eyed the troops as they drew closer. "No, Aren. And even if we did, how would they have come down from the Falls so quickly? That's further up the river than Ayleris."

"I don't know. Maybe Lady Rayne sent word? Or…Lara, of course, she must have told Perwell what is going on?"

He was plucking at straws. He didn't have to wait much longer for his answer, though. The soldiers on horseback drew their rifles and mounted them directly at Aren's army. His heart once again filled with darkness. Hopeless and tired, he watched as the Hercanian soldiers took their shots, taking down dozens more of his men. How had this happened? How had it happened right under his nose? The soldiers screamed in agony, desperately piling onto each other but it was of no use.

"Look out!" shouted Cyneric, pointing at a bluecoat who'd had his rifle aimed right at him. Aren plunged to the ground, rolling over in the bloodstained mud.

"Stop," said Cyneric. "You're too close."

"And I'll get closer still," said Aren, tugging his arm away. "Where are the cowards? I haven't seen them since the start."

"I want them dead just as much as you do but we can't risk it right now…they outnumber us now, they have the higher terrain, they have the dwellers."

"I don't care. I'll find them." Aren could see nothing but death. Blood.

"No," said Cyneric, yanking his arm back and pulling him backward.

"Let me go!" Aren cried out. "I will end this today."

"Wait…"

One of the armoured cars stopped a little distance away and out walked Perwell Hercan himself. He was surrounded by men with rifles on arm but he himself held a wooden bow. He nocked an arrow on his bow and he drew, hard and fast.

"Surely he's not one of them," said Aren.

"A dweller?" said Cyneric. "Or a bluecoat?"

Perwell shot his arrow, killing a Verenic soldier on the left flank. He quickly nocked another arrow and aimed it at another.

"Well, that answers one of those questions," said Cyneric. "But still, a dweller? Old Perwell? I don't see it."

"Why aren't they using rifles?" said Aren.

Before Cyneric could come up with a response, a pale-faced, grim looking bluecoat lunged at him, his eyes red and bloodshot. He carried a dagger which he held in front of Cyneric's throat. Aren could see his eyes get darker and redder as Cyneric shouted out loud.

"Cyneric, careful!"

Aren pointed his rifle at the creature's back, waited for the right moment and then pulled the trigger. The dweller bled, his blue coat suddenly stained vermillion, and he rubbed over his wound with his hand. Aren shot again, twice, with no inhibitions. He watched in shock as the pale skin around the dweller's wounds closed again, slowly but surely, and the creature drew closer to Cyneric. The Panderer's expressions turned to horror as he frantically pushed the creature directly in front of Aren. Aren looked in astonishment, as an arrow pierced through the dweller's chest, and he stumbled. The arrow hadn't come from Cyneric, nor was it intended for the dweller. He looked past the dying dweller at Perwell Hercan, who had his bow aimed directly at Aren once more, and he rolled over. Perwell was out of sight, so he was safe, for now. He looked over at Cyneric who nodded back at him seriously.

"He's dead!" shouted Aren.

"Well spotted."

"No, I mean…he's *dead*. The dweller. How?"

Aren looked back to see Perwell Hercan again, already loading his next arrow. He was stood beside the car, taking cover behind its armoured door.

"Let's get out of here," said Cyneric. "It isn't safe for you anymore."

They made for the watchtowers as fast as they could, staying clear of stray bullets and arrows. Cyneric held the shield up above Aren as they edged closer. There was a sudden scream from the flank. Aren turned to see where it had come from. It was Perwell, grabbing onto the door of his motor as his knees buckled, his leg bloody.

"Traitor scum," said Cyneric. "Deserves it."

"Thought so too," came a deep voice. The shot had come from Laris Hontren, who stood just behind them, grinning, rifle still pointed.

"Well that settles that. He isn't a dweller," said Cyneric. "He's bleeding."

Laris' grin quickly faded.

"What is it?" said Aren.

"Nothing," he said. "Just – have youse yet seen any of 'em kill?"

"What?" said Cyneric.

"Ah nowt. Just the dwellers – have youse seen any one of them actually *kill* someone? Take someone's life?"

Aren wasn't sure that he had. "What do you know of them?"

"Nothin'. Just noticed that every time one of 'em gets close to killing me his eyes go all red and he stops," said Laris. "They've got weapons, the lot of 'em, but I ain't seen any one of 'em actually kill. Arrgh!" That was all he could get out before he dove to the ground.

"Take cover!" he yelled. Aren turned, a stampede of bluecoats was on its way.

"Come!" yelled Cyneric, grabbing him by the arm and hiding him behind a burning motorcar. "That should buy you a bit of time."

Laris hadn't said a lot, yet he had said a great deal. *They couldn't kill anymore*. Key of blood. Stone of sacrifice. Shield of mankind. Had the pendant done this? Was it Olivia's sacrifice that the prophecy spoke of? He hadn't time for prophecies right now. Yet… if the dwellers couldn't kill them? They were just acting as shields… as distractions.

There was another bang and bodies flew up into the air, flashes of red, brown and black flying in every direction as the soldiers turned to ash.

"The watchtowers," said Aren. "We can't stay here, they're almost upon us."

As they got closer, the smoke had mostly risen and Aren could see a lot more clearly now, but the sun had all but set and darkness was setting in. Aren stopped as he caught glimpse of a familiar face in the thick of the enemy forces.

"Cyneric, is that – is that…Jaspyn?"

It was definitely him, but Aren had to ask to be sure his eyes weren't deceiving him.

Cyneric cleared his throat. "Yes – yes that's him."

Aren watched in awe as his friend single-handedly took on two men, bashing their heads into each other before driving his tattered old steel sword into the heart of a bluecoat. It wasn't just any bluecoat though, the man was armed with a bow. The same pale face, red eyes. This man was a dweller. A dead dweller, now.

"Aren, you know what this means?"

"Jaspyn!" shouted Aren, ignoring him. But it was too late. His friend had disappeared into the crowds just as fast as he'd emerged.

"He's gone," said Cyneric. "Looks like he can handle himself pretty well, too. But he killed that dweller with a sword."

"And Hercan killed one with an arrow," said Aren.

"They can't be killed with guns, nor artilleries," said Cyneric. "Looks like we need a change of weapons."

"And *they* can't use guns either," said Aren. "That's why not a single one of their dwellers arms himself with a rifle."

There was a sudden roar above them and a deafening crack as the skies darkened. It happened in a heartbeat, and there was a white flash. Suddenly, the Hercanian stars were set ablaze as burning men ran for cover, crying and yelling in anguish. And then, another. It was difficult to see what had happened, but massive flames rose from the thick of it, as soldiers flew in every direction.

"I thought all the aces burnt," said Aren.

"Those weren't aces."

"Wait, is that–" Aren caught a glimpse a pale, black haired boy limping through the crowds of bluecoats towards the eastern watchtower.

"Is that him again?" said Cyneric.

Aren was mistaken as well, for a moment or two.

"No."

"Aren, no don't –"

But Aren was gone. He set off behind Eyan Ashcrest, not a care in the world of the people around him, arrows flying all over the place, the sounds of swords clanging together, the screams of men dying. This time he wouldn't listen to Cyneric. He left him behind and sprinted, just one thing on his mind. The thick of the enemy was behind him now too, he drew closer. He looked up at the towers before tripping over the body of a dead soldier.

There was a sharp twang and a great weight fell upon his side, bloody all over.

"H-help…"

Aren looked around him in a hurry. It was Perwell Hercan who'd shot the arrow. The traitor nocked another on his bow and pointed towards the dark woods. He hadn't seen Aren.

"Help me…p-please," the feeble voice croaked. A short man, scruffy and scarred. He had only one brow, the other burnt or skinned. "It h-hurts…so, s-so bad." The idiot's longbow had broken as he'd stumbled into Aren, the sharp broken wood of it planted firmly in his thigh. Aren eyed the peculiar soldier. It wasn't one of his. Beneath the little man's muddy, bloodstained bluecoat, a crest. A familiar crest. The burning phoenix of House Ashcrest.

Aren scrambled to his feet, his hands muddy, stained with blood.

"No…n-no, p-please help me!" the idiot wailed but Aren simply stepped over the fool.

Eyan had made for the watchtower, so Aren wasted no time and darted towards it. He would get his justice today. He was sure of it. A loud bang startled him as a bluecoat opposite suddenly dropped his gun – a gun that had been pointed right at Aren. The soldier writhed and screamed in pain as he moved his head wildly to see who had stopped him from killing the king. There were another two loud bangs. The bluecoat fell to the floor, two gunshots in the back of his skull. Aren looked up to see Mentos Jeffyrs holding his rifle steadily at the body. He'd saved Aren's life. That was the second time today Aren had stared death in the face.

"Uncle –"

There was a twang and then his uncle's eyes went wide, and an arrow stuck out through his neck. His skull hit the ground hard, as he fell, his body stiff on the cold ground.

"Arrrrggghhhh!" Aren yelled, dejected and broken. He peered behind Mentos' fallen body to see Perwell Hercan once more, his sights this time set on Aren.

"You coward!" Aren yelled, but Hercan was suddenly out of sight. A motorcar drove in, blocking his view of the traitor. It bore a different crest. A sight he welcomed, when his heart was sunken in the lowest depths of despair. The stallion of House Dresden. He looked around him as many more motors drove in, horses too. Lady Rayne had delivered on her promise. He looked at the Dresden troops as they hit the ground, covering the left flank and drawing the enemy in towards the watchtowers. *The watchtower.*

Aren turned around, ready to set off into the eastern tower. He stopped to pick up a bow and a quiver from a dead dweller. If he was going to do this, he needed to be prepared – for anything. He knew it was probably a mistake, he knew Eyan had had quite a head start, that he could be waiting with a gun, ready to take his life, or maybe he'd be stood with dwellers, ready for an ambush. He doubted he'd be fast enough with his bow, they were faster than him. Stronger too, from what he'd seen. In this moment though, he didn't care. He wanted to kill Eyan. He wanted to watch the life leave his eyes as the traitor took his last breaths. He wanted this over anything. He set aside his rage and darted for the door at the bottom of the tower. Just as he stepped inside, he glimpsed something in the corner of his eye. Something that glistened in the last embers of the dusk sun. He turned around and the masked figure stared back at him. The one who'd buried a knife in Olivia's neck. The silver veil had caught the light of the sinking sun, sparkling as the coward ran.

Suddenly, Aren was faced with a tough choice. It dawned upon him just how much he wanted to see both of these people dead. There was no time to weigh out his options though.

He jumped down from the steps of the tower's entrance. Eyan could wait. He'd get his justice too, Aren vowed to himself. With the Dresden forces, the battle could be won – he'd be safer heading towards the woods, the bluecoats were retreating.

Aren used the cover of the Dresden troops to escape the gunfire as he darted after the murderer, making for the dark woods. He'd been spotted. The figure ran faster, turning back to take blind shots at Aren every so often. But Aren was faster. Maybe it was his thirst for vengeance. He could barely see now, in the cover of darkness as the last embers of sunlight faded away.

Aren decided to take a chance. He was close enough now to attempt a clean shot. Was it worth the gamble? He didn't know. He decided to do it anyway. He stopped, nocking an arrow on his bowstring, and he pulled far back. He let the thumb of his right hand gently caress his cheek as he released the arrow. It missed. His heart sank. Stopping had wasted time. It'd been stupid. With little to lose, he loaded another arrow and tried again. Another miss. Not completely wasted, though. The arrow had hit the ground just in front of the killer's feet. The masked coward tripped, stumbling and rolling in the mud before quickly getting up again. It was enough for Aren to catch up though. He stopped beneath a large aspen tree at the edge of the woods, not too far from where the camps had been set up earlier on in the day. Night had fallen now. He panted loudly as he nocked his arrow. He stood in front of the murderer, his bow at full draw, staring down the barrel of his opponent's rifle. There was something about it all that made him care little about the fact that he was looking death in the eyes. Olivia had been killed in cold blood. Without reason. As an act of sheer hatred and treachery. His best friend. His eyes welled up as he remembered the look on her face. He could see it clearly, even now.

"You don't scare me," said Aren. "Kill me if you want but as soon as you pull that trigger, my arm will loosen, and this arrow will be headed your way." There was a cold silence. "A clean death, too quick for the likes of you," said Aren. He knew though, that his arm would give way soon. This was a much heavier bow than the kind he'd trained with. If he were to shoot his arrow, it would have to be now. He'd get no answers, though. Why Olivia? How did the bluecoats know about the Key of Blood? Maybe it wasn't worth it, maybe killing Olivia's murderer would be enough.

Aren wasn't quick enough. There was a loud bang and a puff of smoke came out of the barrel of the gun. He hadn't felt any pain though. He looked down at his body and couldn't see any blood. That's when he realised that he hadn't been the target at all – the barrel was pointed behind him. He heard the hoofbeats first, before he turned to see Jaspyn on a horse, his side stained red.

"Are you okay? You're hurt!" Aren bellowed.

"I'm fine – watch out!" shouted Jaspyn as he came up beside him.

The masked murderer's gun fired once more, this time wounding Jaspyn's pale horse. The horse bucked, launching Jaspyn forward to the ground in front of him, kicking Aren's arm. There was a twang and the arrow flew into the ground a few paces to the right. A wasted chance.

With a fierce jolt forward, Jaspyn swung his sword hard and fast at the murderer's arm. There was a loud clang as the sword hit armour, but the impact was enough to throw the gun to the floor.

The murderer leapt wildly at Aren, punching him in the face, before kicking the quiver off of him. He struck back, using the bow to push the attacker away, before Jaspyn sprung over and ripped off the figure's silver veil. Beneath was a black metal mask, which Jaspyn tore off revealing the murderer's pale face.

Jaspyn stared in horror. Aren's own mind stuttered for a moment, as he stood in awe, motionless and broken.

"I'd hoped not to meet again like this," said Éline Nazeris.

"Why?" the words finally came out of Aren's mouth.

"Oh, because I was hoping to have a grand reveal on my own terms, not Jaspyn's."

Aren's veins burned with rage. "Why did you kill Olivia?"

The treacherous bitch just smiled at him silently.

"Do you work for the bluecoats?" said Jaspyn. She shook her head solemnly.

"Who do you work for?" Aren screamed. "Why did you kill her? Why *her*? I took your family into my home. I believed in your innocence – all of you, despite all the warnings. You fucking traitor."

She laughed at him. "I'm no traitor."

"You…you…" Aren couldn't get the words out. "Did Ashcrest make you do it?"

"I don't serve the bluecoats."

Aren wanted to hurt her. His head pounded and throbbed. He wished he still had his arrows. No worry, he'd strangle her to death if it came to it. He was done with her. He didn't care for what she had to say, she would get no trial. She would get no mercy.

Jaspyn held out his sword in front of her neck. "Then who do you work for? Do you work for Daxian?"

Her eyes went thin. She stopped smiling and looked Jaspyn dead in the eyes. "No, you idiot. I don't serve anyone. The bluecoats bow to me. The dwellers bow to me."

"Why? What do you hope to gain from all this? The Federation?"

"A Federation, of sorts, perhaps," she said, smiling sadistically again.

"Enough of this, Jaspyn. Finish her," said Aren.

She chuckled. "Listen to your friend, Jaspyn."

"Not another word out of you!" shouted Jaspyn.

"I don't *work* for Daxian, I *am* Daxian. I *am* the one who will remake the world from the ashes of its cruel past. I made the Order what it is today–"

"I don't care what you are," said Aren. Her face suddenly changed again, her eyes seeping with hatred and anger rather than the insanity that had dwelled before. There was something not right about her, something terrifying, and he wished he'd seen it before. "What are you fucking waiting for Jaspyn?" said Aren, agitated. He couldn't let her slip through his fingers. He wasn't going to let her out of this alive.

Jaspyn pulled his sword back, ready to pierce her heart with it, but his face suddenly changed, paler than ever, his eyes wide and red. It couldn't be. It *couldn't*. Aren watched as Jaspyn's knees gave way and he fell, dazed and in pain. He threw the sword hilt-first to Aren though as he went down and in a clean and swift manoeuvre, Aren plunged it forward towards her, but she wasn't there. She'd already disappeared into the woods.

A False Sanctuary
Lara

The night had gotten dark and the sound of guns and artilleries had faded until there was nothing but silence. Even the Aspen trees stood still as the fires in the far distance fizzled out and the smell of smoke and soot was all but gone.

Lara waited anxiously. It had sounded terrifying from where she'd sat. Even Jeryn had left her as the battle began, irritated that she'd refused to let him fight. He'd spent the night in his own tent. She'd let him, because how could she have stopped him? But when it had gotten cold, when the thunder had raged above, that is when she wished she'd had someone by her side.

There was a rustling noise outside. She got up, dagger gripped tightly, and walked to the front of the tent. Nobody should be on this side of her camp, all the women and children who had come with them were on Jeryn's side. Perhaps it had been an animal of sorts.

There it was again. A scurrying, sort of like a fox or a lynx. She tightened the grip on her blade, knowing well that she'd never used it on even a rabbit.

"Lara," came a whisper. It was a strange accent, not one she'd heard much up here.

"Lara, trust me."

"Who…who is there?"

She took a deep breath.

The tent covers swished and she plunged straight forward with her blade, jabbing it blindly at nobody at all. A hand gripped her wrist tightly and twisted it out, making her curse out loud as the dagger fell to the burnt grass below. The figure before her wore a mauve cloak.

"Step back!" Lara shouted. "Far back. They will be back any moment now."

"I am not here to hurt you," said the woman. "Far from it, in fact."

"I said step away!"

The woman took off her hood. She had dark skin and thick curly hair that was neatly tied back.

"Who are you?" Lara shouted.

"My name is Azara Urisci."

Azara Urisci. She'd heard it before.

"I work for two incredibly powerful, fair women," she went on.

"I don't care who you work for. Why are you here? Get out!"

"I'm not here to hurt you," said Azara, putting her arms up. "I'm here to help you, in fact."

"Help me?"

"I work for Zenara Itris and Develyn Asellar," she said. "It is Zenara who has sent me here today."

And that is when it hit her.

"Why?"

"Do you know of a man who calls himself Rhedas Sandaerzi?"

"No," said Lara. "I don't."

"Well, he believes you are in danger and when he believes something as strongly as he does, he is rarely wrong."

"What? Why would I be in danger?"

Azara slipped her hand into a pocket inside her cloak.

"Don't come any closer!" she yelled.

"Relax." Azara pulled out an old key and held it out to her.

"What is this?"

"A key," said Azara laughing. Then her face grew serious. "You will be imprisoned, Aren Aryssen will give the order himself."

"Imprisoned?" Lara laughed loudly. "By Aren? On account of what?"

"Don't laugh. He will imprison you on account of your father's treachery."

Lara gulped. "My father's…*treachery?*"

"He is a traitor," said Azara. "He has fought for Ashcrest today. I expect his men will be on their way here now in the darkness of night to rescue you, in fact."

"R-rescue me? From whom?"

"From Aren Aryssen. But you mustn't let them."

"I mustn't let them what?"

"Rescue you, girl. You mustn't let them rescue you."

"But…"

"We don't have a lot of time. Take the key, hide it well, in your blouse if you must. You mustn't part ways with it. When they come to arrest you, let them. That key, it will be your way out of the dungeons beneath the Malysor."

Lara's heart raced. "Where did you get it?"

"You don't worry about such things, you just keep yourself safe. And remember, when your father's men come here, *do not* go with them. It is a false sanctuary that they offer you."

She took the key. She didn't know why but she took it, and she tucked it safely inside her blouse.

There was a thunderous roar outside, a low rumble high above them.

"What is that?" Lara cried. None of it made sense.

"Don't be scared," said Azara. "They won't hurt you. They are here to help too."

"Why can't…why can't I come with you?" said Lara. "If I am truly in danger with Aren or with my father."

"Because he needs to believe that you escaped on your own accord. Let him arrest you, let him question you and speak your truth to them, to the king's men. And when they least expect it, run. Run far and run fast."

"Aren is fair," said Lara.

"Yet a great madness is waiting to descend upon him," said Azara. "This you must trust me on."

"He would never imprison me, not like this. Not without a fair trial. He trusts me. He trusts all his closest."

"All his closest?" Azara laughed. "The usurper's son? Or the puppets that controlled his mother?"

"No," said Lara sternly. "Me, Olivia. Jaspyn."

"Olivia Berywen is dead. And your friend Jaspyn, well…"

The words pierced through her and for a moment time stood completely still. She felt weak, she breathed in and out sharply until she felt like she was going to faint.

"Sh-she…" she couldn't get the words out. "Olivia…"

"She was never going to make it out alive."

Lara didn't want to be here anymore. She wanted to run as far as her legs would take her. She wanted to hurt them, to hurt all of them, the ones who'd played a part. She shuddered at the thought of it. *Her own father*. How could he? How could any of them?

There was a quick swish and suddenly Azara was gone.

"Hello?"

There was no response. Lara felt an immense pain in her body and yet she was more eager than ever for their return. Eager and scared. She needed to hear it from Aren himself. She could barely walk over to the chair. She dragged herself to it, one leg at a time and slumped herself in it, letting her heavy arms dangle from the rests. She suddenly felt numb, completely free from it all. Had it been minutes or hours since the cloaked woman had left? She didn't know. In the distance, the noises grew louder but it didn't bother her at all. In fact, she could barely hear it now. Even as the thunderous footsteps approached her tent, she closed her eyes. She wasn't here, really.

"Where is she?" came a voice.

"Hold on, hold on," came the reply. It was Jeryn's voice this time. "She's in there, I think."

The tent swung open once more and Ysser Banlin marched in, bloody and dirty, limping on one leg.

"You..."

He charged at her, grabbing her by her arms and shaking her but she did not care. She did not utter a single word.

"Did you know?!" he shouted. Again, she didn't say a word. "Of course, you must have," he shouted.

"Where is Aren?"

"Answer my questions," said Ysser. "Your friend is dead. Half our people are dead. Do you even care?"

Who was he to put her on trial?

"Tell me, did you know? How much did you tell your father?"

The tent opened once more and Cyneric walked in, a deep gash on the side of his cheek.

"Don't," said Cyneric. "Just arrest her."

"Now?" said Ysser.

"That is what the king has said."

The True Enemy

Aren

The morning light filled the large, empty hall. Aren stood at the window, watching the clouds over Ayleris.

"Does it still hurt?" said Jaspyn, looking at his wounded arm.

Aren just held it up at him, not looking him in the eyes, still gazing out at the city below. The trees in the castle's lawn outside swayed ever so gently in the wind.

"Aren, they've finished questioning him. The dweller."

Aren remained quiet, his arm throbbing in pain.

"Do you want to hear what they got out of him? Garlen?"

"Not particularly."

Jaspyn walked up to him. "I know it won't bring Olivia back, nor Mentos, nor any of the others we lost...but it brings us that much closer to getting justice."

"We almost had our justice," said Aren. There was pain in his voice. "We let her slip through our fingers. Worse still, it could've been avoided if you'd just been honest with me the moment you arrived. When were you going to tell me?"

Jaspyn sighed softly. "You had enough to worry about. I didn't know how to tell you. It all happened so quickly–"

"You could have just been honest. Did you think I was going to kill you for it?"

"I didn't know what to think, Aren. All I knew is the dwellers were your enemy and–"

"The bluecoats are my enemy. The usurper Develyn Asellar is my enemy. Daxian is my enemy. I have a lot of enemies, but you are *not* my enemy, Jaspyn."

"I'm sorry, Aren. I'm so sorry... You know I am."

"It doesn't matter anymore," said Aren, looking away from him again. "Did they find them? Arcadius and Ylor?"

"They're gone," said Jaspyn softly. "The lot of them."

Aren took in a deep breath before turning to face him again. "What hurts the most about all this is it all happened right under my nose. I don't care, I will hunt down every last Nazeris and I swear it – none of them will have an easy death. The Ashcrests too." He meant every word.

"Aren, I really think you should speak with Cyneric."

"Why?"

"Well, after him and Laris questioned Garlen back at the camps, they asked him about them, about Arcadius and Ylor. He spat on the ground and called them blood traitors."

"What's new there?"

"No, you don't understand," said Jaspyn. "He said they were traitors of the Order. That they didn't want to see progress, they believed in the old ways. From what he said, Éline acted entirely alone. The Daxian Order didn't have anything to do with Arcadius nor Ylor."

Aren rolled his eyes. "Don't you see? Of course he'd say that. The man's probably trained for this exact thing and of course Éline would want to protect her family."

"Did she seem like the kind of girl who'd want to protect her family? Last night on the field? In fact, now that I think of it, has she *ever* seemed that sort?"

"Then why did they run? They could've stayed here and helped bring Éline to justice. Arcadius is a part of my bloody council, Jaspyn. Well…he *was*."

"Yes, I couldn't quite make sense of that either," said Jaspyn. "But word spreads fast, that I've learnt for sure. Maybe they feared for their safety, maybe …" He broke off and drew in a deep breath.

"Maybe what?" said Aren.

"Maybe they feared you. Your *justice*."

"They'd be right to fear it."

"And you wonder why I didn't tell you what had happened to me," said Jaspyn.

"Don't be daft. That's not the same thing. You've never done me harm."

"I suppose I haven't yet, have I?"

"How did it happen, Jaspyn?" said Aren, seriously.

"How did *what* happen?"

"You know what I'm asking. How were you blooded? Turned? Who did it?"

"You know, *them*. One of the looters. It all happened really fast, I didn't know what was going on…it was just…really painful. The worst pain you could possibly envision." Jaspyn went silent for a minute, his eyes wide and his face white. "Imagine your eyes being boiled in their sockets and your blood raging with fire, burning through each one of your veins. Your skin being peeled off of your body… and you can do nothing. Just endure it."

"Was it just like the stories then?" said Aren.

"In a way, yes."

"Did he bite you? Did he have fangs?"

"God Aren, yes he bit me. Yes, he had fangs and I'll never ever forget the sight of them looking down at me." He shuddered, probably thinking back to that night.

"Who else knows?"

"No one," said Jaspyn. "Aside from Laris, I mean. And–"

"Aren?" came Cyneric's voice from the door. "Can we come in?"

"Yes."

"I have some news for you," said Cyneric. He wasn't alone. Ysser Banlin stood beside him.

"Where's Pennyn?" said Aren.

"Still with the prisoner," said Cyneric.

"Well, Jaspyn's already told me about what this Garlen said about the Nazeris family being innocent," said Aren. "Which, by the way, I do not believe for a moment."

"Well – there's more actually. Ysser, he recognises the dweller, from when he was captive." Ysser Banlin nodded and bowed his head.

"And?"

"He was vile," said Ysser. "Even killed his own man. He kept talking about something, or someone, I couldn't quite understand what exactly. But I know someone who might."

Aren shook his head. "I have nothing to say to her. She's not leaving her cell until the trial."

"Aren, we strongly believe that she's innocent in all this," said Cyneric. "A victim, actually. Rayne's spies have heard from Éterin, they played us all."

"What do you mean? Who played us?"

Cyneric sighed. "Olivia's death, it was going to happen no matter how things went down last night. It was a test, a test that Lord Berywen failed."

"What sort of test?" said Aren.

"Just tell us from the beginning," said Jaspyn. "Everything."

"Right," said Cyneric. "Ashcrest had started to grow suspicious of Lord Berywen, suspicious of his loyalty. And he had heard that the bloodgate was at the Halls, likely from Lord Hercan."

"He is no lord."

"Fine, Aren. Hercan," said Cyneric. "Now, we think that Hercan got wind of this from Lara. The only mistake she made was trusting her father."

"A costly mistake," said Aren.

"One which we can't really blame her for, can we? We never asked her to hide anything from her father, who could have known? We're just as much to blame as she is."

"I never said we weren't to blame," muttered Aren.

"But Ashcrest used the situation to his advantage. He devised a rather bold plan, if not foolish, to test Lord Berywen's loyalty and to get control of the Panderer's bloodgate. Two birds, one stone."

"And how did he do that?" said Jaspyn.

"He asked that Lord Berywen allow his daughter to be taken captive by Ashcrest's men. He assured him that she'd be safe in their hands and that the whole thing was just a ploy – a ploy to get the Crown to pay ransom – the ransom being the bloodgate."

"He allowed his own daughter to be taken captive? I simply cannot believe that," said Aren.

"No, heavens no. He dismissed it outright. But if the rumours are to be believed, Ashcrest offered the *same* deal to Hercan, who obviously was also working for him."

Aren couldn't believe it. "Hercan was willing to do that? To Lara?"

"Well, the day they were taken…her father was the one that wanted her to go to the Halls, specifically on that day, at that time. It wasn't on her own accord."

"You mean he helped orchestrate the attack on them?" said Jaspyn. "What a swine…"

Aren was silent. He was beginning to doubt every move, every choice he had made. How much did Hercan know?

"Aren – when we were tied up in there, Garlen wouldn't let the others touch her," said Ysser Banlin. "He killed a man because of it. They kept saying it… *he will have our heads*."

"And so Hercan passed the test. He proved his loyalty," said Cyneric. "Because he was willing to gamble on his daughter's life, Lara was to be spared."

"And that's why the Berywens feared for Olivia's safety." said Aren. "They must have had an idea something like this would happen."

"We think so," said Cyneric.

"Why don't we ask Chrysan? He can get in touch with Harvus before the funeral," said Aren. "Harvus might be more trusting of Chrysan than he is of us."

"Aren, Chrysan is gone," said Cyneric.

"Perfect," muttered Aren.

"It's why we lost in Medlanta too," said Ysser. "I told you then and I'm telling you now, sir. It was an impossible battle, we were outnumbered by hundreds."

"Yes, and now we know why," said Cyneric. "Hercan, he smuggled his troops across the Strait. That's how they got in, that's how they defeated the City Guard."

"Hercan will get his justice," mumbled Aren. "As will Ashcrest. They all will, I'll be sure that they do. Now, was that all?"

"Just the matter of setting a date for Garlen's trial, sir," said Ysser.

"There will be no need for that," said Aren. "Kill him."

Jaspyn looked at him in horror.

"Aren are you sure?" said Cyneric.

"Certain. Anything else?"

Cyneric and Ysser shared a knowing look. Cyneric gave him a nudge and the soldier took a step forward and cleared his throat.

"As you know, Develyn Asellar is gaining support by the day," said Ysser.

"The healer, yes, yes, I know. What of it?"

"Well," said Ysser nervously. "She's asked to meet you, on her terms."

"Meet me? A parley?" said Aren. "Who does she think she is?"

"Those aren't precisely the words she used," said Cyneric. "Nonetheless, she has reached out."

"To discuss the terms of her surrender, I hope," said Aren.

"One cannot tell," said Cyneric. "It certainly didn't seem like surrender. Anyway, that is something to worry about later."

"There's been more claims of sightings in the far north," said Cyneric. "Beyond the Nevebaris…"

"Sightings?" said Aren. "More dwellers? All the way up there?"

"No," said Cyneric. "Sightings in the sky. Skyverns."

"More insanity," said Ysser. "But then, I don't suppose we can rule anything out at this point, after everything we've seen in this land."

Certainly not, Aren thought. It would be foolish to do so. In fact, it had gotten him thinking.

"Ysser, you mentioned something earlier," said Aren.

"Hmm?" Ysser gave him a confused look.

"You said that Garlen killed a man while you were down there, was this other man a dweller too?"

"I can't say for sure. His skin, it had a warmth to it, a touch of life. But I cannot say for sure."

"And when Garlen killed him, that was before or after what had happened…with Olivia?"

"Before." Ysser raised his eyebrows. "They turned to hunt Olivia right at the end of it all, when all hope seemed lost."

Aren had suspected as much. He stopped and passed his hand over his pocket once more. It was still there, as cold and jagged as ever. He cast his mind back, far back. To Olivia's sweet voice. To the wretched book. To the words he himself had said out loud that day. They came back to him. They filled his thoughts with dread and with anguish.

When the land stains red with the blood of the free, the blood of the shadows, the blood of the winds and the blood of the flames. The end will be nigh, and dawn shall set from destiny's stone itself.

It echoed in his head. It seemed a stretch, hard to fathom, but prophecies had rarely been known to be frank. The land stained red with the *blood of the free, the blood of shadows*? It was war, it had to be. Why else would the land be tainted by the blood of the free? But then…what if it wasn't? *Stone of sacrifice, key of blood…*

"Ysser," said Aren. "Do you remember that man, the Sandaerian."

"Which one?" said Ysser.

"Rhedas Sandaerzi, I think was his name."

Ysser gave him a look of dismay. "Yes, the mad one."

"What did he say about the Key? The Key of Blood?" said Aren.

"He said a lot of different things and very little of it was coherent, Your Majesty," said Ysser. "Blood magic nonsense, sir."

"Not nonsense," said Aren. "You aren't a believer, Lord Ysser, and you saw my enemy – the true enemy, and you believed, didn't you?"

"Well, yes, but it is one thing to believe in the threat of a dweller when his cold eyes are looking down at you – and it is something else entirely to pay heed to riddles from a mad zealot who seeks nothing else but to plague your mind with the broken ideals of his twisted faith."

"*Blood of the Free, Blood of the Shadows…*" Aren was trying to piece it all together in his head. "What do you know of Olivia's heritage?"

Ysser looked confused. "Well, House Berywen has held Éterin for generations, her father is–"

"No, I mean her blood."

"She was Weslin, sir," said Ysser.

"Indeed. Blood of Tilas Jerton himself, some would say. There's very few who can make that claim." Could it be? "But she isn't purely of Weslin blood, Lord Ysser, rarely anybody is these days, are they? Zaldroni blood also runs through her veins."

"I didn't know that," said Ysser. "But I'm afraid I'm struggling to see what you are trying to say."

"As am I," said Jaspyn.

"What do they say of the Zaldroni in the south, my lord?" said Aren.

"They say many things about many people."

"But the Exile, why did it happen? Why are the Zaldroni *still* not trusted in the south?"

"Allegedly, the dweller blood runs through their veins," said Ysser, with a sudden look of realisation.

"The key of blood, it would vanquish my greatest foes…*Blood of the Free, Blood of the Shadows,*" said Aren. He pulled out the pendant from his pocket. "Olivia's blood. Berywen blood. Zaldroni and Weslin. Blood of the mortal and blood of the dweller."

Ysser looked at the old thing with widened eyes, but Cyneric was sceptical.

"I don't understand, how can that be?" said Cyneric. "And the prophecy in that damned book, it also spoke of *blood of the winds* and *blood of the flames*. What in hell do you suppose that means?"

Aren scowled. He hadn't a clue.

"As her blood fell to the ground, it cast an enchantment through the pendant," said Jaspyn suddenly, a knowing look painted across his face. "I read about it – erm – when I was studying. An ancient spell. The one that they say defeated the dwellers in the First Age of Shadows. That's what stops dwellers from killing on this land."

"On this land?"

"This country," said Jaspyn. "But only this land, from sea to sea. It's sacred. Not Zaldron, not Penuelas. That was why the Exile happened…they were sent to their island, to rot. Even the innocents."

"Olivia saved us all," said Aren. "'*Great peril*' he'd said – do you remember? '*Great peril under the stars of deceit*'. He'd been warning us from the beginning."

"Who?" said Jaspyn. "Who warned you?"

"Rhedas Sandaerzi."

"Oh," said Jaspyn. There was an eerie silence as Aren watched out of the window once again, his back to the three of them.

"Sir, as for a speech… A royal address, to your subjects," said Ysser.

"For what?" said Aren.

"The battle, sir. We won back New Castisa."

"At what cost?" said Aren. "There will be no speech. Cyneric, can you send word to the North Parydon. I want to see Rhedas. I want him here as soon as possible."

A Long Road

Eyan

Eyan pressed against his leg where Chrysan Berywen had shot him. He winced sharply, squeezing his eyes shut. A hard, sharp lump of sorts. The bullet, or at least part of it.

Damn. He knew he was lucky though, one of the luckiest. He looked around at the crying men and women, corpses strewn across the hall like dirty laundry. More and more arrived each day. Just bloody cloths for cover. The metal in his leg stung, worse than ever now. Fuck. He'd need Renut's help in getting the damned thing out. *Renut.*

Eyan looked at the little man, the anguish in the poor thing's eyes. He'd scarcely spoken a word in the days that had followed. The days since they'd lost New Castisa. He sat in the corner of the hall, the same corner every day since they'd set foot in Jertonshield. He watched over the bodies, rarely uttering a single word to Eyan. It was as it had been at the very beginning. When they'd first taken the idiot. Brought him into their home. He caught the little man's eyes wander over to Eyan and then swiftly on, to the other Ashcrest soldiers that had survived the brutal slaughter. The little man rubbed the stump where his leg had been, his eyes misty. He did it every day. Every day since they'd set foot in Jertonshield.

Eyan had had enough. If his father wasn't going to address his people, it'd have to be him. He hated it, but he knew there was no way around it. His father was on the other side of the country in Lyndan. It fell to Eyan, now, all of it. Either him or Fraston…and he certainly didn't want it to be Fraston. He stood up and cleared his throat. Not a stir. Everything carried on as if he hadn't made a sound. He clenched his fists and stormed off, stepping over a dead soldier as if she were a rotting piece of meat.

Perwell's chambers were just around the corner from the hall with the dead. Fitting. He'd taken up residence in what had once been a private study belonging to the gatekeeper. The gatekeeper was no more, of course. Eyan thought it best to catch a quick word with Perwell before his departure. Maybe ask *him* to speak to the survivors instead. He was older, stronger. And he wasn't a pompous tool like Fraston Spenler, not as much anyway. It seemed though, much to Eyan's dismay, that somebody else had had the same idea. He put his ear to the door.

"Yes, yes, we'll round 'em all up," said Perwell Hercan. "Every last one, don't you worry."

"Good, good…I'm not worried." It was Fraston's revolting voice. "I just thought, you know…all things considered."

"Yes, well, you thought right."

"And I…erm…well I suppose I wanted to thank you," said Fraston.

"Hmmm?" came Hercan's voice. "It was my duty, an honour, really." But there had been no honour in what had taken place that day.

"No…" said Fraston. His voice dropped to a loud whisper. "What you did for me, the shot you took. At the idiot."

"Oh? Who?"

"You know…" said Fraston. "The idiot. The little one, it's a pity he only lost a leg, really. But at least he won't be able to follow him around anymore, Soren's boy."

Hercan laughed cruelly and Eyan's heart sank. "Oh, well, as luck would have it the idiot fell on his own bow. I shot to kill but the bastard was behind the smoke."

"Well, there's always next time," said Fraston. "He makes Soren's boy weak, a coward. We can't let that happen."

That was all Eyan had needed to hear. He fought the urge to burst into the room, he fought it with all his might. He stepped backwards, away from the red door, still facing it. His mind raced wildly, thinking over each potential outcome. There was only one which made sense to him. Only one choice that he'd be able to live with. He all but ran to his own chambers, tripping up the steps of the narrow staircase, no care for the wound on his leg.

He stood in his room alone, the thick curtains drawn so not a sliver of light made its way in. With each breath, he drew deeper and deeper, faster every time, until he was practically panting. He

364

looked at the boy stood before him in the cracked, grimy mirror. Not much had changed, yet everything had. He was older. Crueller? He didn't know. Weak?

He made for his cupboard, pulling out shirts and tunics and breeches at random. Most were dirty, there was no time to get your clothes washed and pressed in war, moving from city to city, marching into battle day upon day. He pulled out an old, torn rucksack from beneath his bed. Without thinking, he shoved in as many pieces as he could fit. There was a rickety echo from down the corridor. Damn, not now, he was almost done. He reached beneath his pillow and pulled out the gun, putting it into the bag between a compass and a pair of brown boots. He felt for his dagger, passing his palm blindly over his belt, his eyes still fixed on the rucksack. It was still there. Perfect. He heaved the hefty bag over his shoulder, panting and sputtering. And then the rickety steps grew louder than ever and the doors to his chambers swung loudly open, slamming on the wall adjoining. There was no knock.

"Just w-what do you think y-you're doing?" said the one-legged figure in the doorframe. "Master Eyan."

"Now isn't the time, Renut," said Eyan. "Leave me." He tried to brush past the little man, but Renut stuck his wooden leg out wide, tripping him.

"What the hell did you do that for?!" yelled Eyan. The little man eyed the bulky weight on Eyan's back.

"You're l-leaving," said Renut. "Why?"

"Stop it," said Eyan. "Stop being my shadow, stop following me everywhere. Just...just go." He turned away from the little man, tears in his eyes.

"I haven't...h-haven't been speaking to y-you because I was embarrassed," said Renut. "It's...it's h-humiliating. I d-didn't...I couldn't...do a-anything." The stuttering was worse than ever.

"I don't care what you could and couldn't do," said Eyan. "Let me pass, or I will break your other leg."

The little man lowered his wooden leg. "The p-people," he said. "They don't t-trust you...nor y-your family."

For good reason. "Yeah? Why is that?"

Renut sighed. "Olivia Berywen...she w-was killed in cold blood...in f-front of everyone," he said. "Who's t-to say anybody is truly s-safe here?"

"Nobody is safe anywhere, these days. That is the world we have created, all of us."

"So, you seek a b-better world?" said Renut. "A s-safer one? I thought…I thought that w-we would create a safe world." The little man looked down to the purple carpets, sullen. Let down. "Well, i-if you are leaving, at l-least tell me where you are headed."

"So that you can hobble along?" said Eyan. Renut went red, and suddenly Eyan's heart filled with remorse for what he'd said. "I don't know where I am going. Just that it'll be far from here."

"Not the e-enemy's camp I hope?" said Renut. Eyan said nothing. He'd be shot on sight there, no questions asked. Eyan wouldn't be of much use in helping shape a better world dead.

"I told you; I don't know."

"I m-might," said Renut suddenly. "Before the b-battle…I told you that serving Aren Aryssen is n-not the only alternative…you r-remember that?"

Eyan frowned. Then who? And then it suddenly dawned upon him. "The Asellar girl? A delusional fanatic is no better than a power-hungry tyrant."

"And w-who told you that she is a d-delusional fanatic?" said Renut. "The v-very people you are running from."

Eyan paced around the narrow hall, the rucksack heavy on his shoulders. Sweat trickled from his brow, he wiped it away with his sleeve.

"You aren't safe here either," he said suddenly, turning to face the little man. "Pack a bag, it is a long road to Veytora."

"Nynnevor," said the little man. "It is a long road to Nynnevor."